FERRYMAN

THE THIRD SEAL OF THE KRYPTEIA CONSPIRACY

MICHAEL KOOGLER, JED QUINN, & JAREN RILEY

FERRYMAN

THE THIRD SEAL OF THE KRYPTEIA CONSPIRACY

BY MICHAEL KOOGLER, JED QUINN, & JAREN RILEY

ISBN: 978-1-943519-06-4

Book editing by Elizabeth Humphrey
Bookworm Editing, Littleton, Colorado USA

Book cover art, packaging and design by
Kreative Storm Press, Coralville, Iowa USA

Author Information at:

www.michaelkoogler.net
www.jedquinn.com

For Our Beautiful Children

Revelation 8: 6

"And the seven angels which had the seven trumpets prepared themselves to sound."

PROLOGUE

Supai, Arizona: The old Indian's eyes fluttered open and he shivered as the dream ended as it always did, evil uniting with evil at the beginning of time to dethrone God Himself. He had lived the same dream a thousand different times on a thousand different nights and he awoke the same way every time—alone and afraid. He lay silently on his ragged blanket, the bed he had thrown down beside the old saguaro just a few hours before, his body covered in a sheen of sweat born not from the oppressive desert heat but rather from unrelenting horror. He had hoped to gather a few more hours of sleep before confronting what he knew awaited him, but sleep was scarce these days.

With a deep sigh and the creaking of old bones, he slowly climbed to his feet, the cool night air washing over him, drying his sweat-soaked body. He reached down and gathered his thin blanket, draping it around his shoulders. He shivered again in the night air and cast his eyes toward the heavens. It seemed as if every star in the heavens was shining down on him, but John couldn't see their beauty. All he could focus on was the darkness between the stars, in itself a living entity hiding a deadly secret, crawling and snaking since that fateful day, thousands of years before.

It was a secret that was not so secret anymore.

The dreams told him that much. They told him the curtain was about to be raised on the last act. They told him the final player had at last stepped onto the field.

Cain was abroad.

The slaughter was about to begin.

John slowly walked the last few hundred yards up the dirt path toward the small hut tucked up against a sheer rock face, giving it shelter from the elements. Unfortunately, it had not sheltered the inhabitants from what had crawled out of the dark. John knew what he would find, having seen it in a vision almost a week ago. It had been a vision like so many others and they always ended the same—in savage death. He pushed open the door and was met by the strong, coppery scent of blood. Bowing his head, he pushed back the tears and whispered quietly in the darkness. "Why, Father? Why do the innocent suffer so? Why have I been commanded to stay my hand from giving aid, when I have the power to save so many?"

"You are not wrong to ask such questions, John," came a quiet voice, and suddenly the interior of the hut was bathed in a soft white glow of light. "That does not absolve us of our duty, however."

John looked up, his eyes immediately settling on the figure that stood before him. He was not at all surprised by the presence of the visitor and he nodded immediately in recognition. "It has been many years since I last cast my eyes on you, Gabriel."

The angel nodded, his perfect features a mask of stone. Robed in white, he stood as tall as any mortal man, but the power of God within him made the air about him thrum with energy. "I have had no reason to show myself to thee until now, John," the archangel answered gently. His eyes, blue as sapphires, glittered as he spoke. "The time has come, my old friend. You know of what I speak."

"I have had millennia to ponder that which I was shown but could not share," the old man said with a weary sigh. "I confess I am no closer to understanding it today than I was then."

"It is not for you to understand," Gabriel replied. "It is only for you to follow what you know is true and do what has been asked."

"How can I help when I no longer know the path?" John begged, looking up with tears in his eyes. "We fight and die and evil triumphs. I tell them to hope and believe and all will be made right, yet they are like lambs to the slaughter."

Gabriel said nothing.

"I have been tasked by the Almighty Himself to help these mortals in these last days, to protect them against the marked one, but I am constrained by His will. The adversary, however, is bound by no such rules," the old Indian continued. "Even now, he changes the game and the unthinkable becomes the reality."

As if to answer, Gabriel turned and pointed toward the corner of the hut, the light surrounding him illuminating the darker corners of the room. The soft light fell upon the body of a young woman, her skin pale and lifeless. Her eyes were open in death, staring without seeing and her throat was like the others—the flesh torn away, the jugular exposed and ripped open. Blood still glistened on her neck and the ground, but most of it had been consumed. "Do not let your vision be limited by what your earthly eyes show you, my old friend. Tonight, she sits at her Heavenly Father's feet," he said softly.

"But the cost…" John trailed off, unable to finish.

"Humanity is threatened like never before and the plan has been altered, but we are never without hope. God's children need a champion," Gabriel finished quietly.

John shook his head. "You know as well as I that these mortals will be no match for what is coming. The favored son of our adversary now walks the earth and his creatures are about, feeding on the blood of innocents. I know what that means, Gabriel, and I fear what must be done. I fear I will not be up to the challenge placed before me."

"You are allowing your fears too much sway, John. Trust in God. He knows what He must sacrifice to save His children," Gabriel said gently.

"When doing so will guarantee that Lucifer will win in the end?"

Gabriel smiled, but it was a sad smile. "Even in this, we do not know what the final outcome will be. Only the Father knows this, John, and He will keep His own council regarding it. But do not give up on humanity. They might surprise us all."

John nodded and shuffled past the heavenly messenger. With a groan of age, he slowly knelt beside the body of the young woman. Reaching out, he gently closed her eyes for the last time. Then, bowing his head, he spoke again. "You know I will do the will of the Father," he said softly, "but I confess I do not know not what that is anymore."

"Bring forth the spear, John," Gabriel said reverently.

John looked up, weary resignation in his eyes. "So, it truly is time."

"The end is nigh, my friend," the archangel replied softly.

John bowed his head, understanding completely what it meant, even if he did not know how it would all end. "There is someone who will wield it?"

Gabriel nodded.

"Who will be His champion?"

After a long moment of silence, Gabriel placed his hand on John's stooped and weary shoulder and spoke. "The time has come for you to see the rest of your vision. You will still have many questions, but you will receive some of the answers you have long sought after. I am afraid, however, you will not like everything you see."

And with that, he showed him.

CHAPTER 1

Belfast, Ireland: James Ford, former Admiral of the United States Navy and current acting New Army general over the entire European theatre, stood atop Cavehill surveying the arrayed battlements below. He could see clear to Belfast from here, or what remained of it. He had topographical maps, city maps, and up-to-the-minute troop movement data, but what really drove the devastation home for him was the actual view. The proud city harbored the last remaining sizable resistance in Ireland, if not most of Western Europe.

Things had progressed easily around most of the Mediterranean, where governments and economies had collapsed to such a degree after the chaos of two years ago that sweeping in and seizing control was more like a relief mission than an actual invasion. The new regime provided sufficient food, safety, and shelter, and the New Army had swiftly restored rudimentary local communications once resistance was eliminated. In a well-guarded truth, all advanced communications—phone, internet, and satellite—still functioned well, but access belonged solely to the New Army. For the citizens of those occupied cities and countries, that loss was viewed as minor. The army had established a modern-day Utopia of sorts, free from hunger, fear, and crime, and for many, that was better than anything they had seen in a long time. For the general population, the initial freedom from strife engendered gratitude and a sense of peace. As the months wore on and the deep wounds of war, hunger, and cold healed and lost their sting, most of the people had grown content and found themselves at least nominally devoted to the New Army.

Most, but not all.

Two areas of resistance had developed early in the European theatre—one in Edinburgh and the other in Belfast. Edinburgh would be dealt with in due time. The resistance in Belfast would end today, one way or another. The psychology of it baffled Ford. The small pocket of pugnacious Irish had refused every diplomatic offer from the New Army. They cherished their freedom on a deep level, caring more for the hope of future choices than the comfort of present safety. It was almost a part of their DNA and it blinded them to the reality of their situation. Above the necessities to sustain life, they prioritized, fought, and died by the thousands for that freedom.

"Disgusting idiots," Ford spat to no one in particular. "I offer them more freedom from the horrors of this world than they could imagine. Their families would be healthy and safe. I end conflict over religion, nationality, and society and these maggots scream 'freedom' with each dying breath."

The four officers flanking the former admiral kept their eyes on the battlefield, knowing his monologue almost verbatim by this point. They had heard it enough. All four had served in highly ranked positions in their former nations' militaries. When those militaries had been absorbed or disbanded in favor of the growing multinational forces, they had rapidly climbed the ranks of the New Army, thanks in some part to their brilliance, but more due to their allegiance to the one who had built the forces arrayed throughout Europe.

On this morning, each man, including Ford, resolutely ignored the fetid air arising from the valley and bay below. Last week, Ford had purposefully demolished the Lagan Weir, allowing the normal tides to expose the mudflats to the long and unusually hot days. The resultant odor was suffocating and nauseating. He had hoped one more ounce of misery might break the spirit of the rebels, causing them to surrender without the massive death toll an all-out attack would bring to both sides. But all it did was kill the appetite of everyone in his army, including himself.

Ford had finally had enough of this rotten island and its stubborn inhabitants. "I end this today," he said through gritted teeth, his knuckles whitening in anger on the billy club held behind his back.

"Beware of pride, James," warned an unexpected voice from behind all of them.

Ford froze as fear filled his soul. If an avalanche could be quiet, it would sound like the voice of the giant standing behind him and it caused Ford to grip his club so tightly, his fingers could have split like overcooked hot dogs. While the Admiral commanded all troops in the European theatre, seeking to unite the world under a single entity by promising peace and prosperity to all who would embrace his vision, in truth he answered to a being that sought peace in an entirely different manner. Known throughout the New Army simply as the Marshall, he was the last person Ford wanted here.

"You have exhausted the allotted time given you with your misguided goodwill," the Marshall continued. "*I* will end this today. *You* will depart immediately."

The Marshall was a monster of a man, his face distorted, almost hazy, making it difficult to discern any of his features. Ford couldn't even make out the color of his eyes, the shape of his nose, or the size of his mouth. The edges of the man, or where edges should be—the tips of fingers, the outline of clothing, where the man ended and the rest of the world began—seemed to blur, never appearing where they should. His voice was even harder to describe. It had the tendency to blend, as if a dozen different voices were speaking together at the exact same time.

And yet, what distressed Ford the most was not the Marshall's appearance or his terrifying voice. It was his proclivity for bloodshed. In more than a few instances over the past twelve months, the Marshall had asserted himself personally on a battlefield. The resulting slaughter of soldiers and innocents alike was nothing short of horrific and Ford had never been able to reconcile that with his mission of eventual peace. The Marshall had said repeatedly that the sins of the world could only be washed away with blood, but Ford was not so convinced.

He fought to control his own voice and in a testament to his courage, he did. "My allegiance is to the One and my orders are quite clear. They do not include departing before my mission is secure."

"Your new orders come directly from the One, through me."

The revelation confirmed a long held suspicion of Ford's, one he had maintained since receiving the plum assignment of subjugating all of Europe as he saw fit. The Marshall was not just an acting commander with similar forces and orders of his own. The Marshall outranked him. It had never been overtly disclosed to him, but Ford had noticed the Marshall's forces acting in near parallelism to his own as the campaigns through Europe had progressed. Yet here, on Cavehill, on the brink of owning Europe, the truth of his command had just been laid bare. He was being demoted in front of his four top commanders. Honor and rank meant everything to Ford, which meant he had to obey, but being supplanted when he was about to win the hardest fought victory of his military career was too much to bear.

"I assure you I'll depart in twelve hours when I stand victorious on the steps of Belfast City Hall," Ford said stiffly. "If the steps remain." It was the closest he had ever come to disobeying an order.

The Marshall proceeded as if Ford had not spoken, issuing his own orders to the four commanders. "Commander Tad, you will lead your battalion personally and attack immediately. General Ademov, order your wings in the air and commence with the aerial assault. Admiral Jeps, I know your ships are already in position. Begin shelling immediately. Concentrate your fire on the city center and pull the fighters toward the sea as planned. Colonel Chen, you and your men will await my orders."

As all four displayed their obedience with crisp salutes, Ford could only feel his fury grow exponentially within him. This had been planned and he had realized it too late. "This is mutiny!" he shouted angrily, whirling on the man who had come to rob him of his glory. "You dare to plan this attack with my men without my orders?! I'll have your traitorous head on a pole, no matter who you claim to serve!"

"Stop yourself right there, Admiral," the Marshall said quietly without diverting his attention from the battlefield. "You can still be useful to me, regardless of your tirade. You will go to Asia and police the populace there as you have here. Your talents in that area have not gone unnoticed."

Ford advanced, ignoring the warning. "This is my campaign!" he growled. Standing face-to-amorphous-face, Ford felt suddenly overwhelmed by a mass of bone-melting energy emanating from the man and he fought hard not to shrink back in terror.

"These people will not submit, so they must be destroyed. Your campaign would let this open wound in our new empire fester for years to come. But the world has changed, Admiral. There is no place for compassion for those who stand against the One. You are to leave immediately and attend your new duties in Asia. I will finish this."

"And how do you plan to finish it?" Ford dared to ask.

"Extermination," the Marshall gave no intonation, no expression to the phrase describing genocide. "First by air, then we'll push them into the mud and then the sea."

Emotionless.

For the first time in quite a while, Ford felt his own emotions stirring. "There are thousands of people still in the city, including women and children. Many are non-combatants," he said quietly. "What do you intend…"

"You are dismissed," the Marshall's deep voice had grown colder.

It was unthinkable. The entire purpose behind all of his hard work these last two years was to establish peace and freedom. Ford had no problems at all eliminating those soldiers who opposed him. He did so without compunction, freeing innocent people from the plagues of this world and the sorrow resulting from other people's poor decisions. These stubborn Irish deserved the same, whether they wanted it or not, and they would have gotten it after he annihilated the rebels standing in his way. Now they would not get that chance, for what the Marshall was proposing was not a military campaign. It was genocide. And he had done it before.

"I won't allow…," he began, but was cut off again. This time, though, there were no words. The monster spun and threw Ford to the ground, an impossibly strong hand tightening around his throat and choking off the end of his declaration. Heat seemed to pour from the Marshall's twisting face and Ford felt the skin of his neck begin to burn. The Marshall's face was no longer ambiguous, but showed clear as crystal.

It was the face of the One.

"I order you, in the name of the One, to depart," the Marshall said with a voice that implied he would accept nothing short of complete and total compliance. "Under his orders, I cannot kill you, as much as I would enjoy such a diversion. Even after your abject failure here in Belfast, he shows you mercy."

The face blurred again and Ford was free. The Marshall was once again standing, his back to him as he returned to his observation of the battlefield. Ford climbed slowly to his feet. He salvaged what little remained of his pride and straightened his uniform. With his head high, he stepped up beside Legion and turned to face him. "I will follow my orders, of course," he affirmed, his voice wavering only slightly. "But I ask for permission to speak freely."

The Marshall didn't hesitate, his voice firm as stone. "No." The conversation was over.

His features stricken, Ford nodded in defeat as he turned and walked away, leaving Ireland to its doom.

Commander Nicholas Tad was dying. Although young for a New Army battalion commander, he had spent years training for close combat and knew how his body should perform in any situation. At rest, his heart beat forty-eight times per minute, he breathed ten times per minute, and his blood pressure averaged a hundred over sixty. He could raise his heart rate to one hundred-eighty at a dead sprint and maintain it at one hundred-twenty while running ten miles per hour for almost ninety minutes. At this moment, the monitor on his watch registered a pulse of one hundred-thirty. "Mild hemorrhagic shock," he concluded stoically, speaking under his breath and to no one but himself. "About one point five liters of blood lost." There was no need to look at the wound in his abdomen. He knew it was there, knew it was oozing blood, and knew he had less than an hour of life left.

What really galled him was the way it happened. Ademov had performed admirably, leveling the vast majority of what remained of the city with the air assault. He had made the bombing of Dresden during World War II look like child's play. The surviving Irish had holed themselves up in the shattered buildings throughout the remaining city and Tad and his troops now patrolled the streets, eradicating any opposition they found.

While traversing one such street, his point man had tripped an IED planted deep under a pile of broken concrete pieces and scrap metal. Although the detonation had been thirty meters away, Nicholas

Tad had not been spared. A small piece of shrapnel had penetrated his abdominal wall and lodged deep into his gut. He could feel it ripping his hip flexors every time he stepped, but he could tolerate pain. What he could not tolerate was the branch of his deep circumflex iliac vein that had been lacerated. "No glory in this death," he muttered through clenched teeth as a spasm of pain again tore through his abdomen. The fact that the rebels proved so much more resilient than expected did nothing to help his mood.

His personal platoon, an experienced and skilled group in their own right, continued to move forward and had arrived at the final block to be cleared before any remaining citizens could be pushed into the open mud flats abutting the sea. Radio reports detailed close to two thousand rebels already on those plains fighting for their lives against Tad's brigade of five thousand.

"Give me two more hours," Nicholas Tad prayed aloud. "I can cleanse this island for you in two hours, Lord."

"Sir?" one of his men, Lieutenant Exan, spoke up questioningly.

"I just need two hours," Tad repeated. "Two hours to take the city."

"Commander, we're in the city," the lieutenant spoke politely, but with great concern.

Nicholas Tad shook his head and sighed painfully. "Give the orders, Lieutenant," he said softly, embarrassed. *Confusion. Moderate hemorrhagic shock. Two more hours, Lord! I beg.*

"To the flats!" bellowed the lieutenant. The soldiers immediately began to advance in perfect order, harrying the fleeing rebels as they went. The man turned back to his superior. "Commander, let me help you."

Morgan Exan, nicknamed "Max," followed orders as well as he gave them, was of superior intelligence, and had served under

Commander Tad in six campaigns throughout the Middle East and Asia. They had been together long enough that they had formed a tight bond, a friendship forged in battle. Brothers in arms.

"Get the ABDs out of my kit," Tad said, pausing to lean against the shattered remains of a concrete wall. He opened his jacket, exposed the small area between his chest and waist armor. Max eyed the bleeding wound clinically and did not react, despite its apparent seriousness. *Yes*, Tad thought, *he is a great soldier.* "Shove one in, place the other over the top with pressure, then tape and follow with an ace wrap."

Max silently did as ordered with the addition of soaking the ABDs in alcohol. There was no hesitation, no odd facial contortions. He simply followed orders.

Nicholas Tad, on the other hand, saw stars for a time and focused everything he could into just breathing. "I had no…idea it would hurt…this bad," he gasped, eyes tightly closed in agony.

"I'll radio for evac," Max said quietly as he began winding the wrap around his officer's lower torso.

"No, Max," Tad countered. "Help me to the mud flats. Let me see the end of this."

"Commander, you've lost a lot of blood. You need immediate surgery or you'll die."

"I'll die regardless, Max," Tad replied with a dismissive wave of his hand. "You already know that. Help me die victorious."

Max kept his face neutral, though internally he was fighting a difficult battle. Nicholas Tad was his commander and friend, as close to him as his own brothers. Part of him screamed to do what was right by his friend, while the other part of him demanded he obey the orders of a superior officer. Without a word, he pinched Nicholas' fingers, one by one, and watched them blanch and sluggishly turn pink again. Just like that, it no longer mattered. Tad was right. It was too late for evacuation. Steeling himself against the inevitable, he helped Tad back to his feet and together, they moved toward the city's edge where the battle raged on the mudflats.

"He's answering my prayers, Max," Commander Tad finally said after a while, his voice considerably weaker. "I can see everything from here. I'll witness the final victory after all."

The battlefield was simple, a broad expanse of mudflat with no cover, with his brigade landward and the rebels with their backs to the sea. In the bay behind the rebels sat the multinational New Navy, four battleships and a carrier along with numerous support craft, all of which had spent a good portion of their larger ordinance earlier in the battle, helping pound the city to rubble. Only their presence was needed now. They would stand watch over the end of the insurgency, which was even now being desperately fought for and decided in the stinking mud of what used to be the Lagan Weir.

The flats themselves favored the rebels. Vehicles of any kind were too heavy for the soft ground, forcing men and women into gun battles and brutal hand-to-hand. The tactic forced Tad's infantry to spread apart to effectively engage their enemies, which considerably weakened their ability to roll over the rebels en masse. In addition, the Irish had erected small platforms in the rear and on the edges of the flats, from which rebel snipers were picking apart the infantry.

Another scan of the field shocked Nicholas and his euphoria faded. "Max, how many men do we have left?" he asked incredulously, seeing hundreds of New Army casualties lying in the mud and very few rebel dead.

The lieutenant paused only for a few seconds to scan the battlefield. "I estimate two thousand on each side," Max replied quietly. "That would mean we've lost more than half our men."

"There," Tad suddenly said, looking toward the edges of the battle. His own New Army soldiers already fought desperately in the flats, but thousands more were moving toward the fighting. "They descend from Cavehill, led by the Marshall himself."

"Why would he risk being so close to the battle?" Max asked, following his commander's gaze. Indeed, the entire infantry, leaders included, pressed the rebels away from the base of Cavehill toward the sea. "I've seen him do this before," Max went on. "It's like he can't help himself. He has a bloodlust."

Nicholas didn't know exactly what the Marshall was, but he had seen him in combat enough to know he was something special. Seeing him once single-handedly lay waste to a well-trained platoon of enemy soldiers had convinced Nicholas to join him and swear fealty. The man was a force only God could have created. And Nicholas' greatest desire was to fight for God.

"Don't mistake him, Max," he said and was interrupted by a wet cough, one that sent a trickle of blood running from his mouth. "It isn't a bloodlust. He's as much a weapon as he is a leader, and he's wise enough to recognize this. He uses himself to best serve God."

Max answered him with a subtle shake of his head, his features seeming to show a sense of betrayal. "My friend," he said quietly, "I have served, trusted, and supported you through numerous wars and the transformation of the world. I envy your love of God and the confidence you have in your convictions, but, I don't share your views here."

Nicholas merely shrugged indifferently. His friend might be a lot of things, but in this, he was wrong. Nicholas Tad knew better and had seen it firsthand. But he had little time left and none for proselytizing. He turned his gaze back to the battle, where he could see the infantry pressing the rebels closer to the sea, bolstered by the reinforcements from Colonel Chen's troops. The rebels gave ground methodically, taking more lives than they were losing. "Tell me what you see out there, Max," he whispered, his voice capable of little more now.

Max analyzed the field again and immediately recognized the ploy. "The rebels give ground needlessly," he answered. "Our men advance, drawing the noose tighter, but it's by the rebel's design and not our own." He stopped to look at his commander. "They're luring us in."

Just as he finished speaking, thousands of Irish began pouring out of the holes and crevices that gave Cavehill its name. Their movements were disciplined and orderly, the cold precision of a battle-hardened battalion who understood they were fighting their last battle. They had made peace with whatever end awaited them and that made them the most dangerous enemy of all.

They opened up with their weapons as one.

In just a few minutes, hundreds more New Army soldiers had been wounded or killed, their bodies sinking slowly into the oblivion of the of the stinking mud. Nicholas Tad fell to his knees, dizzy and confused, his breathing ragged. "Help me up, Max," he gasped. He had only minutes left and could barely even hold up his own head anymore.

His friend obeyed silently, helping his commander back to his feet one last time. The bandages around his midsection were soaked with blood and his breath rattled in his lungs. As one, their eyes settled on a single hulking figure walking purposefully across the fetid mud. Dressed in the dark grey and khaki of the New Army, the Marshall was a monster of a man, kicking aside the dead and dying without a thought, before plunging into the fray.

An Irish fighter wielding a bloody combat knife moved to intercept him and the Marshall barely broke stride in the time it took him to spin the surprised man around, relieve him of his blade, and slash the knife across the man's throat. He threw both the dying man and the knife to the ground. A sharpshooter's shot took him in the shoulder, but it registered only a barely discernible jerk from the bullet's impact as he continued walking toward the greatest concentration of rebels. As he walked, shadows seemed to gather about him and soldiers on both sides shrank from his presence.

"He doesn't even bleed," Max stated in awe as he watched the spectacle unfold, an uneasy feeling growing within him.

"He's God's destroying angel," Tad whispered, his bloody lips forming into a peaceful smile. "You must see that, my friend."

Max saw nothing of the sort. He had seen enough to believe that the Marshall might indeed be some sort of supernatural being, but he also knew that this was not of God. If there was no other proof, the shadows circling around this warrior like dark, ravenous birds of prey were enough to tell him the Marshall was evil incarnate.

Below them on the field, the Marshall took a gunshot wound to the hip and finally paused in his purposeful march. Bowing his head, he slowly knelt in the mud, one hand raised into the air and the other pressed into the stinking muck. The nimbus of shadows and chaos that surrounded him seemed to swell until the clouds eclipsed the sun. He did not move a muscle. The surviving fighting men of Tad's battalion reeled and charged to surround their leader, the New Army now fighting on two fronts as Chen's soldiers joined the battle en masse.

As the sounds of war rose to an unholy crescendo, a resounding scream suddenly split the heavens and the two men looked upward as the sky blackened in a swirling mass of screeching chaos. It took them only a moment to realize what it was.

Birds.

Thousands of them.

They were merlins, Irish falcons with wicked talons and hooked beaks, and they seemed to come out of nowhere. They circled momentarily as a biologic tornado and then the chaotic swarm descended on the mass of humanity below, attacking Irish rebels and New Army soldiers alike with a murderous rage. Men swung rifles and knives ineffectively at the maelstrom of talons and beaks, which slashed them to ribbons. Men fell by the hundreds, losing eyes, fingers, and blood as their master alone stood firm among them, one hand still raised to the sky. Then, as suddenly as they had arrived, the birds ascended of one accord and dove, every last one of them, into the sea.

Leaning heavily against his friend, Commander Nicholas Tad smiled euphorically and uttered his last words. "I am…delivered," he gasped as his body shuddered and his head slumped forward.

His heart heavy, Max gently lowered his fallen friend to the ground, brushing a hand across Tad's bloody face to close his eyes. He said a silent prayer to a God he hoped still cared about His children, praying that his friend would be forgiven for being deceived as he was. It was a deception that he, too, had originally fallen victim to and had only recently realized. He wondered if both of them were already damned.

The hot sun emerged once more, unnoticed by the majority of men across that expanse of mud. In stark contrast to the masses of doubled-over, frightened, and wounded men, the Marshall stood slowly until fully erect, once more towering above the field. Of the gunshot wounds he had suffered, nothing more could be seen. Max saw him pause for only a moment and then the Marshall was moving, not as a man anymore, but as something entirely alien to his senses. His body blurred as he exploded into the foremost ranks of rebels. So quickly did he move that Max could only see the outcome. Wherever he struck, he divided men's bodies. Two and three at a time, he harvested them like wheat with a scythe. He transitioned from one kill to the next with surgical precision and choreographed grace, every movement producing death. The rebels finally broke, the slaughter of the New Army soldiers stemmed, and the Marshall continued forth, driving the enemy toward the sea.

With nowhere left to run, the doomed rebels turned one last time to face their executioners. The sea at their backs, the Marshall and his New Army soldiers before them, they let loose with a final rallying cry. But the Marshall stood tall, a monster of a figure now, and a resounding cry, like that of a dying sun, burst forth from his mouth. The voices of a thousand souls rolled out of him as one, forcing men from both sides of the conflict to cover their ears in terror and despair. And twisting in and out of the ungodly scream, rising in strength and volume, was one sentence repeated over and over by each of those thousand voices.

"We are Legion!"

Max fell to his knees, praying for death, his eyes still glued to the spectacle before him as he finally understood the doom before him and the identity of the Marshall became clear. Legion dropped to his knees as well and plunged his hands into the muck once more. Almost instantly, the beach began to move beneath the feet of the rebels. For a moment, Max thought it had become quicksand and the rebels were sinking into it. But then as the screams of agonized horror began to rise up from the enemy soldiers, he realized it was much worse for those who stood against this monster.

He could think of no worse way to die.

Leeches by the millions were boiling up from the sand and mud, driven by hunger as they covered boots, then legs, then torsos, and finally faces. They found any and all exposed body parts and attached themselves to feed. They burrowed under clothes and then into bodies themselves, gorging on fresh blood. And while the abominations fed, Legion came for them. Every step crushed a skull or decapitated a man. Every grasp dismembered a victim. Death spread from Legion like a plague and the rebels were slaughtered to a man. In a few short minutes, it was finally over. Legion had indeed done what he said he would do.

The end of Ireland had come.

From a quarter mile away, Morgan "Max" Exan knelt and stared in spellbound horror at the aftermath of the battle. Near the sea, what remained of the bodies was being consumed by the churning mass of leeches. Even from such a distance, Max could hear the moist sucking sounds as the creatures continued to feed. Closer to him, thousands of New Army soldiers—those who were not wounded or dying—had prostrated themselves in the mud, their faces pressed to the muck as they held out their hands in supplication toward their leader, the man who had delivered them and brought victory in a way they could not comprehend. The chant began in almost a whisper, before rising to a crescendo of sound that drowned out everything else. The mass of New Army soldiers were chanting only one word.

"Legion!"

Max pulled himself to his feet, daring to stand in the presence of whatever it was that had claimed victory in the rotting mud of the Lagan Weir. Legion, who had been surveying the battlefield and the troops who were now openly worshipping him, snapped his gaze up to look directly at the standing lieutenant. Even from the distance, Max could see those awful eyes with perfect clarity—eyes that narrowed in conviction and told him he was going to die.

"Thank God for that," he said softly to himself. "There are much worse fates than death." Without another thought, Morgan Exan turned and climbed down from the rubble heap he had been standing on and disappeared into the ruins of Belfast.

The eyes of Legion watched him go.

CHAPTER 2

Rikers Island, New York City, New York: It came out of the darkened hallway with frightening speed, fanged jaws gaping wide as it closed in on its prey. But Tom McCain wasn't just any victim and he calmly whipped his Sig Sauer P226 around and pulled the trigger. The creature let out an inhuman scream as the bullet took it in the gut, rupturing its distended stomach and shattering its lower spine as it exited the monster's back. Bright red blood splattered across the floor and wall as the thing went down and writhed in agony. McCain shook his head in anger as he holstered his weapon. The blood of these monsters was black. The red blood slicking the floor meant it had recently fed.

A lot.

Reaching behind his back, he unsheathed the long blade he had strapped there. The razor-sharp katana sliced through the monster's neck with little resistance and this time only black oily ichor splashed across the floor. The head rolled away and the monster ceased moving. McCain transferred the sword to his other hand and pulled his Sig again. Dropping to a crouch, he peered down the darkened hall.

"What do we do now?" a quiet voice sounded from behind him.

McCain didn't answer right away, keeping his eyes focused intently on the darkness before him, alert for any type of movement in the shadows that would signify another attack. The power was out across the entire grid and even the emergency lights were non-functional. The only light available was the ambient night-time glow from the city that filtered in from the high-set and barred windows at the tops of the wall. That they were in over their heads was not lost on the former New York City detective. He knew there were more out there, hidden in the darkness of the prison and waiting to come at them again. They had been through four such attacks in the past thirty minutes and had still not reached the prison proper.

He doubted they even would now.

If New York City was hell on earth today, Rikers Island had become the Seventh Layer. It sat on more than four hundred acres of land surrounded by water and, in normal times, it housed some of the state's most violent offenders. All contact with the prison had ceased three nights prior and the two teams that had originally been sent to ascertain the problems had not returned.

That's when he had received the call. Tom McCain was a veteran police officer—at least he had been before the events of two years ago. He was in his late fifties and while he kept himself in excellent shape, age was starting to creep up on him. He felt aches and pains a little longer, took a split second more to react in a fight, and generally felt like Father Time was finally catching up to him.

Two years ago, he had returned to New York City—his city—and taken up the shield again. But it had been a short-lived homecoming to law enforcement. New York City had been dying for years and unfortunately, the rise and fall of the undead and the death and destruction they had caused world-wide had hastened the decline of his city considerably.

Today, the Big Apple was but a shell of the past. After the horrifying events brought down upon the world by Hade, shops and stores had closed down en masse and a sizable portion of the population had moved away. Still, the city had not been completely abandoned. Local and world government remained and so had a couple of large-scale industries and businesses, including the prison. The city still functioned at a basic level, but the heart of New York City was largely gone and that pissed Tom McCain off.

A year ago, he had hung up the shield for good and gone into business for himself, hooking up with a private company run by several local government contacts he had known for years. Ironically enough, as a hired mercenary he found himself in a better position to fight the decay of his city. He'd been fighting on a much larger battlefield for most of his life as part of an ancient struggle very few people knew about, much less could have understood, and under his new employers, he had managed to infiltrate their ranks. History was full of conspiracy theories surrounding groups like the Illuminati, the Trilateral Commission, the New World Order or any one of a hundred different secret societies, but the truth was that there really was a secret organization bent on taking over the world.

Krypteia.

There were layers beneath layers of corruption within that ancient association, and he was thoroughly enjoying his time these days doing his level best trying to pull it down from within. This was why Tom McCain found himself this evening toting his Krypteia-issued Sig around and blowing holes in Krypteia-created monsters as he worked for the very entity he was fighting against. If that wasn't irony, he didn't know what was.

He chanced a quick look behind him, forcing himself to focus on the task at hand. Of the four-man team that had entered the prison facility, only he and Baker remained. The man was a hired gun, a former Navy SEAL known for his government-sanctioned wet work. But McCain wasn't complaining. He was good in a fight and had proven it already. The other two members of his team were gone—no less talented, but dead just the same. Marcus Donaldson, a young Australian security officer in the employ of the United Nations, had been killed in the first attack, the blood-thirsty creatures completely eviscerating him before they had been neutralized. Baker had ended Donaldson's suffering with a mercy bullet to the head. There had been no other way.

The other member of his team, Gale Trudeau, a former member of the Armoured Engineer Battalion 1 in the Swiss Armed Forces, had been dragged off screaming into the shadows when four of the creatures had attacked them from behind. They had tried pursuing, but lost her when they ran into several more monsters and were forced into yet another fight. By then, Gale's screams had been silenced.

McCain had not expected to see their foe in such numbers, and now his last remaining companion was asking the same question he was asking himself. What now?

"We get paid to find the answers," McCain finally answered Baker's unspoken question in a whisper, as much to himself as to the ex-soldier.

"Going to be hard to get paid if we're dead," the former SEAL answered.

McCain ignored him as he returned his focus back to the hallway. He'd studied the layout well enough to know that the hall ended in a processing center, a large room dedicated to getting prisoners ready for general population. Normally, the room would be locked down as it was the point of entry into the prison itself, but as they had found out earlier, all the locks and precautionary measures in the entire complex had been disengaged and all the guards had vanished. In fact, the only thing they'd seen had been blood, and a lot of it at that.

"I think we can assume the worst, McCain," Baker went on. "Other than these things, we've seen no one else."

"That's what bothers me. There were over ten thousand prisoners housed here and five thousand working personnel. That's a lot of people to pull a David Copperfield with. Where'd they all go?"

"Do you really want to find out?"

McCain shrugged. "What I want is irrelevant," he replied. "What our employer wants is what pays the bills." It wasn't exactly true, but it was enough to convince Baker to press on.

Baker moved up in a crouch and turned around so that he was back-to-back with the former police officer. He kept his eyes and his weapon on the hall behind them as he spoke. "Two years ago," he said quietly. "What'd you see?"

"I was in Salt Lake City when it happened," McCain answered as if expecting the question, his voice soft. "I've seen a lot of crazy things in my life, but those were a couple of days I'd just as soon forget. You?"

"I was on an assignment in Sao Paolo," the man answered. "I didn't see anything. Brazil didn't go through it like the rest of the world."

"Consider yourself lucky," McCain grunted.

"I did until tonight," Baker nodded. "What I want to know is how does this compare?"

McCain chuckled sourly. "Two years ago, I was fighting slow and uncoordinated zombies in a bizarre Night of the Living Dead remake come to life. That was cake compared to these things."

"I can believe it," Baker scoffed, his voice wavering for the briefest of moments, enough that only someone like McCain would have noticed it. "I've seen the briefings on these things," he added. "Most of it has been your work. Where'd they come from?"

"Don't know," he lied. "I saw my first one about six months ago. I've hunted down the few that I could find, but they were always alone."

"And this?"

"This?" McCain repeated, waving a hand through the air as if to encompass the entire prison complex. "This is a nightmare." After a few seconds of silence, he reached back and tapped the SEAL on the shoulder. "Come on," he continued. "We'll check out the processing center and then evac. We've got enough intel to at least get a bigger squad in here. I'm pretty sure they're going to need some heavy artillery."

"Roger that," the soldier replied with a nod.

Without another word, the two men began to move down the hall. It took them several minutes of careful and silent movement to reach the open doors of the processing center. What they found inside would give Tom McCain nightmares for the rest of his life. The bodies of a dozen prison guards were hanging upside down, their feet tied and chained to a thick steam pipe that ran the length of the ceiling. Their hands were also bound, zip-tied tightly behind their backs. Each had their throats torn out, though there was little blood on the floor to attest to that.

They also found Trudeau. Leaning against the far wall, her eyes were open and glazed over and her mouth moved in a silent scream as one of the creatures fed on her, its mouth rending the flesh of her throat as it drank her blood. Baker's Sig popped once and the top of the creature's head disappeared in a spray of black blood and flesh. McCain was moving even as the SEAL took the shot, bringing his katana to the ready position. Baker's second shot took off the remainder of the monster's head at the neck, sending its body skidding away from the dying woman.

Sword out and at the ready, McCain hurriedly crossed the room and knelt beside the fallen army officer. Her throat was mostly gone and he knew she had mere seconds of life left. "I'm truly sorry," he whispered, his voice choking as he looked into her tortured eyes.

Her lips moved again for a brief second and then her body shuddered once and she was still. Baker was beside him in a moment, anger flashing in his eyes.

"This is beyond wrong," he snapped, his voice brittle.

McCain turned a cold gaze on the man. "It's what they do," he said quietly.

"Are they really vampires?"

"Yeah," answered McCain. "Nearest I can tell."

Baker placed the barrel of his gun against the dead woman's forehead. "Is she going to come back as one?" he snapped angrily.

McCain reached out and gently pushed the gun away. "No," he answered. "Doesn't seem to work that way."

The former SEAL remained unconvinced. "Then where are they coming from?"

McCain was silent for a bit, his eyes roaming the shadows about them, feeling the hair on the back of his neck begin to stand up. "I don't know," he finally answered at length. "We know they used to be human, but that's about all we know. Six months hasn't given us a thing to work with."

"Any chance our bad guys are using some sort of chemical reaction to turn normal people into blood-drinking monsters?" Baker went on. "They've done it before."

McCain shook his head. "No," he replied, considering again the incredible magnitude of what Hade had brought upon the world two years ago. Baker's suggestion that it was happening again was one of the first things he had thought of, too, but this seemed different. Darker. "This is more than that," he finished.

"Then we're done here," Baker said angrily, standing up. "I'll run point in any firefight, but I'm not going out like this. Trudeau didn't deserve this."

McCain couldn't argue. He'd seen enough. He stood as well and began to turn as a vampire shot out of the darkened hall behind them. Baker's weapon came up automatically and he put two bullets into the thing's chest, the impacts sending it slamming up against the wall with an unholy scream of pain.

Two more shadows burst from a darkened holding cell and three more came at them from the center's main office. The vampires were unnaturally fast, but Tom McCain moved quickly himself, bringing his gun to bear even as he sent his katana out in the opposite direction. The blade sliced through the belly of the nearest monster as he put a bullet into the head of another. The disemboweled creature howled in fury and pain as it frantically tried to hold in its blackened organs. Whatever they were now, they had once been human and human biology still ruled them to an extent.

Several more of them were coming out of the shadows and he saw Baker spin around, bringing his own gun up to kill the closest thing to him. Unfortunately, the SEAL missed the shadow dropping from the ceiling and claws tore into the man's hand, ripping the gun from his grip. With a snarl of rage, Baker threw an elbow and connected with the attacking creature's jaw, snapping bone. The vampire dropped to a crouch, a murderous look in its red-rimmed eyes as its broken jaw hung limply.

McCain could see quite clearly the elongated teeth, red with fresh blood. That told him there were other survivors somewhere in the complex. Without another thought, he put a bullet between the creature's eyes.

"McCain!" Baker shouted.

He spun toward his partner who had one creature wrapped around his legs and another on his back, bearing him to the floor. McCain brought his sword up high to strike when he was hit from behind himself. He went reeling into a nearby desk and the blade was jarred from his hand, clattering to the floor. He turned, bringing his gun up when another creature leapt over the desk at him. McCain had just a split second to dive to the floor, where he quickly rolled to his back and opened fire. Two more vampires went down under the hail of bullets, but even as they fell, more appeared, darting out of the shadows to surround him.

Tom McCain knew then that he was dead. Tightening his resolve, he swore he would take as many with him as he could. He fired his Sig again, taking another creature through the heart, but clawed hands tore the weapon from his hand. Balling his fists, he shouted a string of obscenities and prepared to take on the creatures hand-to-hand.

That was when a voice cut through the melee with a single word. "Cease."

The vampires looming over him turned their heads toward the voice and, a moment later, they melted back into the shadows of the holding cells. McCain climbed to his feet and turned to survey the room. Baker was on his feet and doubled over, holding his arm close to his body. It was clearly broken above the elbow and blood dripped from the claw marks on his weapon hand and arms. He was turned away from McCain, his eyes on a new shape.

Standing in the main entry to the prison proper was a figure, huge and imposing. A long black leather trench coat hung open, revealing a black tee-shirt complete with a shoulder rig housing an enormous Desert Eagle. His long dark hair was pulled back into a ragged ponytail and his beard was matted and unkempt. Black pants and boots capped off his appearance and when he smiled, white teeth flashed in the gloom.

Tom McCain knew him immediately.

"Hello, Thomas," Hade greeted him almost warmly, his voice low and deep.

"Hade," McCain replied curtly. "I should have known."

Baker swiveled his head from the newcomer to McCain and back again, and then charged toward Hade, pulling a combat knife from his belt with his good hand. The huge man lashed out as quick as a snake, his fingers closing on Baker's broken arm in a vise. Baker screamed in agony. With a twist of his wrist and the sound of tearing flesh, Hade snapped the arm in two, tearing it completely from the man's body.

The soldier's eyes went wide in shock as blood pumped from his severed arm, arterial spray coating the floor and walls and causing a rumble of hunger to come from the shadows around them. Hade's other hand snapped out, closing on the soldier's throat in a grip of iron. With no effort at all, the huge man lifted Baker off his feet and pulled him close. "You, I don't need," he said and then flung the soldier into one of the holding cells. Baker screamed for only another few seconds as the vampires fell on him, tearing at his body in their frenzied effort to feed.

As Baker died in the dark, Hade turned his full attention to McCain, who stood frozen, watching and wary. "I wondered when I would see you again, Thomas," he said and chuckled, the familiar sound of boulders rolling down a mountainside.

McCain glared. He knew the man—if he was indeed a man—as much more than just the architect of the horror two years ago. McCain's history with Hade went back much further than that, almost to the day he had decided to believe the fantastic story from John about a secret society bent on not only taking over the world, but taking over the beyond as well.

"I was wondering the same thing," McCain said quietly, his eyes on the huge man but his senses wary for an attack from the shadows. "Can't say I'm surprised to see you here. Or happy, if we're sharing our feelings and all."

"I appreciate the honesty, Thomas," Hade replied with a smile, performing a grotesque salute with Baker's severed arm, which he still held. "You didn't think I'd throw a party and not come back for an encore, especially after you didn't show up for the grand finale of the first one."

McCain didn't take the bait. "It wasn't my fight," he replied icily. "You killed an innocent man, but he beat you, Hade. Owen DiConte shut you down."

If Hade was angry, he didn't show it. He simply continued to smile. "Innocence is such a subjective term, my old friend. We're all innocent in our own ways at our own times, at least when we're not anymore," he went on. "Owen followed the dictates of his heart and, while his life may have ended heroically, depending on one's perspective, it wasn't too much earlier that he was all about killing our friend, Petr. Is that the innocence you speak of? You do remember what God said about sinning in your heart."

"That's not the same."

"Oh, but it is," Hade replied smugly. "The only thing that separates Owen from the creatures running around this complex is that Owen didn't have what it takes to finish the job. Of course, that's not to say he didn't try," he finished with a laugh.

"You don't have much respect for your creations, do you?" McCain asked, changing the subject in order to keep his adversary talking while he tried to figure out how he was going to escape. He knew Hade well enough to know that the talking part would not be an issue. Surviving, especially if Hade had already marked him for death, would be very problematic, no matter how long the big man decided to ramble.

"These old things?" Hade scoffed, sweeping Baker's severed arm around to encompass the room and the shadowed movement around them. "Oh, they're a little more durable and reliable than the model we unveiled a couple years ago, but these are definitely higher maintenance."

"And here you are building an army of them." It was a question more than a statement.

Hade laughed. "Not a chance, Thomas," he answered. "The upkeep is too high and if we got too many of them, we'd run out of go-juice, if you get my meaning. Besides, they're mindless animals that do a great job of terrorizing the locals, but aren't much better at carrying out detailed plans than the first batch of toys we created."

"Then why have them?"

"Shock troops," the man replied with a wink and a grin. "That and they make great sheepdogs."

McCain looked at him quizzically and Hade only smiled.

"I see the wheels are at least turning, are they not, Thomas?" he asked slyly. "Too bad you aren't going to live long enough to figure things out."

"I didn't exactly expect a sporting chance, Hade," McCain replied drily, but tensing up just the same.

"You escaped me before, Thomas," Hade said with a chuckle. "But not this time, I think. I had my reasons for not killing you and your daughter twenty years ago when I had the chance—not the least of which was my respect for you and the love you had for your daughter. But I'm not as soft-hearted today as I was back then and the stakes are now much higher. I intend to eliminate your existence tonight and then as soon as I catch up with that little minx daughter of yours, she'll be joining you."

Now it was McCain's turn to smile. "You forget yourself, Hade," he smirked. "I put you down once before."

"You got lucky that night, Thomas," Hade corrected him, the smile never leaving his face.

"Maybe," McCain shrugged. "But I think you and I remember that night differently."

"We can agree to disagree, then. Still, you know me well enough to know I'm a fair man," Hade went on easily. "As I see you're unarmed, let me give you a hand." He tossed Baker's detached arm on the desk in front of the former detective. "Your friend won't be needing it anymore." Turning to the shadows, Hade gave the command.

"Kill him."

What happened next took less than two seconds.

McCain was moving before Hade uttered the death sentence, spinning and snatching up Baker's severed arm. He continued the turn even as the shadows began detaching themselves from their hiding places and he drove the jagged end of the arm's shattered bone into the throat of the first vampire coming at him from the doorway. The creature did a horrible spastic dance in the air as it fell to the floor, clawing at its throat with a hissing, bubbling sound.

McCain leapt over the body and into the hallway, even as he yanked a hockey puck-like canister from his combat belt. He activated it and dropped it behind him as he broke into a dead run. The flash-bang grenade went off a second later, the concussion throwing him forward slightly and the explosion ringing in his ears. He regained his balance and raced on, aware of the pursuit closing in behind him. He knew the grenade would only slow them down slightly. If he planned on getting out of this alive, the rest would be up to him.

Thomas McCain had been fighting the minions of evil for decades. He had senses and abilities that most seasoned soldiers would be envious of. He didn't need to see the creature leap at him to know it had happened and he vaulted himself up as it came at him, turning in the air as the faster vampire caught him. His hands closed on the creature's head and he used his own momentum to turn the monster beneath him as they fell. He ignored the gaping jaws that could easily rip out his throat and used every bit of his weight and momentum to slam the back of the monster's head against the concrete floor as they went down. It broke open like a melon with a sickening crack of bone.

McCain was up in an instant, running hard. The next vampire caught him as he raced through an open security door. Instead of continuing on, the wily fighter spun and caught the edge of the door, slamming it shut. It caught the monster full in the face, driving it against the door frame. Before the monster could move, he slammed the heavy steel door again, this time directly into the vampire's head and body. There was another crack of bone and the monster's red eyes rolled back in its head, a large grotesque crease suddenly dividing its face.

McCain hurried on, not bothering to look back. He already knew that a third vampire was closing in on him. As he turned the corner of a hall and raced toward another security door, he reached to his belt and took hold of his second and last remaining flash-bang. With the monster nearly upon him, McCain stumbled and went down, letting his momentum carry him into a roll to lessen any damage to himself. The creature flung herself on top of him, her jaws filled with predator's teeth opening wide.

McCain brought his hand forward as hard as he could, slamming the flash-bang into the beast's open mouth. Teeth shattered and the monster leapt away in a terrible rage, thrashing herself against the floor and wall in agony. A second later, the grenade went off, blasting most of the creature's jaw and face away.

He was already running as the explosion went off and he quickly reached a third security door, slamming it shut. The electronic latches would not catch, but McCain pushed a nearby desk up against it. He knew it would never hold back his pursuers but it would buy him a few more seconds than it took him to set up the barricade. He would need those few extra seconds to reach the outer doors and the safety of the early morning sun. He still wasn't sure he'd make it out alive, but he was starting to like his chances a whole lot more.

Deep inside the darkened prison, Hade leaned back in a chair and kicked his black alligator-skinned boots up on the desk. His entire bulk dwarfed the furniture. The black-clad and well-armed man standing next to him was surprised the whole thing did not collapse under him.

"Seems to me our intrepid police officer has escaped," Hade rumbled as he casually jacked a bullet into the chamber of his Desert Eagle, while several of the creatures slunk through the shadows of the room, vanishing into the depths of the prison where the real work was taking place.

"I can hunt him down," his companion replied, his voice low and dangerous. "I told you to let me handle him in the first place."

Hade made a show of carefully examining the firearm before pointing it directly at the forehead of the man.

For his part, Marcello Tuono did not shrink back in terror. Instead, he simply stared back at Hade, his own dark eyes piercing. "I only meant I could have had him killed long before he stepped foot on Rikers," he continued

"Had I wanted him killed, I would have done so myself in this very room, Marcello," Hade countered.

The man raised an eyebrow in confusion. "But you sent your playthings after him."

Hade chuckled. "Tom McCain is a seasoned warrior, Marcello," he explained. "But he's no match for me. No man alive is." Hade raised the gun toward the ceiling and looked directly at the assassin for a moment. Then with a movement almost too fast for the naked eye to see, the gun was back in his shoulder holster. "You must understand that everything has a purpose," he continued, adopting his professor-like tone. "Plans evolve and new ones take shape. You're a piece on my chessboard, Marcello, just as Thomas is. He just doesn't know it." He paused to look directly into the assassin's eyes before he finished. "At the moment, I have no intention of sacrificing either of these two prized pieces in a pointless power play."

"So you knew he'd escape?" Tuono asked, keeping his voice even. He had no problem recognizing the threat in his employer's words, but he was not about to give Hade the satisfaction of knowing that it sent a chill through him.

"I would have been disappointed had he not," Hade answered.

Tuono folded his arms in contemplation. "This was for my benefit, wasn't it?" he finally ventured.

Hade smiled and stood up, towering over the assassin. "I was beginning to think it would take you all night to figure that out, Marcello," he replied. "Tom McCain is as formidable an opponent as you would ever face in my employ."

"You underestimate my abilities, sir," Marcello said quietly, his voice betraying no emotion at all.

"Actually, it is you who underestimate our enemies," Hade replied coldly. "Doing so would not only get you killed, but could certainly compromise our operations. Trust me, Marcello," he went on. "You have not stayed alive for so long in your line of work thinking that those around you were not dangerous. Do not make that mistake now. Do you understand?"

"I understand," Tuono replied. "But if he's so dangerous, why let him leave alive?"

"Because sometimes the right enemy can be the most valuable asset," Hade answered with a grin. "Particularly if they don't realize it."

The assassin took a deep breath and nodded his head once. "Very well," he said. "What's our next move?"

Hade looked toward the darkened doorway. "We'll make sure the remainder of our recruits are taken to sea," he replied. "Then you'll go pay a friend of mine a visit."

"Who would that be?"

"Have you ever met President Jose Maria Wilson Nunes da Silva dos Santos of Brazil?"

Tuono shook his head. He knew President Wilson by name and reputation only and he also knew that the man could have someone killed just for using his full name in his presence. "No, I haven't had the pleasure of meeting him personally."

Hade smiled. "Then I think it's high time you two meet. I believe our esteemed president has a job for you, my friend."

Two days later, Tom McCain stood outside of Rikers Island as the United Nations battalion commander, an aging Somali, finished his final report. Row upon row of refrigerated trucks were lined up in every parking lot on Riker's Island, many already filled with recovered bodies, some awaiting dispatch destinations and others already rolling out. More bodies were being brought out of the prison every minute, hidden under bloodied sheets or zipped up in black body bags.

Rikers Island prison was a blood-drenched tomb.

After McCain's narrow escape forty-eight hours earlier, more than two hundred heavily armed soldiers from several different countries and under the orders of the United Nations Secretary General himself, had descended on the complex.

They need not have bothered being armed.

Every room, every cell, every hidden corner of the prison had been turned inside out. Nothing alive remained and no trace of the monsters could be found, except for a few withered corpses McCain and his team had left behind.

Nearly twelve hundred bodies in all had been found, including the remains of McCain's team and the two groups that had visited the prison before he had gone in. Most of the victims had been gathered together and butchered in gyms and cafeteria and showers—any place large enough to pack them in like cattle. Then they had been violently torn apart. Many others had been killed the same way McCain had found the first bodies—hung from steam pipes and cell bars like so much meat and drained of blood. That left well over twelve thousand more prisoners and prison personnel completely unaccounted for. McCain was waiting for the final tally, but he knew the estimate was close. A hundred here or there made no difference. That many people gone signified something big—much bigger than what Hade had brought down on the world two years ago.

The question was, what was it?

CHAPTER 3

Kigoma, Tanzania: Petr Zhugravinsky leaned wearily over the worn, wooden table as he slowly swirled the dregs of his most recent drink. He was settled where he sat every afternoon in the back of the Sun City Bar and Restaurant in Kigoma, just up the road from David Livingston Sumbawanga's old house in Ujiji. Every day for the past year, Petr had made the hour walk up Lumumba Street in the heat of the midday to reach the establishment. Bright yellow inside and out, with blue and white waves painted on the plastered adobe walls, and covered by a red sheet metal roof, it seemed both inviting and forbidden at the same time. He would walk up the five red concrete steps, past the blue chairs with pink hearts painted on the backs, through the narrow veranda and past the rest of the tables in the darkened room to what had become "his" table in the back by the white tiled kitchen.

Today was not unlike any of the other nameless days he had spent here over the past two years. As he took another drink, he looked up and caught his reflection in a mirror recently placed on the far wall. Thinned down considerably, his still muscular frame showed what his size must have been in the past and how far removed he was from that time period. His jet-black hair, uncombed and falling past his shoulders, blended in perfectly with a long, shaggy beard. If he had been in a National Geographic documentary, there probably would have been an ape sitting next to him picking through it.

He allowed himself a small self-depreciating smile as he wondered how long he would have to sit in Sun City before he made it into the tour books for the region. He could imagine it reading, "Stop by Sun City and see the crazy half-man, half-ape, every day between one and four. Pick through his beard for only Tsh500." Shaking his head, the rare moment of levity fleeing almost as soon as it had arrived, he turned his undivided attention back to his drink.

Most days, Petr would spend a few hours every afternoon at the bar, reading and drinking, then settle his tab and catch a dala-dala van out to check on David's sole remaining child and the one person he had sworn to protect—the elder Sumbawanga's daughter, Chuike.

There were some days, however, when he'd walk out to the more touristy Bangwe Beach Bar on the road up to the Kigoma Hilltop Hotel, where he would spend a few hours drinking too much vodka as he watched the vibrant sunset from the beach. When he went and how much he drank sometimes depended on the heat of the day, but more often than not, his decision to get really drunk depended on the severity of the nightmares that haunted him each night.

It was always the same dream, always the same reality. It was unfair, really, that he dreamed of that moment so often when all he had to do was close his eyes and he was instantly back on the mountain in the driving rain, surrounded by people he had trusted and people he should have known better than to trust. He had almost died that day; perhaps he should have. There had definitely been many days since then that he wished Alexis Kennedy had pulled the trigger and put a bullet in his head. But she hadn't, and he hadn't died.

Instead, Owen DiConte had died in his place.

Owen DiConte, so intent on ending Petr's life because of his own failings, had overcome his demons in the end and told Alexis not to shoot. She had listened to Owen's plea and Hade had killed him for it. Petr had never forgiven himself.

Yet, despite the horror of that day, Petr hadn't been driven to drink solely because of what happened on the mountain. While that was certainly the most troubling, there were others that pulled at him, raking his psyche with painful reminders of his own failures. He would find himself stumbling over his repeated attempts to woo Alexis to his side, only to fail and see her constantly out of reach. He continued to blame himself for Rene's death, wondering if there was anything he could have done to save her. He would rewind, word-by-word, his conversations with Hade and mentally scan through the pictures of his family, all of them now dead at his brother's hand. He would find himself reliving the moment he was forced to kill David Livingston Sumbawanga, the one person who always saw the good in Petr.

Still, as traumatizing as those memories were, he could compartmentalize all of that and find peace, even in the loss of family and friends. He knew death intimately, and knew the world had a long history of violent struggles where perhaps the one person least deserving of death, ended up being the one claimed by its icy tendrils.

No, what kept Petr awake late at night were the questions that haunted him constantly and it had become nearly impossible for his broken and battered psyche to move past them. What if Owen had not been the hero? What if he had told Alexis to shoot Petr instead of spare him? Would she have listened and pulled the trigger? Would Owen have survived if Petr had died? Petr had always wanted to be the hero, but he had failed that day, choosing his own survival over that of the others. Had he finally exposed the true Petr to the world? Was he the monster he had always believed himself to be? Was there any chance of redemption? To all of these questions, he had no answers, and was beginning to believe he never would.

Until finally, after a year of spiralling further and further down the rabbit hole, an old Native American named John had arrived on his doorstep with a message.

At first, Petr had told the stranger to get lost, but John had insisted Petr hear him out. The Russian had reluctantly agreed and, as he silently worked his way through a bottle of vodka, John had shared a tale that was nearly impossible to believe. Or it would have been if Petr had not personally lived through it. John spoke for two hours while Petr said absolutely nothing. The old man told him who Hade really was and what his plans had been for that day. He explained the true nature of the conflict up on the mountain, and how his actions and the actions of Owen, Alexis, and the priest, Michael Dalacourt, had spared the world from evil that day.

John had ended by calling Petr a hero, but the Zhugravinsky son felt nothing of the sort. While John's words had answered many of his questions, it had also opened his eyes to just how much he had been used. Everything had been carefully calculated and the seeming randomness of that day had turned out to be just a façade for a great orchestration played out for only one purpose. No, he had not stumbled up that mountain path of his own free will. He had been led there and pushed there, controlled the entire way. He had always thought of himself as a man making his own decisions, but it turned out that he had never been anything more than a puppet whose strings were pulled by others—a puppet not only meant by Hade to die, but one offered up by John as a test for the moral character of another.

In fact, John turned out to be one of the principal architects of that day. He had led Alexis to that mountain, had spoken to her in the same cryptic way Hade had spoken to Petr, and then left her there to her own devices, shivering and shaking in the rain and completely at the mercy of Hade.

Hade had tried to convince Alexis to kill Petr. John had hoped she would not. And Owen had died the hero because of them. They had all been used. They had been played—not just by evil, but also by those who called themselves good. Hade's plans had been bad enough, but Petr had no reason to expect anything else from the man. John had claimed to follow the dictates of God and yet he had been willing to stand by and let it all happen in the name of free will.

Petr reacted in the only way he had left. He snapped.

The fight had only lasted a few brief moments. He had thrown the nearly empty bottle of vodka at the door, shattering it, and then gone after John with the very real thought of killing the old man. The next thing he remembered, though, he was sitting on the floor, the breath driven from his lungs, and no fight remaining within him.

He remembered John kneeling in front of him, his bones creaking and knees popping. He leaned in close and said slowly, "There is still a great deal you don't know or understand, Petr Zhugravinsky," the old man explained. "But if you truly knew the depth that God loves all His children, you included, you would be astounded at what God would do for His children; what more He would sacrifice for them. Though you may not see it or understand its significance, what you sacrificed on the mountain may have saved a great many more, living and not yet born, from a thousand years of hell on earth."

Petr laughed. "Wait. You just said it *may* have," he repeated venomously, his voice slurred. "Did our sacrifice even do any good?"

"The future is never set," John answered gently. "Free agency is a gift, but we are all bound by its consequences. You, me, and everyone else that lives, has lived, or will live are beholden to the history that free will dictates." He paused for several seconds before he finished, his voice barely more than a sad whisper. "So, too, is God."

John stood and offered a hand to Petr. The young Russian slowly took it in a daze and John gently helped him into a nearby chair. "I am not your enemy, Petr Zhugravinsky. I'm your brother and an emissary of God. We are in the final days," he said softly, leaning forward to look into Petr's haunted eyes. "The adversary is not done with you, as you clearly have a part yet to play. When next you see Hade, take care to remember who you truly are."

And then he was gone, leaving Petr alone with his nightmares.

Petr had thus spent the last ten months, not coming to grips with the past, but growing angrier and angrier because of it. He hated Hade for what the man had done to his life. He hated John for forcing him to see things he didn't want to see. He hated Owen for dying the hero and escaping this horrible world. He hated his brother for what he had done to their family. He hated Michael Dalacourt for his blind faith. And he hated Alexis Kennedy for ripping his heart out at the same time she had saved his life. Most of all, he hated himself for the truths he knew in his heart were real, but couldn't stand to face.

So he had remained in Africa, drinking and brooding. At least here he could keep his word to David and protect his daughter and now her husband, Hashim. In many ways, that was what David had died for—to let his sole remaining child live a normal life. Petr had to respect that. He also had to protect that.

And so Petr sat at his table in Sun City, just as he had every day for the past two years, knowing there was no point in hiding or running from his own demons, but hoping that perhaps they might one day forget about him. That's when a cold shadow fell across his table. He didn't need to look up to see who it was. Somewhere deep within him, he already knew.

His demon would never forget about him.

Heavy footsteps tromped slowly across the creaking, wooden floor, coming in his direction. Petr closed his eyes and let all the anger, resentment, frustration and bitterness lying just under the surface swell through his soul like a rage-filled tsunami before picking up his drink and downing the rest of it in a single gulp. He turned the glass over in his hand and slammed it down on the table, before finally looking up, murder in his eyes.

"Hello, Hade."

CHAPTER 4

Cedar City, Utah: The irony was not lost on Alexis Kennedy. She could still remember that evening several years ago when she had gazed through rose-colored glasses at the sleep-deprived surgical residents of Primary Children's Hospital hurrying through trauma bays in the Emergency Department during the early hours of the morning. It had been about two in the morning and she'd been there to support a friend whose young child had been one of those patients the doctors were trying to save. It had all been strangely romantic; residents and doctors sacrificing sleep, food, and a normal life to diagnose and treat children in dire need. What she would give to go back to those innocent days.

Now, a few years later, it was two in the morning again and she was entering the trauma doors of Valley View Medical Center from the helipad where she just quietly deposited an explosive linked to a cell trigger in an awaiting non-medical helicopter.

Stacia McCain had already cut power to the facility, ensuring that the only generators still running were those supplying the ICUs, ORs, and the now dimly lit emergency room, requiring Alexis to walk with a careful yet deliberate pace past the trauma bays and central nurses' station. She proceeded through the busy halls, ignoring the harried medical professionals and acting for all the world like she belonged despite the two concealed M9 Berettas holstered under her form-fitting jacket and the Mossberg shotgun in the shoulder bag slung over one shoulder. The weapons only needed to remain hidden until she reached the next hallway, where security cameras would have been shut down along with all other non-medically necessary electrical equipment. Contrary to the placid expression on her face, adrenaline roared through her, quickening her pulse and respiratory rate, raising blood pressure, dilating pupils, and tensing her muscles.

All to my advantage, she thought. *Use it.*

She scanned the department methodically and then moved deliberately down the hall. There was no immediate threat and she drew no attention to herself as nurses, aids, techs, and doctors rushed about, checking on patients in the suddenly blacked-out hospital. Amazingly enough, things were going according to plan.

Taking the next hallway to the right, she hurried down it and took her next left, before coming to a halt. This part of the hospital was practically empty and she knew it should remain so all the way to their target. She removed her black nylon jacket and armed herself with the shotgun from the shoulder bag. Despite assurances from intel that they would meet no resistance, she nestled the Mossberg in the crook of her shoulder and, pointing it forty-five degrees to the floor to maintain her line of sight, she advanced again using an urgent yet careful toe-to-toe gait to keep herself quiet and balanced. It was fifty feet to the "T" intersection where she would meet Stacia.

Four doors on each side between here and there. Administrative offices, which should all be empty this time of night, she thought and then froze. They should have been empty and probably were, except for the slowly turning knob at the end of the hall on the right.

Hidden in the shadows of the darkened hallway, Alexis tucked herself into the first open doorway and lowered herself to a crouch. She raised the barrel of the gun and sighted, making certain she was a safe distance from the doorjamb in order to allow herself full movement. Keeping her elbows tucked to present a smaller target to her enemies and to avoid bumping them on anything that could alter her shot, she focused on the door. It opened inward and a man's head turtled out of the doorway in an unsafe and unpracticed manner.

Non-combatant, she silently concluded, but did not lower her weapon. Training had taught her to never lower her guard for any reason.

The man's head disappeared into the dark room and she heard him whisper, "It's empty. I'll go first and you can follow in a minute." True to his words, he rushed out of the room, retying his scrubs and shutting off his suddenly beeping pager. He never saw Alexis, clad in shadow, Mossberg trained on his chest, watching him rush past. Alexis remained motionless and twenty seconds later, a young blond woman exited the same room in a greater rush, frantically trying to pull her hair back into a ponytail as she also headed to the ER.

Neither of them would ever know how close they had just come to dying.

With the amorous couple gone, the hall once again fell silent. Alexis detached herself from her shadowed doorway and continued toward the rendezvous point. Stacia would be coming from the hallway on the right, so Alexis distanced herself from the wall to improve her line of sight around the corner and into the left hallway. Grateful for the adrenaline fortifying her body, she slowly crept from left to right, watching the hallway stretch out before her into darkness. This was always the worst part. Anyone at the end of the hall would certainly see her first and she knew it.

I should have switched to the M9, not this stupid shotgun, she silently lamented to herself. Another half step and she froze. A whisking sound coming from the end of the hall startled her back to disciplined attention and reset her edge.

"It's clear," declared a hushed voice directly behind her. It was Stacia. "The vent turns on for thirty seconds every five minutes to circulate," she continued to whisper. "Let's move while it masks your noise." There was a short pause before the other young woman finished. "And next time you clear the corner of a long hallway, Lex, use the M9."

As if I didn't already know, Alexis thought furiously to herself, fighting the urge to twirl her hair. She was deeply grateful her long hair was bound up tightly. Stacia knew what it meant when she played with her locks and Alexis detested showing weakness to her. So she settled for firing as fierce a look as she could muster toward the other young woman—her mentor and friend, and yet a woman who loved to pretend she was so much older and wiser than her.

"Just switch guns and let's move." Stacia remained focused as a wolf. She missed nothing. "And release that ridiculous death grip on your stock. Your hair is pulled so tight you couldn't twirl it in a tornado anyway."

Still angry with herself, Alexis flipped the shotgun around and back into her pack. She did not bother zipping it, knowing she might need to quickly get it back into her hands. A moment later, armed with one of her M9s, they cleared two more hallways, working flawlessly as a team. They encountered no resistance.

Finally, only one door remained between the two women and their objective. It stood at the far end of the hall and, with the power cut to all non-essential hospital functions, both realized immediately that too much light was emitting from the crack at the floor. Alexis shot her companion a smug look and holstered her M9, pulling out her Mossberg once again. Stacia ignored the look and held up three fingers, then two, then one. At one, Alexis blasted two shells through the area between the door's handle and the doorframe. She was moving immediately, rushing forward almost simultaneously with her second trigger pull. Three steps later, she kicked in the shattered door, her shotgun leading the way.

Seamlessly, Stacia rushed past her, barking in a dominating voice, "On the floor! Hands behind your head or you die!"

Behind her, Alexis had dropped the shotgun to the floor and pulled her M9 again. The shotgun would only hinder her in a firefight if one broke out. Staying low, she hurried into the room, keeping her back to the wall until she was in one corner nearest the door. Stacia already occupied her spot in the other corner. Both women faced the same direction, minimizing the chances of shooting each other. "Faces down!" Stacia ordered, her own weapon trained on the targets.

Two men silently obeyed the command and lay face down against a cold steel floor in a room that stood a good three feet smaller in every dimension than the blueprints that the women had studied, indicated. Despite the power loss, the lights worked and the computer screen on the desk gave off its usual glow. A steel door stood behind the desk to the left, where the same blueprints had shown a solid wall. This was the fortress their intel had suggested—cleverly hidden inside a hospital—but it was far more advanced than they had expected.

In silent synchronicity, the two women took a careful step toward the compliant guards. Both men were calm, hands already laced behind their heads. Alexis and Stacia crossed the room to them.

Her gun trained on the back of one guard's head, Stacia dropped a knee to the back of his neck, while Alexis kept her M9 on the other. Stacia holstered her weapon and hastily zip-cuffed the man's wrists, then motioned for Alexis to do the same as she pulled her gun again.

Instead of following Stacia's lead, Alexis pulled her other Beretta and trained it on the desk, keeping her first weapon on the guard. "Out now," she shouted. "Out or I open fire! Hands where I can see them!" The huskiness of her voice surprised even her.

"NO! No, no, no, please!" came a whining voice from behind the desk. Pale, skinny hands showed themselves from beneath the desktop, one wrist encased in standard-issue metal handcuffs. Alexis had heard the man's panicked breathing as they had moved to incapacitate the guards and she anticipated asking Stacia why she had not.

"I'm, um… I... I don't have a gun!" the man begged. "Please don't shoot me!"

"Stand! Now!" she ordered, seeing Stacia from the corner of her eye begin to move sideways so she would have a clearer view behind the desk.

That's when everything fell apart.

The uncuffed guard at her feet lashed out with his hand, grabbing for her ankle as he rolled to his back and reached toward his shoulder holster with his other hand. Alexis , however, was not taken by surprise and easily stepped out of the guard's grasp. She didn't hesitate and put two rounds into his chest and then immediately trained the gun on the second guard. He had not moved, obviously content to stay alive.

Stacia hurried around the desk, her M9 leading the way.

The man behind the desk was all but sobbing. "Don't shoot!" he pleaded again. "No more shooting! Please!"

Alexis did the same, moving quickly around the desk, understanding the urgency of their situation. "Quiet," she snapped. "Hands where we can see them!" She cornered around the right side of the desk to maintain her side of the room and her sight of the door. She could now see the remainder of the panicked man cowering beneath the desk. With his knees pulled to his chest in a protective posture, he shook from head-to-toe. His round thick-rimmed glasses sat askew across a too-large nose, which matched his enormous ears, and contrasted his small chin. He sat with eyes that were tightly closed, bunching up his skin and looking strangely out of place. His left wrist was chained to a briefcase, which was also chained to a metal bar fastened to the underside of the desk.

"Shut up," she ordered.

"Unarmed and immobile," Stacia added, scanning the man's face.

"Not the one we're looking for."

She turned her gaze to the door that had not shown up on their blueprints. It appeared to be solid steel and opened inward, but both women could now see that it sat unlatched and just a hair ajar. Stacia kicked at it, slamming it open.

They breeched it in the same fashion they had entered the first room. But this one boasted pure metal walls, ceiling, and floor. In the center sat a single desk of heavy, dark wood. Their target, a graying, thin Caucasian male, sat in the leather overstuffed chair behind it, armed and ready. Alexis cleared the doorway as the man opened fire, sending bullets whizzing and spinning about the room, ricocheting off the steel until they ran out of energy or escaped through the doorway.

Stacia dove through the doorway and rolled to the right. Bullets came in a flurry from beneath the desk this time, creating a deafening cacophony of metal on metal. Alexis lunged to her left, which showed her that the man had ducked under the desk and was purposefully firing at the walls, making it harder to get close and fire a kill shot. *He was hoping for a stray ricochet*, she thought darkly.

Just then, Stacia bounded atop the desk, reached with her left hand to grab the chair and pulled it close to jam the man under the desk. Alexis found her position just as Stacia found hers and both double-tapped into the target area.

There was no return fire.

Keeping her gun trained on the area, Alexis readied for another shot as Stacia kicked the rolling chair away from the desk. A thin man slumped to the floor out of the darkness, lifeless and facing Alexis with dead eyes. Her M9 trained on the man's head, Alexis moved toward him. She noticed that his gun was no longer in his hand, and the thin trickle of dark blood running from his mouth told her that he was no longer a threat.

She knelt by his corpse and looked closer, her eyes taking in his face. What she saw made her blood run boil. "His hair is died gray," she said, biting down on her anger. "He's way too young. Eyes are the wrong color. This isn't him."

Stacia dropped to her knee beside Alexis and grabbed the dead man by the hair. She turned his face toward her and then slammed his head back to the floor in a fury. "Again!" she snapped angrily. "Our intel is a day late AGAIN! They swore they ID'd him this morning and he hadn't left! And what a stupid fortress!" she growled, looking around in a fury. "This room is a death trap with no escape route!"

"It doesn't make sense," Alexis agreed, looking around as well. Stacia was right. The room was a death trap with no chance of survival. Unless…

Her eyes shot up and met Stacia's. They leapt to their feet simultaneously, moving like cats, but they already knew what they would find.

Bursting back through the steel door, they saw it. Handcuffs, one end empty, still swayed from the bar under the desk in the next room. The frightened man was gone, along with his briefcase.

"We were played!" Stacia snarled and they rushed back into the hospital corridors.

Sprinting beside Stacia, Alexis begged her vision to adjust to the darkened conditions while her mind ran through her mission prep sessions. Four possible exits. The furthest lead to the east and west parking lots, which meant he must have… "He's going for the helipad!" she said as the realization dawned on her. Non-medical helicopter idling on the roof, its pilot speaking with someone on his headset, the passenger door open and ready.

They had known they were coming.

Without waiting for an answer, she turned left and ran hard, Stacia right behind her. Retracing her route through the emergency room and ignoring the frightened shouts and shrieks of patients, nurses, and doctors, the two women rushed forward, desperate to catch their prey. Unfortunately, Alexis misjudged the opening rate of the automatic exterior doors and she smashed through the glass and rolled to the ground just outside. The glass shards reduced her clothing to shreds, leaving her with numerous cuts to her forearms, scalp and shoulders.

Ignoring the pain, she regained her feet and reached inside her pocket as her eyes settled on the helicopter ascending hurriedly into the air from the nearby helipad. She pulled out her smartphone as she looked up for confirmation. There, in the rear passenger window of the bird, she saw the skinny, frightened man who had been cowering under a desk only a few minutes before. Only now, he had transformed into their fifty-five year old target by peeling off the extra-large latex nose and ears he had been hiding behind. Hateful eyes glared at her. With his identity confirmed, she ran her finger in a specific order across the phone screen's image password, unlocking it. "Forgive me, Owen," she said softly as the phone activated.

The helicopter erupted into a ball of white, then blue, then red flames that blinded Alexis, the percussion blast knocking her back to the ground. In pieces large and small, the helicopter fell back to earth with a ground shaking crash.

"Nicely done." It was a rare compliment from Stacia, who had arrived right behind her, but there was a heavy sense of urgency to her voice. "Now come on, Alexis," she went on. "We need to disappear."

Alexis tried to climb to her feet but found that her strength had failed and she collapsed.

"Now, Alexis," Stacia urged her. "We can't stay. They'll bring everything they've got."

Stacia dragged her to her feet and the two women staggered away from the burning wreckage, Stacia taking advantage of the chaos that had descended upon the hospital as she guided her numb friend to the safety of the car she had waiting just down the street. Ten minutes later, they were at the small private airport where their organization's pilot was waiting, engines hot. He wore a stern look as he descended the stairs to help Stacia with Alexis, a look that was particularly severe for a man whose face looked like chiseled stone.

His mouth opened to speak, but Stacia interrupted him. "Not a word, Otis. Not one word."

"I wouldn't dream of it, Miss McCain," he replied with a noncommittal shrug. "I'll make no mention of how clandestine that explosion was. I won't even ask why our young cherub, Miss Kennedy, looks like she caught the business end of a man-sized blender." He effortlessly scooped the injured girl into his arms and carried Alexis up the steps and into the plane. He set her down in the first seat with fatherly care and then proceeded to the cockpit, never looking back at Stacia, who immediately went to work on Alexis' wounds. "I won't tell you the Betadine, bandages, and some Keflex are in the back," he continued. "I also won't tell you that we'll be in the air in five minutes and back on the ground in another forty. And, of course, I won't tell you I'll have the doctor waiting for you when we arrive."

"Enough, Otis," Stacia grumbled. "Just get us to Salt Lake fast."

"That," Otis said as he headed for the cockpit, "is exactly why they sent me."

CHAPTER 5

Los Angeles, California: In May of 1999, construction began on the first Roman Catholic cathedral in the western United States. By the spring of 2002, the magnificent house of God was completed. The cathedral, which floats on one hundred and ninety-eight individual concrete isolators, was built to withstand earthquakes up and into the eight-point range on the Richter scale. In an increasingly godless world, it was a Catholic beacon calling out to those of God's children still listening. It was meant to stand against the heaving of an agitated earth.

Although the cathedral had been built for the people of southern California, Francis De Solei had always considered it his own, personal church. He'd been instrumental in picking the site, in choosing the architect, and in the construction process. And once the cathedral had opened in 2002, even though he had been transferred to the Vatican by that time, he had visited often, knowing that one day he would return for good.

After the last Catholic pope and most of the leaders of the church had been killed in the terrorist attacks that destroyed almost all of Vatican City, De Solei had indeed returned and it was here where he began his new church within the shattered shell of the old. During his two years here, he had turned the area around the magnificent cathedral into a modern day Forum, with church offices, shrines and monuments scattered far and wide across the region and beyond. He had expanded his power and influence, absorbing many other churches and people into his World Church, and he had moved with frightening speed in becoming one of the most powerful men on the face of the earth. It was God's will, after all, and as he was apt to say to those in his inner circles, no man can stand in the way of God's will.

Today, however, as the sun rose slowly over the palm trees and stucco houses below the cathedral, one man had come to challenge that power.

Michael Dalacourt stood at the base of the stone stairs that would take him up to the open walk and from there to the confrontation he knew must happen. It had been a long and winding road that had led him to this moment and he paused briefly to prepare himself for what was to come. He reached into his ragged pocket, as had become his habit whenever he needed some extra resolve, and pulled out a tattered and yellowed piece of newspaper. He looked at the paper, unfolded it and read the headline for perhaps the thousandth time—"Los Angeles the New Vatican?"

His eyes scanned the article again, though there was really no need. He had read the blasphemy so many times that he could recite it word-for-word, even when he was drunk, which admittedly had been a good portion of the past two years.

> "LOS ANGELES THE NEW VATICAN?"—Los Angeles, CA: Parting with tradition has been a hallmark of the newly-appointed pope of the church, even in the short time he has been at its head. From maintaining his own name to actually striking the Catholic name from church doctrine, Pope De Solei has declared that Los Angeles, California, will be the new seat of the Church. "As the final days loom before us, we must be able to move quickly and decisively in all that the Church does," he said in last evening's worldwide broadcast. "The Vatican is gone. We must accept that. The terrible calamities and catastrophes of the past year have tried us all; have changed the very fabric of reality that encompasses humanity. Since then, I have directed the Church from Los Angeles and, for the

> very same reason I have remade God's church into one Church for the entire world, I have decided to remake our location here as the new Vatican. The clock moves toward midnight and we must move with it. We must bring all God's children to us. We must prepare each and every one of you to receive Christ's glory through this, God's Church."

Michael Dalacourt, former priest of the Catholic church, former protégé of Francis De Solei, former pupil of the monster Hade in the guise of Father Dunkirk, crumpled up the piece of newspaper and thrust it back into his pocket. Normally, that would precede the lighting of a cigarette and the opening of a bottle of cheap whisky, but not today.

Today, Michael Dalacourt was on a mission.

He paused to look down at himself and cringed at what he saw. His clothing was in tatters, jeans worn to thread in many places and a thin and patched flannel shirt he had gotten from a kindly old bartender named Gus some time ago. He was barefoot, having walked through his shoes weeks ago, but that didn't matter to him. Pain and suffering of the body was nothing compared to the pain and suffering of the soul and Michael Dalacourt had been hurt like no one else.

In his mid-twenties now, the former priest looked twice his age and he knew it. Appearances were not everything, though, and the scriptures were replete with tales of prophets who were called of God not for their wealth, but for their faith. There were men like Paul, who had persecuted the church as Saul, and prophets like Moses, who came from the least likely of scenarios to lead the Hebrews to the promised land. While he did not put himself anywhere near the caliber of those great prophets, he knew he was still a man of God, even if he had largely forgotten that himself during the past couple years. Apparently, even though he had become a slobbering drunk, God still remembered who he was and, four weeks ago, Michael Dalacourt had sobered up.

He still did not know if it was a dream, an actual vision, or even a hallucination brought on by too much booze. Whatever it was, it had changed his life completely. He could still picture clearly the white-robed personage standing before him, not condemning or shaming him because of his fall from grace, but speaking gentle words of kindness and offering peace to his troubled soul. Was it God or His Son? Was it an angel or some other heavenly messenger? The glorified being had not given a name and Dalacourt was so overwhelmed that he hadn't asked.

The figure had visited him three times that evening in a run-down hotel room above a bar in Broken Arrow, Oklahoma, each time repeating an identical message and asking Dalacourt to repeat what had been given. By the third time, Dalacourt was able to repeat exactly what was to be said and the messenger had departed, not to be seen again.

The very next day, he began his journey. As he had hitchhiked and walked the fourteen hundred miles from Oklahoma to Los Angeles, he'd had plenty of time to repeat the message. He'd translated it into Latin, Italian and French and he could have said it somewhat convincingly in German, Portuguese, and Spanish. He knew what he needed to say, knew who to say it to, and knew how he would be received. He also knew what would happen to him after his message was delivered. But he'd promised he would deliver the message and that was just what he would do. The feeling of peace that had come over him with the arrival of the messenger was like nothing he had ever felt and, for the first time in two years, Michael Dalacourt no longer felt alone.

Four weeks ago, sober but with a splitting headache, he had begun his journey. Three weeks ago, he had smoked his last cigarette. Growing stronger as the miles passed beneath his feet—or the wheels of one of several kind souls who had picked him up in a car or truck and given his feet some rest—he had at last placed a phone call from a kindly stranger's smart phone to the cathedral just three days ago.

He had harbored no illusions he would be given an immediate audience with De Solei himself and had been content to simply leave a message with one of the man's aides. "Tell His Holiness that Michael Dalacourt is coming," he had said. "Be certain to tell him God has a message for him."

He had hung up before the sputtering aide could reply and had passed the last three days with a serene smile on his face. Oh, he knew what kind of a reception he would receive upon reaching the cathedral. De Solei might even have him killed. He had that kind of power. But that mattered nothing to him. All that mattered now was the message.

Now, with his journey nearly complete, he stood at the base of the stairs and paused to look up at the sky. It was a crystal-clear morning, the blue sky of a mostly smog-free Los Angeles stretching from horizon-to-horizon, unmarred by a single cloud. He squinted his eyes in the sunlight, only to see something that nearly stopped his heart.

There could be no doubt.

It was her.

Standing at the top of the stairs was a young girl he had seen only one other time in his life. She looked exactly as she had when he saw her in a dream two years ago—a little eight-year-old girl with beautiful dark skin and deep-set eyes that framed a petite and perfect face, smiling at him just as she had smiled at a much younger Francis De Solei at his confessional, a look of angelic innocence on her face. In the dream, however, she had become seemingly demonic as she accused and convicted De Solei of breaking every one of God's Ten

Commandments. A terrified De Solei had then brutally murdered her before the confessional doors of the long since closed St. Mary's Catholic Church in downtown Los Angeles.

Then she had come back from the dead and convicted him again.

Dalacourt had awakened at that point, but the dream had left him more convinced than ever that his mentor was, in fact, no longer a man of God. And now, just as he had arrived to finally confront Francis DeSolei for his crimes against his flock, this young girl stood before him, reminding him that it had been done before. DeSolei was guilty, of that there could be no doubt, but if his dream told him anything about how today would go, it told him to prepare for his former mentor to attempt to take his life. History, especially in this sort of situation, had a twisted way of repeating itself.

Exhausted, dehydrated, and overwhelmed by his lengthy journey, Dalacourt rubbed his dried out eyes with a grimy hand. When his eyes focused again at the top of the stairway, the little girl was gone. It didn't surprise him at all, as he wasn't sure she was even real. Regardless, she had bolstered his belief in the task at hand. If an eight-year-old girl could proclaim the truth, then surely he could as well.

He steeled his resolve and began his ascent. Each step felt heavier and heavier as he climbed, but soon enough he had reached the top and as he looked up, he beheld the magnificent Cathedral of Our Lady of the Angels. It was modern, yet majestic, almost eleven stories tall in places and with few, if any, architectural right angles. The fifty foot concrete lantern, the holy cross of God's church, thrust out from the building for all to see.

Beneath that stood a procession of people. Upon seeing Dalacourt step up onto the marble walk, four serious-looking men dressed in identical black suits suddenly rushed toward him. He smiled to himself, realizing they had been waiting for him. The two in front had handguns drawn and pointed directly at him. The two behind fanned out so that they were facing him at different angles, automatic rifles aimed at his chest. Dalacourt simply bowed his head and held his hands out before him to show them that he had no weapons.

It made no difference to them. Without a word and without stopping, the first two hit him hard, driving him painfully to the stone walk as they tackled him. One of them drove an elbow into his midsection while the other laced him across the face with the barrel of his gun. Blood ran down Dalacourt's face and onto the marble walk as the first man drove a knee into the back of his neck, pressing his head down while the other searched him for weapons. They appeared to be genuinely disappointed not to find anything because they quickly hauled him to his feet with several muttered oaths.

"He is unarmed?" came a thick voice from the direction of the rest of the group. Dalacourt recognized it instantly. It held the same patronizing and superior tone he had long grown accustomed to, but there was something more to it; something new he hadn't heard before. Dalacourt raised his head and let his eyes focus on Francis De Solei for the first time in two years.

"Nothing on him except this," one of the men said gruffly, holding out the tattered newspaper article Dalacourt always kept with him.

Francis De Solei, dressed in the finest of clothing, stepped forward. In the two years since Dalacourt had seen the man, he had grown substantially in size, his girth now bordering on enormous. De Solei was clad in robes and vestments of black and white, the cloth cut from some of the most expensive velvets and silks. A golden circlet crafted in the image of a crown of thorns sat upon his head and, when he reached for the newspaper clipping, Dalacourt could see that every pudgy finger was adorned with jeweled rings of gold and silver.

De Solei scanned the article and then simply crumpled it and dropped it to the ground. He took a step toward his former protégé, his head turning one way and then another as if he was trying to see who exactly Michael Dalacourt had become.

"Michael?" he finally said, but there was no mistaking the tone of disgust in it.

For his part, Michael Dalacourt wanted to vomit. Seeing the blasphemy before him was almost too much to bear. That the man had single-handedly destroyed the Catholic Church and created his new World Church in its place was bad enough. To see the opulence the man openly flaunted thoroughly disgusted him. But to see the man wearing a golden replica of the crown of thorns that had tormented His savior, as if De Solei himself was equal to or better than Christ, was enough to make him physically ill.

Swallowing the anger that was threatening to rise within him, he did his best to straighten up and he looked the man in the eye. "Hello, Francis," he said softly.

He was rewarded with a slap across the face courtesy of one of De Solei's bodyguards. "You will address him as 'His Holiness'," the guard snarled, raising a hand to strike him again.

"That will be quite enough," De Solei said, stepping forward and casting a rebuking glance at the man, immediately cowing him. "It is not for you to smite the enemies of God unless you are commanded to by me," he went on with exaggerated self-importance.

The man snapped his head down and bowed crisply to the pontiff. "Yes, your Holiness."

De Solei turned his gaze back to Dalacourt and stared for several more moments, before motioning to the guards that held his arms. "Release him," he commanded as he moved back a step, all the while continuing to glare. Both guards stepped to the side, joining the cadre of robed and well-dressed attendants who had accompanied the self-appointed pope. All of them were staring at the vagrant before them with various looks of derision, disgust, and scorn.

Dalacourt simply returned their gazes and smiled.

"So the prodigal son has indeed returned," De Solei finally broke the silence. "Am I to be expected now to call for my servants to bring you my best robe, a ring for your hand, and shoes for your feet?"

"I come for none of those things," Dalacourt replied, his voice calm. "I have come only to deliver a message."

"Ah, yes, so I have been told," De Solei replied smugly. He cast a glance at his entourage, who exchanged smiles and laughed among themselves, almost as if on cue. "You claim to have a message for me from God, is that correct?"

Dalacourt nodded serenely.

"I trust you know that I am God's chosen mouthpiece for the world today and that His communication flows solely through me," De Solei replied. "If He had a message for me, He would simply tell me. As always, you are not necessary to mine, nor God's, plans."

There were several murmurs of agreement from those attending him and he folded his hands together as he watched the former priest.

"God speaks through who He wishes, Francis," Dalacourt answered, having no intention of addressing the man by anything other than his given name. "You are not one of those he wishes to speak through."

A look of rage passed across the older man's face and Dalacourt saw clearly what stood before him. Francis De Solei—a sinful man, full of pride and greed—had used the past two years to feed his every desire and lust. Here stood a frightened man desperately holding onto something he believed was his birthright, who would rather crawl into a dark hole and rot than give any of it up.

"You would do well to curb your tongue, Michael, lest I have it cut out," De Solei replied with a dangerous edge. "I am not above using the ancient methods that were once employed against heretics. I have been polite due to our old association, but do not tempt me past what God would bear. Unless you repent immediately before me as God's true leader on earth today, it is my right to mete out punishment in God's name as I see fit. Do you understand?"

"Nothing you do is in God's name, Francis," Michael Dalacourt replied evenly and he noted that several of the men in suits inched closer to him. He smiled, unafraid.

"You dare to utter blasphemy against me, God's Holy Voice?" De Solei snapped, his face growing red with rage. The pontiff turned and motioned toward his guards. "Teach this heretic a lesson!" he shouted, spittle flying from his mouth. "Beat him until he can no longer speak!"

With snarls of anger, they moved forward, but before they could place their hands on him, they were flung back with the sound of a thunderclap. As the miracle began, Michael Dalacourt never moved. He simply stood and slowly raised his hands and face to the sky. The serene look of peace never left him as everyone's eyes tracked skyward, following his. The rich blue of the morning was fast disappearing and rolling clouds of gray and black began filling the sky with a speed that was both frightening and impossible. They roiled and twisted, shot through with lightning and fire. Thunder boomed out again so loudly that it shook the cathedral itself and drove everyone to the ground.

Except for Michael Dalacourt. He stood tall.

Before him, De Solei's attendants were frantically helping their supreme leader back to his feet. Once standing, he glared at Dalacourt with a look that bordered on rabid. "Shoot him!" he screamed. "God commands that the heretic must die!"

One of his guards pulled a gun from a shoulder holster, but he got no further than that. There was another crash of thunder and a bolt of lightning blasted out of the heavens, slamming through the man's chest. It left a gaping, smoking hole and the man toppled forward dead, the gun clattering uselessly down the marble steps.

Dalacourt locked his eyes on his former mentor and shook his head slowly and sadly. All of this, he had already seen. He knew what was going to happen and what would happen afterwards. "God protects me, Francis," he said softly, at peace and unafraid, "for as long as it takes me to deliver His message. Only afterward, will I be delivered into your hands. Only then can you harm me."

"You are not a man of God!" De Solei shrieked. "I deny you!"

Dalacourt took a breath and then uttered a single word with a power that shattered windows and drove those around him to their knees once again. "SILENCE!"

With but that single word, it was so. All sound ceased. The clouds above boiled and heaved, but no sound came from them. The people before him screamed, but their voices were muted. The sounds of birds and insects were no more. The voice of the world was quieted. All that remained was a deep and unbroken silence.

And then Michael Dalacourt began to speak.

"The Book of Revelation, the eighth chapter, and the seventh verse state that the first angel sounded," the former priest said, his magnified voice sounding for thousands of miles. At the moment, it was the only sound that existed in the world. "And there followed hail and fire mingled with blood, and they were cast upon the earth: and the third part of trees was burnt up, and all the green grass was burnt up."

He focused his eyes on his former mentor, who lay prostrate on the ground. "The anger of God is kindled against His children," Dalacourt said, his voice softer but no less overwhelming. "His anger is kindled against you, Francis. Against your lying and your deceiving and your secret practices."

There was a bright flash of lightning and a crimson bolt blasted down and shattered a stone planter near De Solei. Not a sound was heard. De Solei screamed again, just as silently, and scrambled backward as Dalacourt advanced on him.

"The final chapter is about to be written, Francis. The seventh seal is broken." More silent lightning flashed overhead and still, only the sound of Michael Dalacourt's voice could be heard. "This is the message He has for you, Francis," he went on and raised his face to the heavens.

"This is the message He has for all of His children!" his voice roared out, the sound of it as loud as a thunderclap and heard around the world.

At that, thunder rolled overhead and lightning flashed out of the clouds in a sudden explosion of sound, striking trees, buildings, and even the ground. Fires began to flare up from some of the strikes and the clouds overhead rolled even faster. Voices could be heard within the thunders, the voices of saints and prophets and disciples long dead, condemning the wicked and calling all who would listen to repentance.

"Woe be to any that fail to hear God's voice in this," Dalacourt finished. And with that, he fell to his knees and bowed his head in silent prayer as the heavens opened up and God unleashed His full fury upon the earth. Rain and hail began to pour down upon those before him and across the world. Great drops of blood mixed with the downpour of rain and everywhere that lightning struck, fire sprang up and devoured everything in its path.

With cries of pain and terror, De Solei and his attendants scrambled for cover. He and a few others made it. Several more of his attendants did not, felled by great chunks of blood-red ice. Large hailstones crashed to the ground all around them, some of them big enough that they cracked the marble walk itself. Blood splashed down from the heavens, bright crimson, and orange bolts of lightning struck down again and again, angrily blasting the world.

The wrath of God lasted but a few minutes. When it was over, the world was changed forever. Tens of thousands across the globe were slain, killed in the open by hail or dead in the resulting crashes of automobiles, planes, and other conveyances. Millions more were hurt. Green fields and meadows, lawns and plantings all over the world were suddenly gone, churned up into brown chunks of muddy sod by the great pieces of ice. Countless trees were struck down, shattered by hail or burned by lightning and in some places, entire forests were no more. Many crops all across the world had been obliterated and overnight, food riots would claim thousands more lives. It was the beginning of the end and when it was all over, the land would heave, the seas would die, famines and plagues would come, and wars would span the globe. The world of the past was no more.

God had spoken.

In Los Angeles, California, Michael Dalacourt remained kneeling where he was, surrounded by melting chunks of ice and pools of blood and rain. He knew what was to come next—he would be delivered into the hands of his enemy; of God's enemy. But for the first time in his entire life, he was truly at peace.

Standing across from him, Francis De Solei let his eyes track across the horizon. He listened to the sounds of car alarms and screams of agony and terror. Dogs barked furiously and sirens were wailing in the distance. Robbed of his hearing before the judgment, he now heard everything with startling clarity and he went purple with rage. He had survived and his beautiful cathedral had miraculously taken very little damage. But Los Angeles, his powerbase and the city he planned to turn into the next Rome, was burning.

He turned his gaze downward and fixed a violently hateful stare on the kneeling figure. "Take him," he seethed to those still with him. "Beat him, but do not kill him. I will have him crucified publicly as a lesson to those that deign to blaspheme me."

De Solei's eyes never wavered from watching as, cheerfully and without mercy, his security guards beat Michael Dalacourt into unconsciousness.

CHAPTER 6

Kigoma, Tanzania: Hade stood before Petr in the Sun City Bar and Restaurant, flashing perfectly white teeth in a wide smile. He looked exactly as the Russian remembered him from the last time they had been together. Some seven feet tall with his dark hair pulled back into a thick ponytail and wearing all black, including a long black leather duster, he didn't seem to mind the heat of the African midday, surprisingly cloudy as this particular day happened to be. Hade was a walking nightmare; the bravest of men avoided him at all costs. Petr, however, just leaned back in his chair and folded his arms across his chest. "What kept you?"

"Petr!" Hade bellowed loudly, a great grin on his face. "I come all this way and this is how you greet me? At the very least, you could offer me a seat."

Petr scowled at the man wordlessly, then tilted his head back and whistled. One of the waiters immediately took note and the Russian swirled his hand in the air, holding up two fingers.

Hade pulled out a nearby chair and sat down across the table from Petr. "I'm touched," he rumbled cheerfully. "After all this time, it's nice of you to buy me a round."

"They're both for me," Petr said drily. "What do you want?"

Hade never lost his smile, but he shook his head and laid his tattooed hands on the table. "I think it's pretty clear that I wanted a drink, but I can see that isn't going to happen," he lamented in mock sadness. "Anyway, I was in the neighborhood and I was hoping to catch up on the good old days."

"This is about as far from any neighborhood that anyone could ever possibly be in," Petr replied, without warming his tone at all. "And I'm pretty positive the two of us never had any good old days."

Hade chuckled and glanced around. Several tourists were seated around another table talking and laughing quietly and three waiters were lounging near the bar while one of them prepared the Russian's drinks. The big man turned his gaze back on Petr. "*Comme ci, comme ca.* No blood, no foul, though, right?"

The bartender hurried over and set two shot glasses hastily on the table and then rushed back to his post. Petr picked up the first and quickly drained it. He upended the empty glass and slammed it down, causing the other one to spill slightly and Hade to smile even wider.

"You think this is funny?" Petr asked sullenly.

"Actually, I don't think any of this is the slightest bit funny, with the possible exception of your beard," Hade quipped.

"Get to the point," Petr snapped, ignoring the barb.

"Fine," Hade rumbled. "I want to show you something, but I think we'll want a bit of privacy for this." He reached into his trench coat and Petr tensed, sure a weapon was about to be drawn. Instead, he was surprised to see Hade pull out an envelope. Holding it firmly, he added "Excuse me for a moment," as he stood up and walked over to the group of tourists.

"*Entschuldigen Sie mich,*" Hade said to one of the men in flawless German. "*Wir haben vier Karten für einen Bus zum Gombe-Bach-Nationalpark. Wir haben auch die Reservierungen, zum im Hatari Lodge African Hotel zu bleiben. Wurde Sie mögen sie?*"

The man looked at his companions, who all shook their heads in disbelief as Hade handed him the envelope. The tourist opened it to find that the contents matched exactly what the huge stranger had detailed.

"*Warum benötigen Sie sie nicht?*" asked another of the men.

"*Ah, Unsere Freunde sind ein Tag spät, also benötigen wir nicht die Karten,*" Hade replied.

"*Ja selbstverständlich. Danke*!"

"*Sie sind willkommen, aber Sie müssen jetzt gehen, um den Bus herzustellen.*"

"*Ja, ja*," the first one responded. Each of the men grabbed their packs and hurried out the door, calling back over their shoulders as they filed out, "*Danke*!"

Hade watched them depart and then slowly walked back over to Petr and sat back down.

"What was that all about?" Petr asked, perhaps more perplexed by what he had just seen than by anything else he had seen Hade do.

"Oh, I just gave them four tickets up to Gombe Stream Park and a night's stay at one of the nicest hotels in the entire region. They were more than excited to take them and, in the process, leave us alone."

"Not exactly your style," Petr said carefully, "I expected something with bullets."

"Despite what you might think, I'm not a wolverine," Hade countered. "I don't kill for pleasure—only when it's required. Do we need to rehash our little conversation about the greater good, or can we move past all of that?"

"I would prefer if you actually just moved out of here all together," Petr deadpanned.

Hade ignored the slight, reached into his trench coat and this time pulled out a black mini iPad. He touched the screen to wake it up and scrolled through his apps. "You know, I am so addicted to Angry Birds," he said as he leisurely kept scrolling until he found what he was looking for. "Ah, here we are. This should interest you greatly," he finished, sliding the tablet across the dirty table.

The picture on the screen was of Father Michael Dalacourt, a man Petr had met only once on the mountain in Utah. The picture looked to have been taken well after that fateful day, with the priest now looking emaciated and passed out drunk on the sidewalk in front of a bar as a local police officer looked down at him. "Not surprising," Petr said without emotion. "He was a frail man; a coward. He mattered little to me two years ago and even less now. What's your point in showing me this?" he asked, looking up.

"There's more," Hade replied with a nod toward the tablet.

With a grunt of annoyance, Petr ran his finger across the screen to bring up the next picture. It immediately grabbed his attention.

It was Alexis Kennedy.

Old emotions and desires resurfaced as he closely examined the photo. This was the girl he had desired more than anything, the same girl who had nearly shot and killed him. Alexis had obviously spent the last two years honing her body to near perfection. The picture he was gazing at was a picture of her running along a mountain path, dressed only in tight running shorts and a sports bra. She was tanned and extremely fit, her hair was still long and tightly curled, and she was absolutely gorgeous.

But as he looked closer at the picture, he noticed there was something different about her besides her chiseled physique. Her eyes had changed. He had desired her in large part due to the depths of compassion and understanding he had found behind those eyes when he first met her. Back then, they were the deepest shade of blue he had ever seen, and they conveyed warmth and compassion. Now as he looked at the picture he saw those deep blue eyes had changed. Instead of the kindness of two years ago, they were now as cold as the bottom of the ocean and as hard as chips of sapphire.

His breathing was shallow and rapid as he scrolled to the next picture, this one of her training with another young woman, one he did not recognize. It was winter and they were out running in deep snow. The next showed Alexis and the same young woman in some rundown martial arts dojo, wooden quarterstaffs slammed together in a vicious strike/parry motion. Both women were bruised and their fight looked brutal, but all Petr could focus on were Alexis' eyes. Cold. Hard. Focused.

She had changed, he realized, but then, so had he. They were both damaged goods now. Petr tossed the iPad on the table and laughed, calling up angrier emotions to mask the sudden confusion threatening to drag him down to the depths. "Screw you, Hade," he snapped. "I don't know what this is about, but I honestly could not care less. I'm in no mood to be manipulated today."

Hade raised his hands in feigned innocence. "I wouldn't dream of manipulating you, Petr. I would think you'd remember that from our last encounter."

Petr slammed his fist onto the table. "That's all you do, Hade! You manipulate! Do you think I don't remember what you did to me two years ago? How one of your men killed Rene on the roof of the hotel? How you turned him into a monster and forced me to kill him? I remember it all, Hade! Then I remember how you forced me to kill David!" He faltered a bit at the mention of the elder Sumbawanga, a man he had quickly grown to respect and even revere in the short time they had known each other. "How am I doing so far?" he went on, his voice filling with anger. "Oh, and let's not forget that blasted mountain. I remember how you framed me for the death of Windy, whoever the hell that was. I remember you set me up as the fall guy for killing Owen's friends, too. I remember that's why Owen wanted first crack at killing me. Then when he refused, you tried to get Alexis to kill me instead. And when Owen convinced her to spare me, you murdered Owen in front of all of us!"

The big man remained silent, staring at Petr with a slight grin on his face.

"As if that wasn't enough, you came after my family, too," Petr was nearly shouting now. "We can't forget how you manipulated my brother into killing our entire family and in doing so, turned a relatively unhinged Nikolai into an uncontrollable homicidal maniac!"

"Well, you're wrong about that, my friend," Hade replied with a laugh as he folded his massive arms across his chest. "Nikolai has always been a homicidal maniac."

Inside, something snapped and Petr lunged across the table with an angry shout, his hands reaching for Hade's face. He couldn't help it. He could think of nothing more than killing the man, but he never even got close. Hade barely moved. One arm came up and easily slapped Petr's grasping hands away while the other hand shot forward and an open palm slammed into the Russian's chest. Petr felt as if he had been hit with a sledgehammer. He was driven backward into his chair and continued hurtling backward until the wall stopped him. One of the waiters looked over at the commotion and then went back to wiping down a glass mug, trying hard not to notice.

Hade made a motion of dusting some imagined particle of dust from his shoulder. "Come now, boy," he said, his tone low and dangerous. "You're scaring the locals."

Petr tried to suck in a lungful of air and found it difficult. He wondered if Hade might have broken something in him. Not that it would matter. He was certain the man was going to kill him now.

As if he could read the Russian's thoughts, Hade leaned forward. "If I had wanted to kill you, you'd already be dead," he said quietly.

"What do…you want from…me?" he finally wheezed.

"I want you to understand what really happened on that mountaintop," Hade replied.

"I understand it well enough," Petr said, feeling his breath slowly returning through the dull ache in his chest. "People died. Good people. You can dance around it all you want, but it happened just the way I said it happened. You might know people, Hade. But I know you."

Hade's eyebrow didn't rise, but Petr noticed the subtle tension in the man's face. On any other man, it would be an open expression of shock. "I think you give me more credit than I'm due," Hade finally said, his voice quiet.

"I don't think so. You know more about me than I do," the Russian went on. "That's how you get your power over people. You know who they are. You know what they love, what they want, and you leverage it against what they're willing to sacrifice."

"I suppose you're correct, Petr," he sighed. "I have a great deal of knowledge and I do use what I know to my advantage. I suppose that gives me that power you credit me with."

"False modesty doesn't suit you, Hade. You gain your power because you know what you're doing while no one else does," Petr added. "You play your games, piece by piece, line upon line, precept upon precept, and before the little fly even knows what happened, it's suddenly ensnared in your web."

"I should have you write my authorized biography someday," Hade laughed. "You have a flair with words and you understand me quite well. You also understand something most people do not."

"And what's that?"

"The world thinks holding power over another individual is a bad thing. Society today sees power as something to control, something to box in and never let out. There are so many laws meant to curtail power, but I think you and I are in agreement that power is instead meant to be unleashed and used or it isn't really power at all."

"We're in agreement on no such thing."

"Now you're just contradicting me to contradict me. Listen to what you're saying, Petr," the big man countered. "Of course that's how power is meant to be used. If you can pull your head out of your ass for just five minutes, you'll see that everything I've done has been to help you meet your full potential."

"Oh, so you've been helping me find myself? Is that it?" Petr said scornfully.

"Exactly, but you haven't made it easy. Your problem is that you think education should be painless. The entire history of the world tells us that true learning hurts. No one has ever learned all they needed to know through success, but through trial and tribulation. Remember what Foucault said. 'In its function, the power to punish is not essentially different from that of curing or educating.' You consider this a punishment. I consider it finding truth."

"This is going nowhere," Petr sighed. "Once you start quoting French philosophers, my mind tunes out. Do you need me here for this, or can I leave?"

Hade took a deep breath. "This would go a lot faster if you'd just listen. Think about the last few years. What you see as a punishment has been nothing less than a learning curve. It has strengthened you, just as fire strengthens steel, for what is to come."

"And what is to come?" Petr asked with a roll of his eyes. "Oh, let me guess. You and I are going to rule the galaxy as father and son. I've seen that movie before, Hade, and I'm not interested in your fairy tale."

"This is as real as it gets, my boy, and you will find that everything in life is a matter of perspective and semantics," Hade explained patiently. "For example, you're convinced that I wanted Alexis to shoot you, but I can tell you honestly that your death would have been one of the worst things that could have happened to me that day. We can both agree on what happened, but that doesn't mean you fully understand why it happened."

"I said this before. You can twist your words up and down and all around until they fill up this bar, but I'm not going to fall for your tricks again," Petr retorted. "I'm done playing that game."

"We aren't playing any game here," Hade said as he reached over and tapped the iPad. "Look at them, Petr. Look what they have become. Alexis off playing Xena, Warrior Princess, like she belongs in some video game, and our good Father Dalacourt, a raging alcoholic who can barely stand up on his own. Look what they have done with their gifts. Look at what they have chosen to become. Look at what they have turned their backs on. These are the people you want to throw your lot in with?"

"I never threw myself in with them. You did that for me. I was just along for the ride, it seems."

Hade laughed again. "Hard to disagree with you there, although I know Alexis doesn't see you as the victim in all of this. Remember, she's the one who lost the love of her life. And Dalacourt? Well, if he even remembers his name at this point, I'd be surprised. But I'm certain if he did, he'd also probably feel like he lost the most that day."

"So that's your big sales pitch?" Petr growled in contempt. "Alexis and the priest are losers, so you're here to save me from the same downward spiral? I'm not stupid enough to think for one second that you helping me doesn't really mean me helping you. This is nothing more than a fishing expedition and you're casting your line where you think you can reel me in. Those people mean nothing to me, so whether you're trying to reunite us or split us apart, it doesn't matter. All I want to do is sit here and have another drink and then go home to my family and forget you were ever here."

"Your family?" Hade snorted in disdain. "I would hardly call a dead man's daughter and her workaholic husband a family. They aren't your family, Petr. Your true family still needs you."

"Nikolai needs me like he needs a flower garden to meditate in."

"You're correct, of course, that Nikolai doesn't need you. Not now, anyway. He's doing quite well on his own at the moment. But you need him, Petr. You need him more than you care to admit."

"I'm not interested in your stories or your theories," Petr shot back. "I have no use for you. Go play with your other kings." He was letting it all out now. He refused to be a pawn anymore.

The time it took for Hade to respond seemed like an eternity, but he finally answered with a knowing nod. "I see that John visited you." It was more a statement than a guess. "When did that happen?"

"What business is it of yours?"

Hade simply shrugged. "No matter," he said quietly. "I suppose it was only a matter of time before he found you." The huge man looked directly at Petr. "So you know all about the prophecy, do you?"

Petr could only nod. He actually knew very little, but Hade didn't need to know that.

Hade continued. "I'm certain he told you that you were chosen; that you are the fulfillment of prophecy and you saved the world. I'll bet he even spoke to you about how you had the freedom to choose how you would act on that day, even if the events had been carefully orchestrated to bring you all together."

Petr said nothing, but his jaw clenched tighter.

"It's all true, of course," Hade continued, supremely confident. "So you know that if Alexis had indeed pulled the trigger and put a bullet in your head, I would be very much in control of this entire planet."

"But she didn't," Petr leaned forward, allowing himself his own look of victory. "You lost."

Hade broke into a toothy grin and began laughing. "Me, lose?" he repeated lightly. "My dear Petr, a war is not won or lost on a single insignificant battle. I doubt John told you I really had no expectations of winning that particular battle, that it was merely a gambit, a part of the bigger picture; the greater plan; the culling of the herd, if you will. Did you not hear me earlier when I said that losing you that day would have been a catastrophe for me?"

Petr wasn't expecting that response at all and he leaned back, doing his best to keep the shock from his face.

"No, my dear boy," Hade went on. "Just because I didn't win that one skirmish in this eternal war doesn't mean I've lost. Quite the opposite, actually."

"But if Alexis had killed me, you would have won," Petr said quietly, trying to put the pieces together, but failing.

"I wouldn't expect you to understand," he replied. "John doesn't understand everything I'm doing, either. Whenever he runs out of answers, he'll tell you something vague and cryptic like, 'That's all I'm allowed to reveal' or some other self-righteous nonsense."

Petr nodded numbly at the man's accuracy.

"No surprise there, Petr," Hade nodded sagely. "You see, John doesn't understand what Foucault meant when he said 'freedom of conscience entails more dangers than authority and despotism.' People shouldn't make up their minds about things. In fact, generally it's the worst thing they can do. Still, it always seems a bit dodgy to not answer someone's questions as truthfully as possible. There's really nothing out there except truth. As for hiding it, well, I've never been a fan of that."

"So, let me know if I'm hearing you right, Hade," Petr countered, finding his conversational footing. "You're saying I shouldn't listen to anyone who says they have my best interest at heart? That about get it?"

Hade merely shrugged and smiled. "Do you remember the last time we chatted like this?" he asked. "Up on the top of the Red Lion

Hotel?"

"How could I forget?" The sarcasm fell heavily from Petr's mouth.

"We discussed an experiment played out with cards," Hade explained anyway, "where the observer was looking to see how quickly the participant could figure out the pattern."

"Yeah, 'thin slicing', you called it. You used it to trick me into thinking I had a kind of clarity that would help me make the right choices in difficult situations. All it did was get me into more trouble."

"I'm not so sure you remember that correctly, but that's a discussion for another day. Today, I want to talk about a different card game. I want to talk about the child's card game called War. Have you ever played it?"

"Are you serious?"

"Let me explain how it works," Hade went on, ignoring the Russian's acidity. "You deal half the deck to each person, then each one of you flips over your top card and the one with the highest card wins and gets to keep both cards. Then you flip over your next card and the one with the highest card wins and keeps both cards. There are other components of the game, but that's the basis of it. You continue to flip over cards until one person has all fifty-two cards and that person is declared the winner."

"What does that have to do with anything?"

"For us, today—everything," Hade replied. "You see, the reason children love this game is that it has everything they could want. Suspense, action, the thrill of victory. I've seen children who do nothing but play this game for days. Then, suddenly, the truth behind the entire game hits them and they quit, probably never to play it again. For, you see, the game is rigged. The child eventually realizes that the instant the cards are all dealt, the winner has already been decided. You can't see it in the beginning or even in the middle, but every move gets you closer to the preordained result. There are no choices in the game, only a winner and a loser, and once that knowledge has been gleaned and you realize that all you are doing is marching ever forward toward the inevitable, the game is no longer fun."

Hade crossed his arms and looked at Petr, who stared back at his reflection in Hade's sunglasses. "I suppose you would like me to believe you and I are playing this game?" Petr said carefully. "You would like me to figure out that my life is like a deck of cards, cut in half, and my fate has already been chosen. You want me to just give up and give myself over to you, because the game isn't 'fun' anymore. I don't buy it, Hade. You won't have me, no matter how many silly stories you tell me. I'm not yours and I never will be."

For some time, there was silence, the huge man's cold stare boring into Petr. When Hade spoke again, he was clearly angry. "I was really hoping to avoid this, Petr," he said. "But I can see we're going to have to take this discussion to the next level and unfortunately, we're going to need some real privacy for this next lesson."

Hade stood up and reached into his coat, then pulled out his enormous Desert Eagle. "Everybody front and center!" he practically roared, his voice echoing through the bar.

Almost instantly, two cooks and three waiters emerged from the kitchen, wondering what the ruckus was all about, only to find themselves staring down the barrel of what was probably the biggest handgun they had ever seen.

Hade was about to squeeze the trigger when a little girl, probably not more than eight, poked her head around the corner, peering fearfully at him. Immediately, Hade's countenance changed. He furrowed his brow intensely and closed his eyes for a moment.

Then, instead of shooting them, he said quietly, "Leave before I change my mind."

None of them hesitated and they all scrambled for the exit. Hade didn't watch them go. In seconds, he and Petr were the only ones remaining.

This was not what the Russian had expected and his expression conveyed his surprise. What had made Hade change his mind and not kill the staff? Had it been the little girl? And what was that look on Hade's face? Petr had never seen such anger, rage, and…what else was there—was it anguish? Whatever it was, it was gone as soon as the restaurant cleared out. But it was the first time Petr had seen Hade not in complete control of a situation and it gave him hope, no matter how brief, that perhaps there was a small hole in Hade's armor that he could use to his advantage in the future.

Hade turned back to him. "So we're down to your last chance, Petr," he said, his composure restored as if nothing had happened. "You really want to know why I'm here? Fine. I'm here to recruit you, plain and simple."

"Recruit me," Petr repeated softly, filing his new information on Hade quietly away.

"Correct. I want you with me in the upcoming war," Hade answered. "You're a fool if you think you won't have to choose a side. There's too much at stake and I won't have you fight against me. Sooner or later, you'll choose to serve me. I prefer sooner."

"What could you possibly hope to achieve by asking me to join you now?" Petr countered. "I didn't join you when you had everything; why would I join you now when you have nothing?"

Hade put his hands up in mock surrender. "*Je me rends*!" he scoffed. "We'll just have to agree to disagree on that point. But understand that I'm still very much in the 'taking over the world' business."

"And I'm still very much not for sale," Petr replied, crossing his arms defiantly.

"That's only because you're already bought and paid for," Hade responded forcefully. "I already own you. I have always owned you. And I will always own you. It's simply a matter of time before you realize that."

"You will not have me," Petr said slowly as he reached down and picked up his tumbler of vodka. "So you might as well do your worst," he finished, downing the drink in one shot.

"Doing my worst is when I'm at my best," Hade smiled and then moved so swiftly that Petr never saw the kick coming. His foot connected with the Russian's chest, slamming him backward into the wooden support beam. For the second time that day, Petr's breath had been forcefully driven from his body. Before he could slump to the floor, Hade grabbed him by the throat and effortlessly flung him across the room. Petr smashed into the bar twenty feet away and collapsed to the floor in an explosion of pain. He struggled painfully to his feet as Hade stalked toward him and the look on the big man's face told him he had overplayed his last hand.

Hade reached him and simply flung his arm to the side, backhanding Petr across the face. His head snapped back and the force of the blow launched him over the bar and into the shelves of liquor bottles on the other side of the counter. Once again, Petr crashed to the floor in a haze of pain with shattered bottles, shards of glass, and alcohol raining down upon him. He didn't bother trying to get up this time. He saw Hade coming around the bar and knew the big man would be helping him up anyway.

Hade reached him and leaned down. The massive hand once more closed on his throat, cutting off his air, and Hade effortlessly hauled Petr into the air and then slammed him back down on the counter. Unable to breath, Petr's eyes rolled back in his head in helplessness.

Only then did Hade release him, allowing Petr to fill his oxygen-starved lungs. Ignoring him for the moment, Hade turned around and selected a large unbroken bottle of the tequila, one of the few that remained intact, from the wreckage behind the bar. Turning back around, he spun the cap from it with his thumb and took a long drink. Then without a word, he began pouring it on the bar, walking from one end to the other, saturating everything, including Petr.

Hade reached into his duster and pulled out a cigar. With exaggerated slowness, he bit off one end and then the other, showing elongated canines. Petr thought he looked like a wolf getting ready to slaughter a helpless fawn. "I like you, Petr," Hade finally said, his voice strangely calm. "You remind me of myself so many years ago. So I'm going to give you a chance I wouldn't give anyone else."

"I don't…need your chances," Petr dared to gasp.

Hade smiled and leaned closer. "Ah, yes," he purred with a perfectly evil smile. "You're choosing to exercise your free will. I like that." He straightened and reached back into his duster for a lighter. A moment later, he was sucking the flame into his cigar, lighting the foul-smelling leaf within. "You still don't understand what just happened here, do you," he stated, taking several long draws on his cigar.

"No," Petr groaned, still in pain. He wanted to roll off the bar and back to his feet, but not only did he doubt his ability to stand, he knew another beating might follow if he moved.

"It should be obvious," Hade went on, holding his cigar with one hand and his lighter up with the other. "The main interest in life and work is to become someone else that you were not in the beginning."

"For the love of God, could we be done with Foucault?"

"Call it a weakness," Hade answered with a shrug. "His point is valid, though. We know who you are today, Petr Zhugravinsky. However, do we know what you can be tomorrow? I think I do," he answered his own question, "and I would like to see you become what you were destined to be."

"I will never be what you want me to be," Petr managed to say.

"You will, my boy. I've already killed so many of those you loved just to get you to this point. Do you really think I'll stop at anything now to get you to your final destination? I'll kill everyone you've ever met, if it gets me what I want."

The little amount of blood remaining in Petr's face drained away as he finally understood the leverage Hade would use, and continue to use, to control him. He was trapped, and while he couldn't see a way out now, he knew he had to find one. He wouldn't follow Hade. He couldn't.

Hade thumbed the flint of the lighter and the small flame appeared from it again. "Let's see what tomorrow brings, Petr," he said and touched the flame to the liquid on the bar.

It flared up in blue fire and Petr found himself desperately rolling off the bar as fast as he was able in order to avoid the flames, his body screaming with pain. He found immediately he was right about one thing. His legs would not support him and he fell hard to the floor, quickly rolling over in case his alcohol-saturated clothes had caught fire.

Hade walked slowly around the bar, cigar in his mouth and lighter in hand. It was still lit and his figure shimmered in the heat as he continued walking toward Petr, who was trying desperately to get his legs to work enough to get him away from the growing inferno. "Bravo, Petr," Hade said as he casually tossed the lighter over the counter. It hit a puddle of booze on the floor and the entire back wall of the bar suddenly roared into full flame. "I knew you could pull yourself together if you had the right motivation."

"What are you talking about?" Petr gasped, choking on the smoke as the fast-burning timbers of the walls and ceiling fed the flames. He knew he would have to get out now if he was going to survive.

"When you find out, just remember that it didn't have to be this way," Hade said with finality. "You could have said yes. Now, go home. Your brother is waiting for you."

Petr froze and then his eyes widened in horror. He knew instantly what Hade was inferring. "Chuike," he whispered.

Whether Hade heard him or not, the look on his face said the big man knew exactly what conclusion Petr had come to. With that, Hade turned, his trench coat billowing behind him, and he walked out the door. Petr stumbled out after him, choking and coughing on the smoke, afraid of what he might find as he ran out into the street. But he was all alone. Hade had left as he came; as a shadow.

The Russian paused for a moment and looked up at the menacing clouds, rolling together faster than he had ever seen. He knew a storm was coming in more ways than one. He took a deep breath and then took off running for home, everything else forgotten except for his distant promise to David. He had vowed to protect Chuike.

He prayed he would make it in time.

CHAPTER 7

Salt Lake City, Utah: "I didn't know doctors still made house calls," Alexis offered with a weary, but grateful smile as she rested on the kitchen table. It had been transformed into a makeshift operating room table, meticulously prepared with sterile drapes, upon which rested the tools, sutures, saline, and soaps used to wash and close her numerous wounds.

"I didn't know pretty girls still threw themselves through reinforced glass doors," countered the young physician as he finished applying the last of the wrappings to her injured wrist. Alexis withdrew her hand from his as if bitten and he hurriedly attempted to defuse the uncomfortable situation. "I'm sorry, Ms. Kennedy," he said hastily. "I didn't mean anything by that."

"No, it's okay, Doctor Lem," she replied. "It's just that I…" *am still in love with a dead man*, she thought sheepishly. She closed her eyes and sighed. "Just…well, thank you," she finished, unable to put anything more into words.

Nodding awkwardly, the young doctor hurriedly cleaned up his supplies.

Stacia McCain laughed lightly from nearby and then put her arm around his shoulders. "Oh, Alexis," she scolded in genuine amusement, a warm smile on her face. "I apologize, *Doctor*," she heavily emphasized the title to get Alexis' attention and then turned her eyes to him. "You'll have to excuse Miss Kennedy. She still stares out the window waiting for a lost love, with no medical degree I might add, to come back and rescue her."

Alexis wouldn't give Stacia the satisfaction of knowing how dead center that arrow struck—*don't twirl your hair!*—so she busied her hands by examining the doctor's sewing. Still, she knew the truth cut deeper than anything.

Stacia chattered on. "Some of us, however, know exactly how to treat a handsome, caring, successful young professional." Her flirtatious smile caught his attention as she tucked her arm under his and turned him toward the door. Doctor Lem looked positively entranced. "I'll show you out," she said. "And I don't need to remind you that your significant retainer fee carries with it heavy expectations of confidentiality." Stacia could charm compliance out of most men this way. Too bad it seemed to fail on Otis, the one man whose attention she actually wanted. She would deny it until her dying day, but Alexis could see it all too clearly.

As soon as they rounded the corner and out of sight, Alexis grabbed one particularly tight curl of her raven mane and twisted till the lacerations on her arms and scalp burned. The way Stacia could push Alexis' buttons, it was a wonder she had any hair left at all. Still, the frustration was more than offset by everything else Stacia had given her. Stacia McCain was her mentor, protector, and truly her best friend.

She couldn't hear the rest of their conversation and it was just as well. She needed a few moments alone to collect her thoughts. She stood slowly and once she felt steady enough, she shuffled over to the panoramic window of the corner apartment. As she looked over the stunning vistas of the valley with the white-capped mountains in the distance, her thoughts inevitably went to Owen and the day John had given Alexis over to Stacia's protection.

From here it was easy to see Ferguson Canyon, that crease in the mountains just south of Big Cottonwood Canyon, where it all happened…

A single shot rang loudly from the barrel of Hade's weapon. In the stories and movies, everything would have gone silent, time would have slowed to a crawl. All else would have ceased to exist and Alexis could have sat with Owen, comforted him in his final moments, and loved him openly.

But this was no movie, and as the battle raged below the plateau, she dropped frantically to the mud and hauled Owen into her lap, cradling his head. She tried desperately to block out the chaos, to focus on his beautiful brown eyes, to say something meaningful, something lasting. Her nose filled with the din of smoke and then the warm metallic smell of Owen's blood, warm against her hands. And there was so much of it. The tears came then, her body threatening to shut down from the overwhelming grief.

At that moment, when all seemed lost, somehow Owen coughed, a wet, bloody noise. "Owen?" Alexis cried out. "Owen, I love you! Stay with me! I'll get you to…"

"Stop…talking, Alexis," Owen labored, his voice weak and failing. "There's no time. You have to…be strong. You have…to run."

"I will, but I… "

"Shhh," he whispered. "I love you." He said it simply and a hint of his old crooked smile returned to his lips one last time. "I love…you, Alexis," he gasped.

And then he was gone.

Owen DiConte—her Owen—was dead. And she wanted nothing more than to join him. Just as she was about to vanish into a bottomless pit of despair, a powerful hand gripped her arm and she lashed out while clinging to Owen at the same time. A comforting voice attempted to break through her grief. "Alexis, it's time to go," John said softly.

Where he had come from, and how long he had been there, she had no idea. She looked up to see him standing, alone, above her. She knew a battle was still being fought below them, but she couldn't run. Not yet. The reality of simply leaving Owen's body behind crushed her. "I can't leave him," she sobbed.

"He's gone," John said sympathetically, but with urgency in his voice.

"You can help him, John—you're close to God, you could bring him back," she cried, begging him as her tears streaked the mud and blood across her face.

"Not Owen, not now," he knelt next to her and cupped her face in his wrinkled hands paternalistically, his eyes soft and sad. "I'll explain later. I promise. But for now, we have to go."

But Alexis couldn't. She simply could not leave Owen.

John gently pried her away from Owen's body, ignoring her desperate pleas to leave her with him. As she finally collapsed, sobbing, he lifted her easily and soon, he was bearing her down the mountain trail.

Alexis remembered nothing of the panicked flight for their lives, only what Stacia told her later. Her next memory was of the very apartment she was in now. She lay seemingly catatonic in her bedroom but could hear the conversation in the living room, John speaking to Stacia in hushed tones. "She is your student now, Stacia," he said quietly, his voice almost fatherly.

"But I've never trained anyone before," Stacia whispered, seemingly frightened of the prospect. "And she…she's…well, she's a child. Worse, she's childish—a cherub, a damsel waiting to be rescued! What can I do with that?"

"She is child-like, Stacia, because she has not had your upbringing," John explained. "This has always been your life. But for her, less than a week ago, her greatest concerns were college, career, and marrying the right man. Her world has been turned upside down and the boy of her future is now dead."

"I know, I know," Stacia reluctantly agreed. "And you're right."

"You have to step up to this challenge," John went on. "You must teach her, train her, make her the leader and weapon she was born to be. You must also protect her with your life. She means more now to the salvation of this world than you can know."

To Alexis, none of their conversation made any sense at the time, of course. but Stacia took the charge solemnly. Alexis remained locked in a shell for weeks, never speaking, never indicating she noticed anything outside the abyss behind her eyes. Stacia slept on the floor next to her bed at night; kept her company all day, prattling on about a clandestine organization dedicated to protect humanity. Stacia was always there, always patient, always caring.

Alexis knew John was there at times, too, just as Stacia's father was. She remembered they talked about her, about the world outside, the end of the chaos brought about by Hade, local and worldwide devastation, and the small slow steps toward rebuilding. Most of their concern had been about her, but Alexis, in her self-made prison, didn't care. She never looked in the mirror, never bathed, ate only when forced to, and lost track of days and nights. She never slept, yet she felt as if she were always sleeping. For Alexis, it felt like one endless day.

Stacia later told her it had lasted seven weeks.

And then somewhere in that fog of dissociation, he found her. He quickened her like water in the desert. She had been gazing out the very same window she gazed out now, unfocused eyes oblivious to the scarred city reflecting the sun setting behind her. The apartment was silent as Stacia watched her, and something finally reconnected within Alexis. Something within her stirred. No voice, no wind, no fire, no earthquake—just something...healing, recognizable and compelling. If it had a voice, it would have said, "Look."

And she looked.

The setting sun shone red on the mountains of the Wasatch, making the burnt remains of its trees appear to be ablaze and turning the granite pink. "They're stunning," she whispered.

Stacia was beside her instantly, her eyes anxiously searching Alexis' face, waiting for more.

Alexis focused. "His mountains," she had said.

"Whose mountains, Alexis?" Stacia prodded gently.

Alexis heard her, but another presence, unseen and unheard, felt more real and a well sprang within her chest. It had been so long since she felt anything and the sweetness from it nearly overwhelmed her. She became aware of her surroundings, aware of herself, aware of the vacuous hole in her belly that hadn't been fed properly for weeks. "I'm hungry," she finally answered.

Stacia raced from her side to the kitchen.

Alexis remembered something Owen had said once—something about the mountains looking a certain way, as if they could display moods or convey messages. She saw it now. She felt it. They were his mountains. "His mountains," she whispered again. "Owen's."

The rest would not come. The well within her finally met her eyes and the tears flowed. She could not know it then, but she kept that moment in her heart and, on her first visit back to Ferguson Canyon nearly a year later, it was finally confirmed to her. Owen was there.

Stacia returned with a hot bowl of soup, offering it to her. "Here, Alexis," she said gently. "Start with this."

She took the soup from Stacia as she watched the shadows climb the mountains. For the first time in seven weeks, she did not eat out of necessity. She ate because she was hungry. Once she had eaten, the hunger was gone. The well remained, but she was exhausted.

She slept for three days.

"That was a good day," Stacia's gentle voice brought her back to the present, something she was always so good at doing when Alexis needed it most. Without turning to face her friend, Alexis nodded in agreement and both women stood staring out the window. "There's something about those mountains, isn't there?" Stacia went on, encouraging the memories in her friend. "Show me where it is again."

Alexis looked to the southeast and pointed to a ripple on the south side of Big Cottonwood Canyon. "There," she said with a peaceful smile. "Follow the white water tower up that canyon and you'll be there." It didn't pain her to look at it anymore. It was, after all, not just the canyon where she and Owen had been separated, but also the canyon where they had reunited a year later.

"I remember how beautiful it was in the spring, with the green trees and the river at its highest. You've come a long way since then," Stacia said warmly, placing a hand on her friend's shoulder. "I knew you'd be okay. I had faith you'd be okay," she continued. Her countenance shone with determination. She rarely showed emotion beyond anger or fear, and she was formidable in both states. But when she allowed something more, it made everything else pale in comparison.

"You had faith in me?" Alexis asked quietly, thinking about the path they were forging together.

"In a sense, yes," the other woman answered. "But more faith in what you represent—faith in your role in all of this. It's not easy to explain." She paused, mulling it around in her head. "John could explain it better," she finally continued, her voice contemplative. "He told me simply to believe in you; believe in the plan God had for you. He said that in your darkest hour, you would find hope and take your first step toward something more. When I heard you speak those words here at the window, I knew you'd found it, Alexis," she said, looking at her now. "I knew you'd taken that first step."

"And in Cedar City?" Alexis asked, doubt creeping into her voice. "Killing those men?" She couldn't shake her guilt at what she had done. "Was that another step toward what I must become? Is that the plan that God has for me?"

"Yes and no," Stacia answered plainly. "Yes, because I believe we're following the right path. There is so much at stake here, Alexis, and we have to do whatever it takes to win this war. We have to make tough decisions and we have to find a way to live with those tough decisions."

"And the no?"

Stacia shrugged. "The fact that you're so conflicted about this tells me that this isn't your primary purpose in all of this. It sucks what happened, I know, but I don't think you're going to become an angel of death, if that's what you're worried about."

"But I killed people," Alexis stated flatly. "I killed living, breathing people. It's a horrible feeling, worse than a nightmare." Her hair begged to be tugged and twirled but she resisted. "I shouldn't wield the power of death. What if I make the wrong decision and kill someone innocent?"

"You won't," Stacia answered gently. She took a seat in a chair by a corner desk. She swiveled it so she could look at Alexis, who remained staring out the window. "Tell me about Cedar City," she prompted gently.

Alexis looked at her uncertainly.

"Trust me," Stacia went on warmly. "It'll help."

Alexis looked back out the window. "That man grabbed my ankle, I had no choice but to shoot him."

"No, no, no," Stacia interrupted gently. "Go all the way back. Tell me why we went to Cedar City in the first place."

Alexis nodded, willing to go through the mental exercise if it helped her understand. "It was the intel from our scouts in the southwest," she began.

"More accurately, it was what you pieced together from seemingly innocuous intel," Stacia pointed out. "You're the one who saw what no one else did." She tapped out a command on her phone and the large television on the wall came to life, displaying a map centered on Las Vegas. There were several red dots marking the towns forming a ring around the city. "Explain it to me," Stacia prompted.

Alexis did. "The T.S.S.F.G. had received scattered reports from smaller towns; Cedar City, Mesquite, St. George, Indian Springs, Henderson, Lake Havasu City, Barstow, all rebounding nicely after what Hade did to the world," she answered self-consciously, looking at the map. "They recovered quickly, establishing local governments, energy sources, clean water and hospitals. New growth far outpaced anything we were accomplishing here in Salt Lake or what was happening in any other major city."

"You wanted to know how they were doing so unusually well, so we trusted your hunch and sent in some recon teams. What was the result?"

"These communities were building and thriving, using capital we couldn't trace," Alexis answered. "As our spies dug deeper, their sources shied away and their information lost reliability. No glaring discrepancies, but we noticed them."

"You noticed them," Stacia corrected. "And you give credit for that insight to?"

Without hesitation, Alexis answered, "Owen."

"Why?" There was no ridicule, no patronizing tone—it was a simple question.

"I don't think that way," Alexis answered truthfully. "I can memorize, I can be taught and I can regurgitate what I've learned. But I don't see patterns or put things together." She paused, before finishing. "He could." The past tense stabbed at her. "He can," she corrected herself.

"So he told you?"

"No, he didn't tell me," she answered. "But I knew. Somehow, I knew something I could not have known."

"Regardless of the source, the conclusion was spot on," Stacia nodded. "Continue."

"Our scouts went from town to town and each successive report told the same story," Alexis explained. "But as they tried to tighten the net and zero in on Vegas, we lost communication and our people were compromised. Less than half made it out alive and none of the survivors had any insightful information."

"Some of our best agents were killed or remain missing," Stacia looked genuinely concerned. "So what did you conclude from all of these events?"

"The pattern was unmistakable. This web of well-funded puppet governments, establishing a perimeter of counter intelligence around Vegas, essentially making it invisible to the world, could only mean one thing." As she thought about the men who'd been killed, the lies and deception protecting some evil core, her temper heated up.

"It's Hade," she finally said quietly, biting back the anger that began to simmer within her. "He set up Las Vegas as a hub and established puppet governments in dummy communities all around it to run interference. Vegas is his base and even if he isn't there, his minions will be." The boyish faces of Owen's best friends came to mind. Hade's tool had murdered them all. "Cole Banyon will be there," she finished acerbically.

"Easy on the hair, Alexis," Stacia said gently, stopping her friend before her hand strayed upward. "So we needed to take down Vegas, but we couldn't just drop into the middle of a hornet's nest. We needed to start with more information from one of the towns forming the secure perimeter. Tell me about Mayor Thomas in Cedar City."

"He is…was dirty," Alexis answered with some disdain. "We had intel and then reliable confirmation that he portrayed himself as a hardworking, caring family man, but he also worked out of the hospital funneling drugs, weapons, supplies and money into Vegas. As the only link we had to whoever was running Vegas, it made sense to try to take him."

"The original plan was to take him alive," Stacia pointed out. "What prompted you to put the bomb on the helicopter?"

Alexis turned back to the window, letting her eyes stray across the mountains again. "I had the bomb ready for a complex door breech just like we planned," she answered slowly. "But as we approached the hospital from the north, a thought just kept nagging at me. There weren't any words, just a distinct feeling that I should plant the explosives in the helicopter. I tried to ignore it, but the feeling became more intense, more distracting, and suddenly, I couldn't focus on the mission. So I ran back to the helicopter, planted the explosives, and just like that, the feeling disappeared.

"It wasn't until Thomas almost escaped and we pursued that I put it all together," she continued. "We had failed to capture him; he was escaping with information we desperately needed. He was also escaping justice—he had to pay for the lives he'd taken, and for helping Hade. Lastly, he saw us plainly and could identify us to Hade, putting us and T.S.S.F.G. in danger. If he got to Vegas with our descriptions, the fallout could have been catastrophic. It left us with only one option. So I used it."

"It sounds like a pretty clear choice to me," Stacia stated unapologetically.

"It doesn't feel like it," Alexis lamented.

"But you're ignoring the vast majority of your role in the mission, Alexis. Remember, it was you that sniffed out Hade's compound, uncovered the network of disinformation he set up to protect himself, and then had the guts to step in and take it down yourself. Whether the insight to all of this was yours or not, I don't care. Don't you get it? The world needs you, Alexis. You did exactly what you were meant to do. And you did it the right way," Stacia concluded.

"You really think so?" Alexis asked.

"Well, sort of," Stacia continued with a sly smile. "Over a year of drilling into you the tactics of the IRA, the Afghan Mujahedeen, and the Chechens—the greatest education possible for urban combat—and the success of our mission ends up depending on the assistance of the ghost of a naive boy from Utah!" She threw her hands up in exaggerated exasperation.

"Shows how much you know, Queen of Intel," Alexis interjected, letting herself finally relax. "He's originally from Colorado!"

The two women let themselves laugh at that; let the questions and the anxiety from their mission slide harmlessly away. When the laughter finally subsided, both of them were staring out the window. Both were at peace.

Breaking the long silence, Stacia finally offered soberly, "You understand now, don't you."

Alexis nodded slowly. "So if this really is the right way, why doesn't it feel like it's the right way?"

"I suppose you'll have to find the answer to that on your own. I just know that I've come to peace with it. And, just so you know, I don't worry about your motives, Alexis," she went on. "I know you'll do what we need you to do. It's not destiny, it's just that God knows your potential. He knows He can trust you, so He put you in the position, in this epoch of Earth's history, to do what is needed." She paused for a moment to let it sink in before finishing. "But I really think He's left it up to you to decide how you'll do it. The ability to choose is the greatest gift He gave us and the greatest among us will use it to do the greatest things."

"Thanks," Alexis said softly. "That means a lot to me."

Stacia put her arm around her friend again. "Coming to that understanding is important," she said. "It also means you're ready for the next step."

Alexis looked at her friend through narrowed eyes. "And that is?"

"How would you like to get a closer look at what's going on in Vegas?"

"I thought we were expressly forbidden to get anywhere near there?"

Stacia shrugged. "Things change."

"How are we going in?" Alexis asked, a mix of excitement and fear coursing through her.

"It has to be fast and under the radar," Stacia answered. "Motorcycles at night from St. George to Mesquite, then on to Vegas. We have to get in undetected."

"What about your dad? Shouldn't we wait for him?"

"He said as soon as I thought you were ready, we should do a little recon," Stacia answered and then added with a stern look. "And that's all we're going to do, mind you."

"Why now?" Alexis asked. "Why the urgency?"

"The enemy isn't resting, Alexis," was the answer. "You know that. You see it every day. They're spreading their holdings and their power."

"And now they're preparing something bigger," Alexis concluded. "That's it, isn't it? Something worse?"

Stacia nodded. "We don't know what it is, but we know that Vegas is a part of it."

"Cole could be there," Alexis added thoughtfully. "So could Hade."

"True," Stacia agreed, her look hardening again. "But this is recon only. We go in, we poke around, and we get out. Leave any thoughts of revenge behind. Are we clear on that?"

Alexis glanced sharply at her friend, but knew she was right. "We're clear," she answered. "When do we leave?"

"We'll start studying surveillance and satellite images tomorrow morning," Stacia replied. "If we can pull everything together fast enough, we can head out in a few days. One week, tops."

Alexis nodded silently and cast her eyes back out to the shadowed mountains. Stacia was right. Any thoughts of revenge must be left behind, but that was easier said than done. She knew this was a recon mission with a clear objective. Violence was not to be a part of it, if they could help it. But what would happen if she met up with Cole or Hade? Would she be strong enough to stop herself from trying to kill the men responsible for Owen's death? She knew Owen wouldn't want her to kill anyone in cold blood, but she had just done exactly that in Cedar City with men who were significantly less important in the Krypteia chain of command. And that's what scared her the most in all of this. While she felt a gaping hole in her heart for her role in ending the lives of others that day, she didn't need or want to weigh morality or consider the greater good when it came to Cole and Hade, as that was a decision she had long since made. They would die by her hand, or she would die trying to kill them. There could be no other outcome.

CHAPTER 8

Mesopotamia: Michael Dalacourt blinked, which surprised him since as far as he could tell he hadn't existed the moment before. He remembered delivering God's message to De Solei, remembered getting beaten into oblivion, and then remembered nothing more. He tried to connect with his body, but there didn't appear to be anything there to connect to. What had become of him? Had he died under the cross of Our Lady of the Angels?

His present location only furthered his confusion. He could feel the searing heat of the midday sun, smell the dry sand blowing past him, and see the endless dunes stretching forth before him. This didn't feel like heaven, and if it was hell, then all of his studies about that dark place were misguided at best. No, this felt like something else. What that was, however, was beyond his present abilities to explain or comprehend.

And then, inexplicably, something tugged at him, willing him to move and, with no effort at all, he sailed forward. His spirit flew over the desolate plains until he saw a giant walled city on the horizon. He understood immediately, without knowing how, that this was Uruk, the great city that was both a bastion of light and civilization to the early Mesopotamian world and the scourge of all those who refused to be ruled by the kings within its mighty fortresses.

Without any awareness of how it happened, as if he was skipping through the random scenes of a dream, he was suddenly inside the great chamber of the king's palace next to the great temple to Eanna and just beyond the city's orchards. He was immediately overwhelmed by the decadence of wealth stretched out before him in the great chamber. The entire room glistened and gleamed from the sun's luminous rays streaming through open windows and reflecting on the treasures of gold, silver, copper, bronze and iron stacked in enormous piles throughout the hall. Stringed music was playing slowly, exotic harem girls were dancing gracefully, chained slaves were serving enormous trays filled with all manner of food, and peacocks milled about in all their glorious colors alongside courtesans dressed in hues and shades to match.

Nearly everyone was smiling—and why wouldn't they? The lords and ladies in the room were living surely as the gods must live, with everything provided for them and no concern for tomorrow. Dalacourt might have been tempted to think that perhaps this was the heaven spoken of in so many holy books, if not for the one man who sat alone on an enormous throne crafted of a variety of precious metals high above the gilded crowd. Exceptionally tall and widely built, wearing the traditional Mesopotamian beard and dressed in gloriously multi-colored clothes that outshone those worn by even his most vibrant subjects, he sat alone, a look of scorn etched across his bronzed face. He wore no crown, but it was clear by his countenance that this man was a king. No, the former priest realized abruptly, this was no mere king. He was in the presence of a god.

Dalacourt found it impossible to determine if the look on the man's face signified anger, disgust, boredom, or any other mixture of negative emotions, but it was clear that the ruler was entirely displeased about sitting in a room full of jesters and fools who worshiped him as the most powerful lord in all the lands. A lord? No, he was more than that. In fact, he was more than anyone in that large hall could even imagine. But Dalacourt knew. And that knowledge chilled him to his very core.

The giant reposed before him was none other than Gilgamesh, one of the first kings of the ancient world, a demonic hero who the legends of old claimed was two-thirds god and one-third human.

Dalacourt longed to flee this unholy place, to escape from the presence of one responsible for so much destruction and death in the archaic world, but he knew there was a purpose behind this vision. His spirit floated nearer to this great king of old, only to realize that as he drew closer he was able to hear the thoughts of Gilgamesh as if he were speaking aloud.

"I grow restless again," Gilgamesh thought dejectedly. "I walk in the enclosure of Uruk, where the people prance about in skirted finery, where every day is a day for festival, where the lyre and drum play continually, where harlots wait, exuding voluptuousness and like a wild bull, I make myself mighty.

"But I am not like those who live under my roof, those who know death comes and wait to greet it with open arms. There is nothing to slake my thirst, nothing to sate my hunger, nothing to satisfy my desires. I am nothing, but I am everything. I destroy life and I create life. I release my passions, but I control my cravings. I beg for justice, yet I mete out mercy. I live and I live and I live and I do not die. I have seen the abyss, I understand all and see all, I know the secret things of this world and yet I am alone. I am restless and there is no end to my restlessness. I will never know death. That is not living."

As the great Gilgamesh sat on his mighty throne, deep in sorrowful introspection, the twenty-foot tall cedar tree doors of his grand room swung open and a young hunter rushed in. The musicians stopped playing, the girls stopped dancing, and everyone turned their attention to the man with a wild look in his eyes. Most of the courtesans seemed displeased at the interruption, yet keen to see the sport that might be played out before them. The hunter was out of breath as he rushed to the feet of Gilgamesh and bowed before his terrible lord.

"Arise," the great king commanded and the hunter obeyed. "Speak before I tire of you and rip your tongue out with my own hands," Gilgamesh said idly. There was a murmur of satisfaction through the gathered lords and ladies as they realized blood might be spilt.

"Your worship," the hunter began, desperately trying to gather his composure. "There is a new man in the forest. I saw him for many days and for many days he removed my traps and freed my animals." The hunter waited, unsure if he was to go on. After a moment of silence under the withering stare of his lord, he continued. "He was not a normal man, my king. He was as strong as the meteorite of Anu, as strong as you perhaps, and he walked and talked with the beasts. We prayed to Ishtar to ruin this man so we would not starve and she sent a woman to him. After laying together for one week, the man's powers over the beasts were gone and he was as a regular man again. We ruined him, my king, but we have no cause to rejoice. He is still strong, as strong as many men, and we are fearful he will destroy us in his wrath."

"What is it to me if he destroys you?" came the half-angered, half-bored response.

"Your highness, all Uruk knows Gilgamesh leaves no son to his father; his lust leaves no bride to her groom; yet he is the shepherd of the city, strong, handsome, and wise. We are your sheep and ask for your grace."

"Sheep are for slaughter," was the simple response. "And yet… I have been plagued by dreams of late, one of a shooting star so heavy I could not lift nor move it. A second dream was of an axe that fell over Uruk. The wise goddess Ninsun untied my dreams and told me that both the star of heaven and the axe are one in the same, a companion who is powerful and has incredible strength. Could this man you speak of be such a companion?"

The hunter swallowed hard and looked to his left and right and saw soldiers with large axes on both sides of him, all looking at him, their glares dangerous. "I know little of dreams, my lord, but he could be such a man. He has immense power and is wise as well. You would do well to bring this man here as your companion."

Gilgamesh laughed long and hard. When he finally stopped, he looked down on the hunter and smiled arrogantly. "I am no errand boy. If he is who you say he is, then he will come to me. Perhaps I will kill him. Perhaps together we will kill you. Only the gods know for certain, but you should pray to them that he is the answer to my dream. If not, then your life and the lives of those in your village are forfeit."

"Thank you, my lord," the hunter said quietly and then turned and hurried out from the great chamber, worried that Gilgamesh's anger was kindled against him and he may not live to see the outside of the grand hall again.

But Gilgamesh's mind was on his dreams and what the arrival of this new individual might mean. He thought no more of the hunter.

Michael Dalacourt's eyes snapped open as consciousness returned to him and the vision faded. Pain washed throughout his body—a pain so intense, he desired nothing more than to sink back into the blissful blackness of oblivion. His bones ached, his muscles screamed from abuse, and his lungs heaved, begging for air. He gasped loudly, bringing his hands to his chest and stars exploded behind his eyes at the sudden movement, bringing with it the memory of his last conscious moments, of the brutal beating he had endured at the hands of De Solei's men. He was alive, but he found little joy in that fact at the moment. He knew he was only being kept alive long enough to turn his imminent death into a spectacle for the masses. Such would be De Solei's decree.

He closed his eyes again and tried to relax his body. After a few minutes, his breathing grew easier and his mind turned back to the vision of Gilgamesh. It was so different, in both theme and content, from the vision that had led him here in the first place and unlike that vision, this didn't feel as if it was of God. In the end, as confusing as it was, he had to believe it was nothing more than the disjointed subconscious thoughts of a man in a coma.

With a bone-weary sigh, he forced his eyes open, only to find himself looking directly into the gaunt face of a dead man. Terrified by what he saw, he did the only thing he could think to do.

He screamed.

Ignoring the pleas of his battered body, he attempted to scramble away from the apparition, but a strong hand was laid on his chest and he found himself powerless to move.

"You should not exert yourself," the dead man said softly. "Your wounds are serious. I have tended to you as well as I could, but I was concerned you would not awake. I think now that you have, though, you will survive if given the time to properly heal." The man paused, his deep-set eyes searching Dalacourt's bruised face as if he was looking for something, some moment of tangible clarity. Finding no such recognition, he withdrew his hand, lowered his head and began to turn away.

"You…cannot be," Dalacourt stammered. He stared, his eyes wide with shock. With a great deal of effort, he managed to prop himself up on his elbows so he could better see the man before him. A million thoughts entered his mind at once, but nothing could explain what he was witnessing. Nothing could help him come to grips with what he knew was truly impossible.

"I have often told myself the same thing," the man said slowly, as if he struggled to find and form the words. "Yet, I am."

Dalacourt shook his head, dredging up the memory of their last encounter. "The last time I saw you, you tried to kill me," he went on, absently rubbing his throat. "Do you remember?"

The old Brazilian eyes of Father Francisco Nunez de Oliveira lost focus as he turned inward. "I remember," he answered softly. "It was in the Vatican. I was in darkness."

"You were in one of the catacomb's cellars," Dalacourt corrected.

Oliveira turned his haunted eyes back on the former priest. "No," he said, than placed his hand over his heart. "The darkness was here." Oliveira reached up and touched his head. "And here," he added. "Darkness tried to take me."

"How do you mean?" Dalacourt asked. "I don't understand."

Oliveira thought for a while and then shrugged his shoulders. "I do not know, either," he answered cryptically. "But I remember there were others."

"Other people?"

The old man shook his head. "Other spirits."

"Father," Dalacourt said carefully, leaning forward and peering closely at him. "Who are you?"

Oliveira looked up and shook his head. When he again looked back at Dalacourt, a single tear rolled down his cheek. "I do not know," he answered sadly. "I have no name, no memories, no dreams. I simply am."

"You're not actually Father Francisco Nunez de Oliveira, are you?" Dalacourt guessed.

The living dead man shook his head. "I do not know him," he admitted. "There is a veil within me, something I cannot see beyond. But something is there, just out of reach. If I were truly Father Oliveira, it would not be a mystery to me, I think."

"Yet you inhabit his body."

The old man nodded. "I do," he answered. "But I know not how."

"Do you have a name?"

"No," he replied. "I am aware of no such distinction."

"Well, I need to call you something, so I suppose Oliveira will have to do," Dalacourt sighed.

The man nodded, seemingly pleased at that. "A name," he said softly to himself. "I have a name."

Dalacourt looked closer at him. It seemed impossible that the Oliveira that was before him could be. He had witnessed the chaos of two years ago and seen the dead rise to do the bidding of evil. But the risen dead were dead again, were they not? And if so, then what was Oliveira? How did he get here? The mystery deepened in his mind and reminded him again that with God, all things must be possible. It was that thought that triggered a question. "What do you know of God?" he asked curiously.

Oliveira was silent and thoughtful, before replying. "Everything and yet nothing," he answered truthfully. "I know of Him by knowing the scriptures that I read. But I do not know who He is. I do not know who Satan is. I only know what the Bible tells me of them."

"You've studied the Bible?"

Oliveira reached out and picked up an extremely worn copy of the Holy Bible from a nearby nightstand. "I have been imprisoned for my entire existence," he said. "I have no need of sustenance, of sleep, or of anything else that I am aware of. But I have this." He held it out to Dalacourt, who took it and flipped through it. Every page was tattered; most verses were marked and questions were scrawled on every available open space of every page. "I have studied the Bible every day and every night and I know the passages intimately," he continued and placed his hand on his heart again. "But in here, I know nothing. I have even prayed as the Bible instructs, but the heavens are silent to me."

"You're an empty vessel," Dalacourt pointed out, understanding the man's situation all too well.

Oliveira looked at him quizzically.

"Knowledge will only take you so far," Dalacourt explained. "You say you know the scriptures well, but to truly grow, you must have a passion for something, a feeling. You must have experience. You must gain faith."

"And how will I attain this?"

"Like any other growing individual," Dalacourt replied wearily, his body still wracked with pain, but his mind invigorated by the unexpected conversation. "You'll find your faith by experiencing trials and difficulties like everyone else. You'll make choices and decisions and it's that freedom by which you'll grow."

"How am I to know what decisions to make?"

Despite his aching body, Dalacourt managed to chuckle. "If we all had the ability to know how to make our decisions, there wouldn't be a need for faith now, would there?"

"That doesn't seem like a good way to do things. It confuses me," Oliveira said with a frown. "Does it not make more sense to study all of the information before us and then make a logical choice based on pure knowledge, rather than accept something on faith?"

"There have been days when that philosophy has enticed me, but in the end, it's not of God," Dalacourt answered. "Knowledge is a wonderful tool, but it's not the only tool. Making our own decisions, and more often than not making the wrong decisions and then learning from them and improving ourselves, is the divine way," Dalacourt explained. "God would have us make our decisions based on both faith and understanding, although many times that understanding is limited, in which case we're operating on faith alone. Regardless, he would never force our decisions—even good decisions—upon us. That's the province of another."

"Satan."

Dalacourt nodded and replied, "Satan would have you enslaved to his will, choosing as he would have you choose. He would have you miserable and hateful, eventually being cast into hell with him for all eternity."

"And God would have us choose," Oliveira finished.

"Yes."

"Perhaps in time I will understand as you do," Oliveira said after a thoughtful pause and then after an even longer silence, he added. "May I ask a question of you, Michael?"

Dalacourt nodded, searching the dead man's face, but if he was hoping to find something, anything that would tell him more of who and what Oliveira was, he found only an impassive visage, devoid of emotion.

"Do you believe I am an abomination?"

The former priest looked at the formerly dead priest and contemplated a long time before answering. "I don't know what you are, Father Oliveira," Dalacourt finally said quietly. He reached out and laid a hand on the man's shoulder. "But I believe in time, you'll find the answers you seek."

"How can you be certain?"

"I can never be certain," Dalacourt shrugged. "But I understand things well enough to know that you being here is not by accident. There is a greater purpose for your existence. You must simply discover what that purpose is."

Oliveira was silent and seemed to carefully consider the words that Dalacourt had spoken to him. Then without a word, he stood up and walked to a small desk on the other side of the little cell. He sat down and began to leaf through his worn Bible until he settled on a certain page and began to read, mumbling quietly to himself.

As the dead man read, Michael Dalacourt took a moment to take in his surroundings. The beating at the hands of De Solei's men had been terrible and he was acutely aware of just how much pain he was still in. With a sigh, he sank back down onto the bed and let his eyes wander. He and Oliveira were in a small, but furnished room. There was only the one bed that he was currently lying on and the desk where Oliveira sat reading. A couple of chairs were lined up across from him, as well as what looked like a small cedar chest of some kind, pressed up against the wall. He could see two doors—one was open and led into what looked like a bathroom. "At least I'm not to be treated like a savage," he mumbled to himself. The other door, however, was made of steel and had a small window grate in it, barred and closed from the other side. "But I am still a prisoner," he finished and laid back into the pillow, his eyes closing wearily.

He would get no rest. As his beaten body ached, his mind began to wander over his waking moments, examining the revelations he had received since coming back to the land of the living, as well as the events that had led to him being imprisoned.

Had he really spoken for God and condemned De Solei and those like him? Had he indeed called down the first plague upon mankind—hail and fire and blood? How much had it changed the world? How many had been killed? He had always been well-versed in the last days, so he knew it was the work of God Himself, but his heart broke for the death and destruction that had to be visited upon His children, deserving or not.

Then there was Oliveira. Who was he truly? And why on earth were they now imprisoned together, obviously at the behest of De Solei? Did it have anything to do with his strange dream? Or was it even a dream? The name came to him again, but it brought only more confusion.

Gilgamesh.

As he considered where that had that even come from, something about the name stirred fear deep within him. In his studies as a child, he vaguely remembered the name and the story behind him—a great god-king said the legends. But why would he suddenly dream of him?

So many questions.

So few answers.

And so little time.

CHAPTER 9

Kigoma, Tanzania: Nearing exhaustion, Petr Zhugravinsky slowed slightly as he passed under the broad limbs of the mango trees surrounding the old Sumbawanga house he shared with Chuike, her husband, Hashim, and their newborn daughter. The lights were off and there were no sounds coming from within, which set off every internal alarm he had. Hade had warned him of what he would find when he arrived and he had no reason not to believe the man. Something was wrong here.

Very, very wrong.

He scanned the area and, while he couldn't see anyone guarding the house, he knew they were there. Nikolai and who knew how many of his associates were paying the family a visit and unless a small miracle had occurred, he doubted he would find them alive. It had struck him on his run from the bar that Hade had prolonged their discussion to keep him occupied and away from his protective duties, allowing Nikolai ample time to do whatever he wanted with David's family. This realization had crushed him. He had been set up completely, had fallen entirely into Hade's trap, and once again innocents would suffer for his actions, or lack thereof.

As he came to the house, he knew he needed to stop, assess the situation, and proceed with caution, but there was no time. It was a trap, but he had no choice but to run right into it if he hoped to have even the slightest chance of saving anyone. He therefore consciously committed one of the cardinal sins he had learned never to do as a young Mafiosi: never enter a building you don't know you can get out of. He picked up speed and burst through the front door and into the house, expecting the worst.

He found it waiting for him.

Even with the growing storm outside and the clouds bordering on black, there was enough light coming in from the windows that he was able to make out two figures on the floor in the middle of the living room. The first was Chuike, kneeling just a few feet away, her eyes closed tightly as she rocked back and forth while gently cradling a bundle of blankets in her arms. She was crying softly, a heartbroken lament of loss and hopelessness. Petr's heart fell as he realized she was holding her newborn daughter, Silvi. The tiny girl, only a few weeks old, was not moving. There was no sound at all from her. Then Petr saw the blood on the blankets.

The rage rose up within him and his eyes moved from the heartbroken mother to a figure lying in a heap beside her. Hashim was also dead, his eyes open and staring, a bullet hole drilled into his forehead, fresh blood still trickling from the wound and pooling on the wood floor.

Petr was too late. All of his promises, all of his efforts to protect this family, were for nothing and it left him hollow inside. As he stepped forward, Chuike raised her head ever so slightly and met his gaze. The look she gave him shook him to his core. It was one of utter emptiness.

Before Petr could reach out to her, the attack came from behind, a perfectly timed blow with the flat end of a cricket bat to his lower back. The breath was driven from his lungs and, as he staggered forward, another figure immediately stepped into his fuzzy vision and punched him squarely in the jaw. Stars exploded behind his eyes as the blow connected and he found himself falling to his knees, his legs turned to rubber. A kick to the side of the head laid him prone and, as he struggled weakly to rise, the bat was slammed across the back of his shoulders again, driving him back to the floor once more. His face hit the hard wood and he felt his nose break, the blood running freely.

"Enough," a familiar voice sounded from somewhere in the fog. "He is my brother, after all," Nikolai Zhugravinsky continued, his tone mocking and full of hate. "Help him up," he commanded. "I would see what my dear Petr has become."

As rough hands fastened themselves to his arms and yanked him up to his knees, Petr retaliated. With a violent cry of fury, he shrugged off the grasping hands and leapt to his feet. The cricket bat slammed across his back once more, but he paid it no heed, instead turning and grabbing the head of his assailant. A violent twist snapped the man's neck and Petr threw him to the side like a ragdoll as he whirled and faced his next attacker.

He recognized the man, a Russian hoodlum his brother had dealings with in the past. Petr slapped the man's clumsy grasp away and drove his fingers into the thug's throat, crushing his windpipe. As the man's eyes opened wide in agonized terror, Petr shoved him aside and lunged toward Nikolai. All things being equal, Petr might have had a chance, even in his battered condition, but his brother wasn't about to play even.

Instead, Nikolai shot him.

The .45 slug slammed into the meat of Petr's shoulder just below his collarbone and spun him into a small table causing him to stumble to the floor. As the pain blazed up from the wound, he tried desperately to ignore it, but another of his brother's henchmen kicked him in the face, sending him back to the floor once more in a haze of agony.

"This is a thirteen round magazine and I've still got ten more, Petr. I promise I will put each one of them into you in interesting and painful places if you try that again," Nikolai scoffed, this time quite angrily. "Now get him on his knees," he growled to his thugs, his voice dangerous.

Again, hands fell upon Petr and again he was pulled back to his knees. The bullet wound in his shoulder throbbed and blood flowed from his broken nose. A tall, bald man covered in Chinese tattoos grabbed his hair and yanked his head up, so that he was staring directly at the still sobbing Chuike. She continued to rock her dead daughter as she sobbed, seemingly oblivious to everything around her. Nikolai stood beside her, his silver-plated Glock 21 Gen4 held loosely in his hand.

"Welcome home, dear brother," Nikolai said, stepping forward and looking directly at Petr with a smirk. He cast his eyes about in disdain, before finishing, "If you can call this hovel a home."

Petr spit blood on the floor and glared at his brother, trying to figure out how to murder him where he stood.

"I assume you have questions for me, no?" Nikolai continued. "You wish to know why I am here? You wonder why I waste my time on this trash you live with?"

"I'm going to kill you, Nikolai," Petr snarled, ignoring the question. The hand in his hair tightened, but he paid it no heed.

"And get more blood on your hands, Petr?" he snapped back. "I rather doubt you could handle that. Blood already drips from your hands and stains everything you touch."

"I am no murderer."

"Oh, but you are, my brother!" Nikolai boomed. "Our entire family is dead because of you! So I have come to Africa to repay the favor."

"You killed our family, brother," Petr said. "Now you come here and murder innocent people that deserve nothing like this!"

Nikolai looked down at Hashim in disdain and then pushed the dead man's head with the toe of his boot. "This is exactly what they deserve, Petr," he said plainly. "They mean nothing."

"They were innocent!" Petr roared, but his captors kept him immobile, unable to lunge forward. "You killed a child, Nikolai! A newborn baby!"

The elder Zhugravinsky brother shrugged. "I admit I allowed the blade to fall, Petr," he answered coldly. "But ultimately, the child is dead at your hand."

"You killed them!" Petr shouted again and tears flowed down his cheeks, mixing with his blood. He began to shake with sobs as the ramifications weighed heavily on him. He had failed David to the last and now Chuike's husband and daughter were dead, murdered by his own brother. "You...killed them," he repeated and trailed off, his eyes closing tightly as if the reality could be hidden away somewhere so that it never happened.

"You could have avoided all of this," Nikolai said, his voice suddenly quiet as he knelt before Petr so that they were nearly face-to-face. "You abandoned us, Brother," he went on as Petr opened his eyes and locked stares with him. "You abandoned me," he went on, a slight tremor in his voice. "You let our family plot against me, Petr. You let our father condemn me to death. Did you hope they would kill me? Is that what you truly wanted?"

"We were family, Nikolai," Petr sobbed, looking in desperation at the heartbroken Chuike, still cradling her dead daughter, her life completely and utterly destroyed.

"I am family!" Nikolai fairly screamed, lashing out and slapping Petr across the face. "I am your brother! You abandoned me! You betrayed me!" Nikolai slapped him again and again, raining blows across Petr's face as his rage played itself out. "You..." he trailed off and then suddenly stood, tears in his own eyes now. "Oh, Petr," he continued. "How great we could have been! We, the Zhugravinsky brothers..."

"I never abandoned you, Nikolai," Petr said slowly, his face numb from the beating, but his focus again on his murderous brother. "I only wanted something different."

"Different? You are a Zhugravinsky! We—you and I—were born to be together. To lead together! You abandoned all of that! And for what? This?" Nikolai looked around in disgust and then spit contemptuously on the floor.

"I abandoned our way of life," Petr corrected. "I only wanted better for all of us; for the Zhugravinsky name to be remembered for something more than the way of the gun."

A long, low laugh issued from Nikolai and the sound of it chilled Petr. It was the laugh of a madman. "You wanted better?" he scoffed. "I am the premiere of Russia, Petr! What glory I have brought to the Zhugravinsky name!"

Petr shook his head. "It's not glory, Nikolai," he said softly. "It's shame."

"Shame? To be the leader of one of the greatest countries in all the world is shame?" Nikolai repeated incredulously.

"No," Petr corrected him. "It's the way you attained your power, Nikolai. You were handed everything by the darkest of men, but he deceived you, Kolya. And he still does. I can see in your eyes you know who I speak of. You know who owns your soul."

Nikolai opened his mouth to speak, but found no words. The room was completely silent, before Petr finished.

"Hade."

"What do you know of him?" Nikolai finally asked, his voice barely above a whisper.

"I know him well, my brother," Petr said, easily able to put it all together now. "I know how he manipulates and twists things to get you to do his bidding."

"No," Nikolai said, but his voice shook. He was having doubts and Petr knew it. "You are wrong," he went on. "Hade has been nothing but a friend to me."

"He told you to kill our family, did he not?"

Silence again.

"You know I speak the truth," Petr drove the point home. "This was all about Hade. It always has been and it always will be."

There was a sharp intake of breath and Nikolai suddenly turned away. Petr watched him walk to the back of the room and face the wall. The room was silent, save for Chuike's quiet sobs. Nearly a minute went by before Nikolai turned around. He had completely regained his composure and his face was now a mask of stone as he glared coldly at his brother.

"I have need of you in Moscow," he said, his voice devoid of all emotion. To Petr, it sounded as if death itself was speaking.

"I will not join you, Nikolai," Petr said quietly. "I will not be what you are."

Without a word, the elder Zhugravinsky placed the barrel of his Glock to the side of Chuike's head.

"No!" Petr screamed, but it was too late.

His eyes vacant and emotionless, Nikolai pulled the trigger. The gunshot boomed through the small house and snapped Chuike's head sideways. Her eyes rolled back in her head and her body slumped to the floor, joining her husband and daughter in death.

Just like that, the Sumbawanga name had ended and the failure of Petr Zhugravinsky was complete. Horrified, he glared at his brother with fresh tears in his eyes and raw hate boiling up within him.

Nikolai stepped toward him and knelt down so that they were eye-to-eye again. "You no longer have any ties here in Africa," he said flatly. "You will join me in Moscow or others will suffer the same fate."

"I'll see you dead first, Nikolai," Petr seethed, shaking with rage.

Nikolai was unfazed. "Idle threats from an idle man," he said dismissively. "I will expect you in Moscow in two weeks. If you are not, I will track down Alexis Kennedy and make certain that you watch her die as well. And I promise you," he finished dangerously. "I will make sure she takes a very long time to die."

Petr bowed his head. He was beaten and he knew it.

Nikolai reached up and patted him on the cheek none too gently, some life coming back to his eyes. "I see we have an agreement, brother," he said and then stood and slid the Glock into a shoulder holster underneath his jacket. "I will see you in two weeks. We have much work to do."

The thugs who held Petr flung him roughly to the floor and together, the remaining Russians exited the house. Petr lay still, battered and in shock, his eyes on the corpses of those he had sworn to protect. They were all dead—all at the hand of Nikolai—just like his family. He knew that Nikolai would make good on his threat to kill Alexis, too, and Petr realized he would be forced to attend his brother after all.

Just as Hade had predicted almost two years ago.

No, he thought suddenly. Not quite.

With a groan of pain, Petr picked himself up off the floor. The bullet wound in his shoulder could be treated and his broken nose set. He would survive his encounter with his brother this night. He would even go to Moscow to be with him, per his brother's wishes.

But Petr Zhugravinsky already knew how it would end. He would kill Nikolai. He would kill his brother, even if it cost him his own life.

Without another look at the dead, he turned and staggered out the door. There was indeed work to do and that work would begin this very night. His thoughts set, Petr staggered off into the darkness, never again to return to the Sumbawanga home.

CHAPTER 10

United Nations Plaza, New York City, New York: The loud knock on the door woke the man instantly. Searching for the clock across from the custom-made king size bed in his VIP suite on the top floor of the Benjamin Hotel, he rolled over, saw 11:30 a.m. and called out "Who is it?" in his most irritated voice possible.

"Room service," came the curt reply.

"Ah, yes, breakfast," he said as he pushed himself out of bed, stretched, bent down twice to touch his toes, and put on his Jacquard striped robe. Brazilian President Jose Maria Wilson Nunes da Silva dos Santos, known throughout the world simply as Wilson since his days as one of the shining lights of the Brazilian national soccer teams of the 1960s, looked contentedly around his suite as he shuffled slowly to the door. It had been a meteoric rise for him in the world of politics. He had climbed all the way up from the *favelas* of Recife to the official presidential house, the Palácio da Alvorada, and later today, he was going to join the inner circle of the United Nations Security Council as the leader of Brazil. Staying in a room like this would have been unimaginable even a few years ago. He laughed to himself as he realized that the term "unimaginable" no longer had a place in the world today. Anything could happen. Today was proof of that.

As he arrived at the door, he peered out the peephole to ensure that it was indeed room service and then let the young man in. In a hotel famous for catering to the needs and whims of some of the most powerful and particular people on the planet, even he was surprised by how perfect his Brazilian breakfast was: coffee, milk, French bread and jam, *queijo de coalho*, and a wide assortment of fruits, including papaya, mango, guava, passion fruit, pineapple and even some jackfruit. He sighed as he saw a hollowed out gourd with a silver straw sticking out of it, full of a Brazilian tea called *Mate*. He detested both the taste and the colloquial way of drinking it, but he knew it was a "necessary" part of his companion's morning. Still, he was impressed the staff had managed to find both the drink and the vessel under such short notice. It would make the morning go much better and for that, he would have to leave a larger tip than usual.

He wheeled the tray over to the bed, sat down at the foot of it, turned the television on and changed the channel to WNN, his new favorite source for catching up on world events. Looking at the form nestled under the covers, he shook her softly until she stirred. "*Bom dia, meu amor*," he said with a smile on his face.

The woman next to him slowly pulled the blanket from over her face. "What time is it?" she mumbled sleepily.

"Time for breakfast, *princesa*."

The woman just shook her head, indicating she was going to lie in bed for a while longer before getting up. Wilson nodded and turned to his food. While he was now among the world's elite and had become accustomed to getting whatever he desired, the woman next to him, Tatiana de Moreira, tall and tan and young and lovely, was a former Miss Brazil and Miss Universe, and he had no problem letting her do as she pleased. She reached over for her *Mate*, and then plumped up her pillow to let her incline slightly while drinking.

"What an amazing night of sleep," she said after taking a long sip. "I could stay in this bed forever. Whatever they are paying their sleep concierge, it isn't nearly enough."

"I agree," Wilson laughed. "We will have to bring some of these pillows home with us."

After a few moments of eating and drinking in silence, the segment Wilson had been waiting for came on and he turned the volume up with the remote. The announcer was discussing what was to happen later that afternoon at the United Nations.

"We are here live in New York City on this awaited and momentous day. Almost every important political, religious, and economic leader from around the world is on their way to the United Nations later this afternoon for the historic ceremony marking the end of one nation's leadership on the Security Council and the introduction of a new world power into that increasingly prominent body. As you recall, it was only two weeks ago that Antonio Malvado-Jinete, the United Nations secretary general, announced the change in a stirring speech not soon to be forgotten."

The picture switched from the reporter to Malvado-Jinete, obviously a clip from the already famous speech. "Two years ago our world was turned upside down and while it is right for us to yearn for a return to the bucolic days of old, as we continue to rebuild we must be vigilant to maintain a clear and steady focus on both the present and future. We do indeed live in a new world and the time has come for the most important international organization on earth to reorganize itself to reflect that new world. Long have we looked to the leadership of the United Kingdom to guide us through crises such as these, but the nuclear devastation in London, combined with the collapse of the banking system and civil wars ravaging entire regions, England is now in need of rescuing itself and no longer able to serve as it has done in the past. If we are to look to a strong and vigorous nation to take on a new role of stewardship in the world, we need look no further than Brazil.

"I am therefore announcing that in two weeks' time, when the United Nations General Assembly next meets, we will change leadership of the Security Council for the first time since its inception after the last great World War. I invite all world leaders to join us, as this is your moment as well as ours. Generations from now, the world will look back to this change as the first of many events that saved the human race. May God bless you all."

The screen moved back to the announcer. "And so today we are here to witness this remarkable transfer of power. For many around the globe, this turn of events is hard to believe, but for most, it is only a reflection of the hard realities the world faces today and will continue to face in the future. Coupled with the announcement earlier this week that next year the secretary general would look to add other nations to the Security Council as well, naming South Africa, India, and Japan as possibilities, it would appear that Mister Malvado-Jinete is out to remake the world's entire political dynamic to reflect the current state of affairs.

"Doctor Johan Van Roose, professor emeritus of political science at Ghent University in Belgium, speaking earlier this morning, said that with the United States and China struggling to rebuild their ravaged infrastructures, and France and Russia both just now beginning to function as they had two years ago, it would not be surprising if the move to replace England with Brazil was simply the first domino to fall in creating a new world government. If that is to be believed, then we very well could be ushering in the beginning of a new era for all. We'll be here all day with coverage of this remarkable event."

Wilson muted the television, leaned back on the bed and gave Tatiana a small kiss on the base of her neck. "I can't believe they didn't even say my name in their report," he said, somewhat pained. "Would it have killed them to say who it was that has single-handedly brought Brazil to such glory?"

"You boys and your secret clubs," Tatiana tsked. "I don't understand why you care so much. The UN was never that important and Brazil is now one of the strongest nations on earth. We don't need them."

"You're right, of course, my dear. We could do perfectly fine on our own. Perhaps even better. Yet, I think it's a club that still has a lot to offer us." Wilson sat up, poured himself another cup of coffee, took a sip, and looked back at Tatiana. "Well, it has a lot to offer me, anyway, and I think most of that has to do with the man in charge."

"Malvado-Jinete? You really like him that much? I suppose he is good looking, in his own way. Perhaps I should call him? Maybe he won't make fun of my drink."

"I wish I could say you aren't charming, but of course you are," Wilson smiled. "I've been studying the secretary general for some time, and I'm impressed. Look at how he removed England and put us on the Security Council. But beyond that, it appears that Malvado-Jinete has every intention of making certain that country will never again rise to power. With half the countries in the United Nations either former colonies to England's monarchs or former slaves to England's banks, this is a day a great majority of the world has been waiting years to see. He's made many friends with this move, make no mistake. Brilliant."

"Should I be jealous?" Tatiana asked slyly. "Perhaps you are the one who wants to spend time with him, not me."

"I'm serious, Tatiana, this man is putting something big together and I want in. Did you notice his little addition on Tuesday where he said he might add other nations in the future?"

"No, I must have missed that part. I was busy drinking my *Mate*."

"It was a political move to rival any other the world has ever seen. In one masterstroke he told three of the strongest nations left in the world, India, Japan and South Africa, that if they do whatever he tells them to, they might have a seat at the adult's table. He also let France, China, America and Russia know that if they don't do as he says, he'll send them back to the kid's table. I cannot even imagine what sort of concessions he is getting out of those nations as we speak. If he isn't already the single most powerful man on the face of this earth, he soon will be."

"So, the Security Council really isn't that important after all, is it? If you can be moved on or off if it so easily, it can't be that powerful."

"Excellent point, but it's never been all that powerful in an overt sense of the word. While it has little real power, it's made up of the nations with the largest armies, the biggest economies, the most assets and most influence in the world. Being a part of that lets me attend better parties, be invited to more meaningful meetings, and be involved in the decisions that will let Brazil maintain its rightful place atop the world. Most importantly, though, it gives me access to Malvado-Jinete. There is something about him that tells me he understands the world on a deeper level…"

Tatiana flipped over in bed and scrunched up her nose as she thought about what Wilson had just told her. "So… the club itself isn't that important. It is who is in the club and what the people in the club do together that matters."

"Perfect, my dear. I don't think my entire team of speechwriters could have put it any better. And they said at your last pageant you were all blonde and no brains." Wilson took a bite of papaya and was about to take another drink of coffee when an idea struck him. "Why don't you join me later today at the United Nations? I would very much like you to be there for this."

"Why don't we just stay here in bed instead?"

"You know that isn't an option, as tempting as it is. I've got some things to do beforehand, so I'm going to shower and leave shortly, but I'll send a car for you around three o'clock so you can be my guest."

"And what am I going as?"

It was a question Wilson had never enjoyed answering in the past. The desired response was always as girlfriend, but the truth was always less pleasant. He was president now, and that didn't come without perks, so it was significantly easier for him to come up with something in between legitimate love interest and mistress of the moment.

"How would it be if you came as my new Minister of Culture?"

Tatiana paused, still unsure if Wilson was joking around with her. "Do you really have one of those?"

"If I don't, I should, and if I do, he obviously isn't doing a good enough job and needs to be replaced. I'll call Enrique from the car and make it official."

"I'm grateful, of course, but what am I to wear? I didn't bring anything ministerial."

One more benefit to being the president of Brazil was that there was always someone else to fix the minor details of any problem. "Call the front desk. If they can get you that infernal *Mate* on such short notice, I'm sure they can find you something appropriate for the occasion."

Tatiana climbed out of bed, sashayed over to Wilson and gave him a long, lingering kiss. "Until later then, Mister President?"

"Of course, Minister."

Four hours later, Wilson sat regally in the light blue chair just outside the center of the circle in the Security Council Chamber in the United Nations. For Wilson and his beloved Brazil, inclusion onto the Security Council was validation that his country was finally being recognized as one of the most powerful nations on the planet. Tatiana had been right, of course, that this was all for show and in the end, quite meaningless, but that still didn't mean the spectacle of the thing wasn't something to behold and that it was anything less of a triumph. To the outside world, he was now someone more important and his country was also more important. That did matter.

If he was going to make this day become truly significant, though, he was going to have to make sure he remained as close as possible to the secretary general. The days of the nation state were coming to an end and only those smart enough to understand what that meant would survive the coming years. True power would soon be held here, at the United Nations, and it would be men like he and Antonio Malvado-Jinete, and not countries, that would rule. Wilson had grown keenly aware over the past two years that the secretary general, who was seen by so many as a man of the people, was really a man for himself, with a complete knowledge of what he wanted and how he wanted to get it.

Antonio Malvado-Jinete's story was well known to the world. He had been one of the lost children of the Argentinean Dirty War. During this conflict, more than thirty thousand political dissidents simply vanished. In one of the more shocking betrayals of the people the military junta was claiming to protect, many of the disappeared, or *los desaparecidos*, had their children given to the very families that had made them orphans in the first place. Often, the military would even wait until a pregnant woman delivered and then have her executed before giving the new baby to a leading military family to raise.

Given to a wealthy family of government supporters at the age of two and raised completely oblivious to his true heritage, he had led a quiet life until a fire at the family's mansion killed his entire adoptive family. He had been the sole survivor, orphaned again at the age of seventeen. Two years later, he had found out the truth about his past and had spent the rest of his life fighting for those without a voice. He became the youngest member ever in the Council of Ministries at the Casa Rosada when appointed secretary of social development and, after four years there, he moved on to the global community. Involved in NGO's and an innovator in community building projects around the world, he eventually won the Nobel Peace Prize for his work in building water purification plants throughout the developing world, bringing cheap, potable bottled water to millions of people.

Malvado-Jinete had parlayed that success into a string of United Nations appointments that eventually led him to becoming the secretary general. His campaigning had been vigorous, on a level never before seen, but perhaps indicative of the new role the United Nations was playing on the world stage. He had played off old enemies and made new friends in order to come to power and, during the worldwide upheaval and in the two years since, he had proven himself an able leader. He had kept the world's socio-economic and political systems from caving in on themselves, all while building the United Nations into a true leader on the world scene.

Wilson knew the story well, but he also knew that not all was as it seemed with the secretary general. In his search to better understand Malvado-Jinete, the private detectives he had hired to uncover more information had found slight discrepancies. Old photos didn't quite match up, dates didn't quite equate, and the few remaining documents about his youth didn't quite look authentic enough to be real. Wilson had eventually come to realize that everything he knew about the man was by design. Antonio Malvado-Jinete might well have lived a manufactured past and his true intentions for what he was doing at the head of the United Nations might be unknown, but as long as he saved Wilson a place at the head table, he was content to remain silent on the topic.

As Wilson sat, thinking about what was to come, his attention was grabbed by the entrance into the room of a young woman. Tatiana had arrived and was sauntering toward him.

"I think I said for you to get something appropriate," Wilson sighed, not altogether angry about what Tatiana had put together, but a little surprised nonetheless. She was wearing a low-cut red sleeveless dress that barely stretched down past her hips.

"I disagree," she replied in a smoky voice. "This is quite appropriate. If you had made me Minister of Education, I would have worn thick glasses, pulled my hair back in a bun and worn a brown suit. If you had made me Minister of Defense, I would have worn a military uniform. But you named me Minister of Culture and you have to admit, this is what culture should look like."

"You certainly have me there, *princesa.* Is it me, or is the dress sparkling?"

"It has diamond powder woven into the fabric."

"Do I want to ask how much that cost me?" Wilson asked cautiously.

"Does it matter?" she winked.

Wilson eyed his new minister and smiled. "No, it's worth every penny, although my wife is going to throw a fit when she sees you in the papers."

"Does that matter, either?" she said, winking again.

"No, I'm actually looking forward to it. Oh, it looks like we're about to start. Here, I saved you a seat." He stood up and held the chair for Tatiana, who sat down just as Antonio Malvado-Jinete took his place at the front of the room and in front of the world's elite.

Antonio Malvado-Jinete had been preparing for this moment for seemingly forever and he smiled as he faced the leaders of the world. "Ladies and gentlemen," the secretary general began. "*Senoras y senores, lamen und herren, mesdames et messieurs, gewei xiansheng nushi.* Welcome. We come together on the eve of perhaps the greatest day in the history of our United Nations."

There was a loud round of applause and Malvado-Jinete flashed a winning smile as he allowed it to go on longer.

He looked around the room and took it all in. In the inner circle, clapping and nodding in approval was the United States president, Albert Abrea, and the secretary of defense Anne Marie Banyon. Next to them the Chinese premier, Xu Ziang Po, and chairman of the central military commission, Bo-Lin, as well as French president, Jean-Baptiste St. Claire, and his minister of defense and veterans affairs, Denis Achille Dieudonnee. Seated next to St. Claire were the Russians, President Nikolai Zhugravinsky and his minister of defense, Vanya Zhugravinsky. The seats next to Nikolai were empty, formerly filled by the British prime minister and his attaché. It was now time to change that and usher in a new era.

"President Wilson, if you will," was all he had to say, nodding his head toward the empty seat in the inner circle. He continued to smile as President Wilson stepped forward and took his place in the inner circle along with the newest member of his cabinet, Tatiana de Moreira.

"This is a solemn, but exciting occasion," Malvado-Jinete said, "and I welcome my northern neighbors to the council." There was another round of applause and Malvado-Jinete paused to welcome it once more. "My friends," he stated, "the world is changing and we must change with it. This room, for example, is usually reserved for diplomats and bureaucrats, errand boys at best. Today, however, we see this room filled with the most powerful leaders in the world—and not just political leaders, but religious leaders such as our friend, Pope De Solei, sitting to our right, and economic leaders such as Mister Callithrix Aurita Williams, CEO of Legio Enterprises, sitting next to him. With this group of forward-thinking innovators that we have assembled here, we will rebuild, we will be stronger, and we will be better than ever. We thank you for your efforts and your willingness to work together for the good of humanity."

He stepped back a pace and nodded his head, welcoming the applause that was now aimed at him. He had prepared for this moment for a long time and today, finally, he had the world right where he wanted it.

"My esteemed colleagues," he laid it on thick, holding nothing back. "The wolves are circling, nearer and nearer, the wind is howling, louder and louder, and the sky is growing darker and darker. The tragic occurrences of two years ago have passed, but the environmental devastation that burned cities to the ground and leveled entire regions has told me that there is still much work to do. Additionally, war continues to rage across the globe and despite our best efforts, we lack a unified leader to step forward and take control, a leader that we must have if we are ever to return to a time of true peace and prosperity."

He paused, allowing the applause to begin anew, before holding up his hand and asking for silence. This was the moment he had prepared them for.

"We need a man willing and able to stand up for what is right, to do what must be done, to save our world from itself," he stated forcefully, his very presence dominating the many leaders surrounding him. "Years ago, Franklin Delano Roosevelt saw the role of the secretary general of the United Nations as a 'world moderator.' I think now more than ever, we need the secretary general to become such a leader. I am ready to be that man!"

He finished and stepped back slightly again from the podium as the entire room gave him a standing ovation. He had them. He knew it. And he basked in their adoration and approval.

When the applause finally died down, he laid the groundwork for his New World Order. "In two weeks' time, I ask that you vote me emergency powers in this time of great need—power that I will use for the greater good of the world at large. When the threat has passed and I have ushered this world into a time of peace never before known; when we stand united as one world people, I will restore all power to the Security Council and humbly return to my home in Argentina, just as Cincinnatus of old returned to his fields. Of this, you have my solemn promise."

The room rose again to applaud, this time vigorously, and Malvado-Jinete smiled and nodded, acknowledging their allegiance. He had done what no one in history had ever done before. With honeyed words and a few empty promises, he had united the world under one man, forging his law over the law of the lands. In two weeks, the people in the room would officially make him the first ever dictator of the world, all of them hoping that by giving him all the power, he might share a bit of it with them. It had been almost too easy.

The speech ended and the applause over, President Wilson moved skillfully through the room. He motioned to his personal photographer and began to make the rounds. He shook hands with the Chinese and French presidents, posing for a quick photo. But that was for them, not for him, and he moved on as fast as he could. Their sun was setting and he had little use for them. He slowly made his way across the room and eventually found himself posing for a picture with the secretary general himself. He waved for his Minister of Culture to stand in the picture with them and asked if Antonio Malvado-Jinete's attaché would care to join them as well. It didn't hurt that she was as stunning as the former Miss Universe on Wilson's arm.

Malvado-Jinete smiled as the beautiful young woman attached herself to his arm. "I think you would be better served if you kept *this* little butterfly at a distance, Mister President," he warned with a laugh.

"She's not quite as friendly as she looks."

"I find it impossible to believe a flower so pretty could have any poison," Wilson said smiling, laying on the charm. "Allow me to introduce myself. I am the president of Brazil, but you may call me Wilson."

"*Enchanté*," the young woman said silkily as she held out her gloved hand. "My name is Miss Carestia and I can assure you the secretary general is quite right with his warning."

"Of course I am," Malvado-Jinete said jovially as he put a hand on her shoulder, "but please join us anyway, my dear. It would be nice to have a picture with you in this outfit." His attaché nodded her head, but it was clear she wanted nothing to do with the photo. After Wilson's photographer gave the thumbs up that he had gotten a good shot, she appeared ready to leave when the secretary general gently held onto her wrist.

"I have a wonderful idea," he beamed, a gleam in his eye. "Why don't you take President Wilson's new Minister of Culture around and introduce her to some of the dignitaries here. I'm sure she would love to be in the care of someone so…" he paused as if searching for just the right word. "Helpful."

"Of course," she said coldly, and the two walked away, leaving Wilson and Malvado-Jinete alone for a moment.

"I swear it is feast or famine with that one," Malvado-Jinete grinned and then turned serious. "May I ask you a question, amigo? Between two old friends?"

"Anything, Secretary."

"Where do you see the world in the next few months and years?"

"Ah, and here I thought you wanted an ally and a friend when all along you were searching for a fortune teller," Wilson answered, pleased when Malvado-Jinete smiled at his light-hearted comment. "I know little more than you, but I believe including Brazil in the Security Council is the beginning of something new and wonderful. For everyone," he added.

Antonio Malvado-Jinete leaned closer and chuckled. "You don't actually think this little farce of a ceremony meant anything, do you?"

"Of course it meant nothing. But that doesn't mean it also didn't mean everything," Wilson answered truthfully.

"Well said," Malvado-Jinete said, placing his hand on Wilson's shoulder. "It's a brave new world, a world where a man from Argentina and a man from Brazil can rule the world together."

"Indeed."

"Now, I have others to meet with," Malvado-Jinete added. "We will dine soon, no?"

"Of course, Secretary," Wilson said, shaking his offered, white-gloved hand.

As the secretary general moved away from him, the Brazilian president turned and continued to wander through the room, making certain he exchanged pleasantries with everyone of importance. He shook hands with the monkey-like Mister Williams of Legio Industries, had a brief discussion with Pope De Solei to set up a luncheon, and shared a conversation about trade concessions with Satya Patil, an Indian senator who controlled the increasingly vital technology sector in Mumbai. He embraced his Russian ally, Nikolai Zhugravinsky, with a promise to meet again soon and eventually, only the American president remained to be seen, a necessary exchange of words almost as important as being invited to sit on the Security Council.

Wilson spotted him with his secretary of defense, still at the center table in the inner circle of the room. "Mister President," he said warmly as he walked toward him.

"President Wilson," Abrea said in return, his smile not quite as wide or as sincere.

"Thank you for coming to my party," Wilson said with a wink. "I hope it has been to your satisfaction."

"It's quite a fiesta," the American replied and then turned to indicate his companion. "Have you met my secretary of defense, Anne Banyon?"

"Charmed," Wilson said, shaking her hand. Without waiting for a reply, he turned back to Abrea, still smiling. "I was wondering if you had the chance yet to look over my proposal to merge some of our economic and military institutions to strengthen our position in the world."

Abrea laughed sourly. He had indeed seen the Brazilian president's bold and brash offer, the first attempt of courting favor and laying the groundwork for future alliances. It had made him angry enough to throw his tumbler of whisky across the oval office to shatter against the wall nearest the door. "I'll be frank, Mister President," he said, emphasizing Wilson's title. "I have looked over your proposal and I can tell you that even if I was in favor of it, which I am most certainly not, the American people would never agree to it. What you ask is tantamount to giving you the keys to our house and saying stop in and take whatever you want, whenever you want. I think you forget your place in the world."

Wilson's smile never wavered. "Oh, I know my place, Albert," he said pointedly, his voice hard and cold. "My place is here, at this table with you, as an equal. But that is only for now. There will come a day when you'll need to ask us for help and on that day, as you sit and wait to hear our response—*my* response—you'll look back and realize a different attitude and a different course could have changed everything for you."

Wilson held Abrea's gaze, his eyes never wavering, letting the implied threat hang in the air. As the uncomfortable silence stretched between the two men, his cell phone vibrated with an incoming text. With little more than a slight tilt of his head, he turned and walked away from the fuming American leader and, once he was alone, opened up the message. It was from Hade and it read simply, "Tweedle Dee but not Tweedle Dum."

Wilson chuckled to himself and said to no one in particular, "Say what you will about the man, but his timing, as always, is impeccable." He motioned for his photographer to join him again and together they wound their way through the remaining dignitaries and out through the entrance, where a limousine was waiting for them. The two men slipped inside and, as they drove away, Wilson reached into the bar and skillfully pulled out bottles of vodka, Kahluá and cream. He reached over to the glasses and looked at the man across from him, who gave him a thumbs up as he loosened his tie with his other hand.

Wilson finished mixing the drinks and handed one over to his photographer, who swirled it around slowly and then took a sip. "Where did you learn how to make such a fantastic White Russian, Mister President?" he asked.

"Well, Marcello," Wilson replied. "I didn't make it this far just on my good looks alone."

Marcello Tuono nodded and said nothing.

"I received a message from Hade," Wilson continued. "We are to proceed."

"Am I to kill them both?" the assassin asked, his tone almost bored.

"No," replied the Brazilian president. "It appears that the secretary of defense still has some use to Hade, so for now your only target is President Abrea."

"That makes things simpler."

"For a man of your talents, I would think you'd want more of a challenge," Wilson smirked.

Tuono said nothing, but returned the president's smile as he sipped his drink.

"You know, I will not be sad to see that man go," Wilson went on. "To be honest, I would not be sad to see everyone in that room go. Such arrogance. Such misguided notions of power. It's funny, you know, they all think they're in control, that they have power, but they don't understand what true power is."

His phone chimed. Looking at the screen, he smiled broadly, reached over and pressed the limo's intercom button. "Driver," he said loudly, "we're going to skip dinner. Take us directly to the airport."

Marcello Tuono raised an eyebrow, to which Wilson responded jovially, "I must apologize, my friend, but you have the leader of the free world to dispose of and it appears I have pressing affairs to go over with my minister of culture."

Tuono smiled knowingly and raised his glass. "To order and progress," he said simply.

"To ruling the world," Wilson replied.

CHAPTER 11

Salt Lake City, Utah: Otis Ludlow led the two women under his command—Alexis and Stacia—from their apartment to Elevator C. According to public record, the building they were currently in only had two elevators, A and B. Elevator C did not technically exist and was only accessible from the highest five floors of the building. No button called it and once inside, there were no buttons to direct it as it descended well below ground level.

The elevator finally stopped and the rear door opened to a broad, cool, and well-lit tunnel. Otis stepped out first onto the durable, bright red carpet, and led them to the tunnel's first intersection. Alexis had been down here before, but she had never enjoyed the closeted feelings that overwhelmed her under the earth's crust.

These tunnels were constructed well over a hundred years ago, webbing under the city's surface in an unmarked pattern that was navigable by memorization only. They were an engineering masterpiece, built twenty feet below the city surface, large enough for cars to navigate, the perfect temperature, earthquake-proof, flood-proof, with secure access to essential locations throughout Salt Lake City. During the events of two years ago, civic and religious leaders, as well as select members of T.S.S.F.G. had survived the chaos by taking refuge in these tunnels.

"I still don't get why we have to go this way," Alexis said as they took a left hand turn into another lengthy hallway. "It will take us an hour to march to the helipad from here. We could have driven."

Without looking her way, Otis replied in a tone indicating he'd passed the point of trying to argue this some time ago. "You know why we're going this way. Despite our best efforts, there are still powerful groups out there searching for you. You're a hero, Alexis, or have you forgotten that little bit of important information?"

Alexis mumbled something under her breath, indicating she understood but didn't wish to be reminded of it.

"There are too many accounts of four heroes on a mountaintop in the Oquirrahs, defying an emissary of Satan himself, for those who care about the end times to just ignore," he continued. "And it is not only evil that seeks you, but a great many goodly people are out there searching for you and the others at this very moment."

Alexis cringed at the memories his words dredged up. Thinking about the other survivors from that day was enough to make her physically ill, not to mention extremely angry. In reality, she had little ire for the priest, Michael Dalacourt. She felt he had been deceived from the beginning, just as she had, and while he apparently knew a great deal more about their destiny than what he had told her, it was hard to fault him for not sharing more. They had been on the run for their lives, and hadn't had much time to just sit and chat.

She was quite convinced, however, that Petr Zhugravinsky had a special place in hell set aside just for him, and she was determined that someday she would help send him there. He had lied to her from the beginning and cost her the one thing that mattered most in her life: Owen. Every waking moment, she regretted letting the Russian live, even if it had been the right thing to do.

After the events on the mountain, John had thought it best if the three of them stayed away from each other for the foreseeable future, and she couldn't have agreed more. She was pretty sure she could handle herself on this mission when it came to Hade and Cole, but running into Petr might tax her self-control past its breaking point.

Some heroes, she thought bitterly. Of the three of them, people only understood what they were told in the aftermath. They knew only of the outcome and the victory over evil—over Hade—had become a rallying cry. But these people knew nothing of who they each really were. Humans. Deeply flawed and at least in Petr's case, extremely dangerous.

"They pursue you *heroes* with nauseating fervor," Stacia added with a roll of her eyes, her way of dealing with the unwanted fame Alexis and the others had garnered. For Alexis, it was a matter of modesty and decorum. For her, it was just another distraction and a good way to get them all found and killed by the wrong sort of people.

"But many of them are good souls," Alexis countered half-heartedly, forcing herself back to the conversation at hand. "I still say we could always start bringing them in."

"Really?" Stacia asked with a lifted eyebrow. "For what purpose?"

"To tell them the truth and share what really happened," Alexis answered. "We could marshal people like that as army of good against Hade. You have to admit, there would be strength in our numbers."

Stacia just shook her head. "We've been over this, Alexis. You're not a real person to them, but a symbol; a sign of the times. They assume, and perhaps rightly so, that we stand on the threshold of Armageddon. There are some who would do anything to keep that from happening and others who would do anything to make it happen as soon as possible." She hesitated, looking at Otis for a moment before continuing.

"As soon as you say one thing out of line, use your left hand to eat instead of your right, or forget the word to a sacred verse, they will turn on you. They will no longer see you as a chosen leader, but as a fraud. We just can't risk that. Not now, nor in the future."

"There has to be a way," Alexis began, but then wilted. Deep down, she knew her friend was right, even if she had a difficult time accepting it.

"There isn't, and you know it. Don't forget, we've just been talking about the good people who would be impossible to trust with this. Krypteia is sure to stock the throngs of truth-seekers with people looking to slit your throat. You'd be dead before you knew you were in danger."

"That may be a bit exaggerated, Stacia," Otis said calmly as they continued walking. At an intersection he turned west and continued. "We're pretty good at what we do and we've been doing it for a long time."

"And what, exactly, is *it* that *we've* been doing for a long time?" Alexis knew they wouldn't truthfully answer that question, but she wasn't in a mood to stop asking.

"What we have to," Stacia responded with a voice that said no more questions. They passed a hallway that led north and Alexis saw that it divided several times in the short distance she could see. They must be getting closer to the city center.

Otis shrugged, not wanting to just leave the conversation where it was. "Just remember, Miss Kennedy, the weaknesses we've found in your training. You're still too trusting, too naïve. You've got to learn to be paranoid and suspicious, if you want to stay alive." He gave her an earnest look to emphasize his point and then his gaze returned immediately to scour the tunnel ahead.

A distant noise emanated from another tunnel to the left and Otis immediately dropped into a defensive crouch, moving to a position to better protect her. His actions actually made sense to Alexis, given what she had learned over her time with him. But she also noticed his subtle movement of herding her closer to Stacia so he could shield them both. Alexis knew full well that Stacia didn't need shielding, but she had begun to believe that Otis had feelings for Stacia that moved beyond the professional relationship they shared.

Looking around, Alexis tried to focus her attention on their situation. There was little protection afforded in the wide tunnels, but she scanned the hallways in all directions to familiarize herself with escape routes if needed. Otis stood between her and what was coming toward them, but as the low hum of an electric motor reached them, he let some of the tension out of his broad shoulders. He looked back at the two women with a glance that indicated they would be okay, but they shouldn't let their guard down quite yet. In all likelihood, whoever was coming were allies, but Otis' drawn gun spoke to his practice of the advice he had just given Alexis.

The moment stretched until a white Mercedes golf cart came around a distant corner. There were two men in front, one driving and the other carrying a shotgun. A large man stood behind them, his feet braced on the rear deck of the cart. "Drop your weapons!" the standing man commanded immediately, his authoritative monotone convincing.

Otis held up his left hand, setting his gun down with the other. "Damn self-righteous..." he mumbled, holding up both hands so that they were easily visible. He then declared aloud, "It's me, Otis."

The officer frowned and immediately holstered his weapon. He said something into a microphone on his lapel as the cart came closer. "No need to be armed in the tunnels, Otis. I've told you a thousand times, they're secure," he said firmly, breaking into a knowing smile.

"Which is why you're armed?" Otis didn't smile back.

The guard ignored the barb and nodded at Alexis and Stacia. "Is this man bothering you ladies?" His easy smile widened. He was at least six foot tall, blond with blue eyes and in his early thirties. Wearing a tailored black suit and sporting a dark green tie, he had all the appearance of a member of the Secret Service.

"We're fine," Stacia replied carefully.

"Excellent," he said, still smiling. "And since Otis doesn't seem in the mood to introduce me, I'll have to take care of it myself. The name is Jason Flaska, but my friends call me Captain America. I'm with the good guys, just so you know," he finished with a wink.

Stacia looked inquisitively at Otis, who had picked up his own weapon and holstered it.

"No," Otis answered her unspoken question. "Flaska is not T.S.S.F.G. We aren't the only ones who use these tunnels, but we can trust him. They're on our side."

Flaska turned to Alexis, stepped forward, and clasped her hand. "You must be Alexis Kennedy," he greeted her warmly.

It had become routine in the past two years for people to recognize her, but the young woman had never become comfortable with it. "Pleased to…meet you," she said haltingly, unsure how to proceed conversationally.

"Please don't take this the wrong way," Flaska continued, "but I pray constantly for your safety and guidance and that you may have the courage to fulfill your role in the difficult days ahead."

Alexis smiled. She felt a genuine peace when he spoke, akin to the peace she felt with Owen. "Thank you," was all she could say. It bothered her that he knew so much about her, but at the same time it was reassuring that he honestly believed in her. She wished she had a fraction of that belief in herself.

"The pleasure is mine," Flaska replied genuinely, before turning his attention to Otis with a grin. "It's reassuring that you have such a calm and thoughtful guide. I trust he's being a true gentleman."

"He had the gentleman trained out of him years ago," Stacia cut in with a mischievous smile of her own.

"Alright, that's enough from both of you," Otis growled. "There's a reason we're down here, Flaska. Are you going to move along or are we going to spend all day down here socializing?"

"Of course," came the easy reply. "We're actually here to help you on your way." With that, the two men in the front of the golf cart, who had not spoken nor moved since arriving, pulled themselves out of the cart and stood off to the side. Flaska made an exaggerated bowing motion, indicating the cart was theirs, and joined the two soldiers. "Safe travels," he said. "To all of you." With a final nod of his head, the three men turned and began trotting back down the tunnel the way they had come.

Grumbling to himself again, Otis climbed in the cart, indicating the two women should join him.

"You could have at least said thanks," Stacia couldn't help but grin.

"Never," Otis replied gruffly, but there was no real animosity in his voice. "Flaska would have taken it as an insult and then I would have been forced to shoot him."

Stacia laughed brightly at that. Otis pointed the cart in the right direction and hit the accelerator. Alexis stood in silent contemplation on the back deck of the cart, replaying the latest in a series of cryptic conversations about her role in what was to come, praying the peace she felt could maintain her through the nightmarish mission she now embarked upon. They were headed to Vegas in what to her seemed like a complete contradiction to Otis and Stacia's comments about keeping her safe. But if it gave her the shot she needed at bringing down Hade, she wasn't about to argue the point.

With the aid of the golf cart, they were at the helipad early, and within minutes they were in the air.

An hour later, Otis' diaphragmatic voice was difficult to hear in the headphones over Alexis' ears as he issued their final orders. Alexis hated the relentless noise of the helicopter and Otis made no attempt to be heard above it. The strain to listen combined with the pounding noise of the blades above made her head throb.

"Delta team has been busy since you two left your mark on Cedar City," he was saying, all business now. "They must think you upstaged them."

"They'll deal with it," Stacia retorted, also making no attempt to speak up, further frustrating Alexis. "I've read the Vegas briefing, but what wasn't in the print-outs?"

"Not much," he replied. "As you know, Delta advanced south along I-15, through the desert foothills until they noticed the first highway barricade consisting of two military trucks and flashing barriers. Obviously meant to stop traffic from approaching Las Vegas, the heavily armed men standing watch were there to keep anyone from moving on to Vegas. After months of rumors and a lot of deflection from Washington, it was the first hard evidence we had that Vegas was becoming its own city-state.

"The team moved south and west until they encountered Lake Mead. There, they discovered that the lake was active with patrol boats. The Moapa Valley was similarly deserted but under surveillance, all of which combined to create a vacant dead space between St. George and Las Vegas, and all of it controlled and patrolled effectively by Hade's organization, apparently with the blessing of the United States government.

"Four days ago, the team engaged in a firefight with a well-armed patrol several miles outside of Vegas itself. They suffered several casualties and had to be extracted under heavy fire without being able to recon the city itself. Because of that, there's no doubt the enemy is on high alert, and it's this newly-militarized Vegas that you two are getting ready to infiltrate."

"And we're doing this why?" Stacia said flatly. "I thought we were going in under the radar. This sounds like the exact opposite of that."

"You're right. If Hade knows we're on to him, it's certain he also knows we'll try sending someone in again," Otis added. "And if he controls Vegas as it appears, you're going to be walking into a hornet's nest that's already more than a little ticked off."

Tightening a strap for the hundredth time on her pack—Alexis couldn't stand having gear that bounced around when she was running—she hardened her resolve. "But does that really change anything?" she interrupted.

"Does that really change anything?" Stacia repeated a little angrily. "You know it changes everything, Alexis! We can't scout another way in because we don't have the manpower to send in other recon teams. Not against the hardware and manpower they apparently have. So we're going in blind with the enemy on high alert."

"That's not what I meant," Alexis yelled—not that she was angry, but she was sure Stacia wouldn't hear her otherwise. "I meant it doesn't change our plan. We're still going into Vegas, we'll use every ounce of our training, gather what intel we can, and get out. Those would be our objectives regardless of the obstacles."

"Gee Bambi, is that all we have to do?" Stacia replied sarcastically. "And for heaven's sake, turn on your noise canceler!" She reached over and flipped a switch on Alexis' headphones.

Suddenly the world went beautifully silent, except for the voices of her friends. Alexis winced visibly and mentally chided herself for not realizing it was there.

Otis sat back and smiled, knowing better than to interrupt the two women. Stacia was experienced and smart and knew how to handle her less-experienced friend. Unlike most people, who were motivated primarily by fear or anger, and unlike most T.S.S.F.G. recruits, who were motivated by honor and duty, Alexis was motivated by perceived challenges, the desire to overcome obstacles, and the even rarer motivation of love. That made her an even more effective soldier and leader, but Stacia didn't see the harm in stoking her fire every now and again.

But Alexis stood her ground, her voice a little more heated than she intended. "That's enough, Stacia," she snapped. "You don't have to scare me or intimidate me to motivate me anymore. You've trained me well enough that I won't underestimate the enemy. I'll stay focused and I'll execute perfectly."

"And if something goes wrong?" Stacia stared directly into her partner's eyes, challenging her.

"Something *will* go wrong." Alexis knew Stacia was leading her and she gripped her armrest tightly to quiet her hands. "There will be enemies where intel says they aren't, in greater numbers, and with better weapons. Our own weapons will malfunction. We'll be tired, hungry, and thirsty. Something *will* go wrong. And when it does, I'll deal with it as you have trained me," she finished, meeting Stacia's gaze evenly.

Stacia continued to look at her for several long moments, before nodding. "Well, at least you say the right things. Now for heaven's sake let those armrests come up for air. Your hair won't twirl itself." Looking over her shoulder, she addressed Otis, all business. "What do we know about the south side of Lake Mead?"

"Nothing beyond terrain," he answered, smiling inwardly. "We assume Hade's people are patrolling the obvious approaches to the city most heavily, which means they'll have the airports at Temple Bar and Boulder City covered. And I'm sure the Hoover Dam will be crawling with them, not only as a security checkpoint, but the dam is probably powering their operations in the city. So we're gonna head a few miles downriver and drop you there. It will mean a much longer approach, but I'm afraid we have no choice."

"How'd Vegas get like this without us knowing?" Stacia shook her head in disgust. "This kind of thing doesn't happen overnight."

"It can happen quick enough with the right amount of money and people in place," Otis said helplessly. "You know what we're up against. Krypteia has control over just about everything. That and the information blackout on everything within a hundred miles of Vegas and you've got a perfect storm of hidden activity."

"Well, let's see what we can do about messing things up for them, then," Stacia said, doing a fast check of her gear.

The rest of their low altitude nighttime chopper run was completed in silence.

Midafternoon of the next day found both women lying prone in the desert a short distance from a bustling hive of activity. Stacia slowly lowered her Steiner M830r military binoculars, careful not to disturb the dry dust of the desert mountains above Nellis Air Force Base. "These new glasses work as well as Otis promised. I can see their uniform details from here," she whispered. "Those are full-on American soldiers," she went on, not moving anything but her lips. "Everyone is working efficiently and they're well-trained. These guys weren't thrown together yesterday."

Alexis hadn't moved for almost an hour; the only muscles in motion were those used for respiration and blinking. It felt good to move just enough to talk. "How could they have trained an army so fast?"

"They didn't. I would bet good money the majority of these men were military at the time of Hade's emergence two years ago," she said. "I expected security patrols, maybe a police force, and a fortified city."

She scanned the entirety of the base. Men marched busily everywhere like ants on a hill. They accounted for every necessary task: she saw pilots, aircraft maintenance, drill sergeants, janitors, men checking weaponry, and a score of others. Every uniform was clean, shirts tucked in. "But this? This is a fully operational military base."

As if to punctuate that statement, an F-22 roared down the runway, lifted off and shot perfectly upward, afterburners screaming. An A-10 Warthog pulled onto the runway right behind it. West of the runway sat the tower, the base of which boasted a heavily armed guard of at least twenty men. "What's with the overkill on tower security?" Alexis wondered aloud.

"You noticed that, too. Good," Stacia said with an appreciative nod. "It's not the tower they're concerned about. You see the thickest pole on the roof of the tower? The one with the mushroom-shaped top?"

Focusing her own binoculars, Alexis found what Stacia had described. "I've seen one of those before," she said after a moment. She searched her memory, trying to remember when she had observed the odd device before. "Hoover Dam," she recalled. "The recon team transmitted pics of one of those on the dam. There was another at the barricade on I-15. And others at both of the smaller airports south of Lake Mead."

Under layers of camouflaging dirt, Stacia smiled. "Correct. And what does it tell you?"

Her partner's Socratic tone was the tipoff. Stacia knew what those things were and that meant there was enough information available for her to puzzle out their meaning. "The key is in their locations," she reasoned after several silent moments of thought. "They correspond with the eastern and southeastern edges of the satellite blind-spot that surrounds the city these days. That's why we can't get any info at H.Q.

anymore. It's why we're blacked out now. It's a universal communications jammer." She never knew such a thing existed, but it was the only logical conclusion.

"I'll give you partial credit." Stacia sounded satisfied by Alexis' answer. "Now, ask yourself how these soldiers are operating with such coordination and flying planes if *all* of the communications are jammed?"

"They have to have some way to maintain several open channels despite the jamming and yet they also have the capability to keep those channels invisible," Alexis breathed. She still could not fathom how that would work, but it was the logic path that Stacia was leading her down. "How did they even make something like that?"

"They didn't," Stacia paused, her voice faltering. "That device is in the hands of our enemy because one day in the past, someone messed up. That's why everything we do now has to be perfect. Even the tiniest deviation from perfection can have catastrophic consequences. You have to remember that."

Alexia knew there was more to the story, but now wasn't the time to push her friend and Stacia wouldn't tell her if she didn't want to. So she remained silent, her eyes on the base.

Beside her, Stacia continued scanning the area around the tower. She looked west to the city center, then south toward the desert. It was a large expanse. "We have to change our plans," she finally said thoughtfully. "There's no way we can gather enough intelligence here, then again in the city, then evac and debrief everybody in a short enough period of time."

"What do we do?"

"We have to wipe out this blind spot," Stacia answered matter-of-factly. "We can compromise the whole network if we take this one down."

"Is that wise?" Alexis asked. "If we do that, we ruin any chance we have of picking up any usable intel in the city."

"If we can drop the blind spot, getting satellite eyes on this place will give us more intel in ten minutes than we could gather in a week of snooping around on the ground." Stacia answered, letting her eyes track to the descending sun. "We'll go down tonight. We'll take a path straight in, hit hard and get out fast."

"And you thought *I* would be reckless on this mission?" Alexis asked incredulously. She tilted her head just enough to see the face of her companion in her peripheral vision. She knew that look all too well, the one that said there would be no more discussion. Stacia's mind was made up, and there was no arguing with her. Knowing she was going to regret asking, she said the exact opposite of what she thought she should be saying. "So, how are we going to go about this?" she sighed in resignation. "I can guess how you plan to approach the tower, but how do we get an explosive mounted and detonated?"

Alexis was looking ahead again and didn't see Stacia's childlike smile, but her tone expressed it. "Do you see that A-10 over there?"

CHAPTER 12

Mumbai, India: Callithrix Aurita "Marmoset" Williams slumped down onto the tan, leather sofa and breathed out a long sigh of weariness. It had been a very long day of visiting dignitaries, officials, and industrial leaders throughout the business district, but it had been well worth his time and it did not take much of an imagination to know how much Legio Enterprises and he, personally, would benefit from it.

India had long placed itself among the growing nations in the world and, with the global problems of late, their role in the world's economy had increased dramatically. Mumbai was responsible for half of the exports out of India, making it one of the most important cities in the world today. Marmoset would not have the exact figures for another few days on the benefits of all the signatures and handshakes from the day, but he knew the ballpark figure was more than the gross national product of most third world nations. For some reason, his predecessor, Victor Legio, had never found any interest in India, preferring to spend most of his time working with the Chinese. He could not understand why.

He looked around his room and smiled. As with most five star hotels, the Leela Kempinski was a western style hotel in every aspect. The only way he knew he was in India instead of in New York or Rome or South Africa was that, on the table beside the sofa, there was a golden ox instead of a statue of the Empire State Building or Venus or a zebra. The carpets were a bit more colorful and intricately woven than normal and there was a painting of the Taj Mahal in one of the adjoining rooms, but otherwise it could have been a five-star hotel suite anywhere in the world.

But he wasn't just anywhere, he reminded himself. He was in

Mumbai, the City of Gold, and he was about to become the richest man on the face of the earth. Alexander the Great had gotten to the Indus river and stopped, but Callithrix Williams had not and soon he would build himself an empire that would rival that of even the great Alexander.

"I think," Marmoset said loudly after clearing his throat, "that if ever a day's work warranted a gin and tonic, today would most certainly be that day."

On cue, a short, thin man in a dark blue suit emerged from one of the side rooms. Balding, with dull gray eyes and a facial expression that indicated he might have never smiled in his entire life, he walked over to the bar and began to make the requested drink in silence.

"Thank you, Terrence," Marmoset said, basking in the glory of the day.

"I am at your service, as always, sir," the man replied tonelessly.

"You know, one reads of the olden days when kings and tyrants employed eunuchs as such trusted companions. Yet it seems impossible to me that a man who lost perhaps the most important part of what made him a man could be so faithful, so energetic, and so worthy. But the accounts are true, aren't they, Terrence? What would I ever do without you?"

"Probably wither away and die, sir."

"Why Terrence," Marmoset laughed as Terrence handed him his drink. "In all the years I've known you, I do believe that's the first time I've ever heard you say anything even remotely interesting."

"It won't happen again, sir."

"On the contrary, I quite enjoyed it," he replied. "Feel free to say something interesting again next week, if you're so inclined. It will break up the monotony, I think."

"Of course, sir," Terrence said tersely. "Before I take my leave, though, I remind you of your appointment this evening with the young Indian woman from Punjab."

"Punjab?" Marmoset repeated thoughtfully and then drained his glass and belched. He was positively parched.

"She was most insistent on a personal meeting to discuss how the two of you could work together to improve the cotton industry of the region."

"Do I care about the cotton industry in Punjab?"

"I am assuming you do, sir," the eunuch replied. "She is on your schedule and if she is on your schedule then by that measure, you must care at least somewhat about it."

"I finally understand why I did so poorly in my logic classes back at college," he mused. "Let me know when she gets here. In the meantime, how about a refill?"

Terrence already had a drink in each hand. "I took the liberty of making you two, sir."

"Truly, you are a gift from the gods," Marmoset said with a smug smile.

"Indeed, sir," Terrence said coldly as he walked out of the room.

The knock at the door came some ten minutes later. Marmoset looked over at the three empty glasses and silently chided himself for not waiting until the last meeting of the day was over. He couldn't remember the last time he had had more than one drink in a week, let alone three in one evening.

"Terrence, can you answer that?" he asked lazily, raising his voice enough so his servant could hear him from the other room

"Of course, sir," was the reply as Terrence walked back in. Marmoset stood up slowly and straightened his tie as his servant opened the door and led a young woman inside. "Your visitor, sir," he added, his tone almost bored. "Is there anything else you require?" He was not asking the woman.

"No, that will be all," Marmoset replied with a wave of his hand.

Terrence nodded his head, but got no further as the young woman suddenly pulled a Taser from within her sari and pressed it hard against the back of his neck. His body jerked several times as the electricity crackled and then he flopped to the floor, twitching like a fish out of water as his eyes rolled back in his head.

Had it not been for the alcohol, Marmoset was certain he would have fled, but he was feeling particularly mellow and watched the entire assault with a certain degree of detachment. "What could a eunuch have done to deserve that kind of treatment?" he asked, arching an eyebrow at the woman.

"I have better reserved for you, Mister Williams," she said, pulling a small caliber pistol from the sash at her waist and pointing it at his head.

"While I don't understand what this is about, I'm certain we can resolve it without further violence," Marmoset said calmly, glancing at her weapons and then back to her eyes.

"Actually, I don't see how we can resolve this any other way," she replied, holding the pistol steady.

"If you insist. Might I ask who you are before you shoot me?"

"Nakusa," she answered, her voice firm. "Nakusa Malhotra."

"I assume you're not here to discuss Punjab's cotton industry, are you?" he stated drily. The fact that she was pointing a gun at his head had done little to ruffle him.

"Hardly," Nakusa replied. "You don't recognize the name, do you?"

"Should I?"

"You killed my brother, Rajvir Malhotra, and now I'm going to kill you."

"I assure you I've never killed anyone, Miss Malhotra," Marmoset countered, keeping his voice even. He already knew there was an out here somewhere. Otherwise, she would have shot him already.

"My brother worked for Legio Industries at their plant outside of Jaipur," she went on. "Rajvir was a brilliant chemist. Five years ago, the factory was destroyed and my brother killed."

"That hardly equates to me killing him," Marmoset said. "I truly am sorry for your loss, but what happened in Jaipur was on my predecessor's watch, not mine."

Nakusa took a step forward and pressed the barrel of the gun against Marmoset's forehead, her features creasing with anger. "Do you think I have spent the last five years of my life trying to figure out what really happened, only to show up here by mistake?" she snapped. "Do you think pretending innocence is going to save you?"

"I have nothing to pretend about," Marmoset countered calmly. "I assure you, I've never had anything to do with the factory in Jaipur."

"Your name was on the secret memo ordering the facility disbanded and destroyed," she charged. "It took a lot of time and money to get my hands on it, too."

"That's impossible," Marmoset replied, his cool façade beginning to fracture slightly. "I refuse to be killed by someone over something I didn't do."

"That choice is not yours to make. It was your signature that killed my brother. Whether or not you recall signing the order is irrelevant to me."

"But whether or not I actually did sign it, is relevant," he argued.

Terrence convulsed slightly on the floor, but neither paid him any attention. He would not be recovering any time soon.

"Do you mind if I sit?" Marmoset changed tactics, hoping to get the barrel of the pistol away from his forehead before she accidentally or on purpose pulled the trigger. "I had more to drink this evening then I am accustomed to, and to be honest, my head is a bit fuzzy right now."

"It is about to be a bit bloody."

"I dearly love this little drama, miss," he said a bit impatiently, feeling some of his bravado return, "but since you haven't shot me yet, I'm assuming you want something from me. So, if it is to be an interrogation or a robbery or something of the like, I really do think it will go better for both of us if I sit down for it." Without waiting for an answer, he sat down on the couch somewhat heavily and crossed his arms. "Now, what is it you really want?"

"I want to know why," she snapped, keeping the gun trained on him. "I want to know what my brother was doing and why you felt the need to murder him."

"Ah, so you want meaning," Marmoset smirked in spite of the situation. "Perhaps shooting me is your best option, then, because I'm afraid that I have no meaning to give you."

"You refuse me?"

"If I have learned one thing in life, it is that you can never learn anything from life," he replied with a shrug. "Things happen—sometimes good, sometimes bad—and then more things happen. We live, we die, the next generation lives and dies, and on goes the march. One year we speak Babylonian, then the next year we speak Latin, then the next year English, then the next year Chinese. A hundred years from now, no one will care that you shot me. A thousand years from now, no one will even know we existed. Ten billion years from now, our solar system won't even exist. So, in the grand scheme of things, it won't matter if you shoot me or not."

"So, if nothing really matters, I might as well do it," she said, tightening her grip on the gun. "Perhaps it will save others from dying at your expense."

The young woman might have pulled the trigger at that moment, but the sliding glass door to the balcony opened and in stepped a monster of a man. Marmoset looked up and smiled as the woman switched the gun from his forehead to that of the newcomer.

"Who…who are you?" Nakusa stammered, clearly unnerved at his sudden appearance.

"In due time," the man replied before turning to Marmoset. "I hate to interrupt this little party of yours, but I felt things were getting a little out of hand."

"Impeccable timing, Hade," Marmoset said, not bothering to get up. "I wondered how I was going to keep from getting a hole drilled in my head."

"I have to say," Hade said, staring at Nakusa, "if I was trying to avoid getting shot, I might have taken the conversation in a few other directions than telling her it wouldn't matter if she shot you or not. Listening to you prattle on, I found myself *wanting* her to pull the trigger. Definitely not your best performance, Callithrix," he finished, putting emphasis on Marmoset's given name.

"Perhaps two less gin and tonics and I might have come up with something up to your standards," Marmoset said. "I do happen to still have a pulse, though, so I think we can call that a win."

"Only because yours truly intervened."

"I am happy to give credit where credit is due, of course, so thank you. However, I would like to mention that the young lady is still holding a weapon. Perhaps we could resolve that situation before we begin a celebration?"

"Of course," Hade said with a devilish smile. He waved a hand in the air toward Nakusa and the gun seemed to fly right out of her hand, landing in Hade's own massive paw.

Nakusa's eyes went wide in shock as Hade raised the gun and showed it to her without pointing it. "Now, now, my dear. Why don't you stay a while and chat."

Marmoset, who was just as stunned as Nakusa, stammered, "That was amazing! How did you do that?"

"A magician never tells his secrets," Hade winked. "But then, I'm no magician. I am Hade, and as I have said, that is more than enough." He pushed up the sleeve of his duster to reveal a large metal bracelet. "Directional super magnets," he explained. "Cutting edge stuff, straight out of Japan. I tweaked it a bit, added a little more juice, but you can see that it works. Mostly. If she'd been holding the gun more tightly, she likely could have kept hold of it. I'm half surprised it worked as well as it did."

"Bravo," Marmoset laughed, clapping his hands. "What's your next trick?"

"I believe I will bring a man back from the dead," Hade grinned, bending down and lifting Terrence to his feet with one hand. He eased him into a nearby chair and then, as if an afterthought, he slapped the man across the cheek. The force of the blow was enough to send Terrence sprawling on the floor again, where he lay blinking up in shock, his hand moving slowly to his face.

"Now," Hade said forcefully, pointedly ignoring Terrence as the man slowly crawled back to his feet, "I said I was here to resolve the difficulties between the two of you and I would like to do that. Please," he said, beckoning to the young woman, "come sit down, Nakusa."

Stunned, she allowed herself to collapse into one of the chairs.

Hade cracked his knuckles and grew serious. "Let's cut to the chase, here, shall we?" he stated, looking directly at the young woman. "Marmoset had nothing to do with the death of your brother."

"How do you know that?" she asked.

"Because I killed him," Hade replied evenly.

His statement was met with stunned silence. Everyone sat motionless, staring at the huge man in shock until finally Marmoset spoke.

"While I am glad to have my name cleared, I'm beginning to wonder how I was fingered for it in the first place. Did you frame me, Hade?"

"Of course not," Hade replied. "But perhaps Terrence can shed some light on what happened." He turned his full attention back to the eunuch. "You've been keeping tabs on me, haven't you, Terrence?" he said slyly, his voice dropping several degrees. "Looking into my affairs, pulling up my secrets, invading my privacy."

Terrence looked helplessly at Marmoset, who had gone several shades of pale as well.

"You have something to add?" Hade pressed, turning his attention to the C.E.O.

"Nothing that would vindicate me," Marmoset said with a sigh of surrender. "How did you know?"

"I am Hade," the big man replied easily, clearly not upset with the confession. "Do you need any other explanation?"

"Very well," Marmoset went on resolutely. "Then yes, I had Terrence look into some things for me."

"For what purpose?"

"Professional curiosity, mostly," he answered honestly. "I assumed for years that someone on the outside was helping Victor. When he died and the leadership of the company came to me, I had to know who I would be working with. I had to know I could trust that person."

"And how did the vetting process go?"

"Well enough for me to stop looking," Marmoset said. "You are a terrifying man, Hade—one who gets what he wants and kills anyone that gets in his way."

"Yet, you and Terrence are still breathing," Hade grinned.

"I would like to add for the record, that none of this was ever meant for anything other than my curiosity," Marmoset added. "I never did it for leverage."

"That would have been a neat trick," Hade chuckled. "So how about you show me what you have, Terrence," he added.

"Immediately, sir," Terrence replied as he jumped up and hurried from the room on legs that were still a little wobbly. He returned a moment later, bearing a large manila envelope, which he quickly handed to Hade.

"Hard copies?" Hade mocked, taking the folder. "In this high tech age?"

"Easier to dispose of," Marmoset explained innocently. "A shredded or burnt piece of paper does not have an 'undelete' function. As I said, I never had any intention of blackmailing you. I simply wanted to know who I had sold my soul to."

"Aptly put," Hade smiled and opened the folder. He held up an old photo and laid it on the table before them. "Okay, so here we have a very tall man dressed in dark clothes with long hair standing outside of a plant of some kind in some third world country, I'm guessing. Perhaps the Middle East? Enlighten me as to what this means, Terrence."

"Of course, sir," the terrified man replied. "Twenty three ago you were in Beirut working with a pharmaceuticals company called Chempharm. The plant made various drugs to help with sleep disorders and they appeared to be doing well.

"If I may," Terrence went on as he reached out and picked up a bundle of paper-clipped notes from the folder, which he placed on the table next to the picture. "Chempharm was making a very large profit, but if one looked closely into their accounts, it was clear they were funneling a lot of research money toward other projects. Shortly after this, the factory burned to the ground, killing everyone involved."

"Seventy-four workers died and forty-three were injured, many of them critically," Hade added. "That picture was actually taken the day before I burned it all down."

"So you were working on a project, the project ends, and then the factory and everyone involved goes away?" the young woman spoke up, still in shock at what was transpiring, but understanding the implication.

"Well, yeah," Hade smirked. "This isn't my first rodeo." Turning back to the folder, he pulled out another picture and held it up. "Now this is a great picture of me—one of my favorites, really. If you pay attention to trends," Hade added as he pointed to his left arm, "this was the third most popular tattoo in the late 1980s. I'm guessing this isn't about tattoos, though. So tell me about this picture, Terrence."

"Uruguay. Montevideo. Another slash and burn of a Chempharm company," was the reply. "The corroborating accounting paperwork is the next stack of papers."

"Ah, Montevideo," Hade chuckled. "There were some good times there. I really don't see what any of this proves, though. I've been around when bad things have happened to other people's companies. That in itself isn't a crime, is it?"

"I suppose it depends on your definition of crime. As far as I can tell, you move in on a chemical plant, take over operations, run a lot of secret stuff in and out, and then employ a scorched earth policy where a lot of people die," Marmoset replied, sounding like it was the most logical thing in the world. "We have photos and documents from Uruguay recently, Russia twenty years ago, Israel fifteen years ago, Pakistan twelve years ago, New Zealand, Scotland, and Belize after that and then two years ago at one of our plants in Brazil."

"So you have a whole lot of dots, but nothing to fill in the picture. What's your preliminary conclusion?" Hade asked.

"I've concluded that I probably should have kept my curiosity in check," Marmoset replied evenly.

"That might be the smartest thing you've said yet," Hade agreed. "As far as what you've supposedly dug up on me, I must admit that you've done your homework. I have been doing this a long time and either technology is improving or I'm getting sloppy."

"Or you set this whole thing up yourself," Marmoset added.

"And why would you think that?"

"I'm not entirely sure, of course, but it feels to me like you set all of this up for my benefit. There's a whole lot of damning evidence in that folder, Hade. With all that floating around for anyone to find, there's no amount of money in the world that could protect you if all this got out. I'm guessing there was never any paper trail leading to the man called Hade...until now."

"Until now," Hade repeated.

"So, I suppose this should count as a successful test," Marmoset went on. "You laid out the bread crumbs, we followed them to the correct conclusion, and voila, here we are talking about your greatest hits."

"What a great way of looking at this," Hade laughed. "I love how you've been caught with your hand in the cookie jar and yet you still have the cojones to say you played along as you were expected to, as if doing so warrants a reward. You are indeed a treat."

"Thank you, I think," Marmoset replied, "But I'd like to clear something up, as well, if you don't mind. I really need you to know that I am not at all like Victor. I didn't get where I am today by questioning or worrying about other peoples' versions of morality." Marmoset looked down at the photos and spreadsheets before them and continued. "You did what you felt was correct, so who am I to tell you what was right or wrong? I know you killed Victor and quite honestly, I don't care. But I'm no fool, either. I have no intention of ending up like him."

Hade smiled. "Oh, I promise you that no one in the history of the world has ever ended up like Victor, so I wouldn't worry too much about that. I also know you are a survivor; that you are willing to do whatever it takes to stay alive, which is why you *are* still alive. It's the greatest skill any animal can have, the drive to survive no matter the cause, and one surprisingly few humans possess. But you have it, my slithery friend."

Marmoset inclined his head in an arrogant agreement as Hade turned to face his assistant.

"Terrence, however, is so far removed from that instinct that I know he would take a bullet to the forehead if you told him to," Hade went on. "While that sort of person is useful for a while, eventually they overstay their welcome."

"I serve to the best of my abilities, sir," Terrence said.

"Let's go at this from a different angle," Hade said, rubbing his chin thoughtfully. "Let me ask you a question. Did you personally check up on all of these leads? Did you visit every country, tour every facility, interview every survivor? Or did you just trust the information I was allowing you to find?"

Terrence looked confused. "I looked into everything."

"Everything?" Hade pressed. "What about Belize? If you had indeed checked everything, then it should come as no surprise to you that I concocted the entire story of the Belize operation."

"I had checked on all the other locations and everything else made sense so I saw no reason to use resources to continue looking,"

Terrence defended himself, but his voice was sounding desperate.

"The information on Belize also contained an internal memo that implicated your boss in the Jaipur explosion," Hade drove the point home. "It was a memo that our little would-be assassin here got her hands on. That's bad business, Terrence, and I simply cannot tolerate bad business."

Hade moved with incomprehensible speed, his hand knifing out and smashing into the eunuch's throat, crushing his windpipe and knocking him over the back of his chair where he sprawled on the floor again, hands clawing desperately at his neck, unable to breathe.

Nakusa looked as if she was ready to scream, but Hade silenced her with a look.

"Now, if you would excuse me for just one moment, I simply cannot concentrate with Terrence flopping around on the floor like a dying fish," the huge man said as he stood up. He tossed Nakusa's pistol to Marmoset. "Don't let our friend leave. If she tries to escape, shoot her in the leg. If she insists on fleeing, shoot her somewhere less… recoverable."

Marmoset merely nodded as Hade reached down and took hold of the dying man's leg. Terrence's body shook and convulsed, but Hade paid him no mind and dragged him effortlessly toward the bathroom. He returned a few moments later.

"I have to be honest," he said lightly. "I've seen my fair share of beauty and taste, but my goodness, that bathroom really is stunning. And the rose petals and candles… so romantic! Of course, I can't think of anything less romantic than a dying eunuch in a bathtub, but still, well worth whatever you're paying for the room."

Marmoset shook his head, feigning sadness. "You know, after years without a personality, the man finally becomes interesting today and then you go and kill him. There's something rather unfair in that."

"All life is unfair. But that doesn't mean we can't still make something out of it. Do you mind?" Hade nodded toward the gun and Marmoset carefully handed it back to him. "So, how important is it to you to go on living?"

"You have no idea," he replied.

"Well then, I suppose you wouldn't mind helping me out with a little dilemma."

Marmoset looked at Nakusa, who had tears of fright in her eyes. For the young Indian woman, the whole evening of carefully planned revenge had gone from bad to nightmarish and she was struggling to maintain her sanity.

"We'll get to her in a moment," Hade answered the unspoken question. "This is something much bigger at the moment. I need you to meet a friend of mine and give him any and all the help you possibly can—both on a personal level, as well as professionally, with all the power of Legio Enterprises behind you."

"Sounds mysterious and, to be honest, dangerous," Marmoset dared to reply.

"On the contrary, it's rather simple," Hade explained. "I need you to meet with the secretary general of the United Nations."

"Antonio Malvado-Jinete?" he asked in surprise.

"Do you know of anyone else by that name on the short track to ruling the world?"

"Well, no," Marmoset replied. "What do you need me to do?"

"Arrange a meeting with him," Hade replied. "He'll probably play hard-to-get for a bit, but keep at it. Eventually, he'll warm up to you and make a request to help him retrieve a prized possession he has been searching many years for."

"You're serious?"

"Never more," Hade answered quietly.

"So that's it? Just help him?"

"That's it," Hade replied, "and I need you to keep me posted on your progress."

"And for doing this I get?"

"My everlasting gratitude and respect," Hade answered with a grin.

"In all my years, I've never been offered that," Marmoset sighed. "This sounds like as good a time as ever to try that out."

"Excellent," Hade said. "Now we only have one final piece of business to take care of here." He paused and looked directly at the young woman who had mastered her tears, but still looked like she was struggling to hold her frayed nerves together. "You are in need of a new personal assistant, am I correct?"

"I suppose," Marmoset said slowly, missing the man's meaning.

"Good! Then here she is!" he exclaimed, looking at Nakusa, a wide grin on his face.

"Her?" Marmoset asked in disbelief.

"Me?" Nakusa asked in even more disbelief.

"Oh, don't be so modest," Hade said, reaching out and patting her knee. "You would be a perfect assistant to Mister Williams."

"I've heard it's wise to keep your friends close and your enemies closer," Marmoset replied, "but I don't think this is what they had in mind."

"That is exactly what they meant," Hade replied. "She really is perfect. She's motivated, talented, better to look at than your last assistant, and unlike him, she knows that the worst thing that could happen to her is in the future, not the past."

"What do you mean?" Nakusa asked fearfully.

"A couple years ago, my dear, I unleashed an army of undead upon this world," he answered. "The resulting chaos killed millions across the globe, directly and indirectly. If I could accomplish that, then I can certainly kill everyone you love and everyone they love and everyone they love, before killing you. We could do an entire six degrees of separation experiment and see how many people ended up dead. I'm thinking it would be quite a few."

"But…" she started, only to have Hade wave her off.

"There are no 'buts' here," he said. "As of this moment, you are the personal executive assistant of Mister Williams of Legio Enterprises. Compensation will be commensurate with the top five percent of your job category. I'm sure Mister Williams will have his H.R. department get in touch with you immediately to finalize the details. You'll serve him and, in doing so, serve me. If anything happens to Mister Williams, whether by your hand or another, I will have your head and the head of everyone you love, all lined up on my mantel. Do you understand?" he finished dangerously.

"I understand," Nakusa replied immediately, recognizing the legitimacy of the threat. "I swear I will do as you say."

"Excellent," he finished, turning back to Marmoset. "See, I told you. Perfect." He stood up. "Now, I must depart. There's no rest for the weary and I have much still to do tonight." He walked into the bathroom and emerged with the body of Terrence thrown over his shoulder. "I think you'll find the bathroom has improved dramatically by removing this centerpiece." He then smiled, nodded, and walked out onto the balcony and into the night.

Marmoset and Nakusa sat in silence for a lengthy time, both of them rather shocked at the odd turn of events. Eventually, Marmoset looked at his new secretary.

"So, do you type?" he asked innocently.

She glared back at him. "I'll do what Hade says, but between you and me, know that someday, when the time is right, I will kill you."

"I thought we had been over this. I am not responsible for the death of your brother."

"Perhaps, but I am more convinced than ever that if anyone on this earth deserves death, it's you."

"Pleasant," Marmoset sighed. "I suppose we'll just have to agree to disagree. But while we are busy disagreeing, could you at least get me another gin and tonic? I think Hade scared all the alcohol right out of my system."

"You can get your own drink," she snapped. "He said I couldn't kill you. He didn't tell me I had to tend bar for you. I'm going back to my hotel to pack my things. I'll be here in the morning to take on my new responsibilities." With that, she turned and walked out the door, slamming it shut behind her.

"Perfect." Marmoset said as he got up to pour himself his own drink. "Just bloody perfect."

He made himself two.

CHAPTER 13

Frankfurt, Germany: The Flughafen Frankfurtam Main, like many other airports in the world, still suffered from the lingering after-effects of the chaos that had been unleased on the world two years ago. As had happened with most large international industries, national governments had been forced to step in and prop up the airlines to keep the entire system from collapsing. Passenger manifests were still generally half-full at best, especially on international flights, and the lack of qualified pilots and flight attendants made for expensive tickets and a culture of never-ending delays for the harried passengers.

Petr Zhugravinsky was one of those passengers and as he stood impatiently before the flight board, he noted that more than half of them showed delayed, including his connecting flight to Moscow. Swearing in Russian, he stalked away, venting his hatred of Hade and everything the man had done to him, up to and including his effect on the airline industry.

Noting a small bar directly off the concourse, he walked over and slumped down into one of the few tables available. If he was stuck for a few hours, he might as well sample a couple of German beers during his wait. It was early afternoon and the little bar was busy catering to other passengers who found themselves in the same situation as the Russian. All of them were drinking. If anything, the alcohol industry was the one business doing better now than ever before.

He tossed his bag on the floor next to his seat as a frazzled waitress swung by, took his order for Paulaner Salvator Doppel Bok, and then hurried away. He doubted he would see the drink any time soon. He sighed heavily and closed his eyes, suddenly aware of just how tired he was. He rubbed his face again, still unused to how it felt now that he had shaved his beard. He looked like a completely different man than the one that had called Africa home, but his broken heart told him he was still very much the same. His meeting with Hade and his brother's murderous visit to his adopted home that had severed his last tie with David Sumbawanga had left him empty inside. He would have cried if he had any tears left, but his tears had dried up a long time ago. All that remained was his anger and hatred and, while that fury had initially fueled him, now it left him exhausted.

Eyes still closed and thoughts in a tangle, he heard the slow steps of booted feet approaching his table. "Hau ab," he said wearily in unaccented German, knowing it was not the waitress and not really caring who else it might be. "I prefer to be alone."

"That's okay, Pete," came an easy reply in English. "I usually prefer my solitude, too."

Petr's eyes snapped open, but he remained still as he watched the man pull out the chair opposite him and sit down. The stranger was past middle-age, with very short salt and pepper hair and a couple days' growth on his face, giving him a grizzled look. His face was lined and hard, a lifetime of cares having left their mark. But it was his eyes that caught the Russian's attention. They were a deep blue and piercing and seemed to see right through him.

The man sat silently regarding him, his eyes never leaving Petr's. Finally, it was Petr who broke the silence. "How do you know my name?" he asked sharply. "And it's Petr, by the way."

"I know a great many things about you, Pete," the man replied with an easy smile while raising a hand and motioning behind him. As if drawn to him, the waitress swung by the table and waited expectantly. "Ice water, please," he said pleasantly, "with a slice of lemon."

In a huff and with a muttered oath, the waitress was gone again. The man's eyes had never left Petr's.

"I asked you a question," the Russian snapped. "Now talk. How do you know who I am?"

"Does it matter?"

"It does if you want me to listen."

The man shrugged. "Fair enough," he answered. "I'll cut straight to it then. A year ago, you were paid a visit by a man named John. As he tells it, you never did quite get your head around what he was trying to tell you. Rattles your cage a little, don't he?"

Petr seethed, his eyes cold.

"He shed some light on what happened on the mountain in Utah, right?" the man continued. "That must have been the worst part. The world was being torn apart for your sake and you didn't even know it." The stranger shed his nonchalance and his posture and tone quickly matched the intensity of his eyes. "You were in the eye of the storm, boy, and when that storm blew out, it left you behind. No answers. No understanding. No direction."

"What do you know about any of this?"

"Less than John, more than you," he replied.

"You sound like the old man," Petr growled. "You're either with him or working for…"

"Hade," the man finished knowingly.

Petr started to get up in anger, but the man held up a hand. "Sit down and relax," he soothed. "I'm not your enemy."

At that moment, the waitress arrived and nearly slammed down the bottle of beer in front of the stranger and the ice water in front of Petr. As Petr slowly sank back into his chair, the man slid the bottle over toward Petr and took possession of his water.

"My name is Tom," the man introduced himself. "Tom McCain." He took a drink of his water and eyed Petr, who still glared at him. "I can answer questions and maybe help you understand, if it's understanding you're looking for."

Petr grabbed his bottle and took a long pull. When John had found him, he had offered more questions than answers. When Hade had shown up, he had given him plenty of answers, but no understanding. Tom's arrival might give him more of both and that wasn't something he was willing to pass up. "Okay, Tom," he finally said. "You can start by telling me who you really are."

"Aside from my name?" the man smiled. "I'm a relentless old badger who's spent his life fighting the man you call Hade."

"That isn't a man," the Russian pointed out and took another drink of his beer.

"Oh, he's probably more of a man than he might believe himself to be," McCain countered. "That doesn't change the fact that he's also one of the most dangerous men walking the planet today."

"How do you know so much about him?"

McCain's eyes were suddenly distant. "I've known him for a long time," he said softly. "We've had…business."

"Former friend of yours?"

"Hardly," he replied with a snort, refocusing on the Russian. "Friends don't try to kill each other when they get together."

"Yet, here you are," Petr looked unimpressed.

"Yep, here I am."

"You know, I've meet Hade on several occasions," Petr went on. "He strikes me as the kind of person who would have no problem taking someone out if he wanted to. What do you attribute your survival to?"

"Clean livin'," McCain laughed.

"I'm not in the mood for jokes," the Russian snapped. "You still haven't told me why you're here."

McCain paused to take another drink, sipping his water slowly, seemingly in no hurry. After a few moments, he set his glass down and fastened his eyes on Petr's. The mirth was gone and in its place was a deadly seriousness. "I know why you're going to Moscow, Petr," he began. "Hade paid you a visit not too long ago and, while I don't know the particulars, I do know Hade. I know he wants you and I know he will stop at nothing to get you."

"He'll not have me," Petr replied bitterly.

"Oh, I'm certain you told him the same thing," Tom countered.

"What do you know of that?" Petr seethed.

"I make it my business to know what's going on," McCain answered, leaning across the table. "Particularly when it comes to Hade. But you need to understand something, boy. Hade doesn't force people into anything. He manipulates people and situations to bring about a desired outcome and there's no collateral damage too great to accomplish that. Today, he wants you to go to Russia and, to do that, he made certain your only ties to Africa were brutally murdered."

"I am going to Russia because I have unfinished business with my brother," Petr said coldly, not even flinching at the mention of Chuike's death.

"Correct," McCain agreed. "Of course, it's no coincidence that's exactly what Hade wants."

"You overestimate his influence over me."

McCain laughed loudly this time. "Unfortunately, it's you who underestimates Hade," he replied. "Think about it. This is a man who orchestrated the deaths of millions two years ago for the sole purpose of getting four clueless young people together on a mountain so he could figure out which one wouldn't follow him. He succeeded," McCain finished. "In all of it."

"Succeeded? He set the world back, but I don't see him ruling it."

"That wasn't his objective," McCain replied curtly, "and you're not listening."

"Are you saying we didn't have a choice then?" Petr asked. "That would seem to run counter to what John told me."

"No, it doesn't," McCain explained. "You had choices, Petr. You didn't have to go to the mountain, but you listened to Hade and you did. You didn't have to spare Owen, but you listened to your conscience and you did."

"No good deed…" Petr began bitterly.

McCain slapped a heavy hand on the table. "Let's dispense with the pity party and take a hard look at what happened, Petr," McCain snapped. "You defied Hade! Do you realize how truly remarkable that is?"

"I've already heard that song and dance," Petr shot back. "I didn't believe it when John told me and I'm not believing you."

"There's more than one path in life, Petr, and we can always chose which path we want to follow," McCain said. "Anyone witness to the tragedy you suffered on the rooftop of the Red Lion that night would agree you did what had to be done. Anyone who witnessed what happened on the mountain would agree that you lived up to your potential as a king." He paused and leaned back in his chair again, fixing Petr with a withering stare. "And I would guess that most people who spend more than two seconds with you today would tell you that you're no longer on the right path. You're strung like a puppet, Petr, which is exactly what Hade wants."

"How do you know what Hade wants?"

"Because it's my business to know," McCain answered. "How about you answer a question for me, Petr, and be honest. This stays between you and me."

"Depends on the question."

"Alright," McCain pressed. "Why are you going to Moscow?

Hade's machinations aside, what is Petr Zhugravinsky's reason for going home?"

"You know what happened in Tanzania, right? Then you already know the answer to your question."

McCain nodded, a look of sadness crossing his face. "I know that you blame yourself for what happened."

"Wouldn't you?"

"No," McCain replied immediately. "But I might feel like you and want to exact retribution, even on my own brother. That would take me to Moscow, where I could bide my time and wait for the right moment to strike."

"So what why are you asking me the question for, if you already know the answer?"

"You think that's the right path?" he challenged.

"I think it's the only path," Petr replied.

McCain shook his head. "It's not the only path, Petr. It's but one of the many paths laid before you. More importantly, it's the path Hade wants you on. He wants you in Moscow. He wants you to kill your brother."

"Why? What would he gain?"

"Control," was the simple answer. "He already tempts you; manipulates you in ways you can't even begin to comprehend. You're one of the prophesied kings, Petr. You've heard the story, so I'm not going to bother repeating it to you. But imagine the power he'd possess with one of the three kings marshaling his army across the globe in preparation for the last battle. He learned two years ago that he couldn't bully you and he couldn't tempt you with a pretty girl. He learned to be subtler. He'll appeal to what's good in you, your sense of justice, your need to protect the weak, and he'll twist it. He'll dangle just the right carrots in front of you in order to convince you that the end will justify the means. He'll hammer away at your weaknesses, your anger, and your sense of guilt and responsibility. He wants you to feel the weight of the consequences of your actions until you drown yourself in the guilt of what you've done, until you feel unredeemable. A man with no hope of redemption is easy to lead."

"Redemption? Hope?" Petr snarled. "If I ever had faith in God, I certainly don't have it now. Not after what I saw. Not after what happened." He trailed off and picked up his beer, swirling the contents and looking away.

"Faith is never an easy thing," McCain said, his voice softer. "Not for any of us."

"It seems to be for John," the Russian countered cynically.

"You would be wrong in that," was the somber reply. "For John, it's hardest of all. Everything that you've seen and experienced—that any of us has—it pales in comparison to what John has experienced. But it's a burden he bears willingly."

"Why?"

"Because he sees a better future, Petr. He knows more than any of us ever will."

"Then why let things happen the way they have?" Petr said, his anger surfacing again. "If he is so all-knowing, why not use that knowledge to help people? Instead, people die!"

"John shares what is important and helps us as much as he can, without disrupting our ability to choose as we will," McCain replied.

"So he is no different than Hade."

"You're starting to see the subtlety," McCain nodded. "Hade shares a surprising amount of the truth, enough to be believable. But it is never the whole truth. The difference between he and John that you don't see, is where each desires this thing to end. John wants us to exercise our free will, while Hade's greatest victory would be to rob us of that will." McCain explained. "Hade shares what will advance his ability to manipulate you to a certain end. So while some of the methods may appear similar from the outside, in the end there is a world of difference."

"Not from where I sit."

McCain picked up his ice water and took a long drink before setting it back down. "In time, perhaps you'll see things differently, Petr," he said. "At least, I certainly hope so, for all of our sakes. For now, I'll leave you with this. Of the three of you who survived on the mountain, you were the most heroic. Today, two years later, you are in the most danger. Alexis Kennedy and Michael Dalacourt, while dealing with their own struggles and demons, are at least on the right path. You?" He did not finish.

But McCain's warning was lost on Petr. He had been drawn to another aspect of the man's statement. "You've seen Alexis then?" he asked coolly.

McCain nodded and fished around in his pocket, pulling out a wad of Euro notes. "I have," he replied simply. "She spends her days training with my daughter. Like you, she has cracks and fissures, but otherwise she's okay. She's a survivor."

Petr looked relieved. "I'm glad to hear it," he said, his voice softer. "I wonder if sometimes she blames me for Owen's death."

"I think she might in her weaker moments," the older man replied. "But she knows we can't judge reality by our weakest moments. It was Hade, after all, who pulled the trigger."

"Which is why I'm going to Moscow," Petr replied, his voice hardening once more. "If I can't wipe Hade's stench from this planet, at least I can destroy one of the monsters he created."

"By replacing it with another?" McCain asked knowingly as he stood up. He tossed a handful of Euros on the table. "Drinks are on me, Petr," he added. "But while you wait for your flight, think hard on what I said. Hade is a master at what he does. If you're not careful, you will fall into the trap he has laid out for you. When that happens, you'll be his."

"I'll never be his."

"I've heard that before," McCain said gravely and then turned to walk away.

"There's one last thing," Petr said, his tone even.

"And what would that be?" Tom asked, turning back to face the Russian.

"Berne, Switzerland," Petr replied. "Ring a bell?"

McCain said nothing, only waited.

"Five years ago, I was almost killed by a disappointed buyer to whom I couldn't deliver some sensitive information that I'd promised."

"And you think that was me?"

"Hardly," Petr snorted. "That man is resting at the bottom of the River Aare. Nikolai took care of him."

McCain smiled.

"Your little escapade cost my family a lot of money and credibility that day, Tom. The Zhugravinskys don't forget things like that. If Nikolai ever found you, not even Hade himself could save your life." He laughed mirthlessly and took another drink from his beer. "I'm going to kill my brother, Tom. When I do, I might save your life in the process."

"Then that would that make us even," McCain smiled, tipped an imaginary hat, and then walked casually out of the airport bar, leaving Petr alone at his table with his thoughts and his doubts.

And his demons.

CHAPTER 14

Las Vegas, Nevada: The two women began their slow, deliberate descent of the slope just before sunset. They kept hidden the best they could, taking advantage of the way the setting sun lengthened the shadows of the low, dry brush. They had almost reached ground level as the last bar of sunlight highlighted the peaks behind them.

Twilight was their best cover, the dim light allowing them to move without casting their own shadow. It was also the time when the vision of the patrols was poorest and the floodlights weren't at full brightness. A dry breeze stirred moving sand and dry leaves, creating a pleasantly distracting white noise. The goal was to breach the outer fence before dark, before the searchlights cast harsh shadows and exposed every inch of the featureless ground between the fence and the far side of the open-air hangars where their objective rested.

At the apex of twilight, they lay prone under the cover of the last bunch of desert bush, a mere ten feet from the outer fence. The lights of the base flickered to life, buzzing like cicadas. It would take a few minutes before they reached full brightness. It was time to move.

Or it would have been, were it not for the two guards walking that stretch of fence-line with their massive German Shepherd. Stacia had timed their patrol route for the last hour as they approached. They covered a one-hundred meter stretch of fence, walking at a leisurely pace, but never stopping. It was an unluckily tight pattern. New soldiers had already rotated in to the patrol twice, every thirty minutes, avoiding fatigue and laziness while staying alert. Stacia had chosen a point midway between the ends of the patrol's circuit where a twenty-foot pole anchored the razor wire-topped fence, as well as supporting two security cameras facing opposite directions. The pole was better cover than nothing—the angle of the cameras made this their blindest spot, and here they would have a couple of minutes to work each time the patrol passed.

The two men spoke freely, but were still too far away to understand. They paid too much attention to the fence for Alexis' liking, yet they maintained a safe distance from the fence itself, as did the dog. The instant their backs were to the two women, Stacia slithered silently forward. She gave no signals to Alexis, verbal or visual. As Stacia emerged from the bush, Alexis marveled at how well the new camo worked. There was a coating of sand-colored, sand-textured, moldable grit on every dorsal surface of her body. It erased the wrinkles of clothing and the angles and edges of the human body. To even the most astute observer, it looked like the breeze had stirred some dirt toward the fence. She surged with pride, as the idea had been hers. Well, mostly hers. The basic substance, a grainy, moldable, putty-like material, was commercially available. She knew this because she had played with it at the hospital one day when delivering toys to some pediatric inpatients. All it needed for field use was the right color and application to clothing.

Despite how great it looked, Alexis said a silent prayer before following. Her mind turned briefly to Owen and she knew he was with her. She knew she could rely on his strength without needing to focus on his presence. Concentrating on the task at hand, she followed Stacia, her movement fluid and silent. Being invisible was great, but that would be meaningless if the dog heard her. As she approached the fence, the buzzing from the lights grew louder and she thanked God for the mixed blessing, as the noise would mask any noise she made.

Peeking to her left, over Stacia's body she could see the men and dog about twenty meters away, walking and talking. Both women pulled a pair of double-articulated, carbon fiber wire cutters from their chest pockets and went to work on the fence. The edges would dull to uselessness after five cuts, so they economically chose the links and opened a low arc in the fence. Stacia moved through first, forcing an impossibly low profile under the arc while Alexis prepared plastic fasteners to reattach the piece they had cut out.

Once Stacia was clear, Alexis handed her the piece of fence so she could begin to reattach it the instant she was through. The men were thirty meters away now. Alexis flattened herself and…

"He'll be here tonight, for sure," a man's voice announced from the right. Alexis froze, heart thundering. She saw Stacia's hand flash and dozens of tiny black dots flew several feet to the left, then she pressed near the fence as closely as she could and froze as well. Alexis buried her face in the dirt. Breathing slowly and silently, she pressed her belly into the ground, creating space for her diaphragm to move air and minimizing the motion of her chest. She could not see who was approaching. All she could see was dirt and a few feet of fence to the left. The voice spoke again, closer this time. "It's too bad, really. This place was really starting to run like clockwork."

Their footsteps were audible now, getting closer. "How on earth did an idiot like that get command of this base anyway?" This was a different voice. "Last time he was here, it took us three days to clean up the mess. There were girls everywhere on the base, drugged or drunk out of their minds and he went absolutely nuts at the end. Destroyed an entire barracks!"

They sounded close enough to be standing on top of Stacia. Alexis wanted so badly to see where they were, where Stacia was, where the patrol and dog were, but she dare not move. So far the soldiers hadn't noticed the two women, although they could have a gun pointed at the back of her head and she wouldn't have known.

"Well, we'd better get the word out," replied the other. His voice went from casual to a near shout. "Hey, Specs! Guess who's comin' tonight?"

An enthusiastic reply came from the left, complete with a short bark from the dog. The patrol was still several meters away. The newcomers stayed put, which meant the patrol and the dog were heading toward them. She heard their feet coming at a jog before she could see them.

"What's the word?" one of the men exclaimed as the patrol came into view. Each arrival doubled Alexis' heart rate, but the sight of the dog sent it through the roof. Its tongue lolled to one side as it came closer; then its ears pricked rigidly and its nose went straight to the ground as it began searching. "You guys are fifteen minutes early."

"Banyon is inbound," the first speaker answered. "He's due in tonight any time."

The dog was locked in now and started nosing directly toward them.

"I swear, if there was ever the need for an officer-involved fragging, that dude is it."

A sharp yelp from the dog interrupted the soldier and they all looked in his direction to see the animal reverse its course sharply, shaking its nose and rubbing at it with its paws. "Whoa!" the soldier with the leash barked a laugh as he reined the dog in and rubbed his ears. His thick glasses told Alexis this must be "Specs." "Find another scorpion, Titus?" The dog whined and coughed, continuing to shake his head. Specs patted him down and tried to console him, laughing as he did. "Poor guy. Definitely not the sharpest tool. That's gotta be the third time that's happened this week." Titus blew his nose and gagged.

The other men laughed as well, but stepped closer to where Titus had been stung, eyes trained on the ground next to Stacia. "I don't see no scorpion," one declared nervously.

"I don't see one, either," another replied. "But there's no way I'm getting on my hands and knees to prove it!"

Titus sneezed again and shook, then looked at the men and then at Alexis. Their eyes met. The dog bared his teeth and barked a hoarse, coughing bark. He strained against the leash held by Specs, who reached down and smacked his nose. "Enough, Titus! How dumb are you?" He laughed again and Titus barked and pulled. Specs tugged hard on the choke chain and Titus yelped. "Heel, Titus! Stupid dog. He'll never learn."

The dog finally relented and the other three were laughing heartily now at the misunderstood Titus. Finally, one of them got back to the matter at hand. "Anyway, Banyon is on his way. You two'd better haul ass back to the barracks and take out anything you don't want him to set on fire. You can thank us later."

Specs nodded to the pale-skinned soldier who was patrolling with him. He started to hand Titus' leash over, but the soldier laughed and held up his hands. "Oh, no. You take that crazy mutt with you. We'll have better luck without him."

"Thanks, Jersey. We owe you guys," Specs said and they hurried back down to the tarmac and toward a row of buildings that had to be the barracks.

"That's right! You do owe us," one of the remaining guards exclaimed at his retreating comrades. The two of them were now in full view of Alexis and Stacia. Just like all the others, they wore fitted uniforms, had close-cropped hair, and looked every inch the well-trained soldier. "Well, I guess we have forty minutes of patrol to kill," he went on, turning back to his partner and clapping him on the shoulder. "Look alive tonight," he added. "You know what happens if Banyon gets pissed off."

With that, they walked slowly left, talking aloud about how much of their day tomorrow would be spent cleaning up after their idiot commander.

As the departing patrol's conversation was lost in the drone of the lights, Stacia decided it was finally safe enough to whisper. "To our right, another patrol is headed this way. They'll turn around about the same time as these two. We'll have to wait until they pass by in the other direction. Then we move."

"Copy." Alexis breathed, trying to calm herself down by reviewing their altered mission. She pictured the layout of the base and tried to orient herself. She reviewed their progress to this point, the encounter with the dog, and the split seconds before it. Something suddenly occurred to her. "Pepper?" she asked.

"Yeah."

Alexis didn't need to see her friend's face to know she'd be wearing a self-satisfied smile. So, she stayed silent, concentrating on her breathing and calming her nerves. It took an uncomfortably long time, but she finally saw the men returning. They kept the same distance from the fence that the previous soldiers had and thankfully kept their eyes up, generally scanning the bush line outside the fence. Their conversation about their commander had stagnated and they patrolled more earnestly than Alexis would have liked as they quietly passed.

A whisking sound to her right told her Stacia was moving. Alexis grabbed the arc of cut fence lying on the ground and simply leaned it back against the fence, deciding against zip tying it in place, then moved fast and low behind Stacia. Each shed their camouflage suits as they progressed, ditching them in a bush, and continued through the night in jet-black combat gear.

The grounds were oddly empty and they made good time. Halfway to their objective, they ducked even lower but kept up a rapid pace, eyes darting everywhere, until finally they drew their weapons. Alexis said another silent prayer as they approached two strips of concrete that converged to form a "Y". Each strip held four A-10s, parked and quiet, their cockpits open. She followed Stacia toward the one they had already identified as being perfect for their operation. Within a few feet, Stacia holstered her pistol and started to climb to the cockpit as Alexis covered her back.

"Who's there?" A startled man's head popped out of the cockpit and looked over the edge as an equally startled Stacia reached for her gun. His eyes widened in surprise when he saw her and he quickly reached back into the cockpit, certainly going for his own weapon. He wasn't fast enough and Alexis didn't hesitate. She squeezed the trigger twice on her suppressed Sig Sauer and the pilot's head snapped backward as the bullets took his life, his body sliding back into the cockpit. Both women froze, waiting for some indication that an alarm had been raised. Alexis' heart beat like thunder, palpable to the top of her head. The silence stretched, giving her a terrible moment to consider what she had just done. The conflict stirred in her again, but quieter this time, less intense.

Just when she thought enough time had passed, that surely anyone noticing their presence would have sounded the alarm by now, a siren began wailing in the distance and the nearby control tower suddenly lit up like a Christmas tree.

"Now we're in it," she whispered harshly as Stacia clambered up the ladder and slid into the cockpit with the dead man.

"Just keep your eyes peeled," Stacia replied from the cockpit, her voice cool and controlled as she went to work on the controls of the plane.

"Right," Alexis muttered, dropping to one knee, trying to see everywhere at once.

A few moments later, four Hummers were rolling across the tarmac toward the control tower. Alexis swung her weapon toward the noise, prepared to take out as many as she could before the enemy overwhelmed their position. However, she was greeted by a truly odd visual. From the open moon roof of the lead vehicle, a tall, muscular man was waving his hands in the air like a maniac. His shirt was untucked and he was brandishing an automatic rifle, which he was firing wildly into the sky. Horns were honking, the siren continued, and several women emerged from the moon roofs of the other hummers, all of them scantily clad and all of them yelling and screaming and adding to the lunacy.

Alexis remained low and still as the vehicle's headlights flashed across her and then left her once again in darkness. Still somewhat in shock, she looked around at the sudden activity of the base and it became apparent that not a soul had been alerted to their presence. Cole Banyon and his entourage had arrived and his party had just given them all the diversion they needed.

When Alexis looked up at the cockpit, she saw Stacia looking back at her with a crooked grin. "Better lucky than good sometimes," she said with a wink. "I need a few minutes. Go ahead and scout our exit. I'll be fine here."

"On it," Alexis answered, breathing a sigh of relief. "Anchor the hard line so I can lay it down behind me as I go," she added. She tossed up a spool of wire, which Stacia caught. She disappeared into the cockpit for a few seconds, then reappeared and dropped the spool to Alexis, the wire trailing behind it.

"Go," she said and then went back to work.

Alexis took off toward the fence line and their exit point, letting the wire run out behind her, pausing several times to anchor the line to a rock or a piece of wood littering the desert sand. As she settled into the shadows a safe distance away, the base siren behind her stopped, only to be replaced with a loud subwoofer pounding the beat of Tupac

Shakur's "California."

"Can this guy really be that stupid?" she asked herself as she calmly clipped the line and then began attaching it to an open-ended USB. Several seconds later, she had the lines wired together and then plugged the USB into a smartphone she pulled from one of her pouches. She ran her finger across the display, waking it up, and began searching for the correct program. She had it called up and active less than two minutes later. Out of the corner of her eye, she saw the lights on the wingtips of the A-10 turn on. Looking up, she saw Stacia hurrying toward her, staying low.

A few moments later, Stacia dropped to her knees in the sand beside her friend. "Our aim looks good," Stacia panted, taking the phone from Alexis and looking at the screen. The A-10s primary weapons software was active and her connection with the jet showed green. She had control. "Not a bad plan, eh?" she went on. "No need to get past the tower guard, climb, or get back out. The only question now is when to pull the trigger."

More shots rang out, only this time they came from the fence behind them. Both women spun to see the perimeter security, one man examining the hole in the fence and the other firing a rifle into the air and trying in vain to call for help over the radio. Because of Banyon's arrival, it appeared no one was monitoring the frequency.

For the moment.

"I'd say it's time," Alexis said, surprising herself by how calm her voice was.

"I concur," Stacia agreed and quickly started working on the phone. A moment later, the screen lit up with a two-word command—"Weapons Armed"—and then the parked A-10 unleashed hell on the tower. The 30mm Gatling gun erupted, hurling its projectiles at the tower with unbelievable speed. Next, fire ignited from the fighter's wings as laser guided missiles blasted forward. The tower didn't stand a chance. Exploding metal, concrete, electronics, and soldiers showered down.

It overwhelmed Alexis' senses—the deafening thunder from the ordinance slamming into the tower, explosions and fire lighting up the night, people and body parts littering the ground. The upper half of the tower finally exploded into an inferno. Anything not actively burning, even the steel girders, glowed orange, red, then white. The heat, two hundred meters away, smothered her and felt like it could peel the skin from her face.

Wrenching her attention back from the horrible scene, she looked back to the fence. It was as bad as she feared. Despite the inferno now burning on the tarmac, the well-trained patrol detail had split up. One stood watch at the breach in the fence while the other ran for the live A-10. In addition, soldiers who emerged slowly from the barracks initially, thinking the party had just gotten a little too wild, now spilled from the doorways. Weapons ready, many ran toward the burning tower while others ran toward the parked A-10s.

"We have to run south!" Alexis shouted, but Stacia was already pulling her forward.

The two women sprinted desperately for their lives.

Alexis knew she should have never looked back. But she did and it likely saved her friend's life. While a number of soldiers were firing on the jet, further adding to the chaos, the guard near the fence was now running toward them, his own weapon leveled in their direction. Alexis ducked and tackled Stacia to the ground as automatic weapon fire opened behind them, hurtling deadly rounds over their heads. Then the ground behind them exploded and showered earth over them as a grenade detonated far too close to them for their comfort. As the dust settled, the women jumped up and ran for the building to their right, praying for some cover.

By then, it was too late. Every light on the base was being switched on and in moments, there would be no more shadows to hide them. The din quieted slightly, likely because the soldiers had regained control of the rogue jet, which only meant they would now all be concentrating on finding the people who had perpetrated the attack.

They ducked behind the closest building, a long, narrow brick storage facility. Just as they rounded the corner, the stone exploded as machine gun rounds peppered the edge. "We can't stay here," Alexis fought for breath, fought for calm. They needed help, back-up, rescue.

Both women speedily took stock of their location. They stood on a paved road between two long, low buildings and, for the moment, were out of the line of fire. But more rounds punished the building they were hiding behind, indicating multiple weapons were now firing at them. Apparently the perimeter guard had gained reinforcements. Stacia grabbed Alexis' arm and pointed down the alley. There was only one way to go. Alexis nodded, eyes wide with fright. They were hopelessly outnumbered, incredibly outgunned, and very likely going to die. She had trained hard for a year, been on several live operations, but nothing had prepared her for the helplessness she was feeling now.

Stacia saw the look in her friend's eyes and understood her terror. She'd seen a lot more action than Alexis, but still felt the same dread that was threatening to overcome her.

"We can do this, okay?" she said, leaning close and cupping Alexis' face.

"All right," Alexis replied shakily, taking a deep breath to calm herself.

Nothing more needed to be said. Weapons drawn, they ran. But it was over in seconds. Moments before arriving at the end of the alley, several small objects rolled across the street ahead of them and came to rest only yards away. They exploded even as the two women were diving for cover.

Alexis was instantly flash-blinded and the concussion blew her into the wall of the nearby building. Blind, nearly deaf, and in pain like nothing she had ever felt before, she willed herself to crawl. She had no direction, she had no hope, but she couldn't stop. Her gun was gone. Her friend was, too. She was alone. She tried to continue crawling, but she finally collapsed, her body going numb. The blackness was coming. She lay in the street, dimly aware of approaching boots, but she was helpless to do anything about it. For a moment, panic threatened once more to take hold, but a familiar warmth began to fill her and suddenly she was comforted like never before. In her ears, she heard a voice as clear as a bell.

"Don't worry," the voice said as the warmth surrounded her. "I have you."

Then the blackness took her and Alexis Kennedy knew no more.

CHAPTER 15

Los Angeles, California: Michael Dalacourt was growing tired of dreaming about Gilgamesh and the hunter's warning. He had done so every night for the past several weeks now—always the same dream, and he was no closer to understanding the significance of it, if there was even anything to it in the first place. He was half convinced he was losing his mind, and that was only when he wasn't completely convinced.

He awoke again, not because the dream was ending, but because the steel door to their prison had opened. Dalacourt sat up, his tired eyes trying to focus as an all-too-familiar individual stepped into the room. Oliveira, for his part, looked up briefly at the man with detachment and then went back to reading through the tattered Bible that he held in his hands.

Dalacourt, on the other hand, could not hide his shock.

Or his horror.

"I know visiting hours are over," Hade said with a grin as the door eased shut behind him, "but I simply had to come see how my favorite priest was doing."

"What are you doing here?" Dalacourt asked shakily. It had been more than two years since he had last seen the huge man, but the fear he felt in his presence was exactly what he had felt on the mountain in Utah when Hade had murdered Owen DiConte in front of all of them.

"Is that the polite way to start a conversation?" Hade asked. The big man then turned his gaze to the old Brazilian priest and smiled. "And who do we have here, but our dearly departed Father Oliveira." He clucked his tongue, seemingly fascinated at the dead priest's presence. "I heard about your *resurrection*. Figured it was high time to come have a look-see myself."

Oliveira looked up again, but said nothing.

"You've been the cause of a lot of chatter in my circles, Father Oliveira," Hade went on, crossing the room. "I admit I find myself intrigued."

Oliveira was silent as Hade stepped in front of him and reached out and took his chin in his huge hand. He tilted the old man's head in several directions, peering intently at his face and then into his eyes. "I suppose this is where I should say 'Stick out your tongue and say aah'," Hade said absently as he studied the man. "Fascinating," he finally said, doing a perfect imitation of a well-known Vulcan scientist from Star Trek. He released Oliveira's face and turned to look at Dalacourt. "Do you realize what you have here?"

The former priest shook his head, still shocked at Hade's reappearance in his life.

"His brain is gone," Hade went on, switching to an impersonation of Doctor McCoy. When Dalacourt looked at him blankly, the huge man shook his head in disappointment. "Classic Star Trek, Michael," Hade admonished. "Karl Urban did a great job in the Abrams reboot, but Deforest Kelley was the man. Really, your lack of knowledge or understanding toward the classics is truly dumbfounding."

"What do you want?" Dalacourt finally managed to say. "The last time I saw you was in Utah, when you told me my entire life was nothing more than a lie."

"What happened on the mountain was business, not personal," Hade replied easily, walking back across the room and taking a seat on a battered metal folding chair near Dalacourt's bed. "I don't expect you to believe me, but it's true. By the way, nicely done with the hail and the blood," he added with a wink. "I knew that was coming, but didn't see you being the one to bring down that particular hammer."

"That wasn't me and you know it," Dalacourt replied, finding some strength within. "You know God is speaking, exhorting all to return to Him. I was merely the vessel, nothing more."

"You're correct, of course," Hade replied, never losing his smile. "But that doesn't take away our agency in these sorts of things. We still each have our roles to play, if you will."

"What's your point?"

"Let me play devil's advocate for a second to demonstrate to you how things might look from a different perspective," Hade answered. "We're going to take a little field trip to the New Kingdom in ancient Egypt, so you can meet the cult of the Apis Bull."

"The what?" Dalacourt folded his arms and glared.

"Apis Bull," Hade repeated. "Say what you will about the Egyptians, but they knew how to put a religion together. It didn't make any sense, but the people sure ate it up. The Egyptians would do anything for their gods, but then again, Egypt was always sunny, there was usually enough food, and there were very few battles. I think if I'd been a peasant in Egypt four thousand years ago, I would have had very little to complain about."

"So what is the Apis Bull?" Dalacourt questioned, truly perplexed. "I've never heard of it."

"It was an actual bull," Hade answered, adopting his professor-like tone. "The Egyptians actually considered it the reincarnation of the Memphis god Ptah in bovine form. The bull supposedly had all sorts of magical powers—it could heal people, restore sight, make babies stop crying, defeat your enemies, cure hiccups, etc. etc. So you can imagine how well-treated this thing was. Peasants would be living in small huts and this bull would be pampered in his royal chambers and then led out to the pasture to spend his days with his own harem. Then, after the greatest life of ease an animal ever had, when the bull died, they gave it a royal burial, spending more money on its crypt than on what it would cost to feed a small village for the whole year. After its death, the priests of the god Ptah would then go about finding another bull. Sounds easy, right?"

"I admit that I'm lost," Dalacourt answered, sparing a glance at Oliveira, who was listening intently to Hade's explanation.

"I could say something mean here, but I'll let that one slide," Hade said with a wink. "Anyway, the key to all of this is in the picking of the new Apis Bull."

"If it was truly what they claimed it to be," Dalacourt ventured, "why would they have to pick it?"

"Now you're catching on, Michael," Hade said with a smile. "In ancient Egypt, the god Ptah wouldn't just fill the form of any old animal—it had to be special. The bull had to have a mainly black hide with special white spots on him—a white delta on his forehead, white vulture wing marks on his back, a scarab beetle design on his tongue and a double-haired tail, whatever that means. Oh yes, he also had to have a crescent moon on his right flank as well, also white. Now, with all those requirements, you can imagine how difficult a bull like this was to find."

Dalacourt nodded, but remained silent.

"Of course, if you have a can of white paint, it becomes absolutely easy," Hade said slyly.

"So you're saying they created it?"

"Exactly," Hade replied. "They knew what they were looking for and, considering the enormity of finding something with those exact specifications, they broke out the white paint fairly regularly, so to speak. How many completely normal bulls got their own harems, a pampered life, and a funeral procession simply because a scared priest picked him out of the herd and painted him up?

"Hundreds," Hade answered the question himself. "Seriously,

there are tombs and tombs dedicated to these animals, and almost every single one of them was a fake. Like I said, crazy stuff, but the priests didn't have to worry about anything as long as they had a painted bull and the people were willing to put food on their table because of it."

"So the whole Apis Bull thing was a fraud?"

"By and large, yes," Hade replied. "And yet, every once in a great while, the fraudulent bull would die and they would go out to perform their little sham of a search and low and behold, they would actually stumble upon a bull that met all their specifications. Then the priests, so secure in their little lie, became more insecure in the truth. For you see, the arrival of a real god could only mean that something was starting—something that required the god Ptah to actually come to the earth to direct it. This meant change and the priests didn't want change. A real bull meant they lost their power to a god they had been denying their whole lives."

"Lies have a way of catching up to the liar," Dalacourt added.

"Correct," Hade said. "Nothing scares a man like the thought that there really might be gods out there and nothing drives a man to action like the self-doubt that this sudden realization causes. Unfortunately, this sudden realization causes men to act irrationally and destructively and more often than not, the brunt of their anger falls on the very things they are charged with protecting."

"So what would they do?" Dalacourt asked, intrigued, despite himself.

"The easiest way to ensure that nobody caught on was to make sure they continued to make decisions—any decisions—to prove to themselves and to others that power remained in their hands. The Egyptian priests would put things into motion to keep themselves in power—bad things like self-induced famines, massacres, murders, wars, fires, genocide, you name it. They were forced to break natural, universal laws to conform to their delusional and self-created ones. I've seen it, Michael. I've seen the heartache of the young widow whose husband isn't coming home because of the priests. I've seen the misery of the children whose father died supporting his religious leaders. I've seen entire civilizations destroyed because of the pride of men wearing loose-fitting robes. When the famines are over, the smoke of the battle has cleared, the wars have stopped and the fires are finally quenched, who is still standing in his nice home? The priests. But not the bull, child; no, not the bull. He's too dangerous, so they eat him and find one they can paint themselves instead of one the gods painted for them."

Hade stopped and gave Dalacourt a look that said, "Now figure out what comes next."

Dalacourt sat for a moment, digesting what he had just been told. His mind flashed back to the years he had spent with this man in a small room as he was learning how to be a priest. The meaning in their many lessons was not always clear, but it was there, and Hade never told a story that didn't have a meaning in it somewhere. To Michael Dalacourt, this was classic Hade.

"So," he finally ventured slowly, "It's all about the markings, correct?"

"It is, but I'm going to be completely honest with you, Michael," Hade said, smiling crookedly. "There are all kinds of things in the last days that have significant markings. I'm not a fortune teller and I've never put much stock in prophecies and signs of the times, but I work for and with people who take them very seriously and that's good enough for me."

"Are you saying you have a can of white paint?" Dalacourt asked, already knowing what the answer would be.

Hade laughed at that, a deep, rolling sound. "How very perceptive of you, Michael," he finally answered. "Yes, I admit that I do. But I will tell you this, as well. If you look closely, I wouldn't be surprised if you found a can of white paint in the hands of your old Indian friend, too."

"John?" Dalacourt was startled, clearly unprepared for that statement.

"It's no secret you were meant to be on that mountain a couple years ago," Hade answered, still smiling. "The real question is whether God meant for you to be there or whether John painted you up to fulfill some prophecy."

"I don't believe you."

"Why not?"

"It…it's simply not possible."

"Why? Because John told you?" Hade chuckled. "Must I remind you that John was never truly forthcoming with you?"

Try as he might to blunt Hade's accusation, Dalacourt had no answer to that.

"Me, on the other hand," Hade went on, holding up his own massive hands and wiggling his fingers. "I fully admit that I have white paint on my hands. Do you truly have the markings, child? Or did someone paint you up?"

"I think you know the answer to that," Dalacourt replied, once again finding a point of faith that he could latch on to. "Maybe I do have the markings and you're trying to paint over them and hide them."

"Now that, my good Father," Hade agreed, "is brilliant. You begin to see where I'm coming from."

"Not brilliant," Dalacourt countered. "Maybe 'logical' is the right word for it. I admit that I don't understand my role in everything that's happened, but no one else really does either, including you. Something led you to me—to us—something that has you frightened and something you're fighting against."

Hade just chuckled. "I think perhaps I trained you too well when you were young. Do you have the marks? Or did we paint you?" he repeated. "Like you, I've seen and done things that have shown me there is more to this mortal coil than most could even dream about. But unlike you, I've embraced both sides of this and am using all the colors of the rainbow to paint my masterpiece. And I'm not done painting, Michael. Not by a long shot. Am I a believer? Of course I am. Am I frightened? I haven't been frightened a day in my life. Am I going to win? Absolutely."

"If you're so confident in what you're doing, then why are you here, Hade?"

"To give you a little lesson on painting, boy," Hade answered, breaking into a wide grin again. "A true teacher always desires to share his knowledge. You see, when you know what the markings are and you have the paint, there's nothing you can't accomplish when you're creating your masterpiece," he explained. "It's all about the markings. Real or perceived, you have the markings because that's what we wanted. Owen may or may not have had the markings, but I threw a can of paint on him and then disposed of him as if he never did."

Dalacourt hardened his resolve, refusing to fall into the trap. But Hade spun the web expertly.

"The hail and blood you allegedly called down as if from God himself?"

"That was real!" Dalacourt objected.

"Oh, no doubt," Hade replied. "You and I both know that and the scriptures even talk about it. But we repainted it in the media and now most people think it was just a horrible terrorist attack. Others think it was nothing more than a freakish meteor storm and the blood little more than iron residue. There is a rather large asteroid heading our way that will bear this explanation out in the coming months and people will believe it. There are even more outlandish tales that are springing up and it deepens the confusion, intensifies the distrust, which is exactly what we want. The best way to battle a conspiracy theory is by creating a dozen other conspiracy theories. In the end, the people will believe what we tell them even when it should be plain to them what is really happening."

"I don't understand," Dalacourt said.

"You're a student of the Bible," Hade admonished. "Consider the book of Revelation and everything that will come to pass in the last days. Have you ever stopped to wonder how people could witness all these miracles from God and yet continue disbelieving in Him?"

"You're talking about deception?"

"Precisely. I could paint a nice little farm scene over the Mona Lisa and the Mona Lisa would still exist, but the people would believe it to be a nice little farm scene." Hade reached into his coat and pulled out a cell phone. "Do you recall Revelation, chapter eight, verse eight?"

Dalacourt quoted it immediately. "And the second angel sounded, and as it were a great mountain burning with fire was cast into the sea: and a third part of the sea became blood."

"So here we've got a burning mountain and the oceans turning to blood, right? Do you agree that's pretty clear?"

"It's as clear as any biblical prophecy regarding the last days," Dalacourt agreed. "But it could mean more than a few different occurrences or calamities."

"Exactly," Hade smiled even wider. "So we'll call that the Mona Lisa. Now watch me paint it into a nice little farm scene." He held up his cell and spoke. "Call the artist," he said and the phone immediately started dialing. "Nice touch, don't you think?" Hade chuckled, looking at Dalacourt.

The phone picked up immediately with only a terse, "Yes, sir?" on the other end.

"Activate the Cumbre Vieja," Hade replied. "It's time to ramp up the chaos."

"Yes, sir."

"Is the satellite feed live?"

"Yes, sir," came the reply again, the voice coming back a little shaky. "Coming through now."

Hade said nothing more and ended the call. A couple of finger swipes over the touch screen and he tossed the phone to Dalacourt.

"What's this?" the former priest asked uncertainly as he caught the device.

"What you're seeing is a live shot of our little island, the Cumbre Vieja," Hade explained. "It's an active volcanic ridge on the Isla de La Palma in the Canary Islands. You hear a lot of doomsayers these days talking about global warming, super volcanoes, world-wide storms, government conspiracies, missing nukes—really anything to get a rise out of the nonbelievers. A lot of what you hear today is crap propagated by the tinfoil hat crowd. They take what we give them and run with it, keeping the world stirred up and edgy. Personally, I love those guys."

"The scriptures speak of all that," Dalacourt replied confidently. "The last days are clearly upon us. Even you know this."

"Oh, I certainly do," Hade agreed, "and I can quote the scripture to back it up, too. 'For nation shall rise against nation, and kingdom against kingdom: and there shall be famines, and pestilences, and earthquakes in divers places. All these are the beginnings of sorrows.'"

"Matthew twenty-four, seven and eight."

"Good stuff in the Bible," Hade agreed. "Especially if you know how to interpret it to suit your purposes."

"What's that supposed to mean?"

"Over the years, we've carefully buried a rather considerable amount of conventional explosives deep underground in a number of strategic locations that are important to the stability of this little island. In about five minutes, we'll detonate these explosives, causing approximately five hundred billion tons of rock and debris to slide into the ocean, while triggering a massive volcanic eruption."

"What kind of…" Dalacourt began in shock, but trailed off. What Hade was suggesting was simply too outrageous to believe.

"Damage?" Hade finished the question. "Have you ever dropped a big rock into a creek or a lake? Imagine that, but on a global scale. The ocean is about four miles deep there, Michael. Dropping the equivalent of an island into that will cause a water plume about a mile high. When that settles, the tsunami will start."

"You can't be serious," Dalacourt whispered.

"Oh, I'm quite serious," Hade replied. "This has been a work in progress for decades. We actually had trial runs back in 1949 and 1971, triggering volcanic eruptions in preparation for this particular event. Now the time has arrived for the finale, Michael. The resulting tsunami will travel at nearly five hundred miles an hour. It will cause cataclysmic damage all over the world. If our projections are correct, the Sahara will be hit with a wave over three hundred feet high. The coastal areas of Europe and England would take hits from the wave in the neighborhood of ten to forty feet, depending on the location. However, that's nothing compared to the eastern seaboard of the United States."

"Dear Lord…" Dalacourt began.

"It will take approximately seven hours for the United States to get hit," Hade went on. "In some places, the wave will be upwards of two hundred feet high. Without our intervention, Boston is gone. New York is wiped out. The wave will wash up as far as twenty miles inland in some places, all the way down the coast to Florida."

"But, that will kill millions!" Dalacourt cried out.

"Actually, it will be closer to thirty million worldwide, even with immediate warnings and evacuations and also with us ensuring that the northern East Coast doesn't get hit as hard as projected," Hade explained.

"What do you mean?"

"It means that we still have business to attend to in the Big Apple and D.C.," Hade explained. "Three or four decades is a long time to set up counter-measures and we haven't been sitting on our hands. Let's just say that not all of those missing nukes the conspiracy nuts rattle on about are truly lost."

"You're going to set off nukes?" Dalacourt gasped.

"Only underwater," Hade explained. "Oh, we might get some mutant sharks and a two-headed octopus out of it, but that's small potatoes compared to the benefit. If all goes as planned, the resulting underwater detonations at just the right time will be enough to buffer the approaching tsunami so that places like New York City and Boston and the capitol end up just getting their feet wet. South of Virginia, though? In a few hours, you'll be able to pick up beachfront property on the cheap. It should also take care of this country's Cuba problem, too."

"But why?" Dalacourt exclaimed. "How can you cause the deaths of so many?"

"Actually, we're in the saving business here," Hade answered. "It was going to eventually happen anyway within the next hundred thousand years or so, so we're just pre-empting nature and saving a few million people on the northern East Coast to boot."

"This is insane!"

"It's actually quite brilliant," Hade said. "You see, the resulting splitting of the island will open a fissure into an as-yet undiscovered undersea reservoir of oil. This oil field is massive, Michael, and we've spent a lot of time and money over the years to keep it hidden from the eyes of the world," Hade went on. "As the devastation spreads from the tsunami and the volcano fully erupts, the oil will begin to flow unchecked into the ocean, eventually threatening the entire planet, and ultimately fulfilling the prophecy in Revelation, chapter eight, verse eight. The burning mountain cast into the sea; the seas turning to blood. Earth's blood, not man's blood, Michael. My will, not God's will," he finished, looking hard at Dalacourt to see if he understood.

"But that's just not possible."

"Oh, but it is," Hade replied. "Imagine yourself to be a non-believer for a moment, Michael. Imagine living on the beach and walking outside one morning and seeing that the ocean had been turned to blood—actual, literal, real blood. Knowing that the Bible preaches this, you would immediately fall on your knees and worship God, begging to be saved."

"But…"

"There is no 'but'," Hade interrupted. "Anyone who witnessed such a thing would do exactly that. Anyone who says otherwise isn't playing with a full deck. Now, if we apply our paint to the whole thing—i.e., oil instead of blood—then voila. We have a perfect scientific explanation for things and the world continues to dwindle into unbelief."

"But people would see through it," Dalacourt objected.

"The believers would and they already do," Hade agreed. "But we're not fighting for them, are we? Oh, we may pick up a few of the weaker ones as we go, but ultimately, we're fighting for all those in the middle who are still on the fence, and the longer we can keep them on the fence, the more can be claimed in the end."

"More will side with God than you believe, Hade."

"Maybe," the big man agreed. "But I think you underestimate the gullibility of humanity. While the world reels from this catastrophe and tries to figure out how to recover from it, the oil will continue to pour into the ocean. Several months from now, some of the greatest scientific minds in the world will come to the conclusion—with our help, of course—that the best way to combat this global catastrophe will be to nuke the hole and burn the slicks. Oh, it will be contested and screamed about from every corner of the earth, but in the end, the hole will be nuked. When that happens, a third of all ocean life will be destroyed, as will a third of all global shipping, civilian and military—which you know is also prophesied in the Good Book. Finally, the amount of smoke and pollutants thrown into the atmosphere will be massive, resulting in a world-wide loss of sunlight, thereby fulfilling Revelation six twelve."

"'And I beheld when he had opened the sixth seal, and, lo, there was a great earthquake: and the sun became black as sackcloth of hair, and the moon became as blood,'" Dalacourt whispered in shock.

"It all about how you paint," Hade said, nodding toward the phone in the former priest's hands. "My will, not God's, and prophecy is still fulfilled. Our influence doesn't end with this, either, but it will suffice for the current set of coming calamities. Watch."

Dalacourt's eyes slowly went back to the screen and it did indeed show a satellite shot of a little island somewhere in the middle of the ocean. After nearly a minute of waiting, it finally began. It wasn't a monstrous explosion, but more of a subtle shift of the island itself. Soon it began to gain momentum and suddenly, half of the volcano was sliding into the sea. Flame, smoke, and red lava blasted upwards from the devastated mountain as the entire rock face slid into the ocean. Soon after, the water plume appeared, shooting skyward for hundreds of feet…then thousands, until finally Dalacourt had to look away, unable to watch what was happening any longer.

"Why?" he asked, his voice almost a whisper. "Why would you do this?"

"I could ask you the same question," Hade answered. "Why did you unleash a torrent of hail and blood on the world, causing the deaths of so many? It doesn't matter if either of us or neither of us is right, the truth is the end of the world is nigh, and the signs must come forth as decreed. Whether by your hand or mine, we inch ever closer to that final day. We are in the middle of a war, Michael, one that has been fought on countless battlefields since Cain killed his brother, Abel. It's a war for the souls of all mankind."

"But not for you, Hade," Dalacourt countered, fighting desperately to find his strength again. "Satan is not likely to share with his horsemen."

"You presume much to assume I serve Satan, child," Hade chuckled, but there was no humor in it. "There is only one soul I'm interested in, Michael," he said quietly, rising to his feet. "Everything else is just a means to an end." He walked to the door and opened it, before pausing and turning to look back at Dalacourt once more. "I almost forgot. You'll have another visitor in the coming days and then afterward, Pope De Solei will release you."

"Why would he release me?"

"Because I told him to," Hade replied evenly as only he could. "Besides, with the coming destruction, he'll have far more to do than stand guard over a fallen priest and an undead aberration. So he'll release you and then you can go forth and discover exactly how much paint you have on you."

"I have none," Dalacourt objected, trying desperately to recover from the shock of what he had just witnessed. "I know where I stand and who I serve."

"That may be true, child," Hade answered with what might have been a hint of regret. "But remember the Apis Bull. It was the painted ones they celebrated. The real ones, they ate."

As the big man turned to leave, it was a different voice that stopped him. "Hade," Father Oliveira finally spoke up, looking straight at him. "I have a question."

"I'm sure you do," he nodded serenely. "What is it?"

"Do I have any paint on me?"

Hade was silent for several long moments, before finally answering. "You are certainly marked, Francisco Nunez de Oliveira," he finally said. "But not with paint."

With that, he turned and disappeared through the door, clanging it shut behind him.

CHAPTER 16

Tucson, Arizona: Tom McCain had not lied when he told Petr Zhugravinsky that he preferred to be alone. He was especially grateful for his solitude now, as he sifted through the deeper meanings behind what he had learned over the past weeks. His trip to Europe to meet with an increasingly erratic Petr had been a thankless task that John had felt he was particularly suited for, but one that hardly advanced them in the battle against Krypteia or got him any closer to understanding what exactly they were doing in the prisons across the United States.

His encounter with Hade on Rikers Island still perplexed him. It had been a challenge to escape, especially now that the years were settling in, but he knew Hade had let him live, which meant the man had had a purpose for their discussion. Hade wanted him to know he wasn't creating an army of vampires on the scale of his last endeavor and the logic behind his explanation rang true. Besides, Hade might be a lot of things—all of them terrible—but he wasn't known to lie and it wouldn't be like him to start now. So what was really happening? The only thing Tom knew for sure was that there was an answer out there and he needed to find it before Hade unleashed it on the world as part of Krypteia's final power play in these, the last days.

While McCain was one of those few remaining who understood just what was at stake and actively fought against it, he had never been what he would consider a religious man. He stayed away from churches in general, but he believed in God and the Bible. More importantly, he believed in John. He knew he was on the right side and he knew John was with them at the behest of God. However, despite Hade's defeat and the confirmation of his own faith, the jury was still out on whether or not it would be a millennial reign of Christ or a millennial reign of Satan. McCain's sole purpose in life now was ensuring that it was as the revealed scriptures stated—under Christ.

So he continued fighting the battle in the only way he could at the moment—by fighting in that gray area Krypteia had created as they began to exert more influence over the world. It was no secret to him that Krypteia controlled much of that world now, including a lot of his own country's government. But until Krypteia was fully and obviously in control, those governments still had to appear as if they were watching out for the best interest of their people. That meant, in the case of the United States, they had to investigate Rikers Island and other prisons where odd things were occurring, which gave McCain the chance to go out and poke the Krypteian hornet's nest and see what came swarming out. He knew, though, that his luck would eventually run out. Playing the kind of game he played only ended one way. He only hoped it wasn't here in Arizona.

He was situated on a hillock about a mile from the United States Penitentiary in Tucson, a high-security federal prison for male inmates—the dregs of society; the worst of the worst. The intense sun was slowly descending over the horizon, shifting the sky to shades of reds, oranges and pinks and giving him perhaps thirty or forty minutes of daylight before nightfall. He'd been watching the prison for the better part of twenty-four hours now and, during that entire time, he had not seen a single person on the prison grounds. No prisoners walked the yard; no guards moved about the towers. The place was completely lifeless. With one exception.

He turned the glasses back toward the front gate and again focused on the figures moving around the entrance, pretending to be busy with something. They had been there since he arrived yesterday—no shift changes or changing of the guard. There were four of them, all armed and decked out in black combat fatigues, and they alternated between standing in the guardhouse, milling around the gate, or spending time in the large S.W.A.T. van parked next to it.

As far as McCain could tell, the only thing the guards had been doing was turning the few random visitors who drove up back to the road. He had no idea what they were telling them, but other than a few select government-looking official vehicles they let through, everyone else was sent on their way. The one thing he was certain of was that no one had left the compound. Not a single vehicle or person had come back through the gate.

With a sigh, he set the field glasses down and pulled his cell from his belt. He tapped a single digit speed-dial number and waited. After several rings, it picked up.

"Long time no hear, Tom," a voice answered on the other end, warm and friendly.

"Good to hear your voice, too, Otis," he replied. "How's tricks?"

"Still fighting the good fight."

"Stacia around?" McCain asked, already knowing she probably wasn't. Last contact he had from her was a text telling him she would be pulling some recon duty and would be off the grid for a while. He hadn't heard anything since.

"No, she's not," Otis replied and McCain immediately caught the hesitation in his voice.

"What happened?" he asked, instantly worried in a way only a parent could worry.

"I can't say for sure," Otis said. "She took Alexis to Vegas for some recon and they haven't checked in. It appears Krypteia is using some high-end jamming gear in the area. No communications going in or out."

McCain paused. If Krypteia was using jamming equipment that could cover an entire region, that could only mean they had gotten the technology from one place. And if that was the case, then his daughter was either causing a world of trouble for their enemy or she was in a world of trouble herself. Either way, he didn't like it.

"That's Cole Banyon's territory," he mused thoughtfully. "What are they doing there?"

"Stacia's your daughter, Tom," Otis replied. "You know she's going to go where the action is."

"Yeah, but is Alexis ready? I know she's got a major league beef with that punk. I can't imagine how this thing could go any direction but sideways."

"You're the one who told Stacia to take Alexis out if she felt she was ready," Otis pointed out.

"Maybe to a supermarket or the mall. Not the freaking center of Hade's operations," McCain grumbled. "So how overdue are they?"

"Half a day," Otis answered truthfully. "We're gearing up to send a backup team in to see if they've been detained, but Cole has a lot of soldiers and hardware on the ground. Still, I'm not too worried at the moment and neither should you be."

"Keep me posted, will you?" McCain said, trying to keep the worry out of his voice.

"Roger that," Otis replied and then changed the subject. "What's the status on your end?"

"Unknown at the moment," McCain answered. "The Tucson pen is buttoned up tight. I'm still trying to get a bead on things."

"Intel has Krypteia all over that place. Reports have been coming in for over a week now about it."

"Yeah, I know. The Defense Secretary is pushing this hard and we know she's in deep with the enemy. So, it has to be something. I'm just not sure what it is yet."

"Call it in when you know then. Oh, and Tom?"

"Yeah?"

"Keep the faith," Otis finished, knowing what to say to the worried father. "You trained Stacia well, my friend. She'll be fine."

McCain nodded to himself, ended the call, and set the phone down. Almost immediately, it buzzed. He looked down and smiled sourly. It was his new boss. Perhaps he could get some information out of her that would help. Ever since he had turned in his badge to the N.Y.P.D. in order to better fight Krypteia, he had been working for Secretary of Defense Anne Banyon as a recon specialist. He knew, even if she didn't, that she was part of the many-headed hydra that he was fighting. But he also knew he'd have more success working with them instead of against. Huge organizations were like that and Krypteia—despite its incredible power—was easy to infiltrate.

"Do you have an update for me, Tom?" Banyon said in a clipped voice as he opened the line.

"Negative, ma'am," he replied. "Everything's the same. No one coming out, only a few going in, and the boys in the van are in charge."

"We have to assume this is a repeat of Rikers."

"Rikers didn't have the goon squad out front," he corrected. "No chance of getting in here undetected and finding out what's going on."

There was a lengthy pause on the other end and McCain was about to say something, before Banyon finally spoke up. "Let me get back with you, Tom. I've got some new intel coming in."

Before he could reply she had ended the call. McCain frowned at the phone and tossed it back down beside him. Taking up his glasses, he went back to watching.

And waiting.

Banyon terminated the call and read the message again, nodding as she did. Tom McCain might believe he was hidden in plain sight, but her employer had kept very close tabs on him. They had guided him through Rikers Island and several other similar skirmishes, allowing him small victories while dangling even bigger questions and mysteries in front of him, all the while working toward cracking the tough nut of who he was actually working for. They knew about the T.S.S.F.G. and that he was one of their operatives, but despite all of their numerous resources, they had never been able to locate their main base of operations. It had been a pressing issue for her superiors and they had been working hard at discovering the location for so long they were beginning to wonder if they would ever find it.

But that search was now apparently over. The message on her phone told her they had finally succeeded and they weren't about to wait around deciding what course of action to take.

LOCATION CONFIRMED. TERMINATE WITH EXTREME PREJUDICE.

"We need a decision on Tucson," Robert Aaronson interrupted her thoughts, causing her to look up from her phone at the man sitting across from her. He was a weasel of an individual and his presence never failed to annoy Banyon, but she tolerated him because he was generally useful in gathering intel quickly and was typically spot-on with his analysis. But he was also one of President Abrea's men and had no clue that the country was being run now by a much higher power. With the arrival of the message and the now pending end of the T.S.S.F.G., she believed Aaronson had also reached the end of his usefulness.

"Have you briefed Alfred?" she said easily, referring to the president.

"He knows," came the reply. "He has authorized mobilizing the National Guard and quarantining the prison. You already know this, ma'am."

"Do you realize how long that will take and what kind of an effect that will have on the immediate public?" she countered somewhat angrily. "You know perfectly well what is going on in this country. You know how tightly wound people are. Arizona is still threatening secession. We march in troops and we're going to have a full-blown rebellion on our hands. They're just looking for a reason to pop."

"That's not for me to question," Aaronson said flatly. "The president wants boots on the ground and the situation dealt with. It falls to you to issue the order, Madam Secretary."

"Very well," she replied, picking up her phone. She paused and looked at the man. "Call it a day, Robert," she said as kindly as she could. "We'll have a lot to do tomorrow morning containing the fallout this will generate."

"Yes, ma'am," he said with a nod of his head, before turning and hurrying out the door.

When he was gone and the door clicked shut, Anne Banyon didn't make the call Aaronson assumed she would be making. Instead, she tapped in a series of codes she had memorized before dialing a different number. The phone rang only once and when it was picked up, the person on the other end began speaking immediately. "Was there any part of my instructions you didn't understand?" a deep voice asked sarcastically.

"No, sir," she replied, keeping her voice steady. "I will tend to it immediately."

"Then why are you contacting me?"

"We may have a problem," she went on. "Aaronson is going to return to work tomorrow, expecting the National Guard to be on the scene in Tucson, as per the president's orders. Since we are proceeding with the alternate plan, he will ask questions. That could pose a problem."

There was a pause on the other end before the voice answered. "I see."

"Robert was a good analyst," she went on. "I hate to see him go."

"No you won't and don't pretend you will. I'll see to his removal. In the meantime, complete your assignment in Tucson like you were instructed."

"Yes, sir," she said. "Right away, sir."

The line went dead and she immediately dialed another, this time not needing any codes.

"Fire control," a voice answered after two rings.

"This is Secretary Anne Banyon," she snapped. "Get me Kincaid."

"Yes, ma'am."

Less than ten seconds later, another man answered. "Good evening, Madam Secretary."

"We have a green light, General," she said without bothering with introductions or an explanation. The man was one of hers and was expecting this call. "Launch code bravo zeta alpha…eight five seven one zero."

"Confirmed," Kincaid replied, tapping rapidly on a keyboard in the background. After several moments, he added, "Launch in twelve minutes. Detonation in forty-three minutes."

"Get me a drone flyby at impact," she went on. "I want to see what happens."

"Yes, ma'am," Kincaid replied. "I'll route SatCom Twelve to your personal office."

"We've got men in place," she added. "Get them out, if at all possible."

"Evac is already on its way."

"Thank you, General," Banyon said. She ended the call and ran her hand across the piece of Plexiglas imbedded in her desk. It came to life immediately showing the presidential seal and, after a few seconds, it changed to a bird's eye view of downtown Tucson. In less than an hour, all life in that city would cease to exist. Well, most of it anyway. What remained would form the basis of the new ground forces she would need in the near future.

Tom McCain wasn't part of that plan, or, apparently, any other plan moving forward. Someone high up wanted him dead, and she was happy to oblige. As she watched, she wondered what kind of effect the chemical compound they were about to unleash would have on him. She was somewhat disappointed she wouldn't be able to witness it.

McCain ran his ATV wide open through the desert, heading for the mountains to the north. Less than ten minutes after he had gotten off the phone with Banyon, a military helicopter had come out of nowhere, landing in front of the gates to the prison. The four guards out front were on the chopper in less than ten seconds and the bird was winging its way southward toward the Mexican border. Moments later, there had been multiple detonations all over the prison complex. It hadn't taken long for McCain to realize the explosions were opening up the prison, making it easy for those inside to escape.

After Rikers Island, he wasn't waiting around to see what would emerge.

Thirty minutes later and safely—he hoped—away from the city, he killed his ride and turned to watch. Just as the sun disappeared behind the horizon, the detonation occurred at around five hundred feet above the city, an inverted mushroom cloud reaching down and encompassing the city in a pall of gray-green smoke. As the cloud spread, the shockwave reached him in the form of a strong wind. On that wind, he smelled it.

He had no idea what the odor was, but there was no denying what had happened. The United States had just chemical-bombed one of its own cities. To what end, McCain could only guess. But he knew for certain that Krypteia was fully in charge now.

With a sad shake of his head, he remounted the ATV and kicked it back to life. Pointing it north, he resumed his ride.

In Tucson, the first soldier stumbled through the clouds of toxic dust and out of the ruins of the penitentiary. It was the size of a man, but brutish and corrupted in appearance. It wore pants, but nothing else, its thick scaly skin more than enough protection. Long muscular legs ended in bare feet that were tough enough to run on broken glass and not suffer injury. Its arms, covered in faded tattoos, had elongated, with crooked black-clawed fingers reaching out for something to slice or tear at. What truly made this monster a vision of horror was the former prisoner's face. The shape was no longer human, but diamond-shaped, almost snakelike, and its eyes were reptilian in shape and size, black slits in pus-yellow pupils. Its jaws, filled with jagged, gnashing teeth, had stretched out grotesquely, and as it raised its head and sniffed, a long black tongue flicked between its ragged lips, tasting the bitter air.

A moment later, it began loping awkwardly but at great pace to the north, following its prey.

This creature was only the first. There were dozens more deep within the ruined prison and others scattered throughout the city. Almost all of the city's population was now dead, killed by the venomous plume sent by their own government. Those few who had survived, however, were no longer human.

Tucson had become a city of monsters.

CHAPTER 17

Las Vegas, Nevada: Alexis screamed as ice-cold water splashed forcefully over her naked body. Coughing and sputtering, she shivered violently as she tried desperately to grasp where she was and what was happening to her. Her body convulsed viciously, and if she had anything left in her system she most certainly would have thrown it all up.

"Wake her up, idiot!" a voice shouted, but Alexis heard it as if she was listening from somewhere else, deep underwater. Her ears were ringing loudly and her body ached as if on fire. Her right shin felt like it had been shattered with a hammer and her shoulder and stomach alternated between deep throbbing pain and sharp, piercing agony. She tried to calm herself and quiet the pain to a dull roar, but another sudden fit of shivers brought it all back with a vengeance and she gasped aloud.

The angry voice spoke again, but too softly for her to understand. Her head was pounding and she felt like someone was stabbing her behind the eyes. She opened them cautiously and instantly regretted it. Bright light flooded her vision and the stabbing sensation tripled, forcing them closed again. Instinctively, she tried to cover her eyes with her hands but discovered she was tied down at all four extremities. She realized she was lying supine on what felt like a giant block of ice. Every inch of her was exposed and wet, and nothing in her training had prepared her to mentally overcome just how vulnerable she felt at that moment. She was racked in pain, couldn't open her eyes, could barely breathe, and was tied down, naked, alone in a room with men torturing her. This was well beyond even her wildest nightmares. She was terrified.

Something hard rapped her on the forehead several times and she heard the voice again. She guessed it was asking her a question, but the pain of opening her eyes kept her from looking. The tapping and talking continued, the volume increasing until she could understand.

"Alexis…Alexis…ALEXIS!" Something forced her right eyelid open and the light painfully penetrated her skull once again. A man was holding her eyelid open while firmly tapping her forehead with the butt of a gun he held in his other hand. "Ah, there she is," he said, pure evil shining in his bloodshot eyes. "The angel has finally condescended to look upon us."

He released her eyelid, which Alexis promptly closed again. She was rewarded with a new sensation of pain as the man struck her solidly on her left knee with the butt of the gun.

"Look at me when I talk to you!" he shouted at her.

The pain in her knee was bad, but not as bad as the eyes, so she kept them shut. The next three blows to her knees escalated in force and his voice turned maniacal as he continued shouting, his words indecipherable. The pain was horrific and she was afraid he would ruin her knee permanently, so she finally forced her eyes open, doing her best to ignore the stabbing pain in her head. The man was there, spittle flying from his lips and the veins in his neck bulging as he drew back to strike her again.

"Enough," a deep baritone voice said quietly, but forcefully enough that she could hear him. A hand reached up from behind Alexis and firmly grasped her attacker's wrist, halting the blow. "She's coherent."

Alexis moved her head enough so that she could see the newcomer out of the corner of her eye. He was a well-muscled Polynesian dressed in surgical scrubs, and he was glaring at the pistol wielder with undisguised contempt.

Her attacker glanced only briefly at the other, then turned his eyes back to Alexis, his features going instantly and terrifyingly calm. "You see?" his voice dripped venom. "If you just do what I tell you, things will go much smoother." He holstered his gun with a lecherous grin and ran a hand through his greasy hair as he stepped closer and his eyes roamed hungrily over her bound form.

Alexis felt her training had prepared her for almost anything. But not this and not from him. She knew what was at stake and had been willing to die for the cause. But this? If he touched her or forced himself on her, she wasn't sure she could come back from that. With no way out, and no hope left, she fastened her eyes to a point on the ceiling above her and willed herself to remain calm. He could take everything from her, but she wouldn't give him the satisfaction of knowing he had broken her will.

"You and me," the man went on, delighting in the moment. "We have a lot to talk about. To save time, I'll explain the rules up front." He paused and walked the length of the table, his fingers brushing against the bare skin on her arm as he passed. In her mind, she pictured herself stabbing him through his black heart as she screamed loud enough for the whole world to hear, but all she could do was keep her eyes to the ceiling and do her best to keep from crying. "I'll ask you a question," he explained, stopping to lean over her again, "and you'll answer that question. If you break the rules, you'll be punished—and trust me when I say you'd be amazed how many different ways water can be used to make you scream." He paused to let the warning sink in. "Do you understand?"

She didn't answer.

"Perhaps a demonstration," the man said casually, straightening and nodding toward his partner.

Immediately, a wave of electricity racked her entire body, tensing every muscle to the maximum until it felt like she would break her own teeth or dislocate her shoulder if she squeezed with any more force. The pain was nauseating. She could hear her teeth grinding and ligaments stretching to their breaking point as her body arched in agony above the table. A moment later, the stimulus disappeared and her body crashed back to the metal table—cold, wet, unyielding steel.

Cole Banyon laughed, a wickedly pitiless sound. "You should have seen how high you got, Alexis," he mocked. "You've been working out." The hunger returned to his eyes.

Alexis tried to respond, but her jaw would not relax and her diaphragm wasn't quite working right. She was lucky she was only able to let out a guttural moan. What she really wanted to say would only have brought more pain.

"I'll take that as a 'yes'," he said, straightening and assuming an air of complete dominance. "It's flattering, by the way, that you came all the way out here just to try to assassinate me. Pathetic, of course, as you had no chance of success, but flattering nonetheless. It shows how important I am to this whole thing. Right?" He looked at the big Polynesian, who nodded. "By the way," he said, turning back to Alexis, "this is Ox."

The big man said nothing; he simply glared. However, his eyes were not on Alexis, but on Cole.

Cole ignored it and gestured to Alexis' left, continuing. "Ox claims to be a doctor, so we let him pretend. He is good, however, at administering pain." He pointed again, finally succeeding in getting Alexis to turn her head enough so that she could see what he was gesturing at. It only added to her terror.

Next to Ox was a table, with a half dozen large buckets and an electrical panel with several switches. In addition, there was a tray holding a number of different surgical instruments, all of which could be used for horrendous purposed on the human body. But on the other side him was another table, identical to the one she was strapped to. Lying on that table was Stacia. She, too, had been stripped and bound, but as bad as Alexis felt, it was clear Stacia had been beaten considerably more severely. Her right eye was swollen shut and every inch of skin Alexis could see revealed either a cut or a bruise. But her chest rose and fell rhythmically, causing Alexis to breathe a sigh of relief despite her terrifying circumstances. Stacia was alive.

"I see you've noticed we have your friend here, too," Cole smiled. "You should be thankful I kept her alive. I didn't have to, you know. I was hoping that would help you see just how reasonable I can be," he went on smugly, making it a point to rub his knuckles. Alexis noticed they were bruised, proving that Stacia's injuries had been at his hands. Misinterpreting the look on Alexis' face, Cole strolled over to Stacia, hovered over her for a moment, and then caressed her face with his left hand, all the while looking directly at Alexis. He slowly moved down her neck, lingering on her collarbone until Alexis couldn't take it anymore and she looked away. Letting out a maniacal laugh, Cole lifted his hand and slowly walked back over to Alexis.

"You have a bad knack for choosing the wrong friends, Alexis," Cole continued. "First Owen…now Stacia. I think I'm starting to question that legendary intelligence of yours." Using his fingers, he traced quotes in the air around the word *question*, though Alexis guessed he meant to highlight the word *legendary*. To Alexis, Cole personified crazy and stupid, just as the soldiers at the airfield had described. This was the last man in the world she wanted to be at the mercy of.

"I was there, you know," Cole lowered his face uncomfortably close to hers again. "Did that pansy boyfriend of yours ever tell you how his friends died, before Hade put him out of his misery?" His breath reeked of alcohol and his teeth showed awful black outlines as he bared them. "I killed them," he went on. "I killed them all in that diner while little Owen cowered behind the bar. I watched his face as I cut down every man, woman, and child in that hole and then I made him watch me kill his friends." He leaned forward, leering. "It's not like he could have stopped me, even if he'd tried. I had everything…under…control." His eyes roamed downward again and he laid a rough hand on her bare thigh.

She flinched at his touch and he snapped, lashing out and punching her in the side of the head, causing an explosion of stars behind her eyes. "Ox!" he commanded.

Before she could regain her senses, a deluge of water poured over her face. She spat, sputtered, and struggled, but the water kept pouring, rapidly filling her nose and running down her throat. Drowning, panicking, she felt her soul, tugging from within, twisting and turning as it tried to break free from her broken body. She was going to die.

And then, against all odds, she felt it again—a comforting warmth. Despite the terror of impending death, the familiar presence took hold, wrapping her in a tender embrace, and for some inexplicable reason she felt like everything was going to be fine.

At that moment, Cole delivered another punishing blow to the side of her head and the water suddenly stopped. Then the electrocution returned, longer this time, driving the familiar presence away from her and leaving her on her own to deal with the unimaginable pain. Her teeth grinding together as the current coursed through her, she refused to give in to the temptation to let go. The convulsion wrung her like a wet towel and, when it finally released her, she lay limp and breathless on the table. It wasn't long before she realized that the hum and crackle of the powerful electric current still filled the room. Exhausted, she slowly turned her head and looked at Stacia. Her friend was raised in a tonic posture as the current continued to run through her body.

Cole looked from Alexis to Stacia and back again, his eyes still hungry. "That's right, princess," he laughed. "Take a good long look at what happens when you defy me. She's a lot stronger than you; she can take a good minute of this before she starts foaming at the mouth."

The buzzing finally stopped and Stacia dropped hard to the table. The sight of her tortured friend tore Alexis apart. Cole walked to Stacia, watching Alexis the entire time. Then he spun quickly and punched Stacia viciously in the side, possibly cracking a rib. But there was no reaction—no grunt, no cry, nothing. Alexis tried but could not reach out, could not cry or even scream in frustration.

"But you, Alexis, have one distinct advantage over her," Cole went on. "You have something Hade wants, so I can't kill you until he gets here. Actually, I can't kill you at all. I can't even 'blemish' you. Oh, he made that quite clear, too. But that doesn't mean I can't have a little fun, right, Ox?"

The big man looked irritated and said nothing.

From her own table, Stacia groaned and tensed her hands, then her legs. It looked like she was testing her restraints. Without taking his eyes off Alexis, Cole continued. "Unfortunately for Stacia, she's fair game. In fact, I'm pretty sure the boss is going to be pretty sad when he shows up and she's still alive. So, if you want your friend to live, you might want to try explaining what information a stupid schoolgirl from Utah has that's so important."

Alexis coughed, tasting blood her in mouth, physically unable to answer.

"I'm no idiot, Alexis," he seethed. "I know you're working for someone. Care to share?"

Alexis shook her head weakly, still struggling to draw breath.

"I caught her mumbling the name Otis last night," Cole said knowingly. "I'm sure Hade would have great interest in posing a few…probing questions to your hot friend to find out who that is. If I don't ask her first myself," he finished, grinning lasciviously.

He smiled so sadistically that if Alexis was free and had a gun, she would have no qualms about emptying the entire magazine into him, before reloading and doing it again.

Unexpectedly, Stacia groaned again, this time managing her name. "Alex," she mumbled.

Alexis turned her head again to look at her beaten friend. Stacia managed a smile that lifted the left side of her face, which looked marginally better than the right since her blackened eye was only half-swollen shut. She must have been satisfied by what she saw or too tired to hold her head up, because she laid it back down on the hard table, still smiling, her gaze focusing on the ceiling. "So what do you think of Vegas?" she laughed weakly and coughed.

Alexis wanted to smile at her partner's courage and she took heart. "The concierge isn't as welcoming as I'd hoped," she replied and then chuckled herself. "You?"

"I've had wilder times than this, if you can believe that," Stacia laughed weakly. "Just don't tell my dad…" she trailed off.

Cole slammed his hand down on the metal table next to Stacia's head, his rage-filled eyes darting back and forth between the two captive women. "So glad your girls' night out is going so well! Are we all caught up now?" He spun his pistol from its holster and in an instant, the barrel was resting between Stacia's eyes. "Are you ready for a few more questions, tough girl? I'll bet I can find out what Hade wants to know!"

Alexis couldn't be sure, but it looked like Stacia was laughing and she found it hard not to join in. The whole thing was borderline absurd. They had been captured, beaten, stripped, tortured, and immobilized on tables in the most vulnerable way possible and here they were laughing at their captor like he was the world's dumbest criminal. Which, to be honest, he was.

"Cole," Stacia replied, her voice laced with ridicule, "interrogation from you is like a boy on his first date trying to get to first base. You're clumsy, impatient, and stupid."

"Shut up!" Cole shouted, slapping her hard across the face. Stacia grunted and tensed, but didn't cry out, further angering the psychopath. "Shut up, shut up, shut up!" he yelled louder, delivering a crack across her face after each one.

"Takes a real man to treat a girl like this," Stacia gasped, fighting bravely through the pain to dig at her opponent. "Girl needs to be tied down or she'd kick your pathetic little ass and you'd go crying to mommy in D.C."

Nothing in the T.S.S.F.G. training could explain to Alexis what on earth Stacia was doing. She was dumbstruck by Stacia's bravery.

His eyes wild, Cole grabbed a wet and bloody rag from table and shoved into Stacia's mouth. "I'm done with this. Drown her!" he fairly screamed, looking at the big Polynesian.

With a resigned look, Ox picked up one of the buckets and began pouring water over Stacia's face. As awful as it was when Cole had done it to her, Alexis felt an unparalleled horror at seeing the torture applied to her friend. After half a minute, Ox slowed the pour, but Cole wouldn't relent. "Keep going!" he commanded. "I'll teach this mouthy— "

Disobeying the order, Ox finally broke his silence and threw the bucket to the side. "Look, I'm not gonna kill her!" he snapped angrily, his eyes locked on Cole's. "You know what he said—Alexis unblemished and Stacia interrogated, but not dead. I won't have her blood on my hands. He'll kill us both."

Perhaps she had misjudged the situation, but Alexis had assumed

Ox was the lower ranking man here. Yet, the proud Polynesian stood his ground with authority. Cole tried to match his resolve, but soon turned away. With a grunt, Ox reached out and removed Stacia's gag, allowing her to breathe a little easier. "Lock it down," he said to Cole, throwing the rag to the ground. "If you cross him and screw up, he'll do ten times worse to you."

"Nothing we've done will leave a lasting mark," Cole objected, keeping his eyes averted. "Everything else can be explained by the grenades."

Shaking his head, Ox continued, "He'll know, Cole. He always knows."

"Yeah, and I'll tell him you didn't buy me flowers, either," Stacia added, her voice barely above a whisper.

"You need to learn when to shut up, Miss McCain," Ox warned angrily, turning his eyes on the young woman, but Stacia just laughed weakly at him. The woman knew no fear, even in the worst possible circumstance.

As the two men continued their arguing, Alexis realized this was Stacia's play: take control of the situation, distract their enemies, and give them a chance to look for a way out. Alexis took the opportunity to test her restraints. Solid, but not tight enough to cause ischemia. Not loose enough to work with, either. She looked around to see if there was anything that could help her. The room they were in was plain: painted cinder block walls, two lighting fixtures, one exit (behind Ox, of course), one vent that was too small to crawl into which housed a security camera, and no windows. The lack of any noise from outside the walls told her this could be a lone room in the middle of the desert, or fifty feet under the earth for all she knew.

"For the last time," she heard Cole shouting wildly, "I'm in charge here, not Hade. I'll do whatever I want!"

Now it was Ox's turn to slam his fist down on Stacia's table. "Don't be stupid," he snapped. "You're going to get us all killed for your pride. You know he'll be here soon enough. You won't have time to erase any mistakes."

"I don't make mistakes," Cole growled, his eyes truly crazy now. He whirled around as if he was searching for something, before his eyes finally came to rest on the tray of surgical instruments. His hand shot forward, scattering stainless steel all over the floor, but it came away holding tight to a gleaming scalpel. "Hade doesn't know her condition," he went on crazily, waving the blade in the air. "I can cut her to pieces and he'll never know!"

"Look, just calm down, Cole," Ox said slowly, pointing to the security camera in the vent. "Do you really think he won't look at the footage?" Even as he looked, the red light on the camera went out and the huge Polynesian paused and cocked his head curiously as he looked at it. "What the…" he started to say, but Cole was pacing back and forth with the knife, his eyes showing he had clearly gone off the ledge.

Ox continued to try to calm Cole, but as they argued, Alexis' mind drifted back to where everything had first gone wrong for her. It had been over two years since the tragedy on the mountain, when she had last seen the monster that was Hade. She remembered Owen and Petr fighting; Michael Dalacourt trying desperately to find some thread of sanity; herself trying to hold on to who she was. And then there was Hade, hovering like a tsunami about to break over all of them. She remembered it like it was yesterday; remembered Hade's words to each of them; remembered him murdering her Owen; remembered cradling Owen's beautiful head as he died; remembered Owen's last words to her.

"I love you, Alexis," he had said with his last breath.

And then he was gone.

With tears in her eyes, reality came flooding back to her. "Owen," she cried out loudly.

"Owen's dead!" Cole yelled, whirling back to her and brandishing the scalpel in a frenzy. "And you're going to tell me what I want to know! Now!" Eyes wild with anger, he slashed at her, the razor sharp blade slicing into the flesh of Alexis' bare thigh, opening up a long and very deep cut. Blood immediately started pouring from the wound.

Alexis moaned and started thrashing at her bonds as Stacia screamed, "Alex!"

Cole would have cut her again, but a massive fist slammed into the back of his neck and stopped the attack. Cole fell, his chin slamming into the edge of the metal table as he collapsed to the wet floor. Behind him, Ox looked like a dark shadow, his features creased with anger.

"Alex, stay with me," Stacia went on desperately, fighting futilely against her own restraints.

Ox moved fast, slapping a hand against the gushing wound on Alexis' thigh, holding her leg down even as the rest of her twisted and turned, fighting to get loose. "Calm her down," Ox commanded, casting a hasty glance at Stacia as he grabbed a towel from the surgical table and pressed it against the cut. It quickly turned red as her blood soaked into it.

"Bite me, dough boy," Stacia snapped, but there was only worry behind her voice.

"Look, she's been through too much already," Ox replied, his voice hardening. "Between the concussion injuries from the grenade last night and what Cole has done, she's lost a lot of blood—a fatal amount of blood. And as if that weren't enough, her muscles are beyond their limit from the seizures. They are breaking themselves down. She'll go into rhabdomyolysis and subsequent renal failure soon enough, unless you calm her down."

"Why should I trust you?" Stacia yelled. "You're the one who helped Cole do that to her!"

"Just do it!" Ox boomed, tying the blood-soaked towel tightly around the woman's thigh in an effort to stem the bleeding. "Do you want to save your friend or not?"

Stacia needed no more urging. "Alex! Alex, please," she pleaded. "You need to calm down for me, okay?" Her tone seemed to break through Alexis' psychoses and the young woman slowed her struggling. "Calm down, Alex," she went on, her tone soothing. "You're going to be fine. We'll make it out of this."

Whether convinced or exhausted, Alexis finally relaxed. Ox immediately freed every limb, working rapidly. "Hypothermia, acidosis, hypocoagulability," he mumbled to himself repeatedly. Stepping away from the table, he opened the door and hurried through it. A moment later, there was a whoosh of cold air from the vent, which quickly turned warm, then became positively hot. Ox ran back into the room with an armful of towels, leaving the door open. Still moving with a speed that belied his size, he dried the table and began wrapping Alexis in towels. Her body was limp and she offered no resistance as he moved her around in order to get her tightly cocooned, leaving an arm and her injured leg free.

"What are you doing?" Stacia asked, trying to comprehend how the man could go from water boarding them to saving Alexis.

"I'm not your enemy," Ox said, continuing to work. "Or at least, I'm not…well…it's complicated." He grabbed a stainless steel pole from the surgical cart and attached it to the table. Then he pulled a saline bag from one of the drawers and hung it on the pole. "If you can believe it, in another life, I was a doctor here in Vegas," he went on, laying out a trauma pack next to Alexis. He tied his own upper arm off with a piece of surgical tubing and then unwrapped a needle.

"What are you doing with this guy?" Stacia asked, somewhat disbelieving.

"Long story," he replied, expertly working the needle into a vein in the crook of Alexis' elbow. A moment later, he had it attached to the saline bag and released the stop. The fluid began flowing freely into Alexis. "Unlike this tool," he added, nodding toward the unconscious Cole, "I value my life. Hade said unblemished, and if she dies, I won't survive the day. Besides, this isn't what I agreed to. My family would never forgive me if I let this go on."

"So you're saving us now? Where was this an hour ago when Cole was shattering her soul?"

"We don't always get to make the choices we'd prefer," Ox said forcefully, without looking up from what he was doing. "Now shut up and listen. Alexis has what we call the trauma triad of death: hypothermia, acidosis, and hypocoagulability," he shrugged. "She's freezing. Her blood loss has left the cells of her body starved for oxygen, resulting in acidosis, and her native clotting factors are all used up from today's excitement. So I'm warming her up, replacing lost fluids," he explained, running an alcohol swab across his forearm. A few seconds later, he had a needle inserted into his own vein. "Lucky for her, I'm type O negative." He methodically attached his I.V. to Alexis' and began the transfusion. "This will restore her blood volume, reverse the acidosis, and replace some of the necessary clotting factors."

"Who are you?" Stacia asked, still confused at the stunning turn of events.

"I told you," Ox replied as he turned around and quickly undid Stacia's restraints. He tossed her an unused towel and then went right back to Alexis. "I'm a doctor…or at least I was." From the surgical tray he pulled out a suture kit. In seconds, he had seated himself on a metal stool and was working hastily over the open wound on Alexis' thigh. "Nothing I can do about the scarring," he mumbled as he sewed.

Behind him, Stacia had slowly sat up and wrapped the towel around her body, looking dumbfounded.

"None of this was supposed to happen," he said as he worked. "My job was to keep him reigned in and you in halfway decent shape. Obviously, I failed and for that, I'm sorry."

"When will Hade be here?" This time it was Alexis' voice. It was weak and exhausted, but she was alive and alert.

"Just stay calm," Ox answered.

"He'll kill us," Alexis went on.

"She's right," Stacia added, "and you right along with us. He won't care what condition we're in when he gets here, either."

"Frankly, if it saves my family, I'm good with that," the man replied, his own voice sounding tired. At that moment, the room suddenly went black. The darkness lasted for less than two seconds, before emergency lights flickered to life, casting the room in a dim glow.

Ox looked up wearily as Alexis put words to their fears. "He's here, isn't he?"

"No," he replied quietly, finishing up his work on Alexis' stitches. "Not yet, anyway. Hade wouldn't be shutting down the security network and electricity. It's someone else." With a grunt, he sat down heavily on the stool and began working at undoing his transfusion line. "Maybe they're yours."

Stacia shook her head. "No chance," she answered solemnly, sliding off her table to help him. "Too risky." Together, they undid the lines to both him and Alexis.

They heard the footstep then, rubber soles slapping on tiled floor, too quickly to be walking. Someone was running toward them. Stacia reached down and scooped up the scalpel that Cole had slashed Alexis with.

"No, wait…" Ox's voice trailed off, his speech slurring slightly.

At that moment, an awkward-looking young man stumbled into the room, glasses hanging haphazardly on oversize ears and a gun held loosely in his hand. He had a backpack slung on his back and his eyes darted around the room, taking everything in.

"We have to go," he said. "The girls will come with me. Now. Before he gets here."

CHAPTER 18

Almaty, Kazakhstan: Petr Zhugravinsky stood rigidly in the back of the white UAZ-469, a Soviet era knock-off Jeep. The top was down and he and his brother Sergei were holding on to the roll bars as they paraded through downtown Almaty, the former capital of Kazakhstan and an important industrial town in the old USSR. Their brother Nikolai was in a custom-built stretch Mercedes E550 Cabriolet convertible before them, waving to the cheering crowd of thousands that had come to line the streets. He was joined by Boris Yadislav, the Bulgarian minister of defense and an old friend of Nikolai's, as well as two of his highest-ranking military supporters, Marshal Federov and General Shusinsky. In front of him were three Kamaz trucks, two with anti-aircraft rockets and one retrofitted with a PK machine gun, and in front of those was a small procession of tanks. Following them were roughly a dozen more 469s with many of the dignitaries who had spent the last few days with them finalizing Russia's takeover of the republic. There were three more Kamaz trucks with Katyusha rocket launchers, and then another row of tanks bringing up the rear. It was equal parts conquering army and liberating force, but there were few left in Kazakhstan who cared to make a distinction these days.

While the larger countries of the world had struggled the past few years and were again with the devastation wrought by the recent tsunamis, many others that were already struggling had either become subsumed by a larger nation or fallen into anarchy. Kazakhstan had been one of those that had fallen apart. The country had been ravaged two years ago in the Witching Month, as it had become known in Eastern Europe. Perhaps as many as a fourth of the population had died in the chaos of those times. Unfortunately, those who survived soon found themselves embroiled in a vicious civil war.

The leaders of Almaty, the ancient capital, had led an attack on the rulers of the new, more centrally located capital of Astana. There were few loyalties here, beyond not wanting to be a part of China, its neighbor to the south, or Russia, its neighbor to the north.

Yet, over time, the people of Kazakhstan had come to realize they would never return to former glories without outside help. This, of course, was a fortuitous blessing for Petr's brother. Bringing Kazakhstan back into the fold would be a huge step toward fulfilling Nikolai's goal of restoring the former boundaries of the Soviet Union, and then ultimately surpassing them. The only problem was that Russia wasn't the only option. China shared a long border with Kazakhstan as well and were just as interested in making the broken country a new Chinese province.

So, while Nikolai worked hard to pacify his Chinese allies, he had sent Yadislav to negotiate directly with the Kazakhs. Petr had been doubtful from the start that Nikolai could bring Kazakhstan back under Russian control and had tagged along mostly to see his older brother fail. Nikolai had proven him wrong.

They had spent three days at a small resort on the eastern half of Lake Balkhash with representatives of the Kazakhstani government, including their prime minister, Balta Milokovic. The Chinese chairman of the central military commission, Bo-Lin, was there as well, which meant the decision was far from made. Knowing his brother had all the tact of an angry porcupine, he half expected an eventual war with China over this.

What he found, though, were ministers personally desperate for a way to come back under Russia's protection in order to stop the civil war and to restore the economy of their once emerging state. Nikolai, surprisingly, had exploited that for everything it was worth to get the most concessions possible. There would be no freedom for

Kazakhstan, now or in the immediate future, but with a few good years of harvests and a cooling down of unrest in some of the border regions, including wiping out those opposed to reunification, the rest of the country might just survive—*might* being the operational word.

And so the people cheered as the procession wound past, knowing this might very well be the end of them. Petr waved back, his part in this farce simply to provide a momentary hope that wasn't really a hope at all. As he waved to the crowd, sullen and discouraged by what was surely to come, his eyes came to rest on a young girl in traditional dress waving a Russian flag. Somehow, somewhere deep within him, the sight of this little blonde, blue-eyed girl brought him back to the last time he was in Almaty. It seemed like another lifetime to him now.

Almaty had been the city where he had first considered leaving his family. It had been a girl, of course, who lit the fuse. He was in town on some errand for his uncle and while in a bar having drinks, he had met a young woman named Erobreren. Although she was Norwegian, she had studied Russian literature for her doctoral program at the University of Oslo and, within a few minutes, she and Petr had struck up a deep conversation that lasted until the morning. They had talked of Pasternak, Mayakovsky, and Pushkin, some of Petr's favorite Russian poets and of his desire to follow in their footsteps.

Erobreren had opined that if he wanted to rise to their level, he had to stretch himself, break out and do something new. She had quoted Pushkin himself, saying: "Want of courage is the last thing to be pardoned by young men," and had smiled as she questioned why he didn't leave Russia to find himself and his inner muse. He'd never seen her again after that evening, but as he thought on that night now, he wondered how different the last few years of his life would have been if he had never met her.

Pulling himself out of his thoughts, Petr leaned over to Sergei.

"So, what do you think of the parade?" It was little more than idle chitchat, but Petr was working hard to keep his frustration in check.

"It's something new, I guess," Sergei shrugged. "I do rather enjoy it, though."

"It's only new to us, Sergei. The world has seen this farce before and I'm sure will see it again."

"You're too pessimistic, brother. Why would all these people come out to cheer for us if we are not here to liberate them?" Sergei challenged him. "This is no beginning of a war; it is the end of one. They are coming home, where they belong. This is a time for celebration."

"What we're doing here is wrong," Petr said flatly.

"Why must you always be so dark? It's been two long winters and these people have nothing. We are here to bring them stability, order, and peace. We will bring them food and warmth, for they will get it from no one else. We are saving lives."

"No, Sergei," Petr replied gravely. "We are taking lives. Today is the parade. Tomorrow, we will fly back to the presidential palace and the people here will watch as the exterminations begin. Russian bombers will level Astana because they were less willing to give up their entire country. We'll line up any opposition left along those walls right over there and shoot them and then we'll find their families and shoot them as well. Then our tanks will roll over refugee camps across the country, crushing the last bit of life from the people."

"You cannot be serious."

"The country is reeling, Sergei," Petr said. "Its people are starving and a world that is crumbling around them is not going to step in and help. The easiest way to solve the problem of having malnourished, unemployed, and diseased citizens is to simply get rid of them. In two weeks, perhaps as many as one-third of this nation will be dead. Then

Nikolai will have the region fully under his control and we can sweep in just like Stalin did and take over their copper mines and their industries and we can exploit them for generations. We'll take their uranium and their oil and leave them with death and disease. No, my brother, this is the beginning of a war, not an end."

"And yet the people cheer. They would not cheer if they thought what you think."

"These people know exactly what is going to happen, which is why they are cheering. These people cheer today because they know we are going to kill a great many of them and if they cheer, perhaps they and their children won't be the ones killed. This is the end of Kazakhstan, Sergei. We are witness to their final days. They know it, but they have no other choice and today I mourn for the millions who will not be here in two months."

"I cannot believe you," Sergei said, still waving at the people on the street, "and I will not let you ruin things today, my sour brother."

"I am not here to ruin things. I have no such power. Just don't expect me to smile for Nikolai. It is too much for my heart to bear."

From up in the Mercedes, Nikolai turned his head around and smiled at his brothers as he brought his phone to his ear. Immediately, Petr's phone buzzed and he angrily opened the line, putting him on speaker for his brother's sake.

"You know I have a listening device in your car and have heard everything you said, Petr," Nikolai laughed. "Sergei is right. You are sour!" He roared with laughter and Petr could only glare. "You forget that your place is here, now," Nikolai went on. "You have returned to our family and it is our family that you must protect now, not Kazakh families. I know that there will be death here, as do these people. But they understand how nature works. They grow apples here and they know that an apple tree doesn't deliver the best fruit unless it has been pruned. It is the way things must be. So, shed no tears for these people, Petr. Kazakhstan and Russia will be stronger for it in the end."

"I shed no tears, Nikolai," Petr replied. "But I see the truth for what it really is."

"I think you see the truth for what you wish it to be. Do you remember the ancient Slavic story father told us about the lake?" Nikolai changed the subject.

"Lake Balkhash?" Petr queried.

"The very one," Nikolai replied and launched into a retelling of it, ignoring the cheering people for the moment. "Balkhash was a rich man who had a daughter named Ili. One night, in a drunken revelry, he promised her hand to whoever would win a contest. Ili was in love with a shepherd named Karatel and she helped him win the contest. She thought she could just leave her family and be with whoever she loved, but that is not how families work. When her father found out who had won and that his own daughter had conspired to run off with this poor man, he grew so angry that he turned each of them into a river and then turned himself into a lake between the two, keeping them from ever uniting. And so the two rivers continue to flow into the lake to this day, separated for an eternity due to their reckless and hurtful decision. It is a tragic love story, no?"

"Tragic," Petr repeated. "But I wonder, Nikolai, what would the moral of the story be?"

"Isn't it clear?" Nikolai laughed. "The moral is that family always comes first and that the punishment for forgetting this never ends. Ever." He said nothing more, but his smile disappeared and he stared back at Petr.

Petr understood clearly. Nikolai meant to torture him for the rest of his life for leaving the family and he wanted to make sure Petr knew it. There would be no forgiveness for his betrayal. Ever. Not that it would matter in the end to Petr. If Sergei did not break from Nikolai on his own, he would when Petr exacted his revenge on Nikolai and killed him.

Petr jammed his phone back in his pocket. He saw his brother flash him a perfectly malevolent grin, before Nikolai returned to his task of waving to the people lining the streets of their parade route.

"It's all about family, Petr," Sergei was saying, trying to get Petr to understand. "You must see that."

But Petr wasn't paying any attention. He was watching a commotion taking place in the crowd a short distance ahead. Petr could not hear what was being said over the cheering of the crowd, but he could see what was happening. A woman was arguing with a man, seemingly in hysterics as she frantically pulled on his arm. The man, for his part, was yelling something back to her and roughly pulled his arm free, before turning and hurrying into the road. He was almost abreast of Nikolai's car when he pulled the handgun from his waistband.

The next few seconds were chaos. The man was screaming about freedom as he closed on Nikolai. Had he been smart, he would have pulled up and started firing at the Russian president immediately. As it was, he didn't pull the trigger until he was right next to the Mercedes and by that time, Nikolai had ducked down. Before the would-be assassin could adjust his aim, Nikolai slammed the door of his car open, catching the man in the stomach and doubling him over.

Nikolai jumped out of the car even as Russian soldiers began converging on the scene, their weapons out. In a rage, he grabbed the man by the arm and flung him into the open car door, sending the gun clattering to the pavement. A moment later, he had the man kneeling on the ground, his own pistol pressed against the side of his attacker's head. The woman that Petr had first seen arguing with the man in the crowd rushed out into the street, crying and pleading for mercy. Petr realized immediately it must be the man's wife. A moment later, Nikolai shot her through the heart.

A hush descended on the crowd and Petr climbed out of the car, looking around carefully. The mood of the crowd had changed dramatically and if even a few of them were armed and decided to attack, the whole situation could get completely out of hand. "Stay in the car, Sergei," he said quietly, watching for any sudden movements.

Nikolai had his gun pressed back to the kneeling man's head again as Russian soldiers fanned out around him. "Do you see this?!" he shouted in a voice that was heard by many. "This is one of your people!"

"Nikolai, don't," Petr warned as he cautiously approached.

Nikolai glared at Petr with so much hatred, Petr thought he might turn the gun on him. But instead, he pulled the trigger and blew the man's brains out. "Justice has been served," Nikolai shouted again, his eyes never leaving Petr. "But I am also a merciful man, and will not seek revenge for this attempt on my life. Let this dog lie here in the street to remind the world what becomes of those who would stand in the way of progress. We will continue on to the old presidential home and sign our peace treaty as we planned! Then I will welcome you all into Russia and we will live together again, as we should have before! One big family!"

There were a few cheers and a smattering of applause, but most just looked on in shock. The security guards surrounding Nikolai remained at the highest alert as Petr stepped close to his brother.

"Nikolai," Petr began, but suddenly his brother was in his face, cutting him off.

"Do you know who I am?" he snapped angrily, but in a voice low enough that the masses along the parade route couldn't hear him. "Do you have any idea who I am?"

"You are my brother..."

"I am your ruler!" Nikola seethed. "And you will learn your place, Petr."

Petr started to respond, but Nikolai held up a hand, stopping him.

"I know your heart, Petr," he said coldly. "I have known it since you first left us. You speak grand words and would make the world think you were strong and noble, but when it comes time for more than words, you disappear like a cat in the night. Now, I believe it's finally caught up to you. It's action and not words that make a man. Even the poets of old knew this. I am a man of action, so when you left, I lashed out to make you suffer. To break you. And I would have done more, oh yes, dear brother—I would have done more if I could have. Hade told me to not kill Sergei because he is the only thing you care about; the only thing that keeps you with me. Should we test that? I know you have nightmares every evening about the loved ones you've failed to protect. Should we add Sergei's death to your nightly collection of horrors? Would that finally drive you to action?"

"No," Petr replied quietly, fighting desperately to keep his anger in check. "I am here with you. Leave Sergei out of this. He is the best of us, the only one with a chance to remain good."

"Good?!" Nikolai spat. He looked out at the crowd of people, still clapping but clearly concerned about possible retribution for the attempt on the premier's life. "What a worthless word. It has no place in our language. Look at these people. Do you believe they are good? Have they built roads? Have they fed the hungry? Have they ended a civil war, as I have done today? There are babies in this city who will grow old and see their grandchildren smile because of me. So don't lecture me about good. Where were you, oh noble son, when I was threatened just now? Where were you, my loyal subject, when you failed in your duty to come to my aid? I was forced to save my own life, without your help. Tell me, Petr, using your warped sense of morality, which one of us is good? Which one of us wants to save his brother?"

"I am sorry, Nikolai," Petr replied, realizing there was nothing he could say. He took a step back and bowed his head. "You are correct, of course. It will not happen again."

"No, it will not," Nikolai frowned. "Because if it does, I will personally kill both of you." His demeanor changed, a fake smile widening across his face as he reached out and slapped his brother on the arm as if all had been forgiven, only both of them knew it hadn't. "Come," he stated grandly. "We have a parade to finish and a country to win."

As Nikolai got back into his vehicle, Petr walked slowly back to his. The procession began to move forward again, once more to cheering crowds. The dead were left lying in the street, the incident already forgotten by a people with nothing left to hold on to.

"Do you see?" Petr asked carefully, after he had taken his place back beside a clearly unnerved Sergei, not caring that Nikolai heard. "Do you see what Nikolai has become? His anger? His rage?"

Sergei looked away briefly as if steeling his nerves and then finally spoke his mind. "I don't believe you," he replied, his voice full of accusation. "You left us, Petr. You keep trying to get me to see something that isn't there, as if that will change anything. All I see is that our family is gone. We are all that is left, we three brothers. I am glad you have returned to Nikolai's side, but things are not the same as they were, and they never will be. Nikolai has risen to greatness. He has such dreams. If we band together, there can be no stopping us. We can make the world a better place. We can fix all its problems." He paused, and looked at Petr's, his tone softening. "That is what I see, Petr. Hope. I wish you did, too."

Petr was stunned. Had his brother not just witnessed the same thing he had? A poor soul, longing for freedom, had stood up and fought for what he believed in and had been executed in the middle of the street. The man's wife, desperate for her husband's safety, had sought to save him and Nikolai had put a bullet in her heart. This was not the markings of a stable, thoughtful visionary. This was a madman. Wasn't it?

And then Petr had a thought that froze him. Perhaps he was wrong. Perhaps Sergei was right. Worse yet, perhaps Nikolai was right. Worst of all, perhaps Hade was right. He shuddered, frightened by the implications of what that could mean. Did the world really need pruning? Was that his job—to be the man who brought death to millions in order to bring life to millions more?

He looked ahead at his brother again, watching Nikolai wave at the cheering masses as if nothing had happened. Nikolai had killed almost everyone Petr had ever loved. He was responsible for the deaths of hundreds of thousands already and would soon move that figure into the millions and beyond. And yet, try as he might, he could not help but feel admiration for him. Despite his sins, Nikolai had managed to bring Russia out of the last two years in perhaps better shape than any other country except for Brazil. He was bringing old territory back into the fold and had plans to do so much more. Was this any different than Alexander the Great? Julius Caesar? Peter the Great? Napoleon? Hadn't all of those men surrendered the lives of millions for the greater good? Had not the world improved and increased because of it?

As Petr looked at the crowd, his eyes scanning the faces of the Kazakhs, he realized they were ready to sign over their freedom and their country to Nikolai, not because they had to, but because they wanted to. They believed he would save their country in a way that they could not and they trusted him to do so. The rational side of Petr wanted to shout out to these men and women not to trust his brother; not to let the Russians enter their country. But he couldn't. He couldn't argue because he wasn't sure anymore that it was wrong. The chilling thought came to him again.

Perhaps Nikolai was right about all of it. Perhaps I am wrong.

As he rode in silence, a single tear rolled down his cheek. The world he had built up for himself in his mind, all of his assumptions and beliefs, all of his dreams and aspirations, everything he held dear and precious, had come silently and entirely crashing down around him.

CHAPTER 19

Las Vegas, Nevada: "Cam?" Ox mumbled in surprise. "What on earth are you doing here?"

"I, I…" the boy stuttered, before pulling a phone from the chest pocket of a tee-shirt that read "Bro-grammar" and running his fingers over the surface of it. Almost instantly, the regular lights flickered back to life and Cam squinted as he looked again at Ox. Then his eyes fell on Cole lying unconscious at his feet. Immediately, he raised the gun, alternating between Ox and the comatose killer.

"Put the gun down, Cam," Ox urged. "You're going to hurt someone."

"Who's this Big Bang reject?" Stacia asked, edging closer, one hand at her side and the other holding her towel in place.

"This is Cameron Banyon," Ox introduced. "Yeah, he's Cole's brother," he added, answering the unasked question. "But he's nothing like that bastard."

Cameron paced right to left, left to right, almost tripping several times on untied shoelaces. He looked to Ox, then to Cole, and back. "What did you do, Ox? He looks dead!"

"He's not dead, Cam," Ox soothed. "He was hurting the girls and I had to put a stop to it." He spoke in comforting tones, but there was a worried edge to it. "Cam, you'll hurt yourself or the girls if you keep waving that gun around. Put it down."

"You did this?" Cam stopped pacing and looked at Cole's body suspiciously. "You always think they're dead, but then they're not. In the movies, I mean." He stepped back, waving the gun toward his brother. "Then you get closer to make sure or you turn your back, and that's when they get you."

"He's not gonna get you, Cam. Now put the gun down."

Cam's shoulders relaxed and he looked at his hand, staring for all the world as if he had no idea how the gun had gotten there. He turned the weapon over, examining it, then pointed it straight at his face and brought it close to look right up the barrel.

"Cameron!" Ox reached toward him. "Stop!"

Cameron pulled the trigger. *Click*. Nothing happened. With a geeky laugh, he said, "It isn't loaded, Ox. It isn't even real. I needed it to scare Cole." He shoved the fake pistol in his waistband with a remarkable degree of skill.

"Take the gun out of your pants and give it to me," Ox said in exasperation, his hand still out.

A dejected Cameron finally surrendered the gun to Ox, who tossed it on the surgical tray. Clearly nervous, Cam scratched his nose, then his elbow, his overly large watch sliding up and down on his forearm as he fidgeted. "We have to go," he said. "The girls will come with me. Now. Before he gets here." He spoke as if it was a well-rehearsed speech.

"You're talking about Hade?"

"Yep, he's coming," Cameron replied.

"How are you planning to move the girls, Cam?" Ox sighed. "Neither are in any condition to make a run for it and I'm too weak to help you."

Cam spoke slowly. "I can get them out on my own. He prepared me for this."

Ox looked at him for a long moment, his eyes narrowing suspiciously. "Who prepared you?"

Cameron looked at the girls, the door, and then Ox, getting more agitated by the moment. "We have to go," he said again, but then added, "They won't have to run. I made arrangements."

Ox waited for more. "What arrangements?" he pressed, obviously used to having to push the boy for information.

"If I tell you, he'll get it out of you and find us." Cam slipped off his backpack and handed it to Stacia, who cautiously unzipped it and looked inside. Cam looked more than nervous now, avoiding the big man's gaze. "I have to follow the plan. The girls will put on the clothes." Out of the corner of his eye, he looked at the women to see if they would comply.

"These aren't clothes! I'll have to change my name to Candy to wear this!" Stacia complained as she held up a small, red sequined dress that would cover little more than what her towel currently did. "We need real clothes!"

"You need to blend in," Cam replied as he was overcome by a new fit of itching and nervous movement. "Trust me. Now, get dressed."

"Give me a dress, Stacia," Alexis breathed tiredly.

"You'll look less wretched in the silver one," her friend replied glumly and handed the tiny outfit to her. "Would you boys mind turning around?" she cast them both a withering glance.

Ox nodded and started to stand, but his body suddenly jerked in a racking convulsion and he dropped to the floor with an unceremonious thud.

Cam knelt at his side. He rolled Ox onto his back and checked his pulse and breathing with one hand while holding a Taser in the other. "I'm sorry, Ox," he explained, his voice stronger and sounding truly apologetic. "He said you'd try to help and that I couldn't let you. I had to make it look like you tried to stop us, so you'll live. You'll receive the redemption you seek and your family will be safe. You'll have another chance. That's what he told me to tell you."

Ox's eyes somehow gained depth when he heard this, but his body would not move.

"Telling him that *before* you zapped him may have been the better option," Stacia said as she dropped her towel and slid into her dress. Beside her, Alexis was doing the same, though somewhat slower.

Keeping his gaze averted, Cam touched Ox one last time on the forehead and then addressed Stacia. "You get her to the elevator," he said. "It's just outside the door. I'll open it." There was distinctly less crack to his voice as he stood and hurried out the door.

Stacia helped Alexis finish dressing and then put her arm around her friend. "Can you walk?" she asked softly.

Alexis gingerly put weight on her injured leg and winced. "Barely," she said breathlessly. "Not in heels, though," she finished, looking at the black stilettos that Stacia had pulled out of Cam's backpack.

"Barefoot it is," Stacia replied, looking at her own red pumps. "We can just pretend you're drunk." She looked down at her arm and saw a few puncture marks and winced. "I wouldn't be surprised if we were drugged with something anyway."

Alexis looked over at Cole, and a wave of revulsion rolled over her. She had worried about how she would react if she found him and whether or not she would be able to stick to the plan. But now, with their plan in pieces and after what she had just endured, only one thought ran through her head. She was going to kill the bastard.

Letting go of Stacia, Alexis hobbled slowly toward him. Stacia followed behind closely, unsure what her friend was going to do. As she neared Cole, Alexis reached down and picked up the discarded scalpel Cole had used to cut her.

Realizing Alexis meant to kill Cole, Stacia grabbed her arms and held her tight. "Are you sure about this?" she asked simply, her voice grave. "There's no coming back from this, Alexis. If you kill him like this, the rest of your life, whenever you close your eyes, you'll see yourself killing this man."

Alexis turned her head and stared at Stacia with a wild look. It was clear in the moment that Alexis could care less what the consequences were. She had gone down the rabbit hole too far to be able to think rationally about such an important decision. Stacia held out her hand for the scalpel. "Let me do it," she said quietly.

"There are some days I want him dead, too," Cam said from the doorway, "but he's my brother. Please don't kill him. Not like this."

Ox groaned slightly from the corner, and then fell silent again. Stacia looked intently at the boy. "He could cause a lot of trouble for us going forward," she told him and then added, "if we survive long enough for that to be a problem."

"I'm sure," Cam said firmly. "We have to go. Now. Just the three of us."

Somehow Alexis had managed to stay connected to the world enough to realize where the conversation was going. Single-minded in purpose, she lunged forward to deal the fatal blow to the man she now hated more than all others, but in her weakened state, she stumbled and nearly fell. Stacia held her up and gently took the blade out of her hands, before hugging her close. She looked in her eyes and said quietly, "It will be okay. Not today, not tomorrow, maybe not for years, but I promise you we'll come back from this, okay? And I promise that we'll make Cole pay for what he did to you."

Alexis looked at her, eyes hollow and rimming with tears.

"Stay with me now, so we can get out of here."

Alexis nodded numbly.

Stacia looked back at Cam and did her best to smile. "As much as I want to end this cockroach's life, he's your brother and it's your call. If you want him to live, we'll respect that."

Cam nodded as he scratched his head.

"But that doesn't mean we have to leave without giving him something to remember us by," she added. Smiling grimly, Stacia let go of Alexis just long enough to draw back and kick their comatose captor in the groin so hard that the unconscious man immediately vomited and started making a high-pitched mewling sound.

Her own crisis averted, Alexis slowly lowered herself so that her face was inches from Cole's. She grabbed his face with one hand, her nails cutting into the flesh of his cheek. "You better pray that Hade kills you for letting me slip through your fingers," she said with all the venom she was capable of. "Because if he doesn't, you'll spend every moment of the rest of your life wondering how I am going to slowly, painfully, frighteningly, pull you apart."

She viciously shoved his head into the concrete floor with a thump and then slowly pulled herself back to her feet. For punctuation, and her own personal satisfaction, she kicked him squarely in the face, breaking his nose and leaving him bleeding on the floor.

"We have to leave now," Cam called from the hall. As much as he hated his brother, he couldn't stomach the violence, so he had excused himself to work on his phone out in the hallway.

With a nod, Alexis threw her arm across Stacia's shoulders and leaned heavily on her as they began shuffling toward the elevator as swiftly as they could. Stacia was right. There would be time to process everything later, and if all went well there would come a day in the future when Cole would die and she would be the one to do it. But right now, they had to get out. It took everything she had, but she was able to block out the events of the past twenty-four hours and focus on their present task.

Cam was already at the elevator, his phone being scanned by the control panel screen. An automated female voice reported, "Retina scan cleared for Cole Banyon." The elevator door opened to reveal an ornate, pristine marble and mahogany interior. The dome-shaped camera in the center of the ceiling caught Stacia's attention.

"Don't worry," Cam said, seeing her concern. "It's running on a loop right now that shows an empty elevator. The interrogation room is looping, too, but shows you two lying on the tables. We have to time this right, so do exactly as I say."

"You'll forgive me if I don't just implicitly trust you. What's your plan to break us out of here?" Stacia asked the younger Banyon, looking an odd combination of bruises, swelling, and a skintight cocktail dress.

"No breaking," Cam explained. "You two will act the part of two drunk hookers that Cole just beat up. You only have to stay in character for less than a minute," he went on, his fingers working impossibly fast on his phone. "There's a car twenty feet from the elevator door, on a display pedestal. The doors are unlocked. Hop in the back and hide while I distract everyone." He looked up briefly to ensure they were following his words. "I'll switch all of the security cameras back on as soon as you're hidden. So once you're good, stay put and don't make a sound."

"What about weapons? What if someone comes for us?" Alexis asked nervously.

"Can you hide a weapon in that dress?" Cam managed a little sarcasm, but didn't wait for a reply. "Remember what I said. Get in the car and stay put. It's the only way you're getting out of here alive."

The doors opened to the main casino floor and Cam went to work. He worked his phone again and two slot machines on the far side of the casino suddenly erupted in a cacophony of music, alarms, and dropping coins. The singularity of two slots hitting simultaneously drew every eye and a large crowd began moving speedily toward the commotion to see the event. More than half of the patrons were soldiers. Most of the rest were women dressed in very little, attesting to the atmosphere of the casino. Cameron was right. The two women would fit right in.

"The black Land Rover," Cam said hastily as he walked from the elevator and straight toward a nearby bank of slot machines.

The car did indeed sit on a pedestal ringed by slots and Stacia and Alexis stumbled toward it, not having to try very hard to look the part. No one paid them any attention, particularly with the excitement happening on the other side of the casino. With a quick glance around, Stacia opened the rear door of the beautiful, new black Land Rover Defender just enough to squeeze in. She pulled Alexis in with her, confident that if anyone did actually witness them, they would have thought something entirely different was taking place. She pulled the door closed, the dark tint to the windows and tank-like stance of the vehicle offering them both some much needed comfort.

Nearby, Cameron nodded appreciatively to himself and then worked his phone again. The cameras he had been controlling went live, which he knew would get things hopping in the security room. He had one more card to play, though, and reached out and pulled the arm of the slot machine he was standing in front of. Five digital wheels spun to a stop, showing a row of partial images that lined up to form a picture of the very Land Rover the two women were now hiding in. The entire bank of machines lit up with flashing lights, sirens, and bells, and the excited crowd turned away from the previous winners and began churning toward him. Cameron had no problems looking a combination of bewildered, uncomfortable, and perfectly innocent.

"Cam?" one of the casino security detail shouted as he pushed his way through the milling throng. "Are you okay? Did you just win the Defender?" Cam nodded mutely and pointed to the flashing machine. A smile crossed the guard's face and he added, "Way to go, buddy!"

Cam let himself look queasy, which also wasn't too difficult. Truth be told, he was scared to death. "Paul?" he said breathlessly. "I can't breathe. Get me outta here!"

"You got it, Cam!" Paul replied importantly and took a little too much pleasure in shouting at and elbowing a few drunken casino patrons out of the way, in order to give the teenager some room. Cameron Banyon had endeared himself to the security team at the casino where he and Cole lived. While there was little that anyone found redeeming about their boss, there was nothing not to like about his younger brother. Cameron was always helping the officers out: fixing security systems, bringing them snacks, lots of little things. On top of that, the security men hated the way Cole abused the boy for his apparent autism or mental deficiencies. So, Cameron had achieved a sort of celebrity status with security and casino employees, making them almost excessively protective of him.

"Let's get you out of here," Paul went on. "I'll have Smith take the car around back for you. We'll take care of the paperwork later, when things are a little calmer." He took Cam under his massive arm and spoke into his radio, giving directions to move the car and bring out a different one and reset the game. He then escorted the teen through the chaos and into the control hub where security monitored the entire casino. The mood in the room was just as Cam had hoped—a strong sense of urgency hovered over everyone present.

"What's going on, Carter?" Paul asked as they stepped into the room and he pointed to a chair for Cam.

"We've got issues in detention," the man replied. "What's up with the kid?"

"Cam won the Defender," Paul replied with a genuine smile.

"Really? Good for him," Carter replied honestly. "Hope Cole lets him keep it."

"He better," Paul answered, his smile fading. "What's happening in here?"

"Camera feed is down. We can't bring up detention."

"Wait a second. I got it!" one of the techs suddenly spoke up, just as one of the monitors switched to the detention camera. There was a collective gasp from all five of the men as it showed two empty metal tables and two men, both on the floor. The big Polynesian was trying to pull himself to his knees, but collapsed. Cole Banyon was curled in a fetal position and appeared to be whimpering.

"Oh, this is *not* happening," Paul said quietly in dawning horror of what it would mean if the prisoners escaped.

"Lock down the exits," Carter ordered calmly. "Get images of the prisoners to all active personnel." There was no panic, just an efficient call to arms, and the five men in the room were a blur of motion.

"What's going on?" Cam whined, playing his part as he peered at the monitor and looked suitably perplexed. "Is that Cole? What happened to my brother?"

"I need all cameras up on the monitors," Carter ordered, ignoring the youth. "Elevators, exits, stairs get priority. Two man sweeps in those three areas must be completed in two minutes—reports every sixty seconds." Carter had plenty of experience in this area. "I want visual confirmation of camera blind spots. They're trained; that's where they'll be."

Through the monitors, Cam saw the officers take control of the casino floor. Everyone was forced to the ground, soldiers and all, as the security teams—more than he had anticipated—quickly began following their orders. The Defender was already gone, presumably to the back where Smith was taking it. He suppressed a smile of satisfaction as he realized his plan might actually work. "Who's out there, Paul? What girls are you looking for?" he asked innocently, sitting at one of the control stations and looking suitably scared.

"I need you quiet for a minute, Cam." Paul said brusquely without turning back. "Let us get this taken care of."

Under the desktop, Cam worked furiously on his phone.

"Sir, we just lost the camera in hallway ten near the stairwell," one of the techs said.

"That should be them," Carter said. "Who's in the area?"

"Jones and Barnes."

"Barnes, we need a report from hallway ten now!" Carter barked into his headpiece.

Cam kept working underneath the desk. "I don't feel so good, Paul," he panted, breathing fast.

"Forward stairwell went black!" the tech spoke up again.

"Barnes, Jones," Carter called out. "They're on the move. Forward stairs."

Both men carried out their orders with military-like precision. They all knew what was at stake for them.

"Paul," Cam moaned.

"Will someone get the kid out of here," Carter snapped. It wasn't that he didn't like Cam—he simply had no time for him during what had rapidly become the worst possible situation they could deal with.

"Captain Carter!" the static filled speaker blared.

"Go ahead, Barnes."

"We think we've got them trapped in the stairwell," Barnes answered. "Suggest dropping gas."

"Negative," Carter replied sternly. "I want them coherent. I want to know who helped them. There's no way they are pulling this off by themselves."

Paul chanced a look back at Cam, who was slumped over in his chair, holding on to his stomach. "Go ahead, Cam," he said softly. "Get out of here. Go back to your room and let us get this nailed down. I'll find you later and we'll get the car thing taken care of."

"Okay..." Cam coughed and gagged, continuing with the charade. It almost made it worse for the younger Banyon that everyone was being so nice to him. "Okay," he said again and slid off his chair. He slipped through the door and began walking toward the garages. He had to consciously force himself not to run.

He turned a corner and stepped into a vending alcove, one of the security camera blind spots. He activated his phone again and, in less than thirty seconds, he had cut all power to the casino floor. He didn't have to be there to know that it would send an already agitated crowd into a mad rush for the doors.

Pocketing his phone, he purchased a Twix and then continued walking toward his destination. A few minutes later, he found the Defender exactly where he knew it would be—pulled up in front of the employee's entrance. Smith was nowhere to be found, presumably following orders and helping search for the two escaped prisoners. He smiled to himself and got into the driver's seat, not bothering to look in the back. He knew the women were flat on the floorboards.

"Where are we going?" a voice spoke up softly from the back seat.

"There's someone we need to meet," Cam answered as he started the Defender. Without any more explanation, he drove easily through the lower garage and out into the ruined city. A short time later, they had left the casino behind. Cam realized at that moment that he would never again see the place he had called home for the past two years. He had cut his last ties with his brother, of that there was no doubt. He could only hope it didn't end terribly for the men who had befriended him once Hade got wind of their escape. As far as his brother went, he wasn't sure he cared.

CHAPTER 20

Mesquite, Nevada: The 2006 Night Rod motorcycle raced up I-15 through the isolated Nevada desert at a speed of well over one hundred miles per hour. Its rider was dressed in black from head-to-toe, his long hair whipping freely in the wind behind him. Big as he was, it would have been easy for anyone watching to miss the small rider seated on the back of his bike, arms wrapped tightly around his waist. However, there wasn't another soul within miles. The desert was a desolate waste and the road was completely empty. The only indication that life had ever passed by was in the sand-blasted and weather-beaten remains of automobiles and trucks that for the last two years had been left abandoned on both sides of the road.

Hade finally slowed his bike down as he left the interstate and rolled into Mesquite. He drove through the remains of the city—completely destroyed more than two years ago and still a ghost town—until he got to the golf course, where he finally brought the motorcycle to a stop. As the engine went quiet, Hade's passenger climbed off the bike with cat-like grace. She took her helmet off and long, red hair fell to her shoulders. She was dressed all in black—boots, leather pants and a black leather bodice to go with her trench coat. She walked away from the bike running a hand through her hair, happy to be on her feet again.

Hade dismounted from the Harley with a deep laugh. "You managed to not throw up," he chuckled. "Maybe you're finally getting the hang of this."

"You know I can't stand these infernal machines of yours," the woman replied, casting him a withering glance. "I still prefer a good horse."

"A good horse is still just one horse," he replied. "This infernal machine, as you say, has the power of one hundred and twenty horses."

"Our friends are waiting for us," she said, ignoring his obvious enjoyment at her discomfort. "Do you mind if we join them now or do you feel the need to once more tell me how completely awesome the liquid-cooled, eleven-thirty CC Revolution V-Twin engine is?"

Hade could only laugh again. "I'm glad you paid attention and yes, it is completely awesome," he added. "But you're right, of course. So, after you," he beckoned with a mock bow toward her.

She rolled her eyes at him and then began walking toward a pair of nearby vehicles, an unmistakable sway in her hips.

Hade followed and they approached an older H1 Hummer—a large beast of a vehicle—and a newer Lexus LS. Four individuals were gathered around them in the darkness, lit only by the headlights of the vehicles.

"X!" Hade warmly greeted a man who appeared to be in his late forties with salt and pepper hair and wearing a finely tailored business suit. "I trust everything is well this morning?"

"Of course, Master," the man replied with a polite nod of his head and then turned to face the woman. "And a most wonderful morning to you, my lady," he added, bowing deeply this time.

The other three knelt as well, heads bowed toward the woman. Together, they made up a truly odd-looking group. One of them was a young man wearing surfer board shorts and a tee-shirt featuring a surfboard with shark bite marks. Another man was dressed in torn jeans, a white tee-shirt, and a black leather jacket. The fourth was a pretty young woman, barely more than a teenager. She was dressed in a janitor's jumpsuit with the name George stenciled across one of the pockets.

"Your highness," the girl greeted her, a reverent tone to her voice.

"Rise," said Hade's companion as she shot the huge man a look of mischievousness.

Hade returned a bored roll of his eyes to her and crossed his huge arms. He made a show of tapping his foot in impatience as the woman turned back to the foursome.

"I don't think I've ever seen you look so nice, X," she said, taking his hand. "You should think about keeping the suit when this is over. It favors you greatly."

"I would, Lady Letalis," he replied, "but alas, it's silk, and you know how hard it is to get blood out of silk."

"Indeed," Letalis smiled, her darks eyes glittering "One of the many curses of fine fashion, it seems. And Tin and Narn," she went on, looking at the two young men. "You appear strong and fit as ever. Your time in Vegas is treating you well?"

"Always, my lady," they both said at the same time, nodding their heads simultaneously.

"And Gru, my dear," she finished, looking at the young girl and clucking her tongue in dissatisfaction. "I dare say this is not a good look for you. The gray hardly brings out the color in your gorgeous eyes and honestly, I don't think George himself ever looked good in this. I suppose Hade and his lack of any sort of fashion sense is behind this monstrosity of an outfit?"

"Our mandate was to blend in," Gru replied with a sheepish smile. "Surprisingly, this works quite well. I can get in and out of the casinos without getting hit on by any of the creeps. I guess I'll keep wearing it, at least as long as we're here."

"I suppose it's not without a purpose, my dear," Letalis sighed, giving the girl a quick kiss on the cheek. "Promise me you'll treat yourself to something more lovely when you have some downtime."

"I promise, my lady," Gru smiled, flashing white teeth.

"I want to thank you for meeting us this morning all the way out here," Letalis went on, addressing them all. "Your sacrifices for the cause are most appreciated and you will all be rewarded generously when our business is completed." She paused and cast her eyes toward the south, her face hardening slightly. "There are others, however, who are undeserving of our generosity."

"It is truly our pleasure," X said humbly, taking her outstretched hand and kissing it. "We serve because we love."

"And what better way to show love than to serve," Letalis replied sweetly.

"All right, all right," Hade grunted impatiently. "Let try to wrap up this portion of the mutual admiration society meeting. I need to blow some stuff up."

"Yes, Master," X replied, casting a wink and a smile at Letalis.

"Is everything in place?" Hade asked.

"Yes, Master," X repeated. "The ordinance is placed exactly where you asked for it to be. Look for the red cars along the road. The first will be just beyond the main gate. There's no way you'll be able to miss it, nor the ones to follow." X paused. "May I ask a question, though?"

Hade cocked an eyebrow at him as if to say "shoot".

"Do you really think Cole Banyon is stupid enough to think he can keep you out after what happened?"

"I expect nothing less," Hade chuckled and cast a condescending smile at his companion.

She bit on the bait. "Why are we going to fight our way through an entire army of mercenaries to get to that piece of trash?" Letalis asked. "Surely, there must be a better way."

Hade continued to smile, clearly expecting her question. "X, perhaps you would be so kind as to explain to Letalis why we are here and why Cole will indeed sacrifice a great many men in a vain attempt to protect himself from me. I've tried to explain it myself, but perhaps she might listen better to someone dressed a little more fashionably than I."

"But of course," X said with a grin and began immediately. "As you know, my lady, Vegas basically fell apart after the party two years ago."

"You're still calling that a party?" Hade asked, shaking his head. "It doesn't take much for me to remember why I love you guys so much."

"It was one of the best nights of our new lives," X replied, smiling widely as he licked his lips. "Mesquite can make just about anything taste good."

"Right, right," Hade said impatiently. "Very clever. Mesquite is still empty thanks to you four. But we're talking about Vegas. Stay on topic."

"I apologize, Master," X replied, but he showed no fear—only a fervent loyalty toward the huge man and an almost fanatical love for the woman. Turning back to Letalis, he continued. "After what happened across the country, few people had the time, resources, desire, or ability to live it up in Vegas. It didn't help that most of the southern part of the city had burnt to the ground. To this day, the UNLV campus and surrounding area is nothing more than a ghost town where only the unlucky dare to tread. The northern casinos are all gone, as well.

"In the early going, the gaming industry looked like it was going to go under," X went on. "With no people coming to visit, that meant no money coming in, which meant there was no way to keep the casinos open. Your little gambit, Hade, put hedonism, at least for the middle classes, out of style. In addition, it didn't help that California cut off the water supply going into Vegas, so there was no way to keep the golf courses green or make ice to keep the drinks cold. It looked like the whole city would go under and it very nearly did, until Cole Banyon came to the *rescue*."

Hade chuckled softly and X rolled his eyes so dramatically that they appeared to actually spin inside his head. "That waste of space used his connections to Hade," X continued, nodding in deference toward the big man, "to bankroll buying up most of the casinos. He also used his mother, Secretary of Defense Banyon, to obtain U.S. military supplies and vehicles, so he could set up his own personal little fiefdom here. Somehow, the water got turned back on, too, although I doubt he even knew it was off. The plan, which you know was fully orchestrated by Hade, was to salvage what was left of the Strip and allow Cole to run it. That's the history lesson, but I'm guessing," he paused and looked directly at Hade, "that what you really want Lady Letalis to know is what Cole actually controls at the moment."

"Astute as always."

The surfer—Narn—took up the explanation and held up an old, dog-eared map of Las Vegas. He opened it up and carefully laid it across the hood of the Lexus. "Pardon the old-fashioned map, but wireless doesn't work around here since the towers came down two years ago," Narn said. "You need a hardline, but even then you aren't sure who's watching.

"The northern border of Vegas was easy to set up," he went on, pointing to various locations on the map. "Everything above Spring Mountain Road was destroyed. The Wynn, Encore, Trump, Hilton, Riviera and Circus Circus are all long gone. There's nothing north now for almost a hundred miles, until you get here to Mesquite. Cole used I-15 as the western border, which made sense. It's a shame what he did to the Rio, though," the surfer sighed wistfully. "I used to love that place. Anyway, Koval Lane is the eastern border of Cole's area. Most of the city east of that road was destroyed early on. What lives there now, even his soldiers avoid."

"That brings us to the south side," the other young man spoke up as if on cue, reaching out and tapping the bottom edge of the map. With his grunge rocker outfit, long hair, and boyish good looks, Tin looked as if he had stepped right out of the movie *The Lost Boys*. "When Cole took over, the southernmost casinos were left to their own devices and, despite what everyone thought, some of them have managed to hold on. The Mandalay Bay is pretty much empty, but the Luxor, Excalibur and Tropicana are all still operating. These hotels are for the few remaining locals or for people who want to drive from Los Angeles or Salt Lake City to try and relive the good old days. After these, there is a gate on Tropicana Avenue. Cole has regular soldiers patrolling the area in the name of security, but it's mostly to keep out the people he doesn't want in his inner sanctuary."

"Think Checkpoint Charlie, only without the cheerful, good-natured East German guards," X added with a sardonic smile.

"Right," Tin went on. "The city as it stands now is entirely set up to cater to the world's rich and famous. The casinos inside the perimeter are all still functioning like they used to, if only at a fraction of capacity. But that's exactly what they want. It is simply a playground for the extremely wealthy and depraved now. They fly or chopper into the airfield, which is under full military control, and then they're brought to town to enjoy the new Las Vegas. Twenty casinos to choose from with a million and one vices," he explained, looking up expectantly. "With all the other upheaval going on, the government leaves Vegas alone. There are travel bans all over the place to avoid Nevada in general, but that's not to say some politicians aren't among the patrons here. Plus, it helps to have Mommy Banyon in the highest political circle."

Hade already knew all of this. He had indeed been very active in facilitating the changes, but that didn't mean he liked what the town had become or what Cole had done with it. He had put up with it because it served a higher purpose. Today, however, he was done with Vegas and Cole Banyon's currently wretched existence.

"This cesspool is a pox on the world," he said, more to himself than to those around him, "and it needs to be reduced to rubble."

"Sir, no offense," Tin stammered, clearly not expecting what Hade had just said, "but Vegas always seemed like it would be your sort of town."

"Then I've done a poor job of representing myself," Hade answered sharply. "If there's one thing I abhor, it's vice for the sake of vice. This is hell on earth if ever there was one. God had his fun destroying Sodom and Gomorrah and now I'm going to have a little fun of my own destroying Vegas."

"Do you require any assistance?" X asked, an almost feral look of hunger passing across his face. "We would be more than happy to help."

"Right," Narn added. "We've been stuck in that festering pit for over a year now, keeping Cole under control. We'd really like to let loose and have some fun."

"Any other time, I would welcome you as brothers…and a sister," Hade replied, "but not tonight. I'm afraid your lady Letalis and I need some alone time with Cole and his underlings. But, I'll leave everything north of the Wynn to you. Wait until sundown tomorrow and you can feast on anything you can find."

"Fair enough," X said, doing little to mask his excitement at the prospect.

"But only one night," Hade warned. "From dusk 'til dawn, no sequel. Then I want you in Los Angeles, awaiting your next assignment."

"Yes, Master," X replied, bowing his head in respect. "As always, you can count on us."

"I know I can," Hade said with a smile. "That's why you four have been alive for as long as you have."

"Hade," Letalis spoke up, an oddly pained look on her face. She was clearly concerned with something.

"Yes," he replied slowly.

"You know I'm against the slaughter of innocents, regardless of who they work for."

"I can promise I wouldn't have brought you anywhere near Vegas if there was a chance you would kill anyone who wasn't deserving of their fate, my dear," he said easily. "There isn't a single person in that cesspool who hasn't given themselves over completely to darkness."

"Just how can you know that? I won't have innocent blood on my hands."

"Nor would I let you," Hade smiled knowingly. "Gru, do you mind?" Hade asked, turning and motioning to the young girl.

"Of course not," Gru said, smiling as she held out her left hand, palm down.

Letalis looked closer and noticed for the first time that the girl's hand was marked, but it didn't look like any tattoo she had ever seen. The image was simple, yet intricate, a small purple octopus centered just below her wrist bones. Five of the creature's tentacles stretched down the length of her hand, then encircled each of her fingers and thumb. The other three tentacles wrapped around the young girl's slender wrist. Gru flexed her fingers and the image seemed to move its tentacles as if it was floating just underneath the surface of water. At the same time, its mottled coloring shifted from various purples to hues of brown and gray and then back to purple.

"Impressive," Letalis nodded. "But what is it?"

"It is an electronic device implanted in her wrist," Hade said patiently, "the latest and most sophisticated RFID technology to date, courtesy of our very own Legio Enterprises research and development teams."

"She's chipped?" Letalis asked doubtfully.

"Radio Frequency Identification has come a long way since the days of bar codes and readers, let me tell you," Hade replied. He pointed to the body of the image and then traced a line down one of the tentacles to Gru's finger. "The body houses the transmitter and each of the tentacles contains nano-filaments that store all of your personal data. With this little beauty, you don't need a wallet, a purse, or a smartphone to make purchases, rent library books, or show the bouncer you're old enough to drink."

"I am well aware of how RFID technology works," Letalis said, looking hard at Hade. "Have you forgotten the small library you made me read on the subject? All you've done here is give it a fresh coat of paint."

"Ah, but that's where you're wrong, my dear. This isn't just a system to transmit data. It's controllable to some degree by the individual."

"Explain."

"Let's say you're at a casino in Vegas," Hade went on, "and you want to withdraw a considerable amount of money from your checking account so you can keep gambling." He tapped Gru's hand. "With this, all you have to do is think it and voila—instant cash withdrawal."

Letalis folded her arms. "How does that work?"

Hade reached up and gently pushed aside Gru's dark hair, exposing her forehead. "Do you see the small scar on the right side of her head, near the hairline?"

"Yes," Letalis replied looking closely. The scar was tiny, just a round, slightly luminescent dot.

"That's what takes this to the next level," Hade explained. "It's a simple implant that transmits your brain waves to the hand implant. The technology has been around for a long time. We just made it wireless."

"So the user has complete control over the use of it?"

"To an extent, yes," Hade replied. "For making random payments such as our little example, it works wonderfully. You can cancel your credit cards, open other accounts, pay bills, access your medical records, stuff like that. What the user doesn't have the ability to do is restrict their personal information. The readers are designed to read whatever personal information we need—medical, financial, religious affiliation, etc."

"So, why an octopus?" Letalis changed the direction of the conversation, clearly intrigued by the design of the device.

"The short answer is that the octopus is just awesome," Hade answered with a chuckle. "Did you know ancient Hawaiians actually believed that after the last universe ended and the new one began, the only creature left over from the last epoch was the octopus? So the imagery has meaning for what's coming. But it's much more than just the symbolism. In reality, it comes down to their skin. In the wild, an octopus can change color, opacity, and even its shape. The flesh has chromatophores that contain yellow, orange, red, brown, or black pigments that allow it to change color. The underneath layer of their skin is made up of leucophores, which is a sort of a translucent, colorless reflecting protein. Besides all of its other properties, these leucophores also provide the perfect casing for the microchip. The RFID chip is encased in octopus flesh, which is genetically modified to allow it to exist in your own body without being rejected. The brain implant connects you to your information store and gives you some control over the mobility of the implant. You can actually cause the implant to move slightly under your skin with just a thought and it will even change colors. Depending on your mood, the tattoo can be red if you're angry, orange if happy, etc. It's like no other mood ring on the planet. Just that alone should make it very popular with the younger generation."

Letalis looked at the mark on Gru's hand and asked, "So what does purple mean?"

"It means I'm hungry, my lady," Gru answered with a knowing smile.

Letalis returned the smile and then turned back to Hade. "This is all very interesting, but how does this prevent innocents from being killed?"

"That's actually the easiest thing of all," Hade replied. "All the checkpoints in Vegas are equipped with scanners. If you have one, you can walk right in. If not, the guards will want to have a conversation with you."

"So," Letalis continued, "you're sure everyone in Vegas has one of these?"

"Everyone," Hade affirmed, "including all guards and security personnel. You have to be willing to sign away your personal freedom for the chance to join the club and, while it's a simple procedure, it isn't exactly painless."

Letalis nodded as the pieces began to come together in her mind. "So, everyone in Vegas right now has one of these marks and you have to have money and power to get one of them. Doesn't that mean there are people there who will be missed? This could be a problem for our greater plans."

"No, this is quite literally a blessing in disguise. Getting rid of the vermin in this rat hole is actually going to help us immensely as we go forward. I've gone to great lengths to ensure that just the right people are in the city today. No one is going to miss them: criminals of the worst sort, homicidal degenerates, washed up Hollywood bums and corrupt politicians. I've never said anything more true than this: there is not one shred of innocence in Vegas at the moment."

Letalis thought for a moment, before nodding. "Alright," she answered, "But wouldn't it have been easier without all of them in the city? It would seem to me that the fewer we have to worry about, the better."

"With my schedule, it makes sense to roll as many things together into one as I can," Hade replied.

"You rounded these people up just to have them killed." Letalis wasn't sure whether she should be impressed or horrified, despite who she was.

"Like cattle in a holding pen before the slaughter," Hade admitted. "If you remember your Faust, I am as Mephistopheles, the devil's helper, who didn't search out the souls of the damned, but was more than happy to ferry them on their self-selected paths to hell. Or, perhaps more to your liking, think of me as the coachman in the book Pinocchio, taking little boys to Pleasure Island. I'm rounding up those that have left school and given themselves up freely to all the vices they can dream of, only to be turned into donkeys because of their laziness and poor choices. I'm not making the choices for these people. They're free to choose as they would."

Hade paused and turned to Narn. "If you want to know why I hate this town, it comes down to this. I have no problem with people making whatever decision they want to. I'm as firm a believer in free will as you'll ever find. What I do have a problem with is people thinking there won't be consequences to their actions."

Hade took a few steps over to Gru and held up her hand with the mark spread out just under her skin, his eyes focused back on Letalis.

"Every single person within Cole's walls chose to put this mark into their bodies, knowing exactly what it meant. There isn't a single soul in there that isn't a murderer, adulterer, thief, or purveyor of the worst sins known to humanity, but not one of them thinks there will ever be a reckoning for their crimes. That's the one sin I can't abide: the pride that comes with thinking you're above the consequences of your actions. Everyone has to pay for their sins. For this handful of some of this planet's most vile filth," Hade narrowed his eyes dangerously, "that time is now."

"This mark is how you'll know who is on which side in the upcoming battle," Letalis said thoughtfully and then cocked an eyebrow at Hade as if something had just occurred to her. "This is going worldwide, isn't it?"

Hade touched a finger to his nose. "Welcome to the beta test, my dear," he said quietly. "He will be rolling it out to the world once he has complete control, but we need to get rid of this bunch of scum before we launch it worldwide. It wouldn't do to have the first users be this sort of people."

Letalis finally understood. She understood why they needed Cole, why they needed to take down Vegas in its current form, and where all of this was headed. "After all these years, the end of all things is finally before us," she said softly with a touch of fear and uncertainty in her eyes. If the four companions with them were confused at her emotions, Hade seemed to understand them perfectly.

"It is," he answered solemnly. "And we will be fine if we stick to the plan."

Letalis sighed and looked toward the heavens as if seeking something. When she turned back to Hade, her features had hardened and all traces of apprehension were gone. "So how are you going to sell this to the masses? How are you going to convince twenty-year-olds in

Omaha to sell their souls?"

"Marketing already has an entire campaign ready to go. We're calling it MOTBIE, like potpie. It stands for Mobile Octopus Themed Biotechnological Implanted Electronics," he answered. "In short, we tell them all the cool kids are getting one and they'll line up begging for them."

"Is that really the best you could do?" Letalis asked disdainfully.

"Trust me, I was going for ZOMBIE, but Marketing didn't like Zapped Octopus Mass," he lamented. "I might be able to take over the world, but not even I can override Marketing."

"I can believe that," Letalis sighed. "But it seems like you wouldn't have to be that smart to figure all of this out. Believers all over the world are looking for the mark to show up at any time. I don't see how you could be more obvious. You won't fool anyone."

"We're not trying to, my dear," he said with a knowing smile. "The other side—those that really, truly believe—are never going to allow themselves to be marked, while our side will line up in droves. But the coolness factor and convenience of this is going to get most of the fence sitters to come over to the winning side and, when starvation and panic begins to set in with some of the so-called believers, you're going to see the attrition begin."

"And you?" Letalis asked, turning to Gru. "Why did you get one of these?"

"Our assignment has been all about Vegas for over a year," X interjected before the girl could reply. "When Hade began rolling these out, it only made sense to get them. It's much easier to come and go, that's for certain, and they disappear from view when you want them to, part of the beauty of the octopus skin." He held up his hand and an octopus emerged and then faded to a faint outline.

"I kind of like it, to be honest," Gru added. "Makes us look tough."

"I think you look tough enough as is," Letalis said coldly.

"You haven't seen the goons Cole has running around his little playpen," X remarked drily. "Some of them make us look like girl scouts."

"They might have a change of heart after you go door-to-door tomorrow night," Hade winked, then looked back seriously at Letalis. "Cole's people are ruthless, the visitors are all kinds of sinful, and truly decent people haven't been seen in Vegas in two years. Trust me, we'll sleep well after doing what we must tonight."

"All right," Letalis nodded in agreement. "I'll trust you."

"Good, I'm glad we have that settled," Hade said as he looked back to X. "Now why don't you tell me anything else I need to know before we make our way into town."

"As I'm sure you could guess, Cole is holed up in the Neptune Suite at Caesar's Palace," X explained. "He's been in a drug-fueled funk since the girls got away and he's convinced you're coming to kill him. He's pulled in all of his forces around the Palace and has patrols out with orders to watch for you while he sits and plays cards and waits," X added. "He's not going to be easy to get to."

"We all have a different definition of easy," Hade replied. "I'm sure I'll discuss with Cole his needless preparations and wasted manpower before the night is out. If he's going to be of any use going forward, he's going to need to learn how to think things through much better than he is today."

"You mean you aren't going to kill Cole?" Narn asked in confusion. "I thought all of this was to make an example out of him?"

"Life isn't always as simple as that," Hade replied. "Cole still has a purpose and I need to see if he's up to the challenge. If I just wanted him dead, I would have let you four run amok in Vegas months ago."

That prompted a laugh from the foursome.

"Now if you'll excuse me," Hade said as he opened the back of the Hummer and smiled at what he saw, "I believe it's time to exercise some creative problem solving."

He reached into the Hummer and pulled out a pump action shotgun, ratcheted a shell into the chamber and slung it over his shoulder.

"Will there be anything else?" X asked.

"Nothing more," Hade replied, pulling an old leather bandolier out of the back and slinging it over his other shoulder. There were six very modern looking grenades attached to it. "We'll take it from here. Remember your orders."

"Without question," X replied and then turned and dipped his head toward Letalis. "My lady," he finished.

"Take care of yourselves, my lovelies," she said, then turned away as the group got into the Lexus. A moment later, they were away, leaving Hade and Letalis alone in the darkness of the pre-dawn morning.

"I didn't think they would ever leave," Hade sighed with a smile.

"You were the one who made X give me that infernal Vegas history lesson again," she countered. "Why didn't you tell me about the mark before, though? You don't have to keep treating me like a child."

"I forget sometimes," Hade replied with what sounded like sincere regret. "I promise, I'll make it up to you, though. In the meantime, how about we shake up Vegas a little?"

Hade pulled out a pair of 1873 Colt long-barreled pistols and handed them to her. "I'm sure the aim is horrible, but there's nothing like a little nostalgia to get things started."

Letalis smiled and took the weapons, expertly spinning the barrels on each and examining them closely. "They'll do for the opening round. Do you have holsters?"

Hade grabbed a battered leather belt with double holsters from the Hummer and tossed it to the woman. "So, are you sure you're ready for this?" He asked as he threw his leg back over his motorcycle and held out a hand.

Taking his hand, she climbed up behind him. "As ready as I'll ever be."

"Just remember the plan," he said, his eyes focused on the road before them. "If we follow it to the letter, everything will turn out okay."

Letalis wrapped her arms around Hade as he gunned the motorcycle to life and pointed it toward Las Vegas and Cole Banyon.

CHAPTER 21

Mesopotamia: For the first time in weeks, Michael Dalacourt found himself entering his dreams distant from Gilgamesh's great chamber. Tonight, he was floating, bodiless, within a small hut. While he had no physical connection to his senses, he felt as if he had spent his entire life in this dry, sparsely furnished room. He knew the smell of the constricted space, the taste of the cooling oatmeal on the rickety table, the temperature of the light coming through the window, and everything about the girl shivering alone on the straw mat on the dirt floor. She was Enheduana and he could feel the terror rolling off the young girl as if it were a tangible, material object. Something horrific was about to happen here, and it pained him beyond measure to know he was powerless to stop it.

The door to the one-room hut opened and Dalacourt was not at all surprised to see the huge frame of Gilgamesh enter. He was shirtless, clad only in leather breeches, and wore his weapons openly on a bronze belt. The warrior approached the straw mat and looked down at the girl with a lustful smile that showed his perfectly white teeth.

"It is your wedding night," he said, grinning lewdly.

"Yes, my lord," was all the young girl could say, her voice meek and whispered. She dared not look at him. Dalacourt wished he could look away as well, but there was nowhere to go. The dream forced him to witness what was happening, a silent spirit powerless to intervene.

"It is the lord's right to visit brides before their wedding night," Gilgamesh went on, towering over the terrified girl. "It is my benevolent gift to you—your one chance to have a strong, powerful son instead of a weakling like the poor excuse for a man you have chosen to marry. I am a gracious lord, am I not?"

"Yes, my lord," she repeated quietly, keeping her eyes downcast as

Gilgamesh unstrapped his sword and tossed it to the floor. Desperate to witness a different outcome to what was about to happen, Dalacourt prayed that someone, anyone, would arrive to stop this travesty from happening. But who could stand up to a god? Who could save the girl from the terrible assault she was about to suffer?

And then, against all odds, the door flew open and a giant, nearly as large as Gilgamesh himself, stormed into the room. Almost as if Dalacourt's prayer had been answered, the newcomer threw himself at Gilgamesh with a roar of challenge and both men crashed to the floor in a flurry of thrashing limbs, wild swings and guttural oaths.

The girl, Enheduana, screamed in terror as the two warriors fought, and as the combatants crashed against one of the walls of the hut, she found the strength to run for the door and escape into the night. The epic battle between the violent titans lasted only moments longer, though, as Gilgamesh got the upper hand and pressed his dagger to the neck of his attacker.

"Before I open your throat," Gilgamesh growled dangerously, "I would know who disturbs me from my lordly duties."

"I am Enkidu, he who kneels before Enlil and the Lord of the Pleasant Place," the man replied, breathing heavily but still speaking with powerful conviction. "I am the falling star, I am the axe, I am the man who saves his friend. I am your companion and your equal."

"No man is my equal." Gilgamesh growled.

"I am," the stranger replied without hesitation.

Gilgamesh paused and considered the boast. Was it possible? Was this man truly the answer to his dream? He released his opponent and climbed to his feet. "The hunter spoke to me of you, but I did not believe him," he said as the stranger got to his own feet and faced him. "You look like me, but you are shorter and stronger of bone. I do not fear you, though, for I have slain all who would be my rival."

Enkidu smiled and bowed his head. "I am no rival. There is not another like you in the world. Enlil has given you the kingship, for your head is elevated above all other men."

Gilgamesh was still unsure and turned the long dagger over in his hand in contemplation. "If you know of my kingship, then why stop me from my way with the woman? Do you not know it is my right?"

"My king," Enkidu replied, "I come to you with a warning."

"So you say."

"I was once a wild man, content to live among the beasts," the man explained. "One day I went to drink at the wells when I met Shamhat, who the hunter had sent to subdue me through the woman's power. I fell victim to her powers and now the wild beasts reject me and I am alone. A cry chokes my throat, my arms are slack, and my strength has turned to weakness. You are better without the woman."

"You have great knowledge and a wider mind and are right," Gilgamesh finally nodded and slid his weapon back into his sheath. "You are the one I seek. I am Gilgamesh, the Tree of Godlike Balance. Will you travel with me as we seek after something more?"

"Yes, my lord," Enkidu replied. "I wish for something more as well. I seek after the glory of the gods."

"And who with sense does not?" Gilgamesh questioned. "But who, my new brother, can ascend to the heavens? Only the gods dwell forever in the sunlight. As for humans, their days are numbered; their achievements are but a puff of wind. But perhaps we can leave our mark on this world. I have waited for a companion for many long years to help me in the one quest I cannot complete alone. You will help me defeat an ancient spirit, the roaring lion that men today call Humbaba."

Enkidu faltered. "My lord, Humbaba is a mighty monster. His roar is the flood, his mouth is fire, and his breath is death. Why do you wish to do this thing?"

"I am not merely your king, I am two-thirds of a god!" Gilgamesh exclaimed. "I am immortal. Do you not know me? Do you not know my names? I am the farmer, the wanderer, the cursed one, the lost one, he that harms sevenfold, the first city builder, husband to Awan, father to Enoch, the marked one, the blood drinker, the first murderer. Do you not know me now, brother?"

"I have heard of the marked one," Enkidu said in disbelief. "You are Cain, the brother slayer."

Gilgamesh nodded. "Join me and you will not fear death. Do not let the combat diminish your courage. One cannot stand alone. When two go together each will shield himself and save his companion. A slippery path is not feared by two people who help each other."

"I am lost to women, lost to the beasts, with nothing left but my years. I am with you to the end. I will not fear death. Surely, we will seize and kill Humbaba and throw his body down on the plain. We will destroy this earth and dwell in the sunlight with the gods."

"No, brother," Gilgamesh said with a knowing smile, feeling for the first time in a long time that his fate had turned for the better, "we will stand in the sunlight by ourselves."

The dream ended and Michael Dalacourt snapped awake to find Oliveira kneeling beside him, looking intently at him. Despite their weeks together, he had not gotten used to the dead eyes of the formerly deceased father and he cried out in spite of himself.

Oliveira laid a cold hand on Dalacourt's, which did nothing to calm the younger man down. "You were speaking in your sleep again," Oliveira observed softly. "Are you still troubled by visions?"

Shaking visibly, Dalacourt nodded, and then sat up and swung his legs off the bed. It was the middle of the night and, as usual, the being that was once Father Oliveira had been reading the Bible by the light of a small lamp. "Do you ever sleep?" Dalacourt asked, rubbing his eyes and avoiding the question.

"I have no need for sleep," the old Brazilian answered evenly.

"Even the dead sleep."

"Since I am neither dead or alive…" Oliveira replied and then trailed off.

"I meant nothing by that," Dalacourt mistook the older man's sudden change in countenance to mean his words had insulted him.

But Oliveira was staring at the door to their cell, an odd look on his face.

"What is it?" Dalacourt asked, following his gaze until he felt it, too—a deep bone-chilling cold. It wasn't a coldness attributed to a drop in temperature, but an iciness that began to seep into his body, filling his very soul with dread.

Something was coming.

Oliveira straightened and held the Bible close to his heart, wrapping his arms around it, staring at the door in complete silence.

The lone light in the room flickered and then Dalacourt smelled it—an ancient and musty odor, similar to the catacombs underneath the Vatican. He shuddered as he remembered the last time he had visited those catacombs. Oliveira, freshly raised from the dead, had tried to kill him. But the terror of that moment beneath the Vatican paled in comparison to what he felt now. Oliveira had been an aberration then. Whatever was coming now held within it an evil beyond anything he had ever felt before.

The door handle turned and, with a resounding creak, the huge steel door pushed slowly open. To Dalacourt, what entered the room could only be described as death itself. It was a being, easily taller than any man, and it was draped in robes of black. But the cloth was tattered and rotting, revealing the creature for what it was. Skeletal hands protruded from the sleeves, bits of flesh still hanging from whitened bones. A nearly skull-like face was faintly visible within the shadows of a cowl, but the glowing red points of its eyes seared into Dalacourt and he did the only thing he could think of doing.

He screamed in abject terror.

The specter glided into the room, its head turning slowly from Dalacourt to Oliveira and back as if it was examining them both. For Dalacourt, fleeing was not an option as his terrified body was entirely incapable of movement. Oliveira simply stared at the thing impassively.

"I know you," the old Brazilian said, gazing at the monster.

The thing remained silent, its skeletal head tilting slightly as if it was regarding Oliveira closely. Then it reached out, placing its boney hand on the side of the Brazilian's face. Dalacourt had the distinct impression that if the creature did the same to him, he would die a horrible and agonizing death. But Oliveira continue to look at it, his flesh unaffected.

"Your touch affects only the living," Oliveira stated quietly, his voice one of curiosity. "You have no power over me."

"What…what is it?" Dalacourt finally gasped, mustering up the courage to speak, trying hard to overcome its terrifying presence. The specter withdrew its hand from Oliveira and turned its skeletal features toward him, sending a fresh wave of dizzying terror washing over him.

"It is an ancient spirit," Oliveira answered and turned to face Dalacourt as well. "It is here for you."

Michael Dalacourt could have wilted and collapsed, wailing and screaming in terror. But something within him flared to life—the same strength that had filled him when he had faced De Solei—and he drew himself up straight. "If I am to die," he said slowly, "I will not do it cowering before an emissary of Satan."

I am the emissary of another. The thing replied, but without voice. The words formed in knots and waves within Dalacourt's mind, giving no hint of sound or indication of emotion. The language was not English, nor any other he had ever heard, but he understood what was thought implicitly. It was as if the being had caused him to see the words in his mind.

"What…do…you want?" he stammered, unsure how to respond.

I have come to give you enlightenment, priest, the creature shared.

Dalacourt could feel the scorn in the word "priest" he felt slightly emboldened by the spirit's derision of his former position in the church. "I require nothing from you," he said.

We shall see, it replied. *Behold.*

And Dalacourt saw.

The images assailed his mind like a storm, allowing for no escape. It was nothing like his dreams of Gilgamesh, where he floated along as an observer. With this new vision, time became meaningless. He could see everything—past, present and future—all at the same time. It completely disoriented him and was unlike anything he had ever experienced. It was a kaleidoscope of horror, images woven together from things he knew had happened and things he knew were coming. He saw everything. He was everything.

He witnessed the enormous waves of the recent tsunami crashing upon beaches and coastlines across the world, destroying buildings and sweeping away victims. In the space of seconds, he saw millions and millions die and he experienced each individual's moment of death with a clarity that threatened to drive him insane. He knew their memories, their dreams, and their despair in their final moments. He was a young girl, ripped from her mother's arms and swept out to sea. He was an old man, crushed to death when the building he was in collapsed on him. He was an entire family, separately and yet simultaneously mother, father, and three children, all engulfed in a killing fire when their car plunged into a fissure that cracked open beneath them. He felt each and every one of the dead's full range of emotions as they died. But what crushed him most was that none of them understood why. They did not see that their death was necessary, that each of them had died to move humanity one step closer to the end. They had died to fulfill prophecy. They died because God decreed it. They died because he, Michael Dalacourt, had begun the first woe and ushered in the end of days.

Within the sweeping, eternal scope of the vision, he saw towns ravaged by famine and disease. He saw crops withered and wasted, children malnourished and starving, and the living burning the dead on huge funeral pyres. He was the starving child who would not wake up the next morning. He was the husband crying over his lost wife. He was the grandmother left for dead while her children fled. He felt everything, knew everything, but understood nothing. For a moment, he thought these to be distant lands, foreign peoples, third world nations. Then he saw the signs. Hastings, Nebraska. Mitchell, South Dakota. Carroll, Iowa. Great Bend, Kansas. The list went on and on, into the hundreds, but each city told the same story.

He watched millions die. He felt their pain, their sickness, and their hollowing hunger. He felt their hopelessness. And then he saw the specter. It was always there, lurking in the background, bringing death to each town it visited. For a moment, righteous anger took hold of him, but the creature's words sent his psyche into another tailspin.

I am an emissary of another, it said again, replacing his anger with the cold, clarity of truth. *I bring death to resolve the promise of God.*

Michael Dalacourt's faith was shaken to the core. He could feel his own spirit begin to unravel, breaking apart from the lamentations of the innocent, and he added his own voice to their desperate cries.

But the specter was not done with him and despite his pleas, he was forced to endure more. He saw space. Earth was behind him, a beautiful marbled blue orb. His attention turned outward, taking in the countless stars of creation, and he pondered for a moment, why it was showing him the cosmos—clean, organized, and tranquil. Then he saw the shadow, a giant and ponderous mass hurtling toward him at incredible speed. In space, there was no sound, but he heard it, nevertheless. It spoke to him in a low buzzing noise, the countless voices of the damned whispering of the tragedy yet to come.

The object neared ever closer until he finally recognized it for what it was: a colossal satellite heading directly for the earth. Born of stone and pocked with holes exuding a long trail of poisonous mist, he knew there was no force on earth capable of stopping the destruction this harbinger of doom was set to unleash. As if to prove he still did not understand the true terror behind this goliath, he felt both the effects of the impact and the toxins as the massive comet passed through his celestial countenance. The collision wracked his entire being with unimaginable pain and sickness, far worse than anything he had ever endured. Fever took hold, his stomach heaved and he thought he would vomit out his very soul.

But just as quickly as it had come, the immense rock passed through him and he found himself looking at it from behind. It was then that he realized this was the fulfillment of Revelation, chapter eight, verses ten and eleven: "*And the third angel sounded, and there fell a great star from heaven, burning as it were a lamp, and it fell upon the third part of the rivers, and upon the fountains of waters; and the name of the star is called Wormwood: and the third part of the waters became wormwood; and many men died of the waters, because they were made bitter.*"

This was Wormwood and as he watched, the massive rock—miles wide—entered the atmosphere and began catching fire. Instead of slamming into the earth like a thousand nuclear weapons, however, it began breaking apart as its structural integrity vanished. Pieces of it peeled and flaked away, turning to smoke and dust. Caught by the jet-stream, it was rapidly distributed around the globe. That's when the horror became apparent. The residue of Wormwood began settling upon the earth, laying an oily film on oceans, seas, and rivers. It found its way deep into the earth, filtering into water supplies the world over.

People drank of it and they died by the millions, wracked with agony and overwhelmed by suffering. Again, Dalacourt became the dying and the dead. He felt each one of them; lived their lives and experienced their ends. He felt deeply and personally each and every death and he knew sorrow as never before.

This is promised by God.

"No," he wept, tears in his eyes. "It's not supposed to be like this."

But it is, priest, the thing said in his mind, cold and uncaring.

"Why are you showing me this?" he cried out, wrapping his arms around himself as if frozen to the bone.

I am showing you what has been, what is, and what will be, it replied. *There are few who can understand what God has decreed, and fewer still who can understand why. There are perhaps a handful of souls who can see such things and still believe in God's mercy. You are one of these, but that does not make you special. It makes you weak. You are no king, Michael. You are a dead man, like every other man who has ever walked upon the land.*

And then, with jarring ferocity, Dalacourt felt his whole presence shift to another place as the demon showed him its final vision.

Michael Dalacourt saw himself, his body broken and bleeding among rocks and boulders in a place he did not recognize. A bundle of rags lay nearby, ruffled by an unseen wind. He struggled to draw his final breath, his dimmed eyes staring up to the closed heavens, bloody tears running down his cheeks. He saw his body shudder with a final racking breath and then saw himself go still. Death had claimed him as it had claimed so many others and only one question resonated in his mind, the same one that every dying person felt. Had he done enough in the eyes of God?

You will die and what you possess will pass from you. God has commanded it.

"No," Dalacourt objected again. "There must be something more. There must be a reason for all of this."

There is only what you see; only what God decrees; only His reason. You will bear the burden until your death. Then it will pass to the fourth.

"The fourth?"

She is the hidden one, it replied. *She is the usurper. She is the temptress. She will take it from you and you will fail, just as you must.*

"I just…I don't understand," Dalacourt breathed and looked at the specter with tear-filled eyes. "Who are you?"

I am the companion, it responded simply, its glowing red eyes locked on Dalacourt. *I am the second, the emissary. I am the axe. I am the one that will claim your life in the end.*

Dalacourt blinked and found himself back in his jail cell, alone with Father Oliveira, the steel door shut tightly as if it had never opened. Disoriented and weak, he collapsed to the floor, Oliveira standing over him.

"I believe what you saw is the truth, Michael," the old priest said quietly, understanding Dalacourt's unspoken horror.

The younger man turned his head slowly to regard the old Brazilian. Shock and coldness still permeated his body, but for the first time since they had been imprisoned, he saw something beyond the blankness in Oliveira's face. He saw sorrow marked on the man's face. He saw grief.

"How could you know what I saw?" Dalacourt asked almost

numbly.

"I witnessed what you did, Michael," Oliveira answered truthfully. "I have had the same dreams you have had. I see them in my mind as they are shown to me, just as you see them as they are shown to you. I saw the same visions the specter showed you—the floods, the famine, the meteor. And I believe I am beginning to understand."

Dalacourt finally caught his breath and felt his heart begin to slow. "This…creature. This thing that was here..." he went on, shivering. "What was it?"

"It is an ancient and evil spirit," Oliveira explained. "He fought in the Great War in Heaven; he was cast down along with Satan; and he was chosen by Cain as his right hand, his companion. He is the axe."

"Enkidu called himself the axe in my dream."

"That is correct," Oliveira stated. "He is indeed Enkidu, the companion of Gilgamesh."

"He also referred to himself as the second," Dalacourt said quietly, mulling over the terrifying experience.

"Do you remember he said you would lose what you possess to the fourth?" Oliveira continued.

Dalacourt nodded, the implications clear to him. "He was speaking of the Four Horsemen of the Apocalypse." His mind turned to the first vision he was shown, of the terrible deaths of so many throughout the Midwest. "He is Famine. He is one of them."

"That would make Gilgamesh a horseman as well," Oliveira added. "That would make Gilgamesh the first."

"But Gilgamesh is no longer alive," Dalacourt said, before realizing that he had just been visited by Gilgamesh's companion. "But he would be, wouldn't he. If Gilgamesh is indeed Cain as he said he was in the dream..."

"Then he, too, would exist today," Oliveira finished Dalacourt's thought. "In ancient times, Cain could have taken on the mantle and moniker of Gilgamesh and if he is one of the four horsemen, what better companion for him than Enkidu?"

"So it's all true," Dalacourt said softly, his voice suddenly devoid of hope. "It's really here. The end is close."

"This world has been in the final days since the crucifixion of Christ," Oliveira corrected. "But the four now walk abroad. For that to be so, only a handful of years must remain before the final battle of Armageddon."

Dalacourt shook his head and placed it in his hands. He was not certain he could handle much more before his mind simply broke apart. "It said...Enkidu said this was all decreed by God," he stammered.

"It told you only what it wanted you to know," Oliveira countered. "Do not forget that it is a spirit of great evil and is capable of deception on the level of Satan himself. It seeks to take away your hope, to cause you to dwindle into unbelief."

"But millions of people are dying," Dalacourt pleaded, "and millions and millions more will die. Good people. Righteous people. I know, I have seen into the souls of all of them," he finished, shuddering at the memory. "I am them."

"They will die," Oliveira nodded, "and the righteous will stand at the feet of God Himself, while the wicked will be cast into the fires of hell."

"But the suffering…"

"…is brought about by unbelief of man and by the machinations of Satan," Oliveira finished. "It is not brought about by God. Mankind has always had free will and sadly, innocents suffer when man chooses poorly."

Dalacourt looked up, focusing on Oliveira, looking at him for the longest time. "You seem to be speaking with more conviction," he finally said quietly. "Are you finding your faith?"

"Perhaps," Oliveira replied thoughtfully. "Are you losing yours?"

To that, Michael Dalacourt had to admit he had no answer.

"You will have to answer that eventually, but not here," Oliveira stated, turning the discussion away from the painful visions that Dalacourt had endured. "We will be released on the morrow."

"How do you know?"

"Hade said so," Oliveira answered plainly. "He said we would be released after you had been visited by one more. There was a reason for that visit."

"And what is that?" Dalacourt snapped, letting his anger and frustration show. "To rob me of my faith before I die?"

"Yes," Oliveira replied unemotionally. "You apparently have something important to do yet or they would not bother with you."

"But I have seen my death," Dalacourt lamented.

"Then make it worth something, Michael," Oliveira said softly, reaching out and placing a cold hand on the young man's shoulder. "Do not underestimate your ability to shoulder your burdens. Or God's understanding of those burdens," he finished.

And then Oliveira turned away, saying nothing more to the troubled priest. He seated himself back in his chair and began pouring over the Bible once again.

CHAPTER 22

Las Vegas, Nevada: Hade slowly steered the motorcycle over the cracked and broken concrete, carefully skirting the rusted debris that had been there since the chaos of two years ago. The sun was still safely below the horizon as he idled the bike next to the "Welcome to Fabulous Las Vegas" sign, miraculously still lighting up the entry point from the south to the famous Las Vegas strip. "So, what do you think?" he asked his companion.

"You would think he could have cleaned things up a bit," Letalis said distastefully, her arms still wrapped tightly around his chest. "He's got the money; why not splurge a little? Plant some lilacs or something."

"When you see him, I think you should bring that up as a suggestion," Hade rumbled as he slowly pulled the motorcycle next to the burned out hulk of a stretch limousine. "Since all of the guests are ferried over from the airfield," he went on, "all that matters to him is what's behind the walls. After tonight, of course, it won't matter which side of the wall he's on," he finished, killing the engine.

Letalis smoothly slid off the bike and checked both of her Peacemakers to make sure they were fully loaded. Hade dismounted as well and stood still, quietly looking down the road. Other than the sign, there were no lights in this part of the city, nothing illuminating the streets until one reached the main gate to the city center, which was easily seen from where they currently stood.

In the past year, Cole Banyon had begun fortifying Vegas' defensive abilities. The highlight was the ten foot concrete wall topped by razor-wire that surrounded his compound, complete with guard posts spaced regularly along its length. Everything outside of the walls had been either destroyed or left to slowly crumble in the desert heat, haunted by things the few lived to see and tell about. Sand had covered much of what lie on the outskirts, giving what was left of the city the feel of an oasis that could rival even the greatest cities of the mighty Egyptian empires of old.

Within the fortress walls it was business as usual, with all the lights, sounds, beautiful people, decadence and luxury expected of Las Vegas. The walls encircled an area of roughly twenty city blocks surrounding the considerably shortened Strip and had only three entrances. Besides the one X had dubbed "Checkpoint Charlie" that they were getting ready to exploit, there was a heavily fortified service entrance off of I-15 on East Flamingo and another to the north where people could be shuttled over to the Desert Inn Country Club for some golf.

X had been correct—it would not be easy to get to Cole, but no walls were going to keep him safe tonight from the world's most fearsome predator. Nothing could.

"We have company," Hade said softly, peering into the darkness and pulling one of the grenades from the leather strap of his bandoleer.

"Six contacts fanned out across the road four blocks up," Letalis confirmed, looking into the darkness and clearly seeing the soldiers moving cautiously in their direction. "They're on to us," she added. "I'm sure your motorcycle light had nothing to do with that."

"I wanted to at least give them a sporting chance," Hade chuckled.

The woman gave him a scornful glance. "And grenades are sporting?" She sniffed derisively and without waiting for an answer, brought both her pistols up. In less than ten seconds, she had squeezed off seven shots, firing into the darkness seemingly at random.

Hade laughed, his own vision tracking her targets. "You missed with one."

"Double tap," Letalis replied as she lowered the weapons and began walking forward. "No heat signature. One of yours?"

"Not one of mine," Hade rumbled angrily, considering what it meant. "This might be a little more difficult than we anticipated."

The two covered the distance quickly to the dead guards, passing under the ghostly remains of the Mandalay Bay, the Luxor, and the Excalibur. They reached the first body, a bullet through his forehead, just above his left eye.

"I know you want to check," Hade said, toeing the dead soldier over.

Letalis nodded silently and knelt beside the body. Pulling off the soldier's left glove, she could easily make out the shape of the MOTBIE implant, the color already going gray in death.

"Satisfied?" Hade asked, a little sharper than he intended.

"I told you I trust you," she replied evenly. "But I still wanted to see for myself."

"I know," Hade answered, his voice measurably softer. Then he looked up and asked, "Where's your two-shot kill?"

Without a word, Letalis moved left until they were standing over the body of the guard in question. There was a bullet hole drilled neatly into the man's forehead and another through the center of his throat. Hade knew that second bullet's exit would have severed the soldier's spine, but if the man was supposed to be dead, no one had told him. The guard looked up at them, eyes glittering red in the darkness, his mouth moving soundlessly. Hade knelt down, reached out and peeled a lip back from his teeth, revealing a sharpened canine. He looked up at Letalis and his features creased in anger.

"He's watching us," she ruminated quietly, returning his gaze.

"But he doesn't know anything," Hade replied and reached down and placed a massive hand on each side of the wounded man's head. A quick jerking movement brought a pop of bone and the light went out behind the guard's eyes.

"He doesn't want us here," Letalis pointed out. "You know that, right?"

"I'm about done caring what he wants and what he doesn't want," Hade said, his anger smoldering. "I'm here to get Cole and nothing is going to change that. Not even him."

Letalis stood quietly for a moment, her black leather outfit shimmering slightly as it reflected the light emitted from the 'Welcome to Vegas,' sign. "How many more do you think he has here in Vegas?"

"I can't imagine he would waste too many of his resources on Cole, regardless of what he suspects," Hade replied. "Still, why wait to find out?" He popped the pin from one of the grenades. "Get behind me," he added as he started off toward the gate. At a block out, he simultaneously threw the grenade as he pulled the shotgun. The resulting explosion blew a good portion of the right side gatehouse to pieces, lighting up the night. Shouts rang out and sporadic gunfire began to erupt in their general direction.

"Once more into the breach," Hade said resolutely and began firing at anything that moved on the wall. While Hade used his shotgun and grenades to sow large-scale destruction in front of them, Letalis followed and calmly picked off individual soldiers with well-placed shots from her old pistols, reloading as necessary.

With the threats eliminated at the wall, they moved through the gate and onto the main thoroughfare that led to the Palace. All about them, the lights from the various casinos lit up the night and a combination of pounding music and the electronic sounds of countless slot machines filled the early morning darkness. But now that the gatehouse was burning and gunfire was erupting in the streets, another sound could be heard rising out of the casinos.

Screams.

Hade tossed one last grenade through the window of a nearby shop that appeared closed and then sent several shotgun blasts through the windows of one across the street.

"What are you shooting at?" Letalis demanded as she calmly put a bullet through the heart of a charging soldier.

"Just ringing the doorbells," Hade said and strode purposefully to a nearby red car, tossing the empty shotgun and grenade belt to the pavement. The car was a beautiful Seville and the trunk was already popped. He raised the lid and let out a low whistle as more soldiers began rushing out of the nearest casino—The New York / New York.

He reached into the trunk and pulled out a Heckler and Koch G36 assault rifle with a long clip taped to another, facing the other direction. A two second clip-flip was all that was needed to double the weapon's capacity. He tossed it to Letalis, who had dropped her own empty pistols and leather holsters.

"I don't know, it seems like such a big gun for a little girl," Hade said, playful sarcasm in his voice.

"I'm pretty sure I can handle it," she replied, matching his tone. "What are you going to play with? A rocket launcher?"

"Maybe later," he smirked, reaching into the truck of the car again. This time, he pulled out an absolutely massive weapon, a hand-held M134. "Nothing like a warm helicopter gun to brighten the night," he grinned. "Ol' Painless is waiting!" He smiled at Letalis, who was looking at him as if he was crazy.

"You know…" he prompted. "*Predator*? Blaine? 'I ain't got time to bleed?' This would be more fun if, occasionally, you would watch an action movie."

"I don't watch movies and you know it," she said as she jacked the first round into the chamber of her rifle. Just as she finished speaking, a group of soldiers emerged from past the MGM Grand on their right.

She spun around, moving down the side of the car, firing off bursts from her weapon at soldiers who were hurrying toward the commotion, still sadly unaware of what they were actually facing.

She did not miss.

"Atta girl," Hade grinned as he swung the huge chain gun toward the entrance of the New York / New York. Hundreds of people were hurrying out—soldiers and civilians alike—scattering in the darkness, looking in vain for safety. Hade lit them all up. Bullets tore through people and blasted into the lobby of the casino. In just a few seconds, the front of the casino had been turned into a slaughterhouse. Anyone trying to get out was torn to pieces.

"If I could, I would carry one of these with me everywhere I go," he shouted gleefully. "I'd never have to wait in line for a sandwich again."

"Cute," Letalis replied, "but you missed one."

Hade looked up and sure enough, on the steps of the casino, one soldier still stood, black blood leaking from over a dozen bullet holes. Hunched over, the soldier raised his head slowly, eyes glaring at him. Hade saw the primal hunger in them and knew the stench of blood had sent the man into a frenzy. Without another thought, he sent another torrent of shells into the demon. When he was done shooting, there was little left.

"You keep taking out the babysitters and he's going to be plenty pissed at you," Letalis said.

"That's the general idea," Hade replied dangerously and then swung his weapon back around, pointing it down the street. He laid on the trigger with a vengeance, sending hundreds of rounds down the strip, not caring about casualties or damage. A short time later, the gun's ammo box ran empty and Hade tossed the weapon to the side.

Beside him, Letalis had run through both clips of her own weapon at about the same time. "This is fun," she remarked, looking down the street at the carnage. The bodies of dozens of soldiers and patrons were scattered in the streets, most of them dead, some of them still writhing in agony. "We haven't had such sport in a long time."

"You've never had such sport," Hade corrected, "and I don't want you liking this sort of thing too much."

Letalis smiled at that and motioned forward. "Shall we?"

Hade grunted in annoyance and had only taken two steps forward when the attack came out of the darkness behind them. It was one of the super soldiers, black blood leaking from bullet holes riddled across his torso. He moved silently, grabbing Letalis from behind and slamming her to the broken pavement. Hade whirled around, pulling his massive Desert Eagle from his coat.

But Letalis was already moving as well, kicking herself back to her feet like an accomplished martial artist. The wounded soldier reached for her, but she grabbed his wrist with her right hand and slammed her left hand against his elbow, shattering bone and tearing muscle. Undeterred, he reached forward again with his other hand, but it was Hade who stopped him this time as his own massive hand closed down over the soldier's remaining good arm. Muscles bulged and bone popped as Hade tightened his grip. The soldier's mouth opened in a furious hiss as Hade brought his huge handgun up. He shoved the barrel into the monster's mouth, shattering teeth, and pulled the trigger. The soldier's head exploded into a fine, reddish black mist as the body fell to the ground, legs still twitching feebly.

"I shouldn't have let you talk me into bringing you here," Hade scowled as he wiped blood off his duster. "It's too dangerous."

"I can handle it," Letalis said angrily, placing a hand on his shoulder to regain some stability. "Now, let's finish this." She walked back over to the Seville and took out two Steyr Tactical Machine

Pistols. Hade thought about arguing with her, but instead nodded wordlessly as the two of them started back down the street toward Caesar's Palace. By now, the resistance being arrayed against them was minimal at best. A small group of soldiers broke on them from their right, but Hade just stood watching as Letalis mowed them down with pistols, every burst finding flesh. Hade slid the Desert Eagle back under his duster, knowing he would have no use for it in the next few minutes. Most of the rest of the soldiers and patrons were holed up in the casinos and hotels on either side of the road, unwilling to risk their lives any further. It wouldn't matter in the end. They were all finished.

They approached a red Tahoe and Hade nodded appreciatively as he popped the back open and looked inside. There were two heavy black cases. He flipped open the clasps on one and raised the lid. Inside was the shape of a shoulder-mounted rocket launcher.

"You weren't kidding, were you," Letalis remarked with a smile.

"Nope," Hade answered jovially, his good mood restored. "This is an FGM-148 Javelin fire-and-forget anti-tank missile. It's self-guided with pre-launch lock-on and also does quite well against helicopters and buildings." He lifted the weapon out and slung it over his shoulder. "The other is for you."

"While I'm flattered you thought of me, what could I possibly use this for?"

"X told me earlier that Cole has a surprise for us."

"Cole has to know he can't stop us," Letalis replied.

"He thinks otherwise," Hade said as he pointed over to the Cosmopolitan. "Listen."

"What is that?" Letalis said, her brow furrowing in concentration. "I can barely hear it."

"Concentrate, my young padawan."

A moment later, a look of understanding flashed across her face.

"That sounds like a tank," she said. "Cole has a tank? Whose brilliant idea was it to give him a tank?"

"Who wouldn't want a tank?" Hade answered with a shrug.

"That wasn't an answer," came her clearly perturbed response.

"By the sound of it, it must be an old M1 Abrams," Hade said, as he opened up the second case and handed the rocket launcher to Letalis. He paused and looked at the woman as she examined her new weapon. "Sorry, I couldn't find one in pink," he chuckled.

"I loathe that color," she said, wrinkling her nose in distaste. "Black is just fine." She held up a spare rocket and looked at Hade.

"Armor piercing," he answered her unspoken question. "Top-of-the-line active military ordinance—tandem warhead. It'll cut through tank armor like a knife through butter."

Letalis looked intently through the scope as she swiveled in a circle, taking in the entire Strip. She stopped at one of the few casinos they had walked by that didn't now carry scars from their barrage. "Shall I save one shell for the Bellagio when we're done with the tank?"

"No, leave it be," Hade answered. "I've always loved the Fiori di Como in the entryway. I'd hate to see it needlessly destroyed."

"So, we're leaving it alone because you fancy the thousands of brightly colored glass flowers attached to the ceiling?"

"Of course," he answered. "When Alexander razed the city of Thebes, he ordered his men not to destroy the home of Pliny, one of his favorite poets. They burned the entire city to the ground but left that one house standing. Even in the darkest of times, art, style and culture are worth protecting."

"You never cease to amaze me," she said as she slipped the second rocket snuggly into a belt loop anyway.

"And that, my precious, is what makes this life so very much worth living," he said with a smile. Pointing to the left side of the street, he continued. "What do you say we turn Cole's folly here into a little contest?"

Letalis' eyes lit up. "Oh, I'm liking this already."

"You take the left flank, I'll walk the right," he explained. "Whoever does the most damage, wins."

"And the winner gets…" she trailed off.

"Winner picks dinner tonight," Hade laughed.

"Prepare to lose," Letalis laughed right back.

The two split, each heading for their designated side of the street. "Here it comes," Hade said loudly as the turret of the tank emerged from behind the far wall of the casino. Several strides ahead, Letalis took the first shot and hit the tank in the rear, just above the tread. The explosion was immense, flames charring the side and likely mangling anything inside. The turret continued to spin toward them, however, indicating she had not taken out the gunner.

From the other side of the road, Hade put his own rocket into the left tread of the behemoth, eliminating the tank's ability to move. As the smoke began to clear from the explosion, Letalis saw the turret continue to move toward her. She took aim and put her second rocket directly into the side of the it. Fire and shrapnel exploded in all directions, leaving the Abrams a smoking hulk in the middle of the road. It had never fired a shot.

"That's not fair!" Hade shouted from his side of the street. "You can't use two shells!"

"All's fair in love and rocket launchers," Letalis yelled back over the loud popping of the tank's ammo cooking off inside the ruined hulk. "Looks like I'm picking dinner tonight!"

"Only under protest," Hade growled in mock anger, looking past the ruined tank and toward Caesar's Palace. "Almost there," he changed the topic as he started toward the casino. He stopped suddenly, however, as he caught a familiar scent upon the night air. "I was afraid of this," he said as he stared straight ahead.

"What is that stench?" Letalis asked as she rejoined him in the middle of the road, her nose wrinkling as she, too, caught the same smell.

"Trouble," came the cryptic response. "Ancient trouble."

Hade began walking toward Caesar's Palace, cutting around the far end of the Bellagio fountains and onto East Flamingo, Letalis trying to keep up as he strode forward with purpose. As he walked, he reached within his coat and behind him, pulling out a sword that had been strapped tightly to his back.

"You're carrying a blade?" Letalis asked sharply.

"You're not to get involved in this," Hade said in a tone that told her not to question him. "These are very real and very dangerous individuals and they are most certainly not here at Cole's behest."

Letalis caught the man's tension and quickly tucked herself in behind him as they walked. He slowed his pace as he approached the entrance to the Palace, his eyes scanning back and forth. A few moments later, four men strode out to meet them. These weren't just ordinary men, either. All four were powerfully built and dressed in the military uniforms of the old Roman republic.

"Well, well, well," Hade said, resting the sword on his shoulder as his gaze traveled across the faces of the newcomers. "To what do I owe the displeasure?"

Hade's question was met with silence, as the men stood in a line, shoulder to shoulder.

"Who are these men?" Letalis finally asked, breaking the quiet. She could feel the potent aura surrounding them and knew there was something supernatural about them.

"These," Hade said caustically, "are four of the foulest, pathetic, most degenerative souls to ever take up space on this planet."

"A generous compliment coming from one such as yourself," one of the men finally spoke up, his voice bitter.

"It was not intended as such, Magnus Flavius," Hade said darkly. "I see you're accompanied by your captain, Lucius Publius, and the twins, Tiberius and Caius Antonius, as always."

"And you are where you should not be, as always. We are here to politely ask you to turn back," Magnus said, his tone never changing.

"Says the coward who fled the battle of Carrhae."

"You weren't there, Hade," the centurion snapped, anger rising in his voice. "You didn't have to follow that fool Crassus against Parthia. We had no choice."

"You gave up your brothers in arms for your own gain, Magnus, and were cursed for it."

"One man's curse is another's blessing," one of the twins said maliciously.

"Of course," Hade replied. "And for two thousand years, you've feasted on the flesh of innocents." Hade leisurely spun the weapon in his hand, taking a step forward. "I'll be honest," he went on, "I'm actually pleased to find you here. I can clean up one of the many messes he's created over the centuries."

"You speak sacrilege of the One," Lucius stated hotly. "You are part of the plan, just as we are, Hade. You already know this, so why tempt the fates?"

"A man makes his own fate," Hade replied. "Things are happening fast these days; things you don't understand. And the time has come for each rat to find his own way off this sinking ship."

"We prefer to stay aboard," Magnus chided.

"Then you will die, for I will not be stopped," Hade said, raising and tapping the flat of his sword to his forehead in a salute.

The four men answered by presenting their own blades forward and standing tightly together, believing their strength came in numbers. Against anyone else, they were indeed unstoppable. Against Hade, however, they were lining up as sheep to the slaughter.

With a mighty roar, Hade rushed forward. The four ancient Romans did not break rank, but they were no match for the strength of Hade as he charged in. At the last moment, he slid low, his blade slicing across Caius' leg, severing it cleanly. He rolled to his left and, as Caius came crashing to the ground, he plunged his sword through the Roman's back, tearing his heart apart.

Undeterred by his companion's swift death, Magnus came at Hade and their swords clashed together with such force, they looked as if they would shatter. Tiberius, seeing his twin brother lying dead, flung himself at Hade, making it easy for Hade to redirect his bull rush onto Magnus' sword. The blade pierced through his shoulder and black blood began flowing freely from the wound.

If that was the only damage done to Tiberius, he would have healed quickly enough. However, Hade was far from done. As Magnus pulled his sword from the shoulder of his surprised companion, Hade twisted to avoid a thrust from Lucius, slashing his blade in a wide arc, sending the head of Tiberius tumbling from his shoulders.

Magnus tried to react, but Hade was ungodly fast and buried his sword deep into the Roman's abdomen. The man's eyes went wide and his mouth opened in an unholy scream, baring long canines. His head shot forward, teeth going for Hade's face, but the huge warrior drove his elbow up under the man's chin, shattering his jaw. At the same moment, he drove his right leg backward, connecting solidly with the chest of Lucius, who was trying to thrust home a killing blow of his own.

Lucius spun away out of control, his blade clattering harmlessly on the pavement as Hade ripped his sword upward, splitting Magnus from navel to chin, spilling black blood and entrails. Even an eviscerated vampire of their order could ultimately heal if given sufficient time, but Hade would never allow that to happen. As Magnus fell to his knees, effectively out of the fight, Hade slashed his sword through the air and simply removed the ancient vampire's head, ending the creature permanently.

He turned to face Lucius, who had climbed back to his feet. That the Roman was weaponless meant nothing to Hade.

"Vires et honestas," Lucius said, raising his head proudly.

Hade slammed the blade home, burying it to the hilt through the Roman's heart. "Strength and honor," he repeated in English as black blood poured from the dying vampire's mouth. Lucius red-rimmed eyes fluttered once and closed, before Hade pushed him to the ground, pulling his sword free as he did. A few moments later, he had removed the creature's head, as well as that of Caius.

The four undead Romans eliminated, Hade tossed the sword to the ground next to the bodies. "Are you not entertained!" he roared in a voice that echoed loudly, his arms spread wide. He looked at Letalis knowingly, giving her a wink.

Letalis had never seen this side of Hade before, so visceral and animalistic, and it both frightened and comforted her at the same time. Hade was a demon of the worst sorts, but he was also her protector, and she knew he was not going to let anything happen to her.

"I'm ready to collect Cole," she said, pointedly ignoring the bodies of the dead Roman vampires. "Let's be done with this."

"Agreed," Hade said as he pulled out his Desert Eagles again. "I don't think we'll run into anything else, but better safe than sorry."

Letalis shrugged her shoulders and started forward.

"No gun?" Hade asked pointedly.

She paused, looking him in the eyes with a depth of understanding absent before. "I'm not worried about anything anymore, Hade. Not after that." Without waiting for a response, she turned and walked into the front lobby of Caesar's Palace. Chuckling to himself, Hade followed. The two of them cut an imposing image as they did, their black outfits covered in dust and debris and spattered with blood and gore. They continued walking across the empty lobby toward the elevator that would take them up to Cole's suite. Reaching it, Hade paused for a moment and looked at the statue of three women in the middle of the lobby. "Ah, good art never goes out of style," he sighed.

"You mean naked art never goes out of style," Letalis sniped.

"Well, yes, that goes without saying," he said, but there was no joy in his voice.

"What is it?" Letalis asked quietly, realizing something was amiss.

The giant stood still, thinking upon his words carefully before eventually turning to the young woman. "I need to know you're okay with what is going to happen upstairs. There can't be any doubts. Too much is at stake."

After a lengthy pause, Letalis finally responded. "I'll be honest, I don't understand why we need Cole. What makes him so special?"

"He's special because I've made him special," Hade responded. "And in many ways, his faults of late have been of my doing. He's become scared and unpredictable, which is what we're here to fix."

"I just thought he was an unlikable sociopathic prick," she remarked.

"Oh, he certainly is that," Hade replied, "and I don't blame Cole for trying to cover his assets, so to speak. But, I think he can still be valuable."

"Okay," Letalis sighed. "I only have one last concern. What if he's working for *him*?" she asked, her voice lowering.

At that, Hade tapped the barrel of his Eagle against his shoulder, his forehead creased in thought. "The short answer is, Cole isn't that smart," Hade finally replied. "The long answer is… I don't think he's that smart," he grinned unconvincingly.

Letalis did not return the smile. "I hope you're right," she said quietly. "Because if Cole's working for the other side, we are officially screwed."

"I know," Hade said. "But we're probably screwed anyway, so we might as well go out on our terms. Either way, let's do this right."

"Okay," Letalis said one last time, and reached out to push the "up" button for the elevator. There was nothing left to say as they stepped in, so they rode up the few floors to their destination in silence. A short moment later, the door opened to the opulent Neptune Villa, an eight thousand square foot suite overlooking the Garden of the Gods pool. It was the very picture of pristine splendor and grandeur, a true Venetian paradise, and as they walked into the suite, two things told them that Cole was there.

The first was that his favorite song, "Hotel California," was blaring loudly from one of the rooms off to the side. The second was that the entrance chamber had recently been transformed into an execution chamber. On the floor by the door were the bodies of three guards laying facedown with multiple bullet wounds to their backs. The smell of blood was thick in the air as Letalis rolled the bodies over and saw the names on their uniforms: Costible-Roe, Pearson, and Wurtz. A cursory check showed her they each had the mark on their right hands, but she still couldn't shake the feeling that these deaths were pointless.

"Are you positive you want this psychopathic monster working for you, if this is what he does to his friends?" she asked, staring down at the faces of the dead men.

"We are all monsters in the end, my dear," Hade said almost sadly.

"Come, we have business to attend to."

Letalis stood up and they walked into the master bedroom together.

Cole Banyon was right where they knew he would be and, judging by the careless manner in which he was carrying himself, it was clear he had not been directing the attack against them. In fact, it hardly looked as if he was even aware that a battle had just ensued outside. Cole was sitting at a round, sunken Valley of the Kings poker table with his back to them, his entire attention focused on the card game before him. There were three people playing with him, but their attention was all on their game, and none of them noticed Hade and Letalis' entrance. A row of empty Jack Daniels bottles on the table attested to the fact that Cole and his friends had been doing a fair amount of drinking and that they had been at it for a lengthy amount of time.

Away from the table, the California king bed was still made, the teal spread pulled neatly down at the corners and untouched. An ornate cigar box sat on one corner of the bed, open and showing a half dozen Flor de Cano Cuban cigars still inside. Next to the box was a Beretta 92FS with a high capacity clip, presumably the weapon Cole had used to kills his guards. Next to the bed and against the far wall, an old-style jukebox appeared to be set on repeat, as "Hotel California" ended, only to start over again. An attractive young woman in various shades of purple with numerous ear and facial piercings lounged up against it, soaking in the music while eying the newcomers with detachment. She was the only one who had noticed them, and if she was surprised at their appearance, she didn't show it.

Hade could only chuckle at the absurdity of the situation and raised his Desert Eagle, unloading three booming shots into the jukebox. Surprisingly, the woman leaning against the machine never flinched as the music stopped amid shattered plastic, metal, sparks, and smoke. She just looked up, tapped her forehead and smiled at the two newcomers. "That must be my cue to leave," she said huskily.

"No, stay a moment. I'd hate for you to leave on my account," Hade replied, his gaze going from her to the others seated around the table—a man and two women—and finally settling on Cole. He slid his handgun back into its shoulder holster under his coat and his face turned to stone as he addressed his lieutenant. "Is this a bad time, Cole?"

"You shouldn't be here," Cole slurred. "You gave me Vegas. It's mine."

"What is given freely can be taken back freely, dear boy," Hade replied, tamping down his anger and screwing a false smile onto his face.

"Who's the chick?" Cole asked, pointing at Letalis. "She's hot."

"The chick," Hade said heavily, "has been trying to convince me for the past forty-eight hours that I would be best served by ending your life immediately. I'm beginning to think she might be right."

What little color remaining in Cole's face drained instantly as he realized exactly what was happening. This was not a social call. He was in trouble. A lot of trouble.

"Since we are all getting to know each other," Hade said as he took a few steps into the room, "perhaps you could introduce me to your friends?"

Whether Cole was so fogged by the whisky that he thought he was off the hook or he actually believed that Hade cared at all about his new friends, he brightened. "Sure thing, boss," he said, sweeping an arm around the table. "These guys are from Chicago, flew in the other night to score some change in the casino. They were into poker, so I got a private game going up here in my room."

"Who's winning?" Hade asked as he slowly walked around the

table.

"My buddy Pancakes is," Cole replied, indicating the man sitting next to him. Tall and shaggy, the man's eyes were sharp and he seemed to have his wits about him. In addition, he had a large pile of chips and a stack of cash, more than any of the others combined.

"You're not a card cheat, are you, Pancakes?" Hade asked with a wink.

"Not even on my worst day," the man replied. "And the name is Justin. I'm actually a historian."

"Historian or not, Justin here looks like a risk taker," Hade said to Letalis, before turning back to him. "Justin, are you a risk taker?"

"No, sir," the man replied nervously. Unlike Cole, Justin seemed to have figured out exactly what was going on and was already working on getting out of the situation in one piece. "I'm just here for a game of cards and the chance to walk out of here alive."

"I'll take note of that," Hade smiled. "And you are?" he continued, turning to one of the two girls at the table.

"Everyone calls me Shennondoah," she said calmly.

"Shennondoah?" Hade repeated, turning his gaze toward the woman. On the tall side, she was slender and tanned, with long brown hair pulled into a ponytail. Wearing an elegant black evening gown, with a diamond necklace and matching earrings, she was the only one who actually looked like she belonged in the opulent suite. She returned his gaze with a smile, her eyes clear and aware. Whatever game Justin was playing, he wasn't playing it alone. She had fewer chips, but was still helping separate Cole from his money.

"I'm Samantha," the other girl said, stammering from fear of the new arrivals. Dressed in a form-fitting light blue tracksuit, her most notable feature were her dark hazel eyes that seemed to show all the way into her soul. At the moment, they were showing Hade just how terrified she was of him. "I'm more of a slot junkie, but I'm good for a few hands of poker here and there. I'm with Justin, though, in that I would very much like to leave here alive, as well."

"Wouldn't we all," Hade replied graciously.

"Samantha here dated Johnny Depp a few years ago," Cole added, thoroughly pleased with himself for remembering anything at all about his card-playing friends.

"And your jukebox vixen?" Hade asked, looking up at the woman who had not moved, but was now looking carefully at the carnage wreaked on the ruined jukebox.

"That's Alician," Justin replied for Cole, "but everyone calls her Pierce."

"For obvious reasons," she said in a bored tone, clicking a metal tongue stud against her teeth without looking up.

"Not playing tonight?" Letalis asked coldly.

"I never touch the cards. I prefer to make my money the old fashioned way: robbing everyone else after they pass out."

"A woman after my own heart," Hade smiled. "Well, I suppose I ought to thank all of you for keeping Cole occupied tonight, but I'm afraid the party's over. I would have loved to have granted you your wishes to leave here alive, but that just isn't going to happen."

"Wait," Justin said, putting his hands up defensively. "Keep the money. Just let us leave. You'll never have to see us again. I swear!"

Hade laughed deeply, a sound that sent a cold chill through the room. "I think I'd rather not ever see you again right now," he said, his voice ice. Hade placed his hand on the back of Justin's neck and yanked him up and out of the chair. Justin screamed in pain for just a moment as Hade squeezed, before the sound of popping bone told everyone in the room that Hade had broken the man's neck with one hand. Without a word, he turned and flung Justin's corpse across the room where it slammed into the jukebox, sending Pierce diving for the floor. In the time it took Justin to fly across the room, Hade had already pulled out his enormous Desert Eagle from his coat again.

Pierce looked up in time to see him leveling the gun at her. She had only a second to begin screaming before a bullet blew her heart out her back. At the table, Samantha scrambled out of her chair to escape the carnage, but Letalis caught her, spun her around and sent her stumbling toward Hade. The huge man caught her, both hands—one still holding his firearm—going quickly to her head.

"No..." she pleaded helplessly, her deep eyes showing the even deeper level of the terror she felt at her end. Hade shook his head slowly in the negative and then snapped her neck like a twig.

"Sorry," he said as he dropped her unceremoniously to the floor. He looked down at her broken body and sighed. He then turned to find the one remaining poker player standing, calmly looking at him, seemingly unafraid.

"Make it quick," was all Shennondoah said, a resigned look on her face as Hade centered the barrel of the huge gun between her eyes.

Hade stood silently, mulling over an option that had not been present a moment before, before suddenly holstering his gun and smiling. "Actually, I don't think I will," he said, reaching out and locking his arm around her throat. "This won't hurt much," he said, effortlessly lifting her up, the crook of his elbow locked under her chin. Her eyes went wide with shock and her feet kicked feebly, before she went still and limp. Rather than toss her to the floor with the bodies of the others, he walked over to the settee on the far side of the room and laid her down gently.

"You didn't kill her?" Letalis asked, clearly confused at the turn of events.

"Cole is going to need some companionship where's he's going,"

Hade answered. "I was planning on having Gru or Narn take him under their wing, but this one seemed…perfect. I can have the others do more important work now and besides, I think she has real potential. She could become Cole's next Windy." He turned his full attention to Cole, his smile vanishing. "Now for you," he rumbled.

Cole tried speaking, but all that came out was a garbled plea as Letalis walked over slowly to him, her eyes glittering dangerously. She grabbed him by the back of his neck and threw him across the room as if he weighed no more than a ragdoll. Cole slammed into the wall, sending pictures bouncing and a mirror falling to the floor and shattering. He slumped to the floor, leaving the wall dented from where he impacted it.

"I thought our whole purpose here was to keep Cole alive, my dear," Hade said, shaking his head in mock irritation. In no hurry at all, he walked over to the bed and idly picked up one of the Cubans. He examined it, turning it over between his fingers, before walking toward Cole, who was pulling himself shakily to his feet. Cole grabbed his head in his hands, blood drooling from his lips. He looked up, trying to get his vision to work, but everything was spinning and so he barely saw Hade as the huge man grabbed him by the front of his thousand dollar silk shirt and threw him onto the bed.

As Cole lay there, dazed, Hade looked around at the carnage in the room. "Still think he's working the double agent bit?" he asked Letalis off-handedly as he examined the cigar again. "Flor de Cano…I wouldn't have expected such sophistication from our boy here. This is more of a subtle, day-time cigar, not something for a long night of cards." He bit off the end, took out his lighter, lit it and sucked in a mouthful of smoke. "Mild and refreshing," he finished, "with sweet floral and herbaceous flavors. Not bad at all."

He noticed Letalis waiting for him and nodded. "Get him up," he ordered as he blew a perfect smoke ring and watched it float above his head like some perverse halo.

Letalis reached out and slapped Cole hard across the face. "Wakey, wakey," she purred as his eyes fluttered and he tried to focus again through the pain and the alcohol.

Sputtering, Cole pulled himself up to his hands and knees, his chest and stomach heaving. "Look, man, I'm sorry," he slurred, guessing why Hade had come. "This is about the girls, right? You have to believe me, I couldn't help what happened to them."

Letalis countered, her arms folded in contempt. "I think it's important for a man to take responsibility for his actions. You are in charge here, aren't you?"

"Of course," Cole said, kneeling on the bed and pleading now. "But Ox betrayed me. I can show you the videotape. He knocked me out. I should have killed him months ago!"

"So your non-apology apology is to say that you should have killed the one man who has kept you alive after all of your stupid binges," Hade said coldly. "This warrants death to you?"

"He's a doctor," Cole argued. "It's his job to save my life. Just like the janitor's job is to clean the bathroom. It doesn't mean he deserves more or less than anyone else here."

"I'll remember that when I try to decide whether or not you deserve any more or less than the others here," Hade replied contemptuously, looking at the broken bodies on the floor.

"Look," Cole sputtered, "he knocked me out and helped the girls escape. That's what happened, I swear it."

"Which is exactly what I wanted to happen," Hade added.

"Wha…what?" Cole stammered, his eyes going from Hade to Letalis and back again.

"Now be honest," Letalis pointed out, smiling. "That isn't *exactly* what you wanted."

"Semantics," Hade countered, shooting her a dirty look.

Letalis smiled back at Hade, before growing serious again. "It wasn't the original plan, Cole, but you actually did us a favor by getting yourself beaten up and your nose broken." She placed her hands behind her back and began walking slowly around the bed. "Besides the personal satisfaction I got from knowing that perhaps the world's biggest slime ball got his cojones handed to him on a platter by two battered women, we needed them back out in the wild thinking they had escaped us. And you did that for us."

Cole kept turning his head, trying to keep both Letalis and Hade in his field of vision. "Does that mean you aren't going to kill me?" he asked desperately, clearly not believing that he was actually going to be spared.

"Well," Hade smiled, "that depends on your definition of kill."

"You're so cruel," Letalis smiled again.

Cole had no idea how to respond to that. Letalis pulled a small leather case from a pocket at her hip. She opened it up, revealing a row of six glass vials, all of them containing a black liquid. Cole's eyes grew large, as he had no problem imagining what those could be used for.

"But, Hade," he stammered, trying desperately to find any angle he could use to save his life. "If you kill me, what happens to Vegas?"

"Vegas is done for, regardless," the Hade answered sharply. "After we're done with you, my associates and I are going to tear this place down, brick by brick, roulette table by roulette table, slot machine by slot machine, until there is nothing and no one left. Since you have never worried about anyone but yourself, it should be easy for you to forget about all of this."

"I don't understand," he said, tears starting to form in his eyes.

"Then let me explain so you can. After witnessing your incredible failure here in Vegas, it would appear that perhaps I have not given you the right tools you need to accomplish what I require of you," Hade said, his voice measurably calmer. "It's time I remedied that."

"So..." Cole started and looked up, hope in his battered face for the first time. "So you still need me?"

"I need someone like you, Cole," Hade answered. "And since I already have you, it makes sense to keep you around. But you've gotten sloppy and soft here in Vegas and turned what should have been a bastion of order into nothing more than your own personal Animal House. You have compromised yourself, and worse, you have compromised me."

"I swear, I would never..." Cole began, but Hade interrupted him.

"Hush," Hade said, his voice dropping dangerously. "Your weaknesses control you, so the time has come to remove those weaknesses from you."

"S..so," Cole stuttered, clearly terrified. "What do you need from me?"

"Lots of things," Hade said, allowing himself to smile. "But for now, I have a simple assignment for you. I'm going to need you to kill someone, which I know isn't a problem for you, but I'm a bit concerned with your state of mind right now. I can't have you all strung out and vomiting into your gold-plated puke bucket. I need you at your best."

"My best," Cole repeated, trying to understand.

"Yes, your best," Hade repeated acidly. "I know it's a difficult concept for you to grasp, that you could ever be anything other than what you are now, so Letalis is going to give you something to help you...understand."

Cole started to turn around, but the woman was suddenly behind him, hooking her arm around his throat. She twisted her body, flipping

Cole over backward so that he was face down on the bed. A moment later, she had flipped him over again and was straddling his chest, her legs pinning his arms to his side. He looked up, terror in his eyes as she held up a syringe filled with the dark, viscous liquid from one of the vials in her case. The needle was long—longer than any he had ever seen.

"What…what's that?" he asked, his voice quaking with fear.

"That," Hade answered calmly, "is the elixir of the gods. It will give you the clarity you seek, the capacity to control your basest desires and the opportunity to fulfill your greatest dreams. You won't need drugs to get high, you will no longer need to eat or sleep, and you will have no fear of death from anyone but me. On the downside, you'll have an almost insatiable lust for fresh blood and direct sunlight is going to get a bit uncomfortable. But those are but a trifling compared to what you are about to receive."

"Are you turning me into one of those things?" Cole asked incredulously. "A vampire?"

"You can call it whatever you like," Letalis said as she raised the needle high, making sure his eyes followed it closely. "All I care about is that this is going to hurt you like hell."

She slammed the needle home, plunging it deep, deep into his chest.

Cole's eyes opened wide, his pupils dilating almost instantly to full black as she injected the fluid into his heart.

The agony began immediately…as did the screaming.

Cole Banyon would take a long time to die.

CHAPTER 23

Washington, DC: The Barrett M82 fifty-caliber sniper rifle rested firmly on the half rotten windowsill, six stories up and almost a half mile away from the where the target would shortly be arriving. The distance was unimportant for Marcello Tuono, however, as he had shot people from much further away. Despite the dilemma of not knowing his name or having any photograph of him, Tuono's body of work was well known to the detectives at Interpol, the FBI and Scotland Yard. He had become famous among the many law enforcement bureaus for his surgical, precise kills. From jealous lovers to political rivals, it was always the same for him: two shots to the head from a distance. It was clean, it was quick, and there was no way to trace him to the kill. It was a calling card without an actual card.

As with everyone in his trade, he had suffered through the routine assignments, found meaning in the more difficult ones, and planned endlessly for the moment he was hired for his signature kill—the one that he would be remembered for long after he was gone. After waiting for years for his chance at immortality, the call that would place him in the pantheon of history's greatest assassins had finally come from none other than Hade himself.

Their conversation had been brief, but it was all the Italian needed to know to complete his task. The target was planning on taking in a private show that evening and was to be killed in front of a theater. The shot could come from anywhere, but Hade was adamant that Tuono dispatch the man in his usual fashion and then make his escape. With "when" answered, the questions of "who" and "where" were asked. The answers came smoothly over the phone: "President Albert Abrea. Ford's Theater."

Tuono had paused. Was Hade serious?

"People are calling Abrea the Lincoln of this century," Hade had replied to the unspoken question. "They say he is holding together what is left of this crumbling Union and that he, and only he, can keep it from disintegrating into nothingness. I couldn't disagree more. He has become a liability and has to go. Of course, while he is no Lincoln, that doesn't mean we can't give him a Lincoln style-exit."

Now, it was nearly dark as Tuono waited patiently. The assassin could see exactly where his target would be through the long-range scope on his weapon. He scanned the area and counted off each of the three dozen secret service agents scattered along the street in front of the theater and the buildings adjoining it. The president had a long list of enemies, both sane and not, who were ever-circling like so many hawks waiting for the perfect moment to swoop in and strike, which meant the president had perhaps the most detailed and efficient level of security the world had ever seen. The fact that Hade knew exactly when and where he wanted it done, before the West Wing had even announced where the president would be that evening, was nothing short of astonishing.

The assassin knew that Hade's people had infiltrated the government in a great many places and that they were busy orchestrating things both above and below the counter in an effort to force a move toward a more global government. Even with the recent devastating world-spanning tsunamis, Abrea still resisted that global commitment. The man strongly opposed anything that would compromise his nation's sovereignty, even though his country was falling apart around him. No matter, Tuono thought to himself. In a few minutes, it would no longer be the man's concern. Nothing would.

Moments later, the president's armored BMW arrived at its destination, preceded by a black Cadillac Escalade and followed by two more. They were exactly on time, according to the time table Hade had provided. The assassin smiled as he realized just how much power Hade must have if he could schedule the president for his own assassination so far in advance.

Tuono sighted the rifle on the rear door handle of the armored BMW and waited. As expected, men from the first and last Escalades stepped out, their eyes alert as they searched for possible threats. He was not worried at all—the distance between himself and his prey was well outside of their perceived threat range.

The door to the BMW opened and Tuono took a deep breath, holding his finger against the trigger. From the car stepped a young woman, dark-haired and tanned. It was Abrea's twenty-two year old daughter, Gabrielle. While he had no intention of killing the young woman, the expert assassin had no compunction about depriving her of her father. She reached a hand back into the car and, at that point, time seemed to slow down. President Albert Abrea stepped from the car, holding his daughter's hand, a smile on his face as he spoke to her. Tuono didn't know what he was saying, nor did he care. As the president emerged fully, his head reaching the apex of his height, the assassin pulled the trigger.

The fifty-caliber bullet entered just behind Abrea's right ear and exited out the other side of his skull, taking much of his brain with it. Tuono knew it was a kill shot, but as Abrea's body sagged against the open car door, his body turning slightly, Tuono pulled the trigger again. The second bullet drilled into Abrea's head just above his right eye.

The killer was moving before the president's body hit the pavement, rolling hurriedly to his feet and sprinting the short distance to the rooftop doorway, leaving everything behind for the police to find. It wouldn't matter, however, as there was nothing there that could connect him to the chaos that was happening on the ground below. He opened the door and began walking leisurely down the stairs, shedding his gloves and black jacket. Two flights down, he pushed them into a garbage can and stepped out into an empty hallway.

Dressed impeccably in a black Armani suit, he pushed the elevator button and waited patiently. A few seconds later, he stepped into the car, joining an elderly man and his much younger companion, a beautiful sultry-eyed brunette.

"*È una vergogna che qualcuno così giovane e bella è sellato con un vecchio sfinito cavallo come te,*" he said lightly to the man as the elevator door shut behind him.

The gentleman had no idea he had just asked how a woman so young and beautiful could be saddled with an old worn out horse like him. "I'm…sorry," he replied quizzically, but clearly with a hint of arrogance. "I only speak English."

"I said it's a beautiful evening for a stroll," Tuono lied as the elevator descended.

"Yes, it is," the elderly man grinned as the car came to a stop and the door opened.

"After you," Tuono said graciously, bowing to the woman with a sly wink.

She returned his smile and Tuono followed the couple out of the elevator. He turned in the other direction from them and headed down a hall that ran the length of the building. A minute later, he stepped out into the evening air and paused to listen. The president had been assassinated less than three minutes ago and Tuono was just now hearing the distant sounds of sirens. Everything was proceeding perfectly.

He began walking casually down the street toward an unobtrusive gray Camry parked about a block away. As he walked, he pulled out a phone covered with transparent blue contact paper. He dialed nine one one and waited.

"Nine one one, what's your emergency?" the voice said on the other end after several rings.

"Yeah, I wanted to report gunshots," he said in a thick but believable Southern accent, sounding suitably nervous. "I saw a man coming out of a building just a minute ago, a little north of Capitol City Brewing. Some older guy; had a good lookin' babe with him. He was talking about shooting someone."

"What is your location, sir?"

"Near 11th and I," Tuono answered. "I hear a bunch of sirens."

"Sir, can you remain on the line?" the dispatcher said, tension heavy in her voice. "I have officers en route to your location."

"Sure thing," Tuono drawled. "I'll wait right here." Leaving the line open, he pulled off the blue covering and laid the phone down on the trunk of a parked Volkswagen Passat. Tucking the transparent paper into his pocket, he walked the rest of the way to his own car.

The sirens were a lot louder now as he slid into the front seat of the Camry as a pair of police cars came screaming around the corner and blew past him. After they were gone, he started his own car and began driving away in the opposite direction at a leisurely pace, certain not to attract attention. He would be at Reagan National Airport before anything got locked down. He reached into this jacket and pulled out a second phone.

"Janson," he said, holding it up. The phone put the call through and the other line picked up immediately.

"I need a plane," he said, without waiting for the other person to say anything.

"Where to?"

"Rome."

"When?"

"I'll be there in twenty minutes."

"Not a lot of time," the voice replied. "That will cost you extra."

"It's covered," the assassin said. "Just have it ready."

"It'll be on the tarmac outside of the private hanger. You know the drill."

Tuono ended the call without replying and then spoke again. "Hade."

The call was picked up before it even rang.

"Status?" came his employer's voice.

"It's done," Tuono said tonelessly.

"Sic semper tyrannis," Hade replied easily. "Are you heading to the airport?"

"Yes," Tuono answered. "I'll be at Dulles in forty minutes."

"Good, good. Your plane is fueled and ready, Marcello," he went on. "You'll be in Frankfort tomorrow morning. Take some time for yourself, you've earned it. If I need anything else, I'll be in touch," Hade finished and the line went dead. Tuono rolled down the window and tossed the phone into a small grove of trees along the highway. Smiling to himself, he drove the rest of the way to Reagan International, listening to the operatic strains of the Phantom of the Opera coming through the car's speakers and singing along in his best vibrato.

He arrived at the airport, abandoned his car in the long-term parking lot, and walked out across the tarmac to the idling Gulfstream G650 that Janson had prepared for him. It wasn't that the assassin distrusted Hade—actually, it was, he thought to himself. Might as well be truthful. The first rule of a major assassination was to assassinate the assassin, and despite years of working for Hade, taking chances had never been part of Tuono's makeup and he wasn't about to start now. He knew Hade well enough to know the man could appreciate his caution, so he was not at all worried about retaliation for dropping out of sight. Besides, if Hade wanted him dead, it wouldn't be for covering his tracks. It would more likely be for the rather substantial amount of money Hade had promised him for his services.

He climbed the stairs to the entrance of the sleek business jet and entered the cabin. The G650 was a top-of-the-line business jet, catering to the obscenely wealthy. The cabin had a number of plush leather seats and a couple of small tables, along with built-in touch screens and laptop access. Everything in the plane seemed to be gilded, but Tuono cared nothing for the expensive amenities. It was cool and dark and the pilot's cockpit door was already closed. A single stewardess, wearing a short, black dress, met him with a smile. The assassin was immediately on his guard.

"No baggage?" she asked politely.

"No," Tuono replied, his tone clipped, "and no questions, either." He turned away and walked into the luxurious cabin. "Tell the pilot we can leave immediately."

"Yes, sir," the flight stewardess replied as she headed toward the cockpit.

He sat down, leaned back and relaxed as the plane began to taxi toward the runway. A few minutes later, they were airborne and climbing. Only then did Marcello Tuono allow himself to relax and finally smile. He had pulled off the perfect presidential assassination.

The stewardess reappeared a short time later after the plane had leveled out. "Can I get you a drink?" she asked with a smile.

"Scotch and water," he replied, looking her up and down, feeling considerably more at ease. She turned away to fix his drink and he let his eyes wander over her form, thinking he could find some time to indulge in a little playtime during the flight. He rarely celebrated so quickly after a job, but this one had gone better than even he could have imagined and he was in the mood to enjoy the fruits of his labor.

"It's a long flight," Tuono mused. "Perhaps you'd like to join me for a round or two?"

"Are you talking about drinks or something less…appropriate?" she asked slyly.

"I'm sure we can find something of interest to the both of us," he replied, smiling knowingly.

"I'd like that," the stewardess answered, handing him his glass. "I am ever so thirsty. If you'll just give me a few minutes to take care of my duties…" she trailed off.

"Of course. If you don't mind me asking, what's your name?"

"Shennondoah," the woman replied with a wink, and Tuono raised his glass as she returned to the galley. He took a drink and stretched his legs out. The effect hit him almost immediately. It began with a rapid numbing of his extremities, followed by a shortness of breath. Panic surged through him as the glass fell from his hand to the carpeted floor. His vision began to fade as the stewardess walked back into view, her long hair already let down and a perfectly wicked look on her face.

As she reached down to pick up the glass, he was vaguely aware of movement to the side. He had no idea who or what it was as blackness claimed him a moment later.

Consciousness came back to the assassin, but he kept his eyes closed and his breathing steady, trying to ascertain his predicament without giving away his return to reality. He didn't have to move his hands to know that he wouldn't be able to. He felt the bands constricting them, pinning his wrists to his seat's armrests—zip cuffs by the feel of them. He also could feel the presence of someone near him and realized there was no reason to fake it anymore. Whoever it was, was watching him. He opened his eyes and looked right into the face of his captor.

"Ah, Marcello," the man said, leaning back in a chair that was swiveled around to face him. "Good to have you back. I'd shake your hand, but it appears you're a little tied up at the moment," he laughed loudly.

Tuono took everything in. It had grown dark outside, but the shades had been mostly drawn around the plane. A single overhead lamp was lit, illuminating him and the area around him. His captor was in shadow, but he could see enough to discern that he was dressed in jeans and a black tee-shirt, along with cowboy boots and a ratty, old denim jacket. The man did not appear to have any weapons on him, at least any that were visible, but that hardly mattered since the assassin was completely immobile. The flight attendant, Shennondoah, was nearby as well, seated in another nearby chair. Her hands were steepled together at her chin and she was eyeing the Italian almost hungrily.

The man in shadows leaned forward, smiling. "Please allow me to introduce myself. The name is Banyon. Cole Banyon."

"I know who you are," the Italian interrupted in a voice still slightly slurred by whatever drug he had been given. He knew he was in very real danger, but he needed some time to figure things out. "You're the *uomo pazzo* that Hade kept as a pet in Vegas. To what do I owe the displeasure of this meeting?"

"Haven't you figured it out yet?" the man replied with a smile, seemingly unmoved by the insult. "I mean surely someone like you knows the first rule of assassination."

Tuono nodded. He did indeed. It was exactly as he had feared. "May I ask, how did Hade know where I would be?"

"Hade knows everything," Cole chuckled. "You don't really think your backup plane at Reagan was any big surprise to him, do you?"

"So why kill me?" the Italian asked calmly, not yet ready to beg for his life. "I've never been anything but loyal to him and his cause."

"So I've been told," Cole yawned. "But sometimes you gotta take one for the team, I guess."

Tuono quietly pulled at his restraints, but to no avail. "So you're going to kill me and pin Abrea's assassination on me. Case closed, right?"

"Well, you did kill him," Cole scoffed.

"As I was instructed, and it was a completely clean kill. So why kill an asset like me?"

"How should I know?" Banyon shrugged. "I'm just following orders."

"As was I," Tuono said.

"I wouldn't call changing planes following orders," Cole mocked. "How's that working out for you, by the way?"

"Let me loose and we'll find out," the assassin replied coldly, resigning himself to his fate.

"You heard the man, Shennondoah," he said. "Cut him loose."

"With pleasure," she replied with a sultry voice. She reached out with a long-fingered hand and slipped a nail underneath his bindings. With barely a flick of her wrist, she severed the zip tie and the assassin's hand was free.

Tuono waited patiently for the other. She stood up and reached across, leaning seductively into him as she broke the other tie the same way. The assassin was moving in an instant, his arm lashing out and encircling the woman's slender waist. He was on his feet a moment later, bringing his other hand up and cupping her chin roughly. Surprisingly, she did not struggle, but the Italian had no time to consider it. He stood behind her, poised to break her neck as he looked directly at Cole.

Banyon had never moved from his chair. "Impressive," the former

Vegas dictator said. "Even drugged, you move like lightning. Hade told me not to underestimate you."

"Spare me the false praise," Tuono snapped. "We seem to have a problem, you and I."

"We do?" Cole said in mock surprise, looking around. "Do you have some friends in here that I don't know about? Because I see no one here to save you, Marcello. You're alone," he scoffed, leaning back in his chair.

"I have no problem killing her if you don't do as I say," Tuono countered steadily. "You're going to bring this plane down now and we're going to get Hade on the line and find a way to resolve this amicably."

"Now, that's where you're wrong," Cole countered, his voice still at ease. "I think you would have quite the problem killing this one. Shennondoah? If you don't mind, could you show the poor man what I mean?"

The woman, who was only a muscle flex away from having her neck broken, reached up and grabbed Tuono's hand, peeling it away from her chin as if she was brushing aside a piece of paper. He felt the bones pop as she bent his hand backward and then turned around. He found himself looking into the face of a nightmare.

Shennondoah's mouth was open wide, her lips bright scarlet, long fangs prominently bared. Her eyes smoldered like fire, seeming to glow in the gloom. Her other hand reached up, grabbing his throat, and she lifted him off the ground with no effort at all before slamming him violently to the floor in front of Cole. Tuono felt something snap in his neck and his whole body went dead below his shoulders. The pain vanished as well and he found himself staring curiously upward as Cole rose slowly and leaned over him. His visage appeared exactly as the woman's—sharpened fangs, red-rimmed eyes and a smile of pure malice. Tuono tried to speak, but nothing worked.

"I imagine you must be wondering why," Cole said, kneeling down beside him. He motioned to the woman and she dropped to her knees as well.

Tuono watched as she reached down and picked up his hand, drawing it to her mouth. Paralyzed as he was, he felt nothing when she opened her mouth again, baring impossibly long teeth, before plunging them into the flesh of his wrist, opening up his veins.

"On one level, this is nothing more than business," Cole went on, as Shennondoah began to greedily feed. "Hade's orders. But on another level, you are a gift, as well—a gift from Hade to us for services to be rendered. And since you seem to have lost the ability to speak, let me answer the other question that I know is on your mind." He reached down and placed a hand behind the Italian's neck and lifted him up, bringing his own face close. Tuono could smell death as Cole leered at him, but the moment of escape had long since passed. "You won't be coming back," Cole said, his features now completely ruled by hunger. "For you, this is the end, Marcello." His head flashed forward and Tuono felt Cole's teeth tear into his throat. There was nothing subtle about it, nothing as elegant as vampires were thought to be. Cole tore his throat out.

Tuono choked, blood spurting from his ruined flesh. Cole looked at him a final time, his face dripping crimson. "Hade wasn't kidding," he growled, giving himself completely to the thirst. His face snapped forward again and he buried his teeth in the dying man's flesh.

Tuono's vision began to blur and his last thought was of the thoroughly terrifying idea that he was being eaten alive by vampires. Minutes later, his spirit fled his body.

Cole Banyon and Shennondoah the stewardess spent a long time feasting on what remained.

EPILOGUE

Mesopotamia: It was late and candles were burning, yet there was no one in the tavern save for Gilgamesh and an old woman.

"Siduri," Gilgamesh roared. "More ale!" He had been drinking for much of the night and Siduri, the old woman, had been waiting on him the entire time.

"You're welcome," she said gruffly as she placed another large tankard on the table in front of him. She had lost track hours earlier of how many he had drunk.

Gilgamesh grunted something unintelligible and drank deeply of the ale, following it up with an enormous belch. He looked up through red-rimmed eyes, his gaze fastening on Siduri. "Have you heard what the poets write about Enkidu?" Gilgamesh finally lamented. "They recite his final words as spoken by a lion or an eagle. 'Oh my brother, my dear brother! From my brother they take me. I shall sit among the dead. Must I never again see my brother with my eyes?'" He paused and took another long drink from his tankard. "It is true, what they write," he went on. "He said this and his eyes grew dim and he was no more."

"I still do not understand," Siduri said, familiar with the fall of Enkidu. "How could a man such as he be taken so easily?"

"It is the gods that punish me," Gilgamesh growled. "I am two-thirds god and I cannot die, but Enkidu, mighty as a bull and fully my equal, was but a man. To punish me, they closed his eyes to me. Before we gave battle to Hambaba, the mighty demon of the forest, I said 'Let your voice bellow forth like the kettledrum, let the stiffness in your arms depart, let the paralysis in your legs go away. Your heart should burn to do battle—pay no heed to death, do not lose heart! The one who watches from the side is a careful man. But the one who walks in front protects himself and saves his comrade and through their fighting, they establish fame.'

"We destroyed Hambaba and in our glory we slayed the Bull of Heaven," he went on. "But we were foolish. I scorned the goddess Ishtar, who desired me for my might, and we both suffered for it. She is vengeful and, because she could not harm me, her scorned fury came upon my brother quickly. He was the axe at my side, the dagger in my belt, the shield in front of me, my festive garment, my splendid attire. The evil has risen up and robbed me. Now what is this sleep that has taken hold of him? He has become dark. He cannot hear me, and he does not lift his head. I touched his heart, it does not beat."

"So where do the birds call you?" Siduri asked compassionately.

"I remain alive, but sorrow has come into my belly. I fear death, for it has taken my brother. But I will not rest. I will go to the house of Utanapishtim, the Faraway One, son of the great king Ubar-tutu, and I will learn what I must do to bring back Enkidu and to destroy the gods who took him from me."

"There is no walk back for the dead, my son. You speak folly mixed with ale."

"Do not speak like this to me, old crone. You know I have made that walk and returned to rule this world. I will approach the entrance of the mountain at night with or without your help!"

"This is not the way, my king," Siduri countered. "Let your belly be full. Make every day a day of rejoicing. Dance and play every night. Let your raiment be clean. Let your wife rejoice in your chest and cherish the little one holding your hand."

"That is the way for the dying," Gilgamesh scoffed. "I will bring my companion back."

Siduri sighed again. "I am against this for the troubles that it will bring, both to you and to the world. But if your mind is set and you are to succeed, you will need companions."

"What companion can measure up to the one taken from me?"

"None can, my lord," she replied. "But to reclaim him from the gods, you will need aid."

"Where can I find such aid?"

"Go to the Waters of Death, where you will find Urshanabi, the ferryman," she explained. "He will take you to Utanapishtim, the Faraway One, the very one who survived the flood that the gods brought to destroy the accursed world. But beware, the ferryman is a proud man. You will need to prove to him your valor."

"I am a god and a king," Gilgamesh sneered. "He will do as I say."

Gilgamesh stood on the empty beach, looking out at the black and motionless sea. He had traveled many months to reach the Waters, but now his way was barred and his rage had taken hold. Behind him were two large piles of rocks that had been statues up until a few moments earlier. Now they were only so much shattered stone and rubble. His fury had not been sated, though, and he was contemplating what to destroy next when a giant of a man, nearly an equal to himself, came over the hill and stopped short, looking angrily at the large piles of rocks and then at him.

"What have you done?" the newcomer demanded.

"I have destroyed these lifeless effigies in my anger," Gilgamesh snapped. "I have come to learn what I must do to bring Enkidu back from the dead and I cannot go through the Waters of Death on my own. Where is the ferryman? I must cross."

"You are as an unbridled mule," the large man spit. "I am the ferryman, but these stones are what enable me to cross, for no one may touch the Waters of Death, not even I. You have destroyed your means to cross the Waters."

"You are Urshanabi? You are the ferryman, nothing more," Gilgamesh replied. "I am Gilgamesh, the Tree of Godlike Balance. I have come to seek Utanapishtim, my kin, who survived the great flood and now stands in the assembly of the gods and has found eternal life. Death and life I wish to know. You will help me cross."

"I will do no such thing. Even if I desired it, I could not," the man said angrily, pointing at the broken statues. "You have destroyed the only way."

"Perhaps you do not understand," Gilgamesh threatened, baring white teeth. "I am your immortal king, two-thirds a god, builder of the walls of Uruk, slayer of Humbaba, devourer of the Bull of Heaven and the only man to scorn the goddess Ishtar and live. I command that you take me across, even if it costs you your life."

"Do not threaten me. I know who you are," Urshanabi replied angrily. "You are the marked one, the blood drinker, the first murderer. You are a fallen man and not my king. You have no power over me. I might be a ferryman, but I am my own man and I will not yield to you."

As the two men stared fiercely at each other, each readying to prove who was the stronger and which must submit, a small, solitary figure emerged from a thicket of cedar trees just beyond them. It was a young girl, likely no more than eight years old, with beautiful dark skin and deep-set eyes that framed a petite and perfect face. Dressed in a white linen knee-length tunic, she wore a smile of innocence and childhood purity.

Gilgamesh broke into a knowing smile as he realized that the tense stand-off had just turned completely in his favor. "And who is this pretty young girl?" he remarked slyly to Urshanabi.

The ferryman took a step forward, putting himself protectively between Gilgamesh and the child. "She is from my village," he said dangerously, his eyes never leaving those of his adversary. "You would do well to leave now."

"I greet you," Gilgamesh called out to the girl, ignoring the other man's implied threat. "How are you called, sister of Urshanabi?" he finished, guessing correctly.

"Ninbanda," she replied, naively missing the meaning behind the greeting. She casually walked over and gave her brother a hug, which the big man lovingly returned. She looked back at Gilgamesh, an innocent smile on her face.

Gilgamesh smiled back, but the gleam of malevolence in his eyes was unmistakable.

"You will leave now," Urshanabi repeated his demand, an edge growing in his voice.

"What a pretty name your young sister has," Gilgamesh said slowly, ignoring the ferryman as he pulled his long blade out from the sheath at his belt. "It must be dangerous living so close to the Waters of Death."

"There is no need for this," Urshanabi warned and there was an edge of pleading in his voice.

"Oh, but you are wrong, ferryman," Gilgamesh replied icily, fingering the razor sharp blade. "I have a great need to visit the Faraway One. I must begin Enkidu's heart and you are gravely mistaken if you think there is anything I won't do to make that happen. I will burn this whole earth to fulfill my purpose and I will start here with your precious sister if I must."

With that, he began to stalk forward, but this time the ferryman did not strive forward to meet him in a match of strength and will. The battle was already over.

Gilgamesh had already won.

Coming Soon...

GOD KING

THE FOURTH SEAL OF THE KRYPTEIA CONSPIRACY

The world has changed. The President of the United States is dead and the once-great country is now but a shadow of itself, having lost most of its economic, military, and political power. As America falls into ruin and chaos grows around the world, brutal wars claim tens of thousands by the day and the threat of worldwide nuclear annihilation grows by the second. The inhabitants of the earth begin to lose all hope until finally, a savior arises.

A single man, born from poverty, boldly takes the world stage, promising a peace like none other before in the history of mankind. Against all odds, he unites the world under one rule—his rule. He is Antonio Malvado-Jinete, Secretary General of the United Nations. And he has been waiting for this day for a very long time.

As Malvado-Jinete tightens his hold on the world, the race is on to find a long-lost relic—the spear that pierced the side of Christ as He hung on the cross. With creatures of the underworld rising from the pit, humanity turns to the God King for guidance and protection, while the beleaguered kings of lost scripture wage their own personal battles against an evil that will not rest until they are either enslaved or dead.

www.ingramcontent.com/pod-product-compliance
Lightning Source LLC
Chambersburg PA
CBHW022208010726
47493CB00002B/462
* 9 7 8 1 9 4 3 5 1 9 0 6 4 *